THE TARNISHED LADY
SANDRA HILL

**Winner Of The Holt Medallion
And The Georgia Romance Writers Maggie
Award For Best Historical Novel!**

**Sandra Hill's romances are "delicious, witty, and
funny!"** — *Romantic Times*

ROGUE'S DELIGHT

Eirik scooped Eadyth up in his arms before she had a chance to protest and started to carry her off.

"You are truly a loathsome lout."

"Yea, I am."

"A lecherous libertine."

"Most definitely."

"And a...a...."

"Do not forget horny toad."

Eadyth tried to push out of his embrace, but he held her arms firmly in his embrace. Then he called out over his shoulder, "Good Eventide, everyone. We will see you on the morrow."

"The morrow!" Eadyth squeaked, giving up on her struggles and burying her hot face in his neck. "'Tis only past noon now."

"Yea," he said, smiling with supreme male satisfaction. Then he added in a voice of silky promise, "I have twelve 'peaks' to climb afore then, and I want to get an early start."

"Twel...twelve! Oh, you are outrageous."

"Yea. That is one of the things women love about me."

THE TARNISHED LADY

SANDRA HILL

LEISURE BOOKS   NEW YORK CITY

A LEISURE BOOK®

September 1995

Published by

Dorchester Publishing Co., Inc.
276 Fifth Avenue
New York, NY 10001

Printed in the United States of America.

To Nellie Housel, whose unconditional love inspires all who are privileged to come in touch with her. At eighty-nine, Aunt Nellie is still reading romance novels and cherishing the joy of life and loving. And she can still yodel.

THE TARNISHED LADY

Chapter One

Ravenshire Castle, Northumbria, 946 A.D.

"Bloody Hell! What is *she* doing here?"

Eirik quickly quaffed down the remainder of ale in his wooden goblet, then slammed it down on the high table. All the time, he watched with annoyance as the tall, reedlike figure daintily lifted the hem of her voluminous gown and stepped gingerly toward him through the filthy rushes.

"It must be Lady Eadyth of Hawks' Lair," Wilfrid, his seneschal and longtime friend, remarked.

"I thought I told the guard to turn her away at the gate if she should arrive unexpectedly."

" 'Twould seem the maid finally caught up with you," Wilfrid said with a chuckle. "Surely, her persistence is commendable."

"Hah! I have seen more than enough of persistent ladies and overzealous mothers these two years I have been gone from Ravenshire. All I want is a little blessed peace to—"

Their conversation ended abruptly at the wild yelping of a

dog. Eirik's eyes widened in surprise as he watched Eadyth give the animal another swift nudge of her soft-toed leather shoe as it spread its hind legs and squatted on the floor near her feet. Even through the smoky dimness of the great hall, Eirik could see her lips curl distastefully as she eyed the loathsome "gift" left by the large hound. With her hands on her hips, the impudent wench glared at the whimpering hound until it sheepishly scurried out of her sight.

Eirik and Wilfrid burst into laughter, along with the scruffy knights who lounged below them in the hall. There were no ladies present, other than the serving wenches. Thank the Lord! He hoped to keep it that way.

"The boldness of the woman!" Eirik muttered finally, wiping tears of mirth from his eyes with the sleeve of his threadbare tunic. "First she barges uninvited into my keep. Then she kicks my dog. Shall I lay my boot to her bony arse and send her on her merry way?"

"Oh, let her speak. Mayhap this 'urgent matter' she wishes to discuss will provide good sport to lessen our boredom."

Eirik shrugged. "Perchance. Leastways, I have always wanted to get a closer look at the Silver Jewel of Northumbria."

"Nay, Eirik. Have you not heard? The jewel lost its glitter long ago. Did you not know court gossips now call her 'The Tarnished Jewel'?" He whispered several hasty words of explanation.

Eirik's eyebrows arched with skeptical interest. He knew full well from harsh, personal experience the viciousness of the nobles of King Edmund's court, but still he wondered if Wilfrid's words could be true.

Meanwhile, the woman continued to make her way doggedly toward the dais where they sat. A plump matron and several retainers followed close behind her like ducklings waddling after a scrawny goose.

At one point, she stopped and lifted her arrogant nose, seeming to sniff the air around her. Then she leveled a condemning glare at Ignold, one of Eirik's trusted retainers, and snarled several sharp words his way. The fierce giant of a warrior, who had never been known to back down in a battle, just stared, open-mouthed, at her.

Eirik had a fair idea of what she had said.

After recovering the Norse capital in Jorvik earlier that year, then conquering all of Strathclyde, King Edmund had sent Eirik as his emissary under the Golden Dragon standard to the Duke of Normandy to negotiate the release of Edmund's nephew, Louis d' Outremer. Louis had been captured by the Northmen of Rouen the summer before and then rescued by the Duke of the Franks, who persisted in holding him hostage all these many months. Finally, following months of Eirik's haggling and many setbacks, Louis was restored to his Frankish kingdom.

Many of Eirik's *hird*, his contingent of permanent troops, had straggled in that eve after the long return trip from Frankland. They followed his smaller group of retainers who had accompanied him back two sennights ago. After weeks on board ship and then horseback without bathing, they stunk to high heaven. Even he had noticed the pungent, acrid odor of unwashed male flesh as he passed by earlier on his way to the garderobe. No doubt, the shrew from Hawks' Lair had voiced her displeasure.

The wench continued forward in his direction, ignoring the ribald comments of his men who sat in small groups drinking mead or playing dice. It would seem they had all been too long away from polite society.

A twinge of guilt tugged at Eirik's conscience. Perhaps he had been rude in ignoring her letters seeking aid in an unnamed ''urgent matter.'' But he was bone weary from two years of fighting and carrying messages for his king, not to mention continually dodging the arrows of political intrigue. He wanted naught to do with the cesspit lives of the nobility—men *or* women. Just a little peaceful respite, that was all he asked.

Eirik leaned back in his chair, casually folding his arms over his chest and crossing his long legs at the ankles. He

11

narrowed his eyes and studied Lady Eadyth more closely, barely able to see her body or face under the loose gunna and confining wimple she wore. His eyes teared in the smoke and he squinted even more.

She appeared to have gray hair skinned back tightly under a mud-colored head-rail. No loose tendrils escaped to soften her dour features.

Deep in thought, Eirik brushed his mustache with a forefinger, back and forth, a habit he engaged in when puzzled or deep in concentration. "I had not thought her so long in the tooth."

"Nor I."

They both looked back to the woman in question. She was tall and slender, if the trimness of her ankle was any indication as she lifted the hem of her garment to avoid the muck. Her spinsterish breasts waxed nonexistent on a chest as flat as his battle shield. But it was the scowl on her face that was most uncomely. *God's Bones!* She came seeking favors, yet could not control her sour countenance.

Eirik smiled. He would enjoy playing the cat to this dowdy mouse with her haughty airs.

Clearing her throat, she called out brazenly from the bottom of the dais steps, "By your leave, my Lord Ravenshire, I would beg an audience with you on an urgent matter."

Urgent matter! Urgent matter! That was what they all said when they came seeking favors. Eirik nodded reluctantly, and with a wave of his right hand to a nearby housecarl indicated that Eadyth's companions should be taken off for food and drink.

"Apparently you did not receive the missive I sent," she began in a stilted voice, her lips pinched white with tension. Two little lines between her brows bespoke what must be a permanent glower. Eirik almost burst out laughing as he realized the woman was finding it sore hard to humble herself before him, that she would much prefer to administer a sharp tongue lashing for his discourtesy.

"I received your letter."

When he declined to explain himself further, Eadyth's mouth dropped open, exposing surprisingly white and healthy teeth for one so old. He stroked his mustache thoughtfully and squinted to see better. Despite the age lines that bracketed her eyes and mouth, she might not be as elderly as he had originally thought. In truth, the skin over her delicate facial bones was smooth as new cream in those places where a frown did not crease it unpleasantly. He wished he could see her better; it rankled that his poor vision made him see things less clearly when up close.

"Aaah! An honest man. How refreshing!"

"Didst thou expect any different? 'Tis a virtue I value more than any other—honesty, that is," Eirik snapped, oddly offended by her complacent acceptance of his admission that he had received her summons and rudely failed to respond.

His answer seemed to please her greatly. "Yea, most times I do expect dishonesty. There are not many truly trustworthy men in my experience."

"Or women?"

"Or women," she agreed with a slight nod, appraising him boldly.

A smile tugged at the edges of Eadyth's finely defined lips with their perfectly ridged divot above the center and a small, disconcerting black mole just above the right corner. In truth, the woman was not as horse ugly as he had originally thought. Oh, her straight nose was too strong and haughty for his taste, not to mention that stubbornly jutting chin, but if it were not for the gray hair and broom-thin body she might be passable in looks. Peering closer, he could see now that she would have been a beauty in her youth—the Silver Jewel of Northumbria.

Eirik's hand reached instinctively for his mustache. Something about the lady's appearance struck him as strange. But then he remembered Wilfrid's words on the scandal that surrounded her. She was a puzzle he could not fathom yet. He smiled to himself at the prospect of solving her mystery.

"May I join you?"

"Of course," he said, feeling chastened, like a boy, by her softly spoken words at his failure to offer hospitality. He stood and helped her up the steps to the high table, noting the thinness of her arm under the thick fabric. Lord, where did she find such a God-awful color of russet? She was taller than average but still she barely reached his shoulder, he noted as he introduced her to Wilfrid.

Before sitting, she checked the seat of her chair, no doubt looking for dust. *Bloody Hell!* He had only been home a few sennights and had more important matters to handle than laggard servants. It was one thing for Wilfrid to nag him about opening the purse strings of his fortune to restore Ravenshire, another for this unwelcome guest to look down her long nose at him and his keep.

Reaching for an empty goblet, he looked at her pointedly as he wiped the rim with the sleeve of his undertunic to satisfy her fastidiousness. Then he poured her a drink and offered it to her graciously, hoping to make up for his earlier lack of manners. Eirik saw that she took special care not to let their fingers touch. And, as she sipped the ale, he could not help but notice her nose's slight wrinkle of disapproval.

"You mislike dogs and ale, as well, I see," he commented testily.

"Nay, 'tis untrue. I like dogs well enough, in their place, *outside* the hall and kitchens. And as to your ale, 'tis passable." Her prideful chin lifted a notch higher. "I have been spoiled, though. I make the best mead in all Northumbria from my own honey."

"Truly? 'Tis remarkable. Not that you brew your own mead, but that you sing your own praises."

Eadyth's eyes shot up and locked with his, and the heat of her blush turned her cheeks pink.

Good! he thought.

"I must yield to your wise assessment of my failings, my lord. 'Tis true I am immodest. I have lost the feminine arts these many years I have lived away from society," Eadyth apologized with no embarrassment whatsoever. "Ofttimes I

14

forget that gentle-born ladies are to be ever meek and weak. My father indulged me in my independence.''

Even if he had not already noted her prideful chin, which had a tendency to jut upward stubbornly, Eirik sensed instinctively that she did not often humble herself so. An almost imperceptible note of vulnerability edged her voice, and Eirik softened.

''He was a good man—your father. I met Arnulf years ago when he came to visit my grandfather Dar. Sorry I was to hear of his death.''

Eadyth nodded in acknowledgment of his condolences.

''You have no brothers, as I recall,'' he continued. ''Who runs Hawks' Lair?''

''I do.''

Startled, he choked on the ale he had been sipping, and Wilfrid slapped him heartily on the back.

Eadyth's lips turned up in a condescending smile, and Eirik's attention once more riveted on the small mole near her mouth. He had heard of some women who painted such on their faces. Could that be the case with her? Nay! A woman who skinned her hair back like a nun and wore such drab garments would disdain vain decoration.

''Why is that always a man's reaction? Truly, I do not understand why men ever persist in believing women incapable of more than gossip and stitchery.''

Eirik sat forward and began to look at Eadyth with new interest. '' 'Tis my experience that most women are empty-headed, devious creatures and quite content to do little more than just that. 'Twas certainly so with my wife afore she died. If 'twere not for the need of heirs, I warrant, most men would disdain the marriage bed and get their bed sport elsewhere.''

The bluntness of Eirik's words did not seem to bother Eadyth's feminine sensibilities. In fact, she appeared to appreciate his honesty.

Her fingers traced an invisible pattern on the tabletop as she studied him closely. Why? he wondered. Eadyth licked her lips nervously, drawing his eyes once more to the disarming mole. Eirik watched, mesmerized, as the pink tip of her tongue unconsciously traced a path from one corner, to the divot, to the other corner, then across her full bottom lip. What would it be like to do the same with his own tongue? Eirik fantasized, feeling an immediate swelling at the joining of his thighs.

By All the Saints! he chastised himself. He was behaving like an untried boy. In truth, he had been too long without a woman if an aging chit could turn him hard.

And the impudent wench was scrutinizing him in an oddly searching fashion. Truly, she was a most unusual woman.

"Are your eyes blue . . . pale blue as a summer sky . . . as I have been told?" Eadyth asked unexpectedly, jarring him from his lustful thoughts.

Disconcerted by her odd question, Eirik drew back slightly. "Yea, they are—a legacy from my Viking ancestors."

Eadyth nodded her approval.

God's Teeth! Why would the old crone care one way or another whether his eyes were sky blue, or dirt brown?

"You do not look the Norseman. Your hair is black, is it not?" She asked her question in a casual manner, but Eirik could tell by the whiteness of her knuckles, apparent even in the dimness of his hall, that his answer was important to her.

What was the wench about, asking him foolish questions about the color of his eyes and hair? He leaned back and viewed her suspiciously through slitted eyes. "I am only half Viking. My mother was Saxon." He bit his bottom lip in annoyance as he failed to figure her game, then added mischievously, "Would you like to see my Viking half?"

Wilfrid chortled gleefully at his other side, but Eadyth only colored brightly and pretended she had not heard his words.

"I meant my brawny might in battle," he added mockingly, lifting a well-muscled arm for her to admire, "and my cunning in maneuvering unscathed amongst the Saxon political snakepits." He tapped his head as if to show it was not entirely empty.

Eadyth, apparently lacking in humor, as well as beauty,

failed to smile at his jest. Instead, she thoughtfully compressed her lips to a thin line as she boldly scrutinized him. Finally, she asked, "May we speak in private, my lord?"

Eirik schooled his face to blandness, betraying none of his surprise, before motioning Wilfrid to leave them for a while.

As if pondering some serious problem, she drummed her slender fingers uncertainly on the tabletop before appearing to come to a decision. She waited until Wilfrid stepped off the dais, then looked Eirik directly in the eye.

"I need to marry immediately," Eadyth blurted out without preamble. "Wouldst thou be interested?"

Eadyth watched the dark knight fight to keep his jaw from going slack. After his initial shock over her unexpected proposal, his face froze into an expressionless mask as he tried to understand her bizarre actions.

Hah! Men were so transparent. They thought women incapable of logical thought, and therein lay their weakness. Eadyth had learned over the past eight years lesson after lesson in the power of men over women. But it was not an absolute power, and she had become an expert in outwitting them. Had she not proven over and over her capability in running Hawks' Lair and trading her own products in the marketplace of Jorvik—the best honey and mead and beeswax candles in all Northumbria?

It nettled Eadyth to have to come on humble knee before the handsome, smooth-tongued Lord of Ravenshire. As if she cared whether his finely chiseled features could melt the hearts of maids from Yorkshire to Strathclyde! Or that his slick words could cause a saintly nun to lose her inhibitions. She wanted no man for husband, and certainly not this ill-clothed brute in his crumbling castle who looked down his arrogant nose at her in barely suppressed disdain.

St. Bridget's Breath! The thought of entering the bonds of matrimony made her cringe with distaste. *Bonds!* That was the all-important word here. For all these many years, she had refused to become chattel to any man.

17

But now she had no choice. Time was running out. The best she could do was strike a deal for the best betrothal agreement, one that would benefit her prospective husband but allow her to retain her freedom. Would the Lord of Ravenshire agree?

"Mayhap my ears play me false, my lady. Did you ask for my hand in marriage?" When she nodded and defiantly lifted her chin, he snorted with disgust. " 'Tis unseemly that you act on your own behalf."

"Who would negotiate for me? My father is dead. I have no family." She shrugged. "Are you so strait-laced and fearful of your manhood you cannot deal directly with a woman?"

Eirik sat up straighter, a muscle twitching angrily in his square jaw at her challenge. "You tread on dangerous ground, foolish lady. Heed me well, I fear you not, nor any man *or woman*. You ask for direct dealings. Well, you shall have them. I tell you directly—my answer is 'Nay.' I am not interested in your marriage proposal."

Eadyth felt an annoying flush move up her neck and heat her cheeks. Why couldn't she curb her wayward tongue? Accustomed to dealing with crafty tradesmen and laggard churls, she ofttimes forgot how to be diplomatic. With deliberate care, she banked her rankling temper and forced herself to proceed carefully before speaking again.

"I apologize, my lord, for my hasty words. The urgency of my situation causes my loose tongue, but, please . . . please do not refuse my proposal afore you hear the details."

Eirik poured more ale into his goblet and sipped thoughtfully, scrutinizing her through slitted eyes, and obviously finding her lacking in the attributes he would seek in a wife. That didn't surprise her. In fact, she had tried her best not to attract the lustful attentions of men since her one disastrous mistake eight years before.

"With all due respect, my lady, I have no interest in another marriage—to any woman. Once was enough."

"Ever?" Eadyth asked, surprised. "I thought all men felt

the need to breed heirs. Your wife bore you no sons, did she?''

He shook his head. "My brother Tykir is my heir, and I have no particular desire to propagate my own image." His head tilted questioningly, as if he had just thought of something important. "Leastways, I would hardly consider you of childbearing age."

"Huh?" His comment disarmed Eadyth. It was true that many girls wed by age fourteen, but she had seen only twenty-five winters and was certainly well within the age of conceiving a babe. Not that she wanted to. And certainly not with such a crude oaf as him. But how old did he think she was?

Aaah! she realized suddenly, touching her head-rail, it was her silvery hair that caused his mistaken notion of her age—that and the deliberately loose garment which hid her womanly curves. It was fortunate that he had not seen her this morn as she tried to manage the wild, waist-length curls under her wimple, finally resorting to pig's grease to slick back the unruly mass. Apparently, the lard also managed to hide the golden blonde highlights in the silvery strands.

But then a sudden thought occurred to her. Perchance his mistaken notion of her age could work to her benefit. After her one distasteful—nay, disastrous—encounter with a man's lustful inclinations, she had no wish for any other. Warming to her role, Eadyth almost smiled as she hunched her shoulders slightly and forced a cronish cackle into her voice, evading his question. "Heh! Heh! Heh! 'Twould seem my age is of no importance if you wish to breed no heirs. In fact, it could work to both our advantages."

His interest sparked, Eirik raked his fingers through the coal black hair which reached to his shoulders. He brushed his mustache distractedly, a trait she had noticed several times as he watched her like a wary bird—yea, the raven that he was. And he squinted often. Finally, he arched his eyebrows questioningly over translucent blue eyes.

Holy Virgin! A woman could drown in their mesmerizing

depths, Eadyth admitted to herself, then mentally berated herself for the thought. In truth, Eirik was not as handsome as Steven, the cause of her problems. Steven's polished veneer and delicately proportioned features approached perfection, while Eirik's rugged beauty was too blatantly virile, his sharp edges too powerfully masculine for Eadyth's tastes. In an odd way, he frightened her.

Forcing herself back to the matter at hand, she went on, "Let me be blunt—"

"Why stop now?"

Eadyth shot Eirik a withering look. She would ignore his jibe for now. But she could not stop her fists from clenching and unclenching convulsively as she spoke. Blessed Lord, humility came sore hard for her to swallow.

"I need to marry as soon as possible. My husband must be able to lead men if it comes to fighting, but more important is political cunning—a talent for politics, avoiding a confrontation, if possible. Do you understand my meaning?"

"Why me?" Eirik asked curtly. " 'Tis obvious you are not attracted by my innumerable charms."

He was watching with interest the revealing action of her nervous hands. Eadyth willed herself to composure. He saw too much. At the same time, he did not see her true appearance. How odd!

And his flippant remark about "charms" annoyed her. Did he play with her, regarding her reluctant proposal as an excuse to make sport with her? Of course, he did. To his mind, she was well past the age for being interested in a man's endowments.

Enough! She wasted precious time tiptoeing around the dangerous issue at hand. He said he valued honesty. Well, she would give him a fair dose and show him what she thought of his "charms," as well.

" 'Tis true, I am not overwhelmed with lust for your godly handsome body," Eadyth remarked sarcastically. "Nor do my bones melt in your manly presence. I could even bear to be in your company for a short while without swooning in

20

adoration, I wager. In truth, I would as soon wed your loathsome dog as you, if 'twould solve my problems.'' Eadyth saw the muscles tense in his tight jaw. *Good!* She had his full attention now—no more smirks or veiled allusions. ''But your hound would not suit at all, you see, because it does not have your blue eyes . . . or black hair. Did I not mention afore, those are important requisites for my groom.''

''Blue eyes! Black hair!'' Eirik sputtered. ''Have a caution, wench, you overstep yourself. And you waste my time with foolish talk of physical attributes. I do not wish to wed, especially not to a coarse-tongued, waspish harpy. And that is my final word on the subject.'' He stood as if their meeting was at an end.

Eadyth's hopes withered under his scornful words, and a rush of alarm swept over her. Once again, she had let her repugnance for a forced marriage overshadow her reason.

''Here,'' she said quickly, shoving a document into his hands. ''Mayhap you should consider what you so blithely toss aside.''

Eirik stared at her in stony silence, but finally he looked at the document, holding it at arm's length. He scanned the words and figures briefly, then plopped back down into his chair, exhaling with a loud breath of impatience.

''What in the name of St. Cuthbert is this?''

Eadyth thought the document was self-explanatory since the words ''Betrothal Agreement'' were written clearly across the top in her own neat script. Mayhap he could not read. '' 'Tis the dower I offer if you will agree to the marriage,'' she explained proudly with chin held high.

Eirik gazed at her incredulously for a long moment before turning back to the document, reading aloud, ''Five hundred mancuses of gold; two hundred hides of land adjoining Ravenshire to the north; twenty ells of fine baudekin silk from Baghdad; three cows; twelve oxen; fifteen thralls, including a stone worker and a blacksmith; and fifty queen bees, along with an estimated hundred thousand worker and ten thousand drone bees.'' He looked at her questioningly, a mocking grin twitching at his lips. "Bees? What would I want with bees?"

" 'Tis how I have made my fortune, my lord. Do not be so quick to mock what you do not understand."

He put the document on the table, then steepled his fingers in front of his mouth as he leaned back in his chair and studied her closely. Finally, he spoke, choosing his words carefully. " 'Tis impressive, indeed—the dower you offer. And surprising. I had not thought Hawks' Lair to be such a prosperous keep."

He smiled then. It was a very nice smile, she conceded to herself. And Eadyth noticed how his very expressive eyes twinkled with merriment. Truly, she could understand why women melted at his feet if he turned this lethal charm in their direction.

"Does the king know of your wealth? Surely, his council would be interested in a higher levy for your riches."

Eadyth bristled at his backhanded compliment. "Hawks' Lair is a small keep, but I use every portion of it efficiently. Any wealth I have garnered, however, comes from my beekeeping enterprise. The last few years have been especially profitable as my reputation for fine mead and honey and beeswax candles has grown. My timekeeping candles earn a particularly handsome profit."

"You engage in trade yourself?"

"Yea, that I do. I have an agent in Jorvik, but 'tis always wise to keep a check on those who handle your affairs."

Eirik chuckled and shook his head from side to side in disbelief.

Eadyth bristled. "You find humor in wise business."

"Nay, I find humor in *you*, my lady, and your many contradictions."

"How so?"

"You come barging into my keep, uninvited, bristling like a hedgehog. You insult my dog, my ale, my person and my integrity, and yet you ask for my hand in marriage. You are highborn, and yet you dirty your hands in trade. And . . ." He hesitated, seeming to think he had mayhap gone too far.

"And what? Do not stop now. Let us be perfectly honest with each other."

"Well, I have oft heard you referred to as 'The Silver Jewel of Northumbria' because of your renowned beauty, but I see it not."

Eadyth cringed under his harsh but honest appraisal. In truth, she did all in her power to hide whatever beauty she still had. It should not matter that he found her less than comely, but somehow it did. It was just a remnant of her old feminine vanity, she supposed. She squared her shoulders and asked, "Is there more?"

"Yea, there is." Eirik paused before continuing, "You have the demeanor of a stiff-necked nun who never spread her legs for a man's staff, and yet I have been told you were wanton in your youth. I cannot fathom a woman such as you bearing a man's weight, let alone a bastard child."

Eadyth closed her eyes momentarily, ill prepared for the mention of her son John. She had known the boy would have to be discussed if Eirik agreed to the marriage. He was, after all, the reason for her being forced into such a repugnant alliance. But she had hoped to bring up the subject in her own good time.

"Yea, I have a son," she admitted finally, looking him directly in the eye. "Is John an obstacle to this marriage?"

Eirik traced the edge of his goblet with a long, well-formed forefinger while he studied her further. Eadyth noticed that his smallest finger was missing, cut off long ago at the base, and she wondered idly if he had lost it in battle or an accident. Her speculation was interrupted as he continued speaking slowly, with what seemed to be carefully chosen words.

"If I met a woman I wanted to wed, a child would not deter me from the vows. 'Twould be false of me to say I would not prefer a virgin to wife, but then who am I to judge? I bear the mark of bastardy myself, and I have two illegitimate daughters of my own." He grinned sheepishly at her. " 'Twould seem we share a common bond."

Eadyth gritted her teeth and fisted her hands so tight the

nails dug painfully into the soft flesh of her palms. She wanted to tell him what she thought of his fathering two illegitimate children. It was not her fault that her son was born outside wedlock. But he, an unwed man, could have given his daughters legitimacy. Oh, how desperately she would like to inform him that the only bond he shared was with all unscrupulous, loose-moraled men who thought their male organs were gifts from God to be pushed indiscriminately into every maid who dared to cross their paths. He disgusted her. She, more than any other, knew how women suffered from mating outside marriage, even when promises were made aplenty.

But she could not voice her thoughts. Not now. She had to get his consent to the marriage. Once they wed, if they did, then he would get an earful of her opinions on his begetting two bastards.

Her voice oozed forced politeness as she asked, "Oh? And where are the children?"

"Larise lives nearby with Earl Orm and his family. She is eight."

"Will she live with you now you have returned to Northumbria?"

Eirik shrugged uncertainly. "I do not know yet. It depends on whether I decide to stay at Ravenshire."

How heartless! Eadyth thought. How could he abandon his young daughter to the care of others? The poor child! And what was that about not staying at Ravenshire? Perchance his absence could work to her advantage if they wed. She wanted no bothersome husband around to interfere with her freedom.

"And the other child?"

A brief flash of misery clouded his eyes. "Emma is only six. She lives in an orphanage in Jorvik, has done since she was three. My foster uncle Selik and his wife Rain, my half sister, care for her there." His voice cracked with emotion.

His words puzzled Eadyth. "But why an orphanage for such a young child, and one not a true orphan, at that?"

Eirik's expression turned bleak as he answered bluntly, "I have been away from Ravenshire for a long time and have had no home to provide her. Besides, Emma cannot speak, and she gets special care from Rain, who is an accomplished healer.'' Then he stiffened and said resolutely, ''I do not wish to discuss Emma.''

''And their mother? Could she not care for them?''

''Both mothers are dead.''

Both? Eirik had abandoned not one, but two women to the shame she knew so well. The lusty wretch!

Still, she bit her tongue to stop the spill of ill-advised opinions. She must tread carefully.

''Perchance I could be the answer to your prayers.''

Eirik smiled broadly at her poor choice of words, and Eadyth was dazzled, despite herself, by the charismatic pull of his good looks.

''My prayers? I think not, my lady.''

''What I meant,'' Eadyth persisted, ''was that if you were to agree to the marriage I could care for both your children.''

''With all due respect, methinks a wedding would be too high a price to pay for the mere care of two children.''

Mere care! Eadyth forced aside her repugnance and eyed his samite tunic, once a bright sapphire blue, now faded with age and wear, and the gold brocaded embroidery of his surcoat worn into a meaningless pattern. A fine dragon brooch of beaten gold with amber eyes adorned the shoulder of his mantle, but, in all, his attire spoke of poverty—that, and the crumbling walls of his castle and lack of servants to care for the filthy keep. Furthermore, she had noticed many empty cotter's huts and long uncultivated fields as she approached his manor.

She decided to try a different approach.

''May I respectfully advise, my Lord Ravenshire, that the dower I offered you could be put to good use in getting your manor back in order,'' she suggested, ignoring the look of surprise that swept his face. ''I know much about these things, you see. If you had no interest in the running of your keep and wished to return to court . . . or . . . or wherever . . . I would be more than willing to manage your affairs. You would have coin enough to purchase new fabrics for fine garments and restock your larders and . . ." Her words trailed off as she realized Eirik glared at her with consternation.

"And what would I be doing whilst you do all this . . . *managing*? Sitting around watching my fingernails grow?"

Eadyth just stared at him, unprepared for such a snide response to her kindly offer.

"Lady, you overstep your bounds mightily. Have you so little regard for me that you think I cannot handle my own affairs? How would I pass my idle time? Swilling ale? Bedding every maid in sight?"

Her expression must have betrayed her thoughts that she had, indeed, expected just that, because Eirik let out a loud bellow which drew the attention of several knights below him in the hall. Through gritted teeth, he snarled contemptuously, "Wouldst you find a means to fill your own sheath on the wedding night, as well? For, surely, you have no need of a man."

Crestfallen, Eadyth sighed with resignation. Obviously, he would not wed her now.

"I meant no disrespect, my lord. You are wrong, however, in saying I have no need of a man. I desperately need a husband. Oh, 'tis certain I want no man in my bed. In truth, if we were to wed, you could keep your mistresses for all I would care."

"Just how many mistresses do you think I have?" Eirik asked with amusement, no longer angry.

Eadyth waved a hand in the air as if the number mattered not. "You have a reputation for having many women, and—"

"*Having* many women?" he choked out. "All together?"

"Do not be ridiculous," Eadyth said, but then she felt her face heat at the image. Without thinking, she commented, "I had not realized *it* could be done with more than one woman at a time."

Eirik hooted with laughter.

Eadyth wilted under his ridicule and tried to go on. "I know you have a mistress in Jorvik, and, if there are others, it matters not to me."

He lifted a dark brow in surprise. "You know of Asa? Your spies have done your work well, my lady."

Eadyth shrugged dismissively. " 'Tis of no importance. I see now that you will not wed me. 'Twould seem I will have to begin my search anew to find another highborn man with black hair and blue eyes."

"Truly, you intrigue me, my lady. Explain yourself, if you will. Why those requisites?"

Eadyth hesitated to discuss her son John with this man, but, her chances for wedding Eirik now being nonexistent, she thought he might be able to advise her.

"The boy's father has had second thoughts after all these years of having disclaimed paternity. He petitions the Witan to gain custody of John for his own wicked purposes. I need a husband to protect me in my fight. And"—she hesitated, questioning how much information she could trust him with—"and it could not help but aid my cause if the man swore he was John's father, especially if he has black hair and pale blue eyes, as my son does. As does his true father."

Eirik threw back his head and laughed uproariously. When he finally regained his composure, he shook his head, amazed at her devious mind. " 'Twould seem you have thought of everything. But what makes you think the king's council would heed such a belated request for custody from the father?"

Eadyth leaned closer to explain. "King Edmund has supported me at the Witan against . . . against this horrible man these many years, mainly in deference to my father who served him loyally, as he did his brother King Athelstan afore him. 'Twas the wound my father sustained at the Battle of Leicester, in Edmund's service, that led to his death. My position has weakened with my father's death."

"Edmund is a good man. He does not renege on his promises of protection."

Eadyth raised a hand to indicate there was more. "As you well know, many attempts have been made on the king's life, and Steven, the unspeakable fiend, toadies up to young Edred, who is bound to be his heir since Edmund's children are so young. There is no question Steven will succeed if Edred takes the throne."

She sighed and leaned back in her chair, closing her eyes wearily. She was deathly tired of all the turmoil, and now she would have to start her search all over again. After several moments, she noticed Eirik's odd silence. When she opened her eyes, his dark, angry expression stunned her, all the emotion seemingly directed her way.

"Wha-at?" she gasped as he stood abruptly, without warning, and grabbed her by the upper arms, lifting her out of the chair and up off the floor so she faced him, nose to nose, with her arms pinned at her sides.

"The father of your child—do you perchance refer to that *nithing*, Steven of Gravely?" he asked in a steely voice.

Eadyth nodded, realizing she must have inadvertently spoken Steven's name. And she could not deny that Steven deserved that most offensive of insults, *nithing*—the lowest of all men.

"You spread your legs for that slimy snake and dare to question *my* character?"

He shook her so hard her teeth clicked together. She knew she would bear bruises on the morrow. Leaning her head back, she gazed into his icy eyes. His stormy countenance frightened her, but she refused to defend herself to this loathsome lout. In truth, only a woman could understood what she had done with Steven and why his betrayal had cut so deep.

Finally, he dropped her to her feet. Wagging a finger in her face, he ordered in a voice that brooked no argument, "You will remain in my keep this night. We will talk more in the morn when I have had time to think through all you have told me. God's blood! Steven of Gravely! I can hardly credit the coincidence."

"I do not understand." Eadyth's mind reeled with confusion.

"You need not understand, wench," he told her with contempt, "but know this: you may very well have a marriage pact yet. And may the Good Lord and all the saints have mercy on your hide then. For I will not."

Chapter Two

Eadyth awakened at dawn the next morning. Truth be told, she lay wide-eyed long before first light, thanks to her flea-infested bedding.

Her servant was sleeping on a pallet laid over the dirty rushes near the door. Poor Girta! The vermin had probably held a bloody feast on her plump flesh. On closer inspection, though, Eadyth noticed that her trusted maid was snoring evenly, undisturbed by the pests.

Perhaps Girta's hide was thicker, or more likely Eadyth's fair skin just tasted sweeter, she thought, chuckling softly. *Hah!* The insufferable master of this crumbling heap of a castle would beg to differ on that subject, she would wager.

Eadyth stepped over her prone maid, whose mouth now played a veritable chorus of sounds—soft snores interspersed with a few contented grunts and wheezes. She gazed fondly down at the stout woman who had served her faithfully these many years, first as nurse when her mother died in her birthing, now as companion.

Looking for a bowl of water, she hoped to refresh herself

before facing Eirik's stormy resistance once again. She could find none. In fact, not only had the fire gone cold in her room, but an air of total silence encompassed the halls outside. Surely, the Ravenshire servants ought to be about by now, preparing for the new day.

Pensively, Eadyth donned her dowdy garments and smoothed her hair back under its wimple and head-rail. As an added measure, she grabbed a handful of ashes from the hearth and smeared them carefully on her face to give her skin a grayish cast.

She smiled, remembering Girta's outrage yestermorn when she had deliberately sought out the most drab and concealing garb she could find.

" 'Tis a poor temptation you make for the marriage bed,'' Girta had complained tartly.

"Just so, Girta dear. 'Tis exactly my aim. I would entice a husband with my dowry and my abilities in managing an estate, not my flesh.'' She had shuddered with repugnance at that last prospect, adding, ''I have more than learned my lesson in *that* regard.''

"Ah, child, 'twas one bad experience. Not all men are cut of the same cloth.''

Eadyth's demeanor had hardened then. ''Nay, you are a good woman, Girta, but harsh reality has proven to me that more men than not share Steven's evil designs where women are concerned. They consider us mere chattel to be used and set aside when the pleasure fades. I would have more than that.''

Girta had shaken her head with worry. ''I cannot fathom how you will be able to accept the strictures of wifehood.''

"I will not. My prospective groom must agree to my conditions aforehand,'' she had asserted with more confidence than she felt.

"Oh, Eadyth, dear child, I fear you will be sorely hurt.''

Hurt? Eadyth pondered now as she opened the door of her bedchamber onto the drafty hall. Nay, she had long since hardened her vulnerable heart. But John . . . he was a different matter. She would do all in her power to protect her son from pain—even if it meant marrying the loathsome lout of Ravenshire, or some other equally detestable man.

Eadyth walked through the hall and down the stairs of the two-story, wood and stone keep. Much larger than Hawks' Lair, it had been an impressive castle at one time, or so her father had often said, but crumbling stone and rotted wood bespoke years of neglect. In truth, she hated to see any fine thing, whether person or building, treated so poorly. It said something about the man. Eirik had much to answer for in his abuse of his heritage, Eadyth thought as she shook her head woefully.

She looked for a servant who could direct her to the garderobe, then to fresh water for drinking and bathing. No one was about. Some drunken knights she had seen yestereve slept on wide benches and in bed closets edging the great hall, along with some of the servants.

A few of the women lay naked under the sleeping furs, limbs entwined with the highborn men. Through the partly open door of an alcove, Eadyth saw a red-haired vixen sharing the bed place of Wilfrid, the seneschal she had met yestereve. In the cradle of Wilfrid's arms, the woman's bosom pressed provocatively against his dark-haired chest and a long leg was thrown over both of his massive thighs. More outrageous, her callused fingers lay intimately over his limp man part.

Eadyth's eyes widened at the erotic scene. Then her upper lip curled with revulsion. Knowing what she did of the nature of men, Wilfrid could very well be married and his poor wife asleep above stairs while he fornicated like a rutting rabbit with the servant girl.

Not really surprised, Eadyth knew that bed sharing was common practice in many manors, especially a male-dominated one like Ravenshire. But she did not permit such bawdiness at Hawks' Lair. She encouraged marriage among her churls, and no unwilling maid was ever bedded by visiting nobles in her keep.

She considered shaking them both awake to vent her disapproval, but, unlike yestereve, she vowed to follow a more sensible path today. After all, it was not her keep—nor likely to ever be so. Instead, she headed toward the separate kitchen area, connected to the keep by an enclosed passageway. Even though the castle had no chatelaine, some servant should be in charge of the household . . . perchance the cook.

Pushing open the heavy door, Eadyth gasped with horror at the nightmare of greasy pots, darting mice, spoiled food, unwashed trenchers and goblets, and even two chickens pecking contentedly at food droppings on the dirt-encrusted stone floor. Eadyth grabbed a broom and shooed away one fat mouse feasting on a hunk of mutton atop the table, then stomped over to a pallet near the cold fire where a servant, probably the cook, was snoring loudly through the rotten teeth of her open mouth. She rolled over onto her stomach with a grunt and broke wind loudly. Using the broom, Eadyth gave her a whack across her wide buttocks, and the woman shot upright, rubbing her bottom.

"WHA..AT?" the woman shrieked as she jumped up off the pallet, coming only to Eadyth's shoulder, but twice as wide in girth. "Have ye taken leave of yer senses, bedevilin' an honest servant like me?" Narrowing her eyes—small black pinpoints in her bloated face—the cook asked caustically, "Who do ye think ye be—a bloody queen?"

"Lady Eadyth of Hawks' Lair, you lazy slut. Are you responsible for the filthy condition of this kitchen?"

Obviously frightened now that she realized her insult had been addressed to a noble lady, the woman nodded hesitantly, rubbing the sleep from her beady eyes. When she yawned widely, Eadyth almost swooned from the wave of foul breath that came her way, a combination of bad teeth and stale mead, not to mention a body and clothing that probably had not been washed since Easter. Thank the Lord, she had eaten no food prepared by the grimy hands of this old hag.

"What is your name?" Eadyth demanded in a steely voice.

"Bertha."

"Well, Bertha, what say you of this pigsty of a kitchen?"

"Huh?"

Eadyth snorted with disgust. "How many servants are about this keep?"

Bertha scratched her armpits indolently, then began a mental count on her fingers. " 'Bout twelve inside, mayhap another twelve outside. Many a servant and cotter left durin' these two years the master has been gone."

"Who was in charge in his absence?"

The cook shrugged her bulky shoulders. "Master Wilfrid, but he be gone much of the time, as well, since his wife died last year. Bless her sweet soul!" Bertha looked dutifully sorrowful at the loss of Wilfrid's wife. *Hah!* Wilfrid had not looked to be in mourning when last she had seen him, Eadyth remembered cynically, picturing him with the naked servant.

"I want you to gather every single servant—thrall or churl—in this kitchen immediately. Do you understand me?"

The cook nodded dumbly.

When the scurvy group of sluggards crowded into the kitchen area a short time later, Eadyth already had water heating on the hearth and pots and trenchers and goblets soaking. She gave the servants a tongue lashing they would not soon forget, then specific directions on tasks she wanted accomplished within the hour.

"Bertha, I want the floors and walls of this kitchen swept and scrubbed. All the cutting boards are to be scoured, and fresh flour brought in for baking. I will check the food supplies in the larder for spoilage and worms, which will be considerable, I warrant.

"Lambert, get another man to help you cut and stack a five-day supply of firewood for the cooking fires. Agnes and Sybil will gather the eggs and milk the cows." She hesitated then and looked to Bertha. "There are cows, are there not?"

Bertha nodded her head slightly. "Only one cow be left, and mayhap two dozen hens."

"Good, we will churn some butter when the milk is brought in."

On and on she went with her instructions until a few of the servants rolled their bleary eyes in their heads.

Then Eadyth turned to the great hall, ordering some of the men to sweep out all the filthy rushes and replace them with fresh, herb-scented ones. Others she set to scrubbing the trestle tables and sweeping cobwebs from the walls. Still others lifted dusty tapestries from the stone walls and took them out to the bailey for a good shaking.

Most important, to her thinking, she banned all dogs from the great hall for the time being. Even so, the stupid hound from the night before kept following her around like a love-struck swain. Giving in momentarily, she looked about quickly to make sure no one watched, then bent down and scratched him lightly behind the ears, causing the beast's tongue to loll out in ecstasy. Eadyth shook her head in mock disgust.

" 'Twas a lackwit thing you did yestereve, hound, in front of a gentle lady, no less, but I did not mean to hurt you, even if 'twas only a mild nudge of my shoe." She sat back on her haunches and examined him closely. "Ah, you are a fine breed. I can see that now. Surely, your lineage is impeccable. Do you have a name? Nay? Well, then, I shall call you . . . what? Prince?"

The dog wagged its tail enthusiastically, and Eadyth laughed softly. "You like that name, do you? Well now, we must come to an understanding on another matter." Picking up the foul-smelling animal, she walked outside and deposited him in the bailey. "Do not come back 'til you have bathed, Prince," she advised the dumb beast, whose eyes watched her soulfully as if it understood perfectly.

Turning back to the hall with a chuckle, she saw that some of the highborn gentlemen were awakening groggily from their drunken stupors, and she set them to hunting fresh meat for the table, even Wilfrid, who seemed too stunned by her bullying to protest. In fact, he smiled enigmatically, asking innocently, "Didst the Lord Eirik ask for your help, my lady?"

Eadyth felt herself blushing—a habit she would as soon control, but could not. "Nay, he did not. I presume he still lies abed after swilling ale the night long with you," she snapped back tartly, then turned defensive. "I do him a service setting his lazy servants to their work." She cast a quick, meaningful glance at Wilfrid's bed companion of the night before, implying that Eirik probably did something other than sleep in his chamber, as well.

Wilfrid flashed a knowing smile her way and gave a quick kiss to the maid, who, standing beside him, had managed to cover her nakedness with a fur pelt. "I will see you later, Britta," he said, tweaking the maid on the rump with a lascivious wink.

Britta blushed prettily and looked up at Eadyth with blank innocence.

Eadyth tried to glare angrily at the foolish maid, but Britta was little more than a child, probably no more than fifteen. Truly, she knew no better. "Britta, please cover yourself with more suitable raiment, then remove all the bedding from whatever pallets or chambers are unoccupied. Bring them out to the kitchen courtyard for washing."

Britta nodded obediently. "Be you the new mistress?" she asked shyly. "Will you wed the master?"

Eadyth felt another unwelcome blush heat her cheeks. "I doubt that we will wed, and, nay, I am not your mistress. I merely act as . . . as friend to Lord Ravenshire in getting his keep in order."

Eadyth tried to sit politely then and await Lord Ravenshire, but her body bubbled with its usual restless vitality. She could not bear idling uselessly while awaiting the master's convenience, especially when her hands itched to tackle the vast amount of work surrounding her. She soon gave in to her instincts.

By midday, she felt a glow of satisfaction as she gazed at the remarkable progress already made. The kitchen gleamed. The hall smelled sweetly of fresh rushes and newly crushed herbs. Clean clothing and bedding boiled in large kettles over open fires and lay out to dry on bushes in the neglected kitchen gardens.

Some of the servants had already been sent to bathe at a spring-fed pond behind the keep, and the rest would soon follow. Eadyth had forbidden anyone from breaking fast until they had performed their chores and bathed. She wished they would hurry. Her stomach growled noisily, along with the rest, at the tantalizing aroma of fresh bread baking in the stone ovens to the side of the wide hearth. Newly churned butter rested golden yellow in a large crock atop the massive wood table dominating the center of the kitchen. The grain of the oak had finally emerged after the table's harsh scouring with sand and strong soap, despite Bertha's whining about her raw-skinned fingers.

Admiring the basket overflowing with recently gathered chicken and goose eggs, Eadyth wondered if Bertha knew how to make a good pudding. If not, she could advise her with one of her own receipts.

Eadyth's stomach roiled again with hunger as she heard the sizzle of juice popping in the open fire from a side of salted pork. A small boy, Godric, the orphan of a long dead castle thrall, turned the spit slowly as he looked up at her, his gaze adoring, thankful to be given his own small chore. A stock pot of venison bones and leftover winter stored vegetables had been started in a cauldron at the back of the fire, with a cloth-wrapped pease porridge hanging in its center.

There was still much to be done, but a good start. Eadyth preened with satisfaction. Would Eirik appreciate her efforts? For the first time, Eadyth wondered if perchance she had been hasty in her well-meaning actions.

Eirik awakened to a loud pounding at the door of his bedchamber. Or was the pounding in his head? He sat up abruptly, then fell back down to his bed at the sharp pain in his temple.

God's Bones! He must be demented to have drunk so much ale with Wilfrid yestereve. He had not tilted his cup so much

37

since he was an untried boy experimenting with all the forbidden fruits. He raked the widespread fingers of both hands through his unruly hair and sat up again, remembering the reason for his drinking spree—the aged maid, Eadyth, and her mention of Steven of Gravely. *Blessed Lord!* Would he ever escape that evil beast? Two years away from English soil, and already Gravely's hated specter ruined his homecoming.

With a grimace of distaste, he donned the same tunic and braies he had worn the night before. His servants must wash some clothing soon or he would be unable to bear his own stench. Better yet, he would throw the whole lot in the midden and have new garments made next time he ventured to Jorvik. It was past time he enjoyed his wealth, instead of letting it molder away in its hidden underground room. The tiresome game of pretending to be the beggared lord of a run-down castle wore thin these days.

Perhaps he should restore his grandfather's castle to its former splendor, set the cotters to working the fields again. He drew his lips in thoughtfully at the prospect, one he had been weighing these two sennights since his return.

He smiled then as he remembered Lady Eadyth and her outrageous proposal of marriage. In truth, it was not the first time a maid had pursued him hotly with matrimony in mind. And many a devious plot had been devised to trap him into a betrothal pact—everything from seduction to blackmail. Luckily, he had escaped them all. One bad marriage was more than enough, to his mind. When Elizabeth had died ten years ago, he had vowed never to wed again—with good reason.

But now, the mistress of Hawks' Lair offered him a temptation he might not be able to refuse. He creased his brow with irritation. Oh, it was not her handsome dowry that enticed, and certainly not her physical attributes, *God forbid*, but the prospect of revenge against Steven of Gravely—*that* he might not be able to resist. The means of finally being able to draw Steven out in the open for a fight to the death was certainly worth considering.

The pounding on his door resumed, and Eirik recognized Bertha's whining voice. "Master! Oh, please, master, come afore she turns us upside down and shakes the lice from our heads."

Eirik jumped to attention and walked to the door, opening it on the surprised cook who was about to knock again and, instead, pounded his chest. His stomach churned and the taste of stale mead rose nauseously to his throat. *Bloody Hell!* That was all he needed, on top of the pounding ache in his head.

Then his mouth dropped open in surprise.

"Bertha? 'Tis you?"

He barely recognized his old cook in her clean perse tunic. Her skin had been scrubbed red, and her clean hair lay wetly in snakelike clumps down to her shoulders, framing a face mottled with outrage.

"What is it, Bertha?" he finally asked, choking back astonished laughter.

" 'Tis the lady, Mistress Eadyth. The bleedin' harpy . . . beggin' yer pardon, master, fer me disrespect . . . the lady woke ever'one afore first light with her squawkin' and put us all to work, she did." She held out her red, roughened palms to demonstrate how hard she had labored.

Eirik frowned in puzzlement. "Do you not get up at dawn every morn to start the chores?"

Bertha's face turned bright red. "Well, yea, I mean, sumtimes, but . . . but . . .'tis not *her* place to order us about, and she called us slugabeds and worse. Sez we be so lazy we got to, no doubt, lean against the wall to belch. Claims we got lice, and sez we got 'til this midday to git rid of 'em or she will turn us upside down and shake 'em off."

Eirik laughed despite himself, and Bertha shot him a look of disgust. *Blessed St. Boniface!* The cook's shrill voice could peel the rust off armor, Eirik thought, but she failed to notice his wince as she gasped for breath and huffily straightened her wide shoulders before blathering on with her complaints.

" 'Tis a fine foul humor she be in, I tell you. Mus' be the

time fer her monthly flux, I wager. Ne'er have I heard a fine lady use such words. Why, she sez we smell like hogs, and she made ever'one bathe, sez no one kin eat 'til they be sunshine clean, and—''

"Hold!" Eirik ordered, his lips twitching with amusement.

" 'Tis jist that we . . . yer loyal servants, that is . . . thought ye should know what she be about,'' Bertha added, slowing down as she realized that she had perhaps overstepped her bounds.

"I appreciate your information, Bertha. Now, go back to the kitchen. I will be down shortly.''

Eirik splashed cold water on his face, then dunked his entire head into the deep bowl to sober himself. With a shiver, he shook the droplets from his hair, cursing at the icy shock. Thinking he should probably shave, he turned to a square of polished metal on the wall and grimaced with distaste. He looked like a bloody barbarian. He grinned. It would be good for the dour dowd from Hawks' Lair to see just what she would be getting in her marriage bed—*if* he chose to so honor her.

He smiled to himself as he walked down the steps toward the great hall, remembering her words of the previous night. "Bees!" he muttered to himself. "Did the wench actually try to buy my favors with bees?" He shook his head in disbelief. Well, it was certainly a first for him.

Eirik stopped dead in his tracks at the bottom of the steps. He blinked several times to clear his vision. Everywhere he looked, servants worked industriously—scrubbing trestles and table tops, using long-handled brooms to reach spider webs in the highest corners of the hall, removing old ashes from the hearth.

He stepped forward, and the sweet smell of herbs jarred his senses. He inhaled deeply, then looked down at the clean rushes crunching under his soft leather shoes.

He marveled at the bug that had bitten his lazy servants to bring about this reformation.

Feeling a rush of cool air, he swept his eyes to the open

door of the hall, which led out to the bailey and outbuildings. Wilfrid leaned lazily against the doorjamb, a brace of dead rabbits over one shoulder, and a wide grin plastered across his smirking face.

"Where have you been?" Eirik grumbled as he moved closer.

"Hunting."

Eirik frowned. "Why did you not awaken me? I would have joined you."

" 'Twas no time."

"Why?" The annoying grin on Wilfrid's lips drew Eirik's puzzled attention.

"The lady ordered us from our warm furs at dawn and said we would have no food this day unless we bring fresh meat to the table." Wilfrid paused, obviously relishing the telling of this tale. With a barely suppressed laugh, he continued, "Methinks she said something about you swilling ale all night with me and sleeping off the effects this morn." He tapped the side of his head in an exaggerated fashion, as if thinking deeply, then smirked. "Or did she imply you did something other than sleep in your bed? I disremember now."

Eirik snarled, "Where is the interfering witch?"

Wilfrid shrugged. "Mayhap she is out rebuilding the castle walls."

"I find no amusement in your ... amusement," Eirik growled, putting a hand to his throbbing head. Lord, he needed a drink.

"Does your head hurt, my lord?" Wilfrid asked with mock concern. "Mayhap you need a wife to soothe it with sweet words and a gentle hand."

Eirik said something very foul and turned toward the kitchen. Wilfrid followed closely on his heels, no doubt wanting to witness the inevitable scene.

He passed quickly through the kitchen, noticing its clean condition and the appetizing smells coming from the hearth. The little urchin, Godric, stood diligently turning the spit on a joint of meat the size of a hog. Probably was.

"The mistress set me to this chore, m'lord. Dost want me ter leave?'' Godric offered apologetically at Eirik's frown. Eirik saw the tears brimming in the child's wide eyes and knew he thought Eirik's annoyance was directed at him.

"Nay, 'tis a good job you are doing, Godric. Continue, if you will. Where is the Lady Eadyth?''

Godric pointed to the open door of the kitchen courtyard.

Eirik had not been in this section of the keep since his grandmother Aud kept a fine herb and vegetable garden here years ago. Each time his father Thork or grandfather Dar had returned from a trading voyage, they had always brought her exotic plants from faraway lands, to her delight. The painful memory of his grandmother, long dead of a wasting disease, and the sweet hours spent in her company, weeding the precious thyme and rosemary and chives, held Eirik immobile for a moment.

He shrugged, bracing himself for the fine mess he fully expected to see in the long-neglected yard. Guilt nagged at him like an aching tooth. Like the rest of the keep, it would, no doubt, need a total refurbishing.

At first, the bright sunlight blinded him to the whirlwind of activity surrounding him, setting his head to throbbing once again. When the din of the chattering voices finally penetrated the pounding in his head, he stopped in mid-stride, struck speechless.

Everywhere he turned, his laggard servants had been transformed into vigorous, busy bodies of activity. And they were cleaner than he had seen them since his return. Even their tunics, shabby as they were, looked newly washed. Eirik stroked his mustache pensively. He hadn't realized there were so many servants left at Ravenshire.

Some stirred boiling cauldrons of soapy water. Others removed clothing from those pots and dropped them into clean water. Still others wrung them out and hung them on nearby trees and bushes, which were as overgrown and uncultivated as he had expected. Eirik's eyes almost popped out then as he recognized his own small clothes hanging ignominiously from a mulberry bush.

"Argh!" he choked out, then spied the cause of his distress. Lady Eadyth stood chastising a young housecarl, whose wet hair bespoke his recent return from the bathing pool. Pulling on his earlobe, she shrewishly ordered him back to the pond, exclaiming over the dirt remaining on his neck and in his ears.

"Dost think she will check our ears, as well?" Wilfrid asked dryly at his side.

Eirik shot him a look of disgust, then strode purposefully over to the outrageous woman. Gritting his teeth to gain control, fearing he might do her bodily harm in view of his servants, Eirik finally said with forced calmness, "Lady Eadyth, may I have a word with you?"

The skinny wench jolted to attention and turned. They locked eyes across the suddenly silent courtyard, and Eirik's heart lurched oddly against his chest walls at the questioning vulnerability on her face which she quickly masked with its usual hauteur.

The servants froze in a tableau of frightened curiosity, but the dimwitted wench did not have the sense to fear him. Nay, she just stared brazenly back at him through luminous violet eyes. Witch's eyes! He had not noticed their odd color yestereve. Mayhap they were just rheumy with age, as his grandmother's had been before her death. Of course, that must be it.

Her cool, unflinching manner irritated him sorely. That, and his unexplainable, but undeniable, attraction to the older woman. Cursing himself disgustedly, he caught her by the arm in a pincerlike grip and steered her back to the keep, ignoring her sputtering protests.

"Sit," Eirik ordered when they were in a small, private chamber off the great hall, under the stairs. Having no windows, the room was dark and musty with neglect. He lit a candle but could see little except the thick layer of dirt and grime that covered every object in the room. Eadyth apparently had not attacked this room yet. *Bloody Hell!* What had his servants been doing while he had been gone these two years?

Eadyth grumbled under her breath and rubbed her arm where he had grasped her. Then she pulled a small scarf from her girdle which she used to dust the chair with wide sweeping motions before sitting down obediently. He noticed that she studiously averted her face and fidgeted with her head-rail, as if she did not want him to look too closely at her face. No doubt because she was so ugly. She dropped her eyes under his steady gaze, but not with humility, he noted.

Eirik sneezed repeatedly at the dust Eadyth had raised. She had probably done it apurpose, just to annoy him. He glared at her, having still another reason to mislike her intensely.

Eadyth pretended to be unconcerned as she shifted in her seat under Eirik's scowling countenance. Then she remembered that he thought her older than her years and pulled her head-rail forward slightly, hunched her shoulders a bit, and averted her face so she was not in his direct line of vision. She pulled one tiny strand of greasy hair from under the wimple to remind him of its "gray" color. Peering up slyly, she saw that her appearance displeased him greatly and knew she had succeeded for the time being.

"How dare you order my servants about?" Eirik finally asked angrily. "You insult me and my home by doing such."

"I meant no disrespect, my lord. Truly, I did not. 'Tis just that idleness sits ill with me. When I saw how your servants took advantage of you, I thought . . . well, ofttimes women notice more of these things than men. And you have been gone a long time . . ."

"Still, 'twas not your place."

Embarrassment overwhelmed Eadyth suddenly as she realized just how inappropriate her actions appeared to him. Had she lost all sense of decorum in her continual fight for independence?

With difficulty, Eadyth swallowed her pride. "I realize now

that I acted out of place. But how can you bear to eat food that comes from that filthy kitchen? Or walk in rushes that squish with animal droppings and bones and spoiled food? Or . . . ," and here she spoke challengingly, looking him directly in the eye, ". . . or sleep in beds so live with bugs 'twould be a real raven's paradise."

A flash of triumph swept over Eadyth when she saw Eirik wince at her harsh criticism. He seemed to choke back a quick retort. Raising his chin defiantly, he refused to explain himself to such as her.

"How I sleep is no concern of yours."

Suddenly, Eadyth sensed the hopelessness of her mission here, despite his having asked her to stay the night. Standing, she told him curtly, "You are right. I should not have interfered. I will be off to Hawks' Lair now. I am sorry to have inconvenienced you."

Eirik put an open hand on her shoulder and motioned her back into the chair. "Hold. Let us discuss the matter," he said in a placating tone, offering her a cup of wine.

"This early in the day? Nay. I have not broken fast yet."

"Nor anyone else in my keep, I understand," he commented drolly.

"Wouldst you prefer to have your food from a filthy kitchen? Hell's flames! The lice fair danced in your cook's hair."

Amusement lit Eirik's blue eyes, but his expression remained annoyed. "Mind your language, maid. 'Tis uncomely for a lady of your station."

Eadyth rankled under his criticism. In truth, she had been amongst tradesmen and their crude conversations too long, but she would not admit such to this humble knight.

"Did you drag me into this room to discuss the manner of my words? If so, I would take leave of your company, for I have better things to do with my time."

"You are quick-tongued, my lady," he said, with a grin. "Most men would not appreciate such from a mere woman. 'Tis the reason you have not wed afore, I wager."

Eadyth gritted her teeth and met his gaze directly. "I have not wed," she said through clenched jaw, "because I chose not to. Contrary to most men's high-blown opinions of themselves, many women are content with the solitary life."

"Did you want to marry Steven?"

Eadyth stiffened at his blunt question. Eirik twisted the end of his mustache between two fingers pensively, watching her like a hawk. She could tell her answer was important to him.

"I find your question rude and personal, and—"

Eirik held up a hand to halt her words. "Nay, the question is a reasonable one for a prospective bridegroom."

Eadyth's eyes shot up in surprise. She had thought the possibility of their marriage doomed. Coloring hotly, she forced herself to reveal an intimate detail of a past life she would as soon forget. "Yea, I wanted to marry Steven of Gravely, fool that I was."

"Did he promise marriage to you?"

"Yea, he did . . . afore he got what he wanted of me."

"And that was?"

Eadyth cut him with a sharp look that said even he was not that lackbrained. She leaned back in her chair, folding her arms across her chest, then immediately wished she had not when his eyes settled on her seemingly flat breasts. She dropped her arms with a small sound of disgust and said boldly, looking him directly in the eye, "He lusted for my body." At the skeptical expression on his face, she added with a shrug, "I had a lust-provoking body in those days."

He snickered.

She glared.

"And did you lust for him, as well?"

Eadyth gasped. Truly, this conversation had gone too far. She pressed her lips tightly together to halt the crude expletives she wanted to hurl at him. Then, weighted by a deep sense of shame, she admitted in a soft, bitter voice, "I mistook lust for love, on both our parts. But I was soon shaken of that halfwitted notion."

"How so?" Eirik persisted, his face solemnly intent.

"When I discovered my pregnancy and went to him, fully expecting a quick betrothal and wedding, as he had promised, he laughed in my face. He disclaimed paternity." Eadyth glared at him stonily, angry that he had forced this humiliating admission from her. It was a subject she never discussed. "I refuse to speak more of that devil's spawn with you."

" 'Tis one subject, at least, on which we can agree—the evil character of Steven of Gravely."

"Yea, 'tis."

"Once you discovered his betrayal, did you not consider seeking a midwife to help you . . ."

"What?" she prompted, failing to understand his meaning.

She noticed his lips tense whitely as he hesitated before voicing what seemed to be an important question to him. "Some women would have found a means to rid themselves of an unwanted child. Did you make such an attempt, and fail?"

"Nay!" she cried out. "How could you even ask? John is the only good, pure thing to come of that hateful . . . liaison." Eadyth tried to bank her anger at Eirik's insulting question. When she was finally able to speak below a shout, she added, "You have a very low opinion of women, my lord. I wonder why."

He stared at her thoughtfully for several long moments, rubbing that infernal mustache. His bemused expression finally faded as he seemed to make a decision. "Wait here," he ordered as he stood and approached the door. "I must get something."

When he returned a short time later, he carried a small, linen-wrapped bundle which he placed on the table. Then he sat down in the chair next to her and drew her dowry document from his tunic. He motioned her to pull her chair closer to the table.

"Afore I call Wilfrid to witness our signatures, I would set my own conditions to our betrothal agreement, my lady."

47

Startled, Eadyth stared at him questioningly. "You intend to wed me?"

Eirik's lips spread over a rueful grin, as if he himself could not believe that he was about to act so foolishly.

"Yea, God help me, I do."

At first, Eadyth's mind failed to register the significance of Eirik's words. Mixed feelings warred within her—relief that John would be protected by the marriage vows, countered by her desperation over the hateful bonds. She did not loathe men, only their lusty ways, and yet she felt herself drawn by Eirik's handsome masculinity.

"Why?"

Eirik threw back his head and laughed. " 'Tis an odd question for a bride to ask."

"I am not the usual bride, and you well know it. 'Tis obvious you find the prospect of marrying me distasteful. Did my dower tempt you? Did you decide you could use it to restore Ravenshire?"

Eirik blinked with surprise, then burst out laughing again. "Mayhap I am more like Steven. Mayhap I lust after your lush body." He wiggled his eyebrows lasciviously.

Eadyth felt a hated blush creep up her neck and across her cheeks, and she snorted with disgust at his making sport at her expense. He was too frivolous, by far.

" 'Tis not my body, lush or not, that will be a part of our betrothal agreement."

Eirik raised one brow in mocking question, his thick black lashes forming spidery shadows over the oddly pale eyes.

"Oh? Will it not? Hmmm. We shall see."

Her heart hammering with alarm, Eadyth looked to see what Eirik meant by his cryptic remark, but his head was bent over the document as he scratched out his own conditions on the bottom.

Eadyth closed her eyes wearily.

Am I making an even bigger mistake, casting my lot with the Lord of Ravenshire?

Chapter Three

Eirik's words about the betrothal agreement finally sank in, and Eadyth bristled. So now she would find out what he really wanted of her.

"Conditions? What is your meaning?" she demanded in a deliberately cronish voice as Eirik painstakingly scratched words at the bottom of her document.

She was pleased to see him wince at the abrasiveness of her cackling voice, even as he ignored her question and kept writing. He held the sheet some distance away from him as he wrote, squinting occasionally.

Eadyth's brow furrowed in puzzlement at his odd motion. Then a soft smile touched her lips as, suddenly enlightened, she realized that he must have difficulty seeing things close up, just as her own father had.

So this was why he mistook her frowns for wrinkles and could not tell ashes from a gray complexion. Now she understood why the color of her hair and the deliberate stoop of her shoulders had fooled him so easily.

She almost laughed aloud with glee. This slight deception

was not something she had planned originally, but any device that forestalled the distasteful touch of a lusty man would be more than welcome.

Eirik did not notice her quickly suppressed smile, so hard was he concentrating on his writing. Finally he expelled a long breath of satisfaction and leaned back in the chair, pushing the betrothal agreement toward her. The expectant gleam in his eyes warned her that she would not like the conditions he had set.

Eadyth carefully averted her face, knowing Eirik was watching closely as she read. His eyesight could not be too dim. After all, it did not lessen his abilities as a seasoned knight, if his reputation rang true. She had to remind herself to bend her shoulders slightly, as well, and occasionally she peered up at him through the open fingers of a hand coyly fanned over her lower face, as if his overwhelming masculinity turned her shy. *Hah!* She would have much to confess in this deceit when next she saw Father Benedict.

"Do you understand the words, my lady?"

"Yea, I can read well enough." She continued to scan his words, then protested, " 'Tis not necessary for you to provide a *foster-lean* for me. My father is dead."

"A husband is expected to pay the father of the bride for past nurture. In his absence, I give you his due."

Eadyth lifted her chin proudly, defiantly, and scratched that provision from the document. "Claiming paternity for my son is *foster-lean* enough for me."

Eirik shrugged.

"And I do not crave any portion of your property as the *morgen-gifu*. My morning gift will be your promise of protection. You have already told me your estates will go to your brother."

Eirik looked her directly in the eyes. "And if we have a son, or sons? What then?"

Eadyth felt her face flush. She wanted to remind him of the nature of this marriage, but could not find the words. *Sons!* "Have you mistaken my proposal of marriage for something other than a business arrangement?''

"A business arrangement! Never have I met a woman like you afore. Never!" he exclaimed, shaking his head from side to side with disbelief. He waved her protests aside with one hand and said, "Let it stand for now. With the dangers my brother Tykir faces daily, I will no doubt outlive him anyway."

Then she read his last conditions and alarm swept over her like a heat flash. "I cannot accept what you ask of me."

"Oh, what do you find objectionable?" he drawled, extending his long legs languorously, crossing them at the ankles. The worn fabric of his tight braies pulled taut on his thighs, and Eadyth stared, open-mouthed, for a lengthy moment at their well-formed contours. His surcoat had fallen back, exposing the wide chest of the same blue tunic he had worn yestereve. A few silky black hairs escaped the parted neck opening, but not her notice.

The edges of Eirik's firm lips tilted slightly in a knowing smile, and Eadyth's mouth snapped shut. She could have kicked herself at her betraying perusal. Willing her rapid pulse back to normal, she grumbled, "Must you flaunt your body so? You may think you can charm the very snout off a pig, but I am not one of your lackwit mistresses to swoon at your feet."

Eirik just grinned infuriatingly. "Methought we were speaking of conditions here. *Betrothal* conditions." He looked down at his thighs, then back at her, goading her silently to react to his taunt.

Eadyth cleared her throat irritably and pointed to the words he had scrawled at the bottom of her document. "Yea, I wouldst speak of your conditions. Firstly, I prefer to live at Hawks' Lair. I see no reason to move myself and John here to Ravenshire."

Eirik arched an eyebrow in question. "Have you no seneschal to serve in your absence?"

"Yea, I do. Gerald of Brimley, but—"

"Is he trustworthy?"

"Yea, but he only serves in my stead. I am needed, if for no other reason than to oversee my beekeeping."

"Move the bloody bees here."

Eadyth smiled condescendingly at his ignorance. "Bees are not like people. They do not just pick up their belongings and move from keep to keep."

Eirik stared at her intently, and Eadyth squirmed under his scrutiny. She wished he would stop stroking the silken hairs of his mustache. It was disconcerting.

"Then leave the bees there. But you, my lady," he concluded flatly, pointing a finger in her face, "will live here with your son or there will be no marriage."

"Why would you care where I live? 'Tis no love match atween us."

"For certain," he said drolly, casting a look of amused disdain her way.

Lord, she would like to smack the silly smirk off his disgustingly handsome face. "Methought you would value the freedom of my absence from Ravenshire."

"What makes you think I would be less free with you here?"

Eadyth stiffened with indignation and pulled her head-rail forward to hide her emotion. Then she asserted, jutting her chin out proudly, "I could not abide having your lemans in the same keep as I."

Eirik's translucent eyes widened with surprise. Then he smiled with irritating mockery.

"My lady, you offend me. I have told you afore, and will not repeat it again. I am an honorable man. I would not disgrace a wife so."

Casting a sidelong glance of skepticism at him, she asked, "Are you saying you would never take a mistress?"

She delighted in the flush that swept across his face and the way he squirmed in his seat. He refused to answer, just watched her closely with arms folded across his massive chest, stroking his infernal mustache the whole time.

"I do not mean to make you uncomfortable, Eirik. I have

not asked you to give up your women.''

''Women! Oh, Eadyth, you do credit me with more endowments—and endurance—than I truly have,'' Eirik remarked, shaking his head incredulously. ''Where do you get these ideas of the many women I have?''

'' 'Tis said you fornicate like a rutting stag.'' *Oh, sweet mother; did I really say that?*

Eirik inhaled sharply at the words she had blurted out without thinking, and his jaw tensed with outrage.

''You heard such said of me?''

''Well, not quite those exact words.''

''Then be more specific,'' he demanded. ''Who would insult me so? 'Twas Steven of Gravely, I warrant, the damned rumormonger.''

''Nay, 'twas not Steven,'' she informed him, wishing once again that she could learn to curb her foolish tongue. Hastily, she added, ''Actually, I think the words I heard in the marketplace were more like, 'The Raven cannot pass a pretty maid without sampling her honey, and the women buzz with satisfaction at his pricking.' ''

She shrugged her shoulders dismissively.

Eirik's eyes almost popped from his head and his mouth went slack-jawed at her frank words. Then he exploded with laughter.

''Oh, Eadyth! The things you do say!'' he finally choked out. ''Ne'er have I met a woman with your blunt tongue. 'Tis too bad you . . . ah, well, a man cannot have everything.''

Eadyth somehow knew he was about to bemoan her age and ugliness. A small part of Eadyth shriveled inside at his unspoken words. The low estimation of this devilishly handsome oaf should not matter to her, but it cut nonetheless.

A thrum of alarm swept over Eadyth at her weakening resistance. What was happening to her usual good sense? Sitting up straighter, she vowed to maintain better control over her oddly churning emotions.

Forcing a bland expression to her face, refusing to show how the implied insult hurt, Eadyth persisted, ''I still would know why you insist I stay here.''

"I wish to bring my daughters home. Remember? You promised to care for them.''

With relief, Eadyth nodded at his explanation, understanding now why he wanted her to live at Ravenshire.

"Well, perchance I could bring some of the bees here. Leastwise, 'tis what I promised in the dower agreement. Let us compromise, though. I will spend half my time here and half at Hawks' Lair, taking the girls with me so that you are free to . . . travel or . . . or . . . whatever 'tis you do.'' She refused to mention his other women again and open herself up for further ridicule.

Eirik grinned at her tiptoeing over the issue of his mistresses. "You will stay at Ravenshire,'' he stated implacably, "and occasionally travel back to Hawks' Lair, at *my* sufferance.''

Eadyth assessed him over the table, weighing her options. "I agree, on condition I may keep all proceeds of my beekeeping in a separate household account in my name.''

Eirik nodded stiffly.

"And you understand that Hawks' Lair is to be held in your guardianship only 'til John reaches his majority.''

He nodded once again, piercing her with a withering glare. "I have no desire to take your piddling coins, nor your son's inheritance. But there is one other condition which I demand, on which there will be no compromising—*ever.*''

His eyes were like shards of blue ice, glittering with some fierce emotion as he spoke. He clenched his fists so tightly that the knuckles whitened, and a pulse beat rapidly, disarmingly, as the base of his exposed neck.

For a moment, his suppressed rage frightened Eadyth, and she wondered once again if this marriage to the Lord of Ravenshire was such a good idea, after all. Truly, she did not know this man. He could be as bad, or worse, than John's father. Was it too late to cry off?

With lightning swiftness, Eirik grabbed her chin tightly and forced her to look into the bottomless pools of his eyes.

"Understand me well, lady. There will be no contact betwixt you and Steven of Gravely."

Eadyth gasped, but before she could speak, he went on in a controlled voice, "If ever I find you have so much as looked at him with yearning, or touched his putrid body, I swear afore the Holy Grail I will kill you both with my bare hands."

The intensity of hatred in Eirik's words momentarily stunned her. Then outrage took over. She stood angrily and sputtered, "How dare you imply I would have aught to do with Steven? I have already told you of his perfidy toward me and his devious plans to take my son John. You insult me by even thinking I could bear his repulsive touch."

"You loved him once," he pointed out accusingly.

Eadyth had explained her actions once. She stubbornly refused to do so again.

Eirik's face remained rigid. "You will not play me false with Steven, my lady. Ever! Swear a holy oath. Assure me of your fidelity."

Oddly, he did not demand that she shun other men, only Steven. She knew her reasons for hating Steven. What were Eirik's? She started to ask, but his implacable expression told her that now was not the time. She sat back down, vowing to explore the mystery later.

"I give you my oath as an honest woman: I will never betray my marriage vows . . . with Steven of Gravely . . . *or any other man.*"

The harsh lines in Eirik's face smoothed a bit, but then he grabbed her wrist and pulled it toward him on the table. She watched, mesmerized, as he laid her hand flat on the hard surface, palm up, and ran a forefinger back and forth lightly over the pale skin of her wrist.

The barest touch of his finger, a whisper of a caress, ignited sweet tingles of sensitivity which ricocheted sensuously up her arm, to her breasts, causing the tips to harden into tiny pebbles of aching need. Eadyth inhaled sharply, alarmed at this new feeling of helpless yearning. She tried to pull away, but Eirik held her hand fast.

His head tilted questioningly and his eyes narrowed as he studied her closely.

"When you are not frowning, you do not look so aged. How old did you say you are?" he asked, without warning, in a suspicious tone of voice.

Eadyth could see the erotic luminosity hazing his eyes and knew the touch affected him as much as it had her. At the same time, he obviously puzzled over his uncharacteristic attraction to an aging woman. Thank the saints for the dimness of the chamber. Before she had a chance to respond or turn her face away from his scrutiny, Eirik suddenly unsheathed a sharp blade hanging from the belt at his waist.

Good Lord! Was he going to kill her just because he felt a momentary lustful impulse for an old crone? She gasped and yanked futilely against his grip. The man had lost his senses.

Before she could guess his next move, he ran the razor-sharp blade across her wrist, then did the same to his own. In shock, Eadyth watched entranced as thin streams of blood pooled on both their wrists. For a long moment, they both gazed at the twin wounds, the only sounds in the room the even, exaggerated echo of their breathing.

Gently, he pressed his massive hand across hers so the blood mingled and their pulses merged, then looked her directly in the eyes and stated in a firm, husky voice, "Blood of my blood, I pledge thee my troth."

Heart hammering, Eadyth stared at him. *Sweet Mother of God!* He truly was a Viking barbarian. At the same time, she felt an irresistible pull toward him, a melting of her defenses that frightened her to the core.

Seemingly unaware of his devastating effect on her, Eirik adjusted his hand so that their fingers twined together and folded, wrist to wrist. Her tingling wound throbbed and changed character, became almost an erotic rhythm, a sharp counterpoint to her pounding heartbeat.

Oh, my!

"Now you repeat the words," he demanded raspily, refusing to let her pull her wrist from its savage embrace with his.

In stunned silence, her eyes locked with his. She could not speak.

"Say the words, Eadyth," Eirik coaxed.

"Blood of my blood, I pledge thee my troth," she repeated softly.

Her world tilted askew then as something new and beautiful—and frightening—blossomed inside Eadyth's chest and unfurled with exquisite, heart-stopping intensity. This was not the usual betrothal ceremony, presided over by church clergy, attended by family and friends, as solemn as the wedding ritual itself. It was better, and its heart-wrenching intimacy shook Eadyth's long-frozen soul.

"Do you think this is binding?" she finally whispered.

"Yea, 'tis," he answered softly.

Still holding her arm fast, Eirik pulled a ring from his tunic and slipped it on the third finger of her right hand. " 'Tis the first of my *arrha* gifts for you. You will move it to your left hand after the wedding, symbolizing that you accept your new position of obedience." He chuckled at his last word.

Eadyth raised an eyebrow skeptically, but she could not fail to appreciate the magnificence of his gift as she closed her fingers to keep the huge gold band from slipping off. Looking closer, she saw the image of a raven, with gleaming emerald eyes, etched into its center.

" 'Twas my grandfather's."

Eadyth nodded at the significance. "I have never heard of *arrha*. It means 'earnest gifts,' does it not?"

"Yea, tradition calls for three bridal gifts. The ring was the first." Then he reached into the packet on the table and handed her a silk-embroidered shoe, proclaiming, "This is the second. It belonged to my grandmother Aud."

"Only one?" she asked with a laugh, pleased, despite herself, that Eirik had taken the time to honor her with tokens.

He grinned. "I get to strike you on the head with it during the marriage ceremony. Normally, your father would hand it to me, symbolizing his transfer of authority over you to my hands.''

"Hah! My father never exerted that kind of control over me. I would not allow such, even if he had wanted it.''

Eirik continued to grin. "On the wedding night, the other shoe is placed at the head of the marriage bed, on the husband's side, to signify the bride accepting her husband's authority.''

Eadyth shoved the slipper back into Eirik's hands. "Keep your bloody slipper. As for the ring," she said admiringly, not wanting to give it up, "I accept it with my own interpretation of *obedience* to my husband." She smiled at him, despite her resolve to develop no fondness for the churlish knight. "Well, if that is all—''

"Nay, you forget. I mentioned there were *three* 'earnest gifts.' ''

She raised an eyebrow.

"The traditional betrothal kiss.''

Before she could demur, he leaned forward. Alarmed, Eadyth turned at the last moment so his warm lips brushed her cheek. Eirik chuckled low in his throat at her maneuver, then put his right hand at the nape of her neck and forced her lips to meet his in a light feather stroke of a kiss. His left hand still held hers in a firm clasp.

Eadyth closed her eyes momentarily to savor the sweet pleasure of his warm lips.

Oh, Eadyth girl, you are in big, big trouble. This man is a dragon, and you are the dry tinder. He will burn you alive. Run, girl, run as fast as you can.

"What is that ungodly smell?" he asked.

Eadyth blinked several times to clear her muddled senses. "Huh?" she said.

Eirik wrinkled his nose and leaned closer to her head-rail, sniffing loudly. "It smells like fish oil. Or hog renderings gone bad.''

Eadyth pulled away from him then and stood shakily, knowing he smelled the grease in her hair. She hunched her shoulders a bit and cackled, " 'Tis a special ointment I have concocted to ease my aching limbs of a cold morn. Would you care to try it? 'Tis good for horses, as well.''

Repulsed, Eirik jerked back. Eadyth smiled inwardly at the look of confusion on his open face. He obviously failed to understand the odd attraction that had shot between them for one moment. An aberration, she vowed, which would never occur again.

"You will call the banns then?'' she asked weakly as she moved toward the door, her senses still churning from his touch.

"Yea. I have no chaplain at Ravenshire now, but I can send to St. Peter's in Jorvik.''

"And the wedding? When will that take place? Time is important if we are to forestall Steven's moves.''

"Three sennights?''

She nodded. "I will be off to Hawks' Lair then whilst there is still light and will return in twenty-one days.''

"Nay, you will not leave today.''

Eadyth stopped dead in her tracks. "Why?''

"We must needs have the betrothal feast tonight.''

"Nay, we will not!'' she cried, knowing she had to put a distance between them to reevaluate this foolish masquerade she had started. At the challenging look on his face, however, she softened her voice and cajoled, "Let there be no hypocrisy atween us in this marriage. Why pretend emotions we do not feel?''

"My men will question my motives, and yours, if we do not at least appear to want this alliance. If we cannot convince my loyal retainers that I cared enough once to breed a babe on you, how will we convince the king that I am the boy's father?''

Eadyth saw the logic in his words but resisted, nonetheless. "*Cared enough!* Hah! You do not know Steven so well if you think that was the motive for the act that brought about John's conception. 'Twas more like, *lusted enough.*''

He shrugged and grinned widely. "Either way. If 'tis the

image of lust you prefer to convey, mayhap I could put a hand on your thigh or a tongue in your ear whilst we are toasting our betrothal this night.''

"A tongue in my . . . !" Eadyth felt her face flame. "Do you dare, and I will put a sharp knife to your precious manhood."

Unamused by her threat, he informed her stonily, "I dare much, my lady, and think again afore you throw warnings my way. You will get more than you bargained for, I promise." When she raised her chin haughtily, he added, "I will win every battle you wage, my lady, whether it be with might or words."

"Do not be so sure of that," Eadyth threw over her shoulder as she walked out the door, and heard him chuckle at what he probably considered childish, feminine defiance.

When Eadyth saw Girta sitting at a table in the great hall, partaking of the newly baked bread and a slice of freshly cooked meat, she slowed down.

"When you are done breaking fast, will you see if my beekeeping veil is in the pack attached to my horse's saddle? I would check for wild bees in the fields beyond the orchard I saw this morn. Mayhap there are some new species I can breed with mine."

Girta nodded and raised an eyebrow questioningly, knowing full well that Eadyth often pursued her beekeeping jaunts when troubled.

"Will there be a wedding?"

"Yea, there will," she said, looking down with wonder at the ring and at the thin wound on her wrist. "In three sennights."

"Will we stay here 'til then?" Girta's brow furrowed as she scrutinized Eadyth with loving care.

"Nay, we return on the morrow at first light and will come back the day of the wedding." She sat down next to her old maid and confided, "Girta, there is one thing you should know. He thinks I am much older than I am, and quite . . . uncomely."

"Why would he think so?"

"Well, he does not see perfectly, like my father. Remember?"

Girta nodded.

"And the hall is dark and smoky. And, uh, the grease in my hair apparently gives it a grayish hue. And my loose garb . . . well, all these things combined, I suppose, have given Eirik the impression I am old. And—"

"How old?" Girta asked suspiciously.

Eadyth shrugged. "Mayhap forty or so. Certainly past the childbearing years."

Girta's mouth dropped open in surprise before she threw back her head and chortled gleefully. "Oh, Eadyth, child, you play with danger here." Then she sniffed and leaned closer to her beloved charge. "Oh, Good Lord, Eadyth, the pig grease in your hair has gone rancid."

They both burst out laughing then, and Eadyth hugged her dear old nurse warmly in companionship. And perhaps desperation.

Eirik stomped off the exercise field later that afternoon, prompted by the wild ranting of several servants who had come to him complaining about the ghost in the orchard come to haunt Ravenshire. Bloody Hell! It was all he needed—an aging wife, a crumbling keep, and now a ghost.

He walked briskly through the fields beyond the kitchen garden, overgrown with gorse and bramble, past the spring-fed pond where he had swum as a child and now used for bathing, and through the long-neglected orchard of apple, pear, peach and plum trees. His grandmother had cultivated and cared for these fruit trees lovingly over the years. He wondered idly if they were diseased beyond salvation.

Finally, he spotted the "apparition" his frightened servants had been complaining about all afternoon. In truth, the witch from Hawks' Lair did look a mite ghostly in a long diaphanous veil which covered her entire body from head to toe, like a ghost, with specially made sleeves from which protruded odd leather gloves that reached up to her elbows. The hound she had kicked the night before lay nearby like a besotted lover.

"By all the saints, woman! What do you out here at this time of day in that ridiculous apparel? 'Tis almost time for our betrothal dinner."

Eadyth swiveled abruptly, just realizing he stood behind her. "Don't come any closer. The bees are swarming and may attack."

Eirik's eyes widened as he noticed the hundreds of bees covering her hands and glove-protected arms. In fact, they buzzed all over her flimsy garment, like live ornaments.

"Are you daft, my lady? Come away from here at once."

"I am in no danger. 'Tis my business, raising bees. I have told you so afore. I just wanted to see what wild species you have available here at Ravenshire afore I bring my bees here. I have had some success in mixing the breeds, but these are of an inferior quality and may have to be moved to another site."

Eirik shook his head in disbelief at this strange woman he was about to wed. Would she continually surprise him? And what was it about her that both repelled and attracted him at the same time? He had never lusted after older women in the past, and yet he did not think he would find the bedding of her as distasteful as he had originally thought.

"Mayhap we will consummate the wedding tonight," he said huskily, not realizing he had spoken aloud 'til he noticed the stiffness of her body and the defiant lift of her chin.

"Mayhap cows have wings," she snorted, sweeping the bees off her garment with jerky motions of her hands as she moved away from their hive. Then she glared at him angrily. "I am going back to Hawks' Lair *now*. I will not stay the night at Ravenshire, you lusty lout. Hah! There must needs be a shortage of women for you to make such a ludicrous suggestion to me."

The dog fell into step behind her like a well-trained foot soldier when she called out, "Come, Prince."

"*Prince*? What manner of name is that for a lowly mongrel?" Then he drew his thoughts back to her annoyance over his suggestion. " 'Tis not so ludicrous. Many a marriage is consummated on the betrothal alone."

Eirik had not really expected her to comply. In truth, he did not know why he had even broached the subject. He did not want to make love with a skinny wench like her. But still her displeasure rankled his pride, and he followed her stomping figure back to the keep, cursing under his breath at his stupidity—not just in voicing the words, but in even agreeing to the wedding.

"I was only jesting," he lied. "Have you no sense of humor at all?"

"Humph! Stop following me."

"Stop walking away from me. And stop that bloody dog from nipping at my heels."

" 'Tis your bloody dog, not mine. He is just being protective of me because you are raising your boorish voice."

"Lady, you overstep yourself. We are not wed yet. Remember that."

She had the good sense to slow down at his warning. After all, she had more to gain from this wedding than he. Or so she must think.

He grinned as he caught up with her and reached for her arm, the dog yipping wildly. She jerked away at his touch, and Eirik frowned. He misliked her touchy attitude. In truth, she was nervous as a pregnant cat any time he got within breathing distance of her.

Deliberately, he placed a hand on her arm, testing her reaction. Leaning back so he could see better, he watched as her eyes flew wide with alarm. Even through the filtering screen of her veil, Eirik could see that she breathed heavily through her open mouth. He watched with fascination as her deliciously full lips quivered nervously behind the white netting. "I have seen such fabrics in the harems of some eastern rulers, though put to much different use," he murmured, then smiled in remembrance.

Eadyth just scowled.

The small mole at the side of her mouth drew his attention. He reached forward, unable to resist the temptation, and touched it lightly through the wisp of material. A jolt of desire rocked his senses and turned him instantly hard.

"Do not touch me," she whimpered, trying to pull out of his firm grasp. "Please. I beg you. I will release you from your betrothal vow."

Eirik dropped his hand and stared at her, puzzled. What frightened her so? After all, she was not a virgin maid, untouched by man. And knowing Steven of Gravely's predilection for sexual excess, he assumed the knave had taught her more than a few tricks in the mating.

"My lady, I do not take my oaths lightly. As far as I am concerned, my betrothal vow is as binding as the wedding ones."

She lowered her gaze and inhaled deeply to regain her composure. It was obvious his touch had distressed her mightily.

Or repulsed her, he thought, and went rigid at the insult. Women found him attractive. It had ever been so. What prickled Eadyth? Something was seriously amiss.

Finally, she raised her eyes, even more luminously violet in their misting of tears, and said in a shaky voice, "I take my vows seriously, as well. 'Twas just that you took me by surprise. I had not expected you to make such a vile suggestion."

"*Vile?*" His brow furrowed. "Are you daft? You ask a man to marry and do not expect him to bed you?"

Her cheeks pinkened becomingly, and Eirik squinted to see her more clearly through the clouding of the sheer veil. Damn his poor sight! He shook his head as if to wipe the fog from his eyes and looked again. *God's Bones!* If it were not for the ashy hair, he could swear she was younger than he, and he had only seen thirty-one winters.

"Stop that."

"Stop what?"

"Looking at my mouth."

He grinned. Raising a hand, he touched her veil-covered lips with the pad of an extended thumb.

She slapped his hand away.

Eirik laughed, low and throaty.

Eadyth, squirming under his intense scrutiny, dodged away from him and put a hand to the small of her back, as if it pained her, then cackled in a manner that raised the hairs on his arms.

" 'Tis just that I did not think a man like you would want to do . . . *such* . . . with a woman of my age, and appearance.''

"Lady, I am beginning to think that a man with the bedlust might overlook your age and . . . shortcomings . . . just because of your delicious lips and that enticing mole.''

That drew her body stiff as a battle pike, and Eirik laughed to himself at her quick rise to his baiting. Better yet, he saw an odd look of pleasure at his compliment sweep her face before she had a chance to draw on her usual mask of chagrin.

Ah! Finally, an inroad into her formidable defenses.

But then she retorted shrewishly, "Good Lord! If a mole makes you hot, I have a whole cartload of aging, toothless weavers at my keep that could turn your manhood rock hard and occupy your time for a score of weeks.''

"My lady, your crudity knows no bounds. Never . . . *never* have I heard a highborn woman use such words afore.''

" 'Twould seem there is a first for everything then, for I have never heard of a normally endowed man who would yearn to take old grandmothers to his bed.''

Eirik clenched his fists.

Do not strike the impudent wench. Do not strike the impudent wench. Do not strike the impudent wench, he repeated over and over to himself, but, by all the saints, he was sorely tempted to put both hands on her slender neck and squeeze the very breath from her bony body.

"You are not a grandmother,'' he sputtered out, then stopped. "Are you?''

Eadyth flashed a strange look his way, and a brittle laugh escaped her lips. "Nay. Not yet.''

As they continued to walk back toward the keep, a thought occurred to Eirik. "Just how old is your son John?"

Eadyth stumbled, but then caught herself and kept on walking. Eirik froze at her reaction to his question, but soon caught up with her. More and more, her actions puzzled him.

"Well?"

"How old do you think he is?" she asked shakily, deliberately refusing to meet his eyes.

Little warning bells went off in Eirik's head. He sensed he was getting closer to the mystery, and answered hesitantly, "I do not know precisely. Mayhap fifteen or so."

Inhaling sharply, Eadyth began a fit of coughing. Eirik slapped her mightily across the back before she finally choked out, "Enough! Dost want to break my bones?"

"You did not answer my question, Eadyth," Eirik pointed out stonily and drew her to a stop outside the kitchen door of the garden courtyard. "I would have the truth."

She looked him directly in the eye. "Seven."

"Seven!" he stammered out. "He is a mere child. Why did you not tell me afore?"

Eadyth shrugged. "I saw naught of importance in his age." Then she studied his face. "Does it matter?"

"Nay," he said hesitantly. "You just took me by surprise."

Now that he had a chance to think about it, it was not so unusual for a woman her age to have a seven-year-old child. She would have been in her early or mid-thirties at the time of her involvement with Steven. He looked up, about to ask her if that was the case, but she had already dashed through the door.

"I will see you at the feast," she called over her shoulder. "Do not bring the dog inside, if you please. I have warned him that he may not enter 'til he has had a bath and learned to behave properly."

Eirik grinned and shook his head at her overbearing attitude, but his amusement soon died on his lips when she added impishly, "Mayhap you could learn the same lesson, my

66

lord.'' Ripples of laughter echoed in her wake.

Eirik stared after her for several moments before he realized that the saucy lady had inferred that he needed to bathe and learn some manners. Hah! He would show her soon enough what her impudent words would gain for her. She was too high and mighty in her own estimation, by far. He would relish the task of bringing her down a peg or two.

A wicked thought occurred to him then. He threw back his head and laughed aloud. Oh, yes, it was a wondrous fine use he had just conjured for that sheer veil of hers.

With a jaunty step, he turned and called after the dog. ''Come, Prince, we go to bathe. The lady says we stink.''

The dog yipped in agreement.

Chapter Four

By the time Eadyth reluctantly left the seclusion of her guest chamber, dusk already hazed the dimness of the closed corridor.

Dust motes danced merrily in the narrow stream of light coming through an arrow slit at the far end of the hallway. In contrast, eerie, moving shadows in the crevices of the stone walls loomed out at her, reminding her of the long history of tragedy that had haunted this keep for three generations.

Would her destiny as the mistress of Ravenshire be as sad?

Actually, Eadyth reminded herself, Ravenshire's history was no more unfortunate than many manors in the vast north, Hawks' Lair included. Northumbria had always been a bone of contention amongst the warring powers, wedged as it was between the Saxon kingdom to the south and the lands of the Scots, Cumbrians and Strathclyde Welsh to the north and northwest.

And the Northumbrians themselves! This mixed breed of different races, Norse and Saxon intermingled, guarded their independence fiercely. They delighted in provoking the supercilious, purebred Saxons by drinking too much, speaking with uncouth accents and refusing to conform to society's standards.

Sometimes these rebel Northumbrians were successful in their revolts. But not of late, Eadyth reminded herself. Oh, no. Not of late. Since the Battle of Brunanburh nine years before, where thousands of Viking, Scots and Welsh soldiers had died attempting to shake the tyrannical yoke, Northumbria had never truly recovered.

Eadyth heard a shuffling noise behind her and almost jumped out of her skin. Startled, she pressed the widespread fingers of one hand to her chest to slow her wildly beating heart, then giggled, realizing it was only Prince following in her footsteps, tail wagging contentedly.

She continued on her way to the great hall, wishing once again that she could avoid the lord of this dreary keep and hide in the protective cocoon of her chamber until morning. But she knew she had to set aside her foolish fears and comply with Eirik's demand that she celebrate their upcoming nuptials with him. Her prospective bridegroom had already sent three insistent reminders that it was past time to join him at the high table.

The last message had been quite blunt, if Godric's artless honesty in the retelling could be trusted. "Tell her to get her malingering arse down here, or I will carry her down on my shoulder. Better yet, I will come up and launch the wedding festivities in my own way, and I do not mean with a cup of ale."

The boor!

She had tried to convince Girta to go down and tell Eirik she suffered from a stomach cramp, but her faithful companion had turned stubborn, refusing to participate in Eadyth's deceit.

" 'Tis unseemly that you shame the lord by dressing so for a betrothal feast," she had clucked disapprovingly before her exit. "And worse that you humiliate him with your tardiness. It smacks of contempt. You could, at least, wash that horrid smell from your hair. Good Lord, Eadyth, even I cannot bear to be near you for more than a few moments.''

Disgusted, Girta had left her presence long ago, presumably to oversee the food preparations, but more likely to escape her dour mood.

If only women had more choices in life!

But Eadyth knew full well that, even if her husband were ugly as a toad, the Holy Church and Saxon law said a wife must submit to her husband. *Submit!* What an ugly word! That was why women like herself were forced to revert to subterfuge in resisting the attention of lust-minded man.

Even so, misgivings hammered at Eadyth's brittle composure. She agonized over pretending to be old and uncomely, despite her perfectly understandable reasons.

Would Eirik consider them reasonable?

Hardly, Eadyth answered herself. How well she knew that men cherished their pride like a precious appendage, and the least thing a woman did to make them appear less than manly could prick them sore. Eadyth sensed—nay, she knew without a doubt—that Eirik would be very, very angry when he discovered she had been less than honest. He would not see the humor in her disguise, and the longer she fooled him, the greater would be his outrage.

But what could she do? Confess before the wedding and take a chance on his canceling their betrothal agreement? Nay, she had to carry off her pretense for at least another three sennights. Then she would devise a clever way to disclose her true self—one that would not demean his pride in any way.

Once she weathered this evening's events, she would be back at Hawks' Lair until the wedding. Even then, she decided, she would tell him her true age but would do naught to enhance her appearance in his eyes, not a thing to incite his lustful impulses. That was not *really* dishonest, she tried to convince herself.

All she had to do was get through this night.

Sweet Mother of God, help me, and I vow to bend my

prideful ways. No more will I make jest of Father Benedict.
Or look down my nose at weak-willed women. Or . . .

Eadyth saw her mistake the moment she entered the great
hall, where scowling men impatiently awaited her arrival before beginning the feast. She had forgotten one major consideration. In her dawdling, she had given Eirik and his knights
excessive time to drink ale on empty stomachs. Annoyed at
the delay, they were in a fine temper to taunt her with their
ribald remarks as she passed, red-faced, through their whis-
tling, snickering ranks to the dais.

"The Raven awaits anxiously, m'lady," one young warrior
called out. "Will you stroke his ruffled feathers smooth?"

"Nay, just that one hardened quill atween his loins," a
gnarly old warrior snickered in a quick rejoinder. It was the
same knight she had chastised yestereve for body odor.

The other men guffawed loudly at the jape.

A handsome, blond-haired knight blocked her path momentarily, a retainer from Eirik's Viking side of the family,
no doubt. All the men were well on their way to being fall-
over drunk, including this handsome Norseman who swayed
on his feet. Before Eadyth had a chance to brush past him,
the arrogant lout belched hugely, then asked, loud enough for
all his friends to hear, "Mistress Beekeeper, will you let the
master taste your honey this night?" Then he fell back, laughing uproariously at his own jest.

"Nay," still another bantered coarsely as she swept past,
"she will teach our lord to make his own honey."

"Bzzz. Bzzz. Bzzz," they all began chanting as they
pounded on the tables with their goblets.

Eadyth finally pushed her way past them all, her chin held
high and her eyes welling with embarrassed tears. Where was
Girta, her only ally here? And why didn't Eirik call a halt to
the indelicate jesting? As her betrothed, he should protect her
from such insult. Truly, he should, she cried inwardly.

Past humiliations flashed through her mind, memories Eadyth thought she had put to rest long ago. How naive she had
been in those days! She had never really expected her peers

to forgive her indiscretion with Steven, but their cruelties had been beyond anything she had ever experienced in her sheltered life. No wonder she had shut herself away these many years!

She lifted her chin defiantly and refused to slink away to lick her wounds. No more would she let such people hurt her.

Blinking her eyes, she searched for Eirik through the eye-smarting smokiness of the great hall. Really, something would have to be done when she took charge about enlarging the smoke hole, or finding some better means of ventilation, she decided, wiping her eyes with the back of one hand. It must be unbearable in the winter months.

Her gaze collided then with her betrothed's, and she knew exactly why Eirik had not intervened on her behalf. Although he leaned back casually in his high-backed chair on the dais and strummed his fingertips idly on the table, his tight jaw and glittering eyes bespoke a blind fury. Eadyth faltered slightly but then proceeded stoically up the steps.

Oh, Sweet Mother.

"Please forgive my delay," Eadyth offered with her customary directness when she finally stood at his side. "I suffered a slight ague of the stomach, my lord."

He looked up at her lazily through slitted eyes, not even bothering to rise, then said something very foul that even Eadyth's trading acquaintances had never dared to utter in her presence.

She stiffened. "Dost make you feel better to show as little respect for your betrothed as your knights do?" she complained waspishly. She pointed with disgust to the lower hall where his retainers ogled them openly, still calling out an occasional lewd suggestion or merely making buzzing sounds. "I may speak too frankly betimes, but I am not accustomed to such rude treatment."

Leastwise, not lately. Especially since I rarely leave my keep.

"And what of the ill-bred manner in which you have treated me and those knights who follow my standard? Your contempt for the betrothal speaks for itself in your refusal to join our toasts.'' He shrugged. "You forced us to do the toasting alone.''

He raised his goblet, draining the contents in one long swallow, and Eadyth realized he had, no doubt, lifted his goblet a dozen times while awaiting her arrival.

Oh, Lord! She had trouble enough dealing with the sober Eirik.

She caught the eye of Wilfrid as he sat down next to his master, regarding him with pity. Eadyth bent her head in shame, realizing full well how it felt to be demeaned in front of others. She had not meant to humiliate Eirik before his men. It was just that she feared his discovery of her charade. And, Holy Virgin, in his present mood, it appeared he would as soon twist her neck like a spring chicken as marry her.

"You do not even deign to dress for the occasion,'' Eirik rebuked her further, scanning her garments disdainfully.

Eirik had bathed and trimmed his mustache. He wore a black tunic and surcoat, somewhat worn but trimmed with gold braid and cinched at the waist with a belt of fine gold links. Perhaps he was not quite as impoverished as she had originally thought. She looked down at herself and realized how drab she must look, standing next to Eirik.

" 'Tis unfair to condemn me for my garb,'' she cried. "I did not bring any other, and how was I to know you would agree to my proposal so readily?''

"How, indeed.''

Eadyth braced herself against his rejection. Self-pity was a luxury she rarely countenanced, and she refused to succumb now. When she felt her emotions were under control, she asked calmly, "Wouldst thou break the betrothal because of my thoughtless actions?'' She closed her eyes momentarily in weariness. Had she come so far only to fail now? Forcing herself to face him outright, she offered, "I will release you from your vows if 'tis what you desire.''

Eirik studied her as she fidgeted, fanning her fingers nervously across her lower face. He seemed to seriously consider her offer, then shrugged his shoulders.

"What I desire has long ceased to be of any importance. And I have told you afore, I do not break my oaths."

"But I—"

Eirik raised a hand, halting her words. "Let us understand each other from the start. I will not abide your obstinate ways as wife. I am not a tyrant, but I cannot tolerate a wife who defies me at every turn. A contest of wills is not my vision of wedded life. I have had more than enough of strife in my time. If this is the path you set for our marriage, I want naught of it. Let us end it now."

Eadyth bent her head contritely. How could she have overlooked the thin skin of a prideful man? She should have realized that even the appearance of scorn for their betrothal would demean him in his men's eyes.

"I was wrong to dally. Actually, I was frightened." Well, that was the truth, in part, Eadyth hedged. She *was* afraid, but for her own reasons.

Eirik seemed to soften then and laid a hand on her arm. "You have no reason to fear me, Eadyth. As long as you are honest with me, I will do you no harm."

Eadyth's heart skipped a beat at his words. Oh, Sweet Mary, he demanded truthfulness—the one thing she could not give him at the present. Hating deceit, Eadyth contemplated baring herself to him. But then she thought of John in the hands of his vicious father and knew she could not take the chance.

Eirik stood suddenly and called his knights to silence with upraised arms. He waited imposingly for their attention without saying a word. Finally, he announced in a deep, grave voice, "My loyal supporters, I would present to you my betrothed, Lady Eadyth of Hawks' Lair."

His men rose to their feet in one swell of motion, despite their drunken state. When a few continued to call out lewd remarks, Eirik raised a halting hand, demanding total silence. Then he commanded, "I would ask that you give my lady the same loyalty you pledge to me. And that you show her the respect due the Lady of Ravenshire.''

He called each man forward, introduced him to Eadyth, then stood solemnly while every individual swore formal allegiance to her. Eadyth slanted thankful eyes toward Eirik, but he did not even look her way. In truth, it would seem he acted, not as a favor to her, but as the lord of the manor demanding *his* rightful due from his men.

Some of the words were a bit slurred, considering the men's sodden condition, and Ignold, the burly warrior with the body odor, had the impudence to wink at her when he was done.

From then on, the evening careened progressively downhill. Despite the hand Girta had obviously played in preparation of a surprisingly sumptuous feast, all tasted like ashes to Eadyth and barely passed the lump of anxiety in her throat. Her nerves jangled constantly, like a bad toothache, and she squirmed in her seat every time Eirik looked her way, fearing this would be the time he would discover her masquerade. She did not truly breathe easily until they were on their way to Hawks' Lair the next morn at first light.

But she knew it was a false respite. She now had three sennights to prepare for her wedding, and Eirik's eventual discovery of her deceit.

''You are annoyed with my brother?''

''Annoyed? More like bloody, eye-bulging, breath-hissing, fist-clenching furious,'' Eadyth said dryly to Tykir Thorksson, who sat next to her on the dais at her wedding feast three sennights later day. Eirik's brother had shown up unexpectedly at the Ravenshire chapel that morning, creating a stir midway through the marriage ceremony.

But he was not the only unexpected visitor. Dozens of other nobles with their wives and retainers had crowded the small chapel and now graced the hall. *St. Bridget's Bones!* It was just what she did not need—more witnesses to her deceit. Even the politically powerful Archbishop Wulfstan and an entourage of his clerics had come from Jorvik to perform the holy rites. Surely some lowly village chaplain would have sufficed for this loveless alliance.

Eadyth waved her hand in chagrin to encompass the crowded hall and highborn guests on the dais. *By the Virgin's Breath!* Somehow Eirik had even come up with white cloths to cover the high tables. Sparkling silver mazers and small hand cloths graced every other place setting for washing fingers between courses. And the vast array of foods, well, he must have spent his last coin to provide this wasteful excess, Eadyth muttered to herself.

"Eirik knew I preferred a quiet ceremony, not this farce of a celebration," she complained aloud.

Tykir grinned.

Lord, did bone-melting handsomeness run in Eirik's family? She would have to hide all the comely maids in the keep over the age of fourteen. Oh, he looked naught like Eirik, but he was wildly attractive in his own way. Where Eirik had black hair and pale blue eyes, his younger brother was a true Viking with long, blond hair down to his shoulders, eyes so light a shade of brown that they almost appeared golden, skin sun-bronzed from riding the waves on his longship, a massive, battle-conditioned body, and a smile that could charm the very teeth from a dragon. Even worse, the rascal had braided his magnificent hair on one side, exposing an ear adorned with, of all things, a thunderbolt earring.

When she arched an eyebrow with amused interest, Tykir jiggled it slightly with a forefinger. " 'Tis a legacy from my father. Eirik got the dragon brooch. I got the earring."

Eadyth could not help but smile and shook her head in mock dismay. "You are just as frivolous as your brother."

"My brother, frivolous? Nay, you do not know him well if you think him so. He has always been stone-cold serious, even when he had only passed ten winters and chose to live in King Athelstan's Saxon court." He tweaked her cheek and remarked, "You wed the wrong brother if 'tis a lighthearted nature you seek in your husband."

Eadyth laughed at his playful attitude, but she was not

amused when she darted a livid glance to her right side where Eirik sat with his back to her. He talked earnestly with Earl Orm, a wealthy Northumbrian landowner of Norse descent whose estates joined his on the south. He had come with his half-Saxon daughter Aldgyth, whom Eadyth had met in the old days when she went to court. Aldgyth was the widow of Anlaf Guthfrithsson, who had been Norse king of Northumbria for a short time before his death. Also joining in the conversation with Orm and her husband was Anlaf Sigtryggsson, the sometime king of all Dublin, and the current aspiring Norse ruler of Northumbria.

Good Lord! "I am surprised he did not invite the king of Norway, as well. Or King Edmund, for that matter," Eadyth grumbled sarcastically.

"Uncle Haakon is hunting wild boar this week and could not come," Tykir said drolly, then smirked, obviously pleased with Eadyth's quick intake of breath. "And Edmund, well, I would not have come if he were here—the bloody Saxon bastard."

Eadyth exhaled loudly with disgust.

"You are upset that Eirik honors you by inviting his friends to your wedding feast?"

"Yea, I am. He humiliates me by pretending happiness in our wedding. Everyone knows just by looking at me that 'tis a mismatch, that there must be some hidden reason why he would wed such as me."

"How so?"

"Oh, really! Just look at us. He struts like a proud raven in all his finery. And me?" She looked down at herself in self-disdain. "I, my friend, am just a crow."

Tykir tilted his head questioningly and reached out to finger the unique head-rail she had designed to match her wedding garment. Girta had helped her fashion the tunic and over-tunic from a deep violet samite fabric, then embroidered the edges with silver threads in a design of intertwined lilies. A narrow silver circlet held in place a head-rail made of double layers of the diaphanous material she used for her beekeeping veils, which she had dyed a pale lavender.

She had known Eirik would take insult if she wore her usual drab garb and so she had compromised. She had even washed the pig grease from her hair, although she had slicked it back under a white wimple with an odorless ointment Girta had made for her.

Eadyth tried to shrug Tykir's fingers from her head-rail. She had practiced before a polished metal the past two sennights how to drape the material across her face to hide her features, how to maintain a constant stoop and a perpetual scowl. She hoped most people would think she was demurely attempting to hide her homeliness. The cackling voice was harder to keep up.

"Why wouldst my brother need an excuse to marry a beautiful woman like you?"

Eadyth gasped and finally managed to pull away from Tykir's fingers, bending her posture. He was too observant by far.

"Beautiful? Heh, heh, heh! There is naught of beauty in me these days."

Tykir snorted rudely.

"You must share my Lord Eirik's dim-sightedness. 'Tis true I had rare beauty long ago. Some even called me The Silver Jewel of Northumbria. But now . . . ," she trailed off with a shrug, looking down at her body as if it spoke for itself.

At first, Tykir just stared at her with a puzzled frown, furrowing his brow. "My vision is perfect, and Eirik's impairment is only slight. Do you jest with me?" Then, as if a thought had suddenly occurred to him, he asked incredulously, "Or do you play this charade for my brother?"

Before she had a chance to mask her dismay, Tykir broke out in a fit of laughter. Eirik and Earl Orm turned their way, but Tykir just waved their curious stares aside, wiping tears of mirth from his eyes.

Eadyth hissed under her breath, "Halt, at once. 'Tis not as you think, you bloody fool."

"Oh, I beg to differ, my lady," he hooted gleefully. " 'Tis exactly as I think. You are playing a grand jest on my brother."

"Nay."

"Yea."

"My hair is gray."

" 'Tis silver blonde under all that grease, I warrant."

"My shoulders are stooped."

"Hah! Your breasts are magnificent."

Eadyth cringed with dismay at his impudent words. "I have age spots all over my body," she said lamely, her spirits sinking desperately.

"If 'tis an age spot that adorns your upper lip, I warrant my brother will pay homage to it with his tongue afore this night ends, or he is not the man I know him to be."

Eadyth groaned aloud. "My skin is wrinkled," she protested, trying to maintain the scowl she had kept on her face the entire day. In truth, her face ached from the strain of her forced efforts.

Tykir's lips tilted in a disbelieving smile.

Her shoulders slumped finally in defeat as she realized she was fighting a lost battle with Tykir. He knew the truth.

"Does anyone else suspect?"

Tykir shook his head slowly from side to side.

"What did I do wrong?"

"You did naught. But you apparently forgot that we met many years ago at Hawks' Lair when I was but a child, accompanying my grandfather Dar. I knew afore I came today that you are younger than me, and I have seen only twenty-nine winters."

Eadyth exhaled on a deep sigh.

"Just how old dost my brother think you are?"

Eadyth waved a hand airily in resignation. "Forty or thereabouts, I presume," she admitted with disgust.

"Forty!" Tykir choked out. "Forty! Surely, he is not *that* dull-headed."

"He is not a lackwit. 'Tis just that I worked hard to portray that image, and we were only together a few times. Circumstances helped my cause.''

''But why?''

''Oh, I do not know. I never planned to deceive him, but when I realized on our first meeting that he thought me older . . . well, it seemed to be a good way of forestalling his . . .''

Tykir arched a brow questioningly.

Eadyth shifted uncomfortably, then blurted out, ''. . . of forestalling his lustful gropings.''

Laughing, Tykir remarked, ''Yea, my brother's 'gropings' do tend to be lustful on occasion.''

''Oh, it has naught to do with Eirik. 'Tis any man. I try my best not to attract men. Any man.''

Tykir seemed about to say more on the subject, then stopped himself. ''How long do you think you can continue this ruse?''

''I do not know,'' Eadyth cried despairingly. ''It has gone too far.''

Tykir shook his head with concern. ''My brother is slow to anger, but a lion when provoked. And, I warn you, sister, Eirik is very sensitive about his poor sight. You play a foolish game.''

Eadyth felt a weight on her right arm and turned to see Eirik's hand laid possessively on her sleeve. She started and forced herself not to pull away in distaste.

''My lady, share your pleasantries with me,'' Eirik demanded huskily. ''I would know what tale prompts Tykir's gales of laughter.''

Eadyth shot a pleading look at Tykir, who hesitated, then nodded at her unspoken plea. He told his brother, '' 'Tis our secret, brother—mine and Eadyth's—one I expect to laugh about with you in years to come. But not now. Nay, not quite yet.''

Eadyth breathed a deep sigh of relief. She was safe. For now.

But then Tykir added mischievously, ''I know a skald in

Dublin with a talent for putting words to true events. Methinks I have the bones of a saga to carry to him next trip."

Eirik raised an eyebrow at his brother's apparent deviltry. "Wouldst I like the saga?"

"Oh, undoubtedly."

Eadyth cringed with foreboding.

"And Eadyth?" he asked suspiciously. "Will she enjoy the tale, as well?"

"My brother," Tykir said, laughing as he patted Eirik on the back, "methinks she will relish it best of all."

Chapter Five

Eirik watched Tykir and his wife suspiciously. She relaxed with his brother in a way she never had with him, as if they shared some great secret.

He had worried sorely over Tykir's fate these past nine years since he had almost lost his leg in "The Great Battle." And then word had filtered to Eirik earlier this year in Frankland that King Edmund had invaded the Celtic kingdom of Strathclyde and overrun all of Cumberland. In the end, Edmund had instilled Malcolm as the new ruler of all Scotland on the condition that Malcolm help him fight the Norse invaders on sea and land. And if anyone could be called Norse invader, it was his brother Tykir.

Thank the Lord, Eirik had been across the channel and able to avoid fighting at his Saxon king's side at Brunanburh and then again in Strathclyde. He had pledged his loyalty to both brothers, Athelstan and Edmund, and had proven himself in many a battle, but he refused to fight his own kin.

Well, Tykir's limp was barely noticeable now. Eirik was delighted to see his brother, though he'd been as surprised as his wife when Tykir interrupted their wedding ceremony.

His wife! Bloody Hell! The words had an awful ring, like a death knell. He turned back to her with a frown, knowing he had avoided this moment too long.

"Eadyth, 'tis time. Get the boy and bring him to me. And Larise, as well."

He saw a look of alarm sweep across her face, but she forced back her fear bravely and nodded her assent. Her eyes scanned the hall and found her son John sitting below them at the first table, his head nodding with sleepiness. Eirik's eight-year-old daughter, on the other hand, who had come with Earl Orm, was enjoying every moment of her first night-time feast. Her head swiveled back and forth on her birdlike neck as she tried to soak in all the wondrous sights around her, and she talked like a magpie to the uninterested young knight at her side.

Tykir slid into Eadyth's chair as she walked stiff-backed off the dais to fetch the children, snubbed by the highborn people she passed on the way. Eirik had already spoken with his knights and vassals about the respect he expected them to show his wife. But Eirik could not control his guests, and he noted the way they eyed Eadyth condescendingly, making no pretense of their disapproval. The women snickered behind their hands as she passed; the men eyed her with disdain.

Eirik's eyes narrowed angrily. There would be some prices to pay when this wedding feast was over, he vowed.

"So, my brother," Tykir drawled, "now that I have spoken with Eadyth, I better understand your change of mind about marriage. Are you happy in the match?"

Eirik raised an eyebrow skeptically at Tykir's approval.

"Did you notice the sway of her hips when she walked in front of us through the chapel doors this morn?"

"Sway! Your mind must be muddled with mead. That woman never swayed a day in her life. Besides, she has no hips to speak of."

"And her lips! By all the gods! They certainly look kissable."

"Did our father perchance drop you on your head when you were a babe?"

"Oh. Mayhap I was mistaken."

Eirik could see the spark of deviltry twinkling in his brother's eyes. "What are you up to now?"

"Me? You wound me, brother, with your mistrust."

"Hah! I would wound your head if I thought 'twould shake up your senses. Where in bloody hell have you been these past years?"

Tykir shrugged. "Here and there."

"I have been worried, you lackwit, especially after I met up with Selik in Jorvik last month. He and Rain told me you were raiding in the midlands with Anlaf. Canst you not stay home in Norway where you belong?"

"Home? I have no home." Tykir's face turned somber.

"Tykir, I have told you repeatedly that Ravenshire is your home if you do not want to live in Norway, but—"

Tykir put a hand up to halt his words, then forced a lightness into his voice as he commented, "Did you know that Rain is breeding again? Hell's flames! Selik walks around like a lackwit all the time with a smile plastered over his face. You would think he had invented the making of babes."

Eirik nodded, with a smile. Their father's friend Selik had looked over them protectively after their father's death when they were only boys. Later, he'd married their half sister.

"Those two breed babes like rabbits," Tykir continued to grumble. "Five of their own, including the one in the oven, and dozens of orphans."

"Yea, the noise in their orphanage is enough to make one's ears bleed, but I give them credit. Selik and Rain seem to love each other as much as the day they wed almost ten years ago."

"Mayhap if they loved each other a mite less, Jorvik would be a little less crowded." Changing the subject, Tykir asked, "Have you noticed how well my leg has healed since Brunanburh? I have only a slight limp now. And the maids seem to like it greatly."

Eirik shook his head in mock despair and gave his brother a playful shove on the arm. God's Bones! He wished Tykir would be more careful. After all, other than his daughters, Tykir was the only close family he had left. He corrected himself immediately. Nay, he had other family now. He had a wife. And a son.

Would they be a blessing or a curse? he wondered.

"You asked if I am happy in my match with Eadyth. The answer is nay, but I have resigned myself to the marriage in the three sennights of Eadyth's absence," he said warily. "You know the true reasons for my decision to marry."

Tykir nodded. "Do you think you will ever be able to put Steven and his evil misdeeds behind you, brother?"

"Not 'til the worms are eating his putrid flesh. Not 'til his soul languishes in hell."

"Selik was able to give up his quest for vengeance. Why cannot you?"

"Would you?"

"Nay, but I am the bloodthirsty brother. Remember?" He flashed a teasing grin, then turned serious again. "Will you use the boy as bait to lure Steven out into the open?"

"Yea. Steven apparently needs a son to ensure his Odel rights to his grandfather's lands in Frankland. I truly believe John will be the means for Steven's downfall. But, Tykir, do not think I would sacrifice the child. John is not to blame for his father's evil. I will guard him well."

"And what of your new wife?" Tykir asked with casualness, deliberately changing the subject as an odd little smile twitched at his lips. "Does her age not bother you? Or her, well, less than comely attributes?"

Eirik was wary. He knew his brother too well, and the secretive gleam in his sparkling eyes bespoke mischief.

"Her age and physical appearance do not bother me overmuch. You know I married a young, beautiful maid of pure reputation once, and soon discovered utter misery. This time I made a choice based on logic." He shrugged. "Even so, 'tis sore hard to accustom myself to the unpleasantness of

85

Eadyth's nature. Does she have to scowl constantly? And her voice! Its shrillness makes my hair stand on end."

Tykir choked on the mead he had been drinking, and Eirik tilted his head in suspicion once again. Tykir was hiding something. What could it be? Did it involve Eadyth and that laughing fit Tykir had just engaged in?

Hesitantly, he went on, "I find myself touched that she has taken some care with her appearance today. Hell's Flames! You should have seen her three sennights ago. Ugly as a mud hen and twice as mean."

"And now?" Tykir raised an eyebrow with exaggerated interest.

"Now, leastways, her silk gown is obviously newly made, and the odd head-rail adds a girlish attraction to the garment, especially when she pulls it over her lower face. Dost think she is basically shy under her arrogant exterior?"

Tykir's mouth dropped open in disbelief. "Hah! More like an houri in an eastern harem I once visited."

Eirik smiled at that unlikely comparison and shook his head woefully. "Eadyth, a harem slave? Hardly. She would, no doubt, cause a revolt within a week."

"Eirik, do not be too harsh in judging your new wife," Tykir advised in a suddenly serious tone. "Despite her facade of strength and self-sufficiency, I sense a deep hurt inside."

"You underestimate my insight, brother. The vulnerability that Eadyth fails to hide on the odd occasion touches me, too. Didst see her face earlier when I introduced her to Earl Orm and his daughter Aldgyth? They treated her with bare civility."

"Yea, if you had not been standing at Eadyth's side, I warrant Orm and his bloody daughter would have snubbed her, but, hypocrites that they are, they put on false smiles."

Eirik shrugged. "They need my support in their political intrigues. I know that well. They will not insult her outright. And Archbishop Wulfstan, that wily priest, look how he works his way amongst the crowd below in his plot to overturn Saxon rule in Northumbria."

"Yea, he performed the wedding ceremony, but even he could barely hide his disapproval of the match and Eadyth's scandalous past. Shall I chop off his head for you?"

Eirik grinned at his brother. "Nay, you bloodthirsty fool, though I, too, feel the urge to protect her. This wedding feast has given me a tiny glimpse of what Eadyth's life must have been these past eight years—snickers, judging stares, shunning."

"And you know all too well how cruel the high-blown Saxon nobility can be, my brother. How you stood it so long I will never know."

Eirik nodded at the unwelcome memories Tykir's words brought forth. "I would be a fool not to be drawn by Eadyth's strength of character in withstanding their ill treatment. I can only wonder what pain my wife has suffered that she holds inside still."

"Mayhap her only armor is the brittle shell she draws around her soft inner core?"

Eirik had not thought of that before, but decided Tykir was probably right.

"And do you wish to discover that inner Eadyth?" Tykir asked with a jiggle of his eyebrows.

Eirik laughed. "Oh, I will discover Eadyth's 'inner' secrets this night. You can be sure of that. But, if you speak of that part of herself she attempts to hide, know this: a man protects those under his shield, and I may not be able to erase past mistakes, but I will make sure that no one hurts her again. And that includes Steven of Gravely."

"And how will you sweeten her unpleasant nature?"

Eirik shook his head at that awesome task. "I will be gone from Ravenshire much of the time. Even now, I await word from Edmund. He moves his armies to . . ." Eirik let his words trail off, realizing he should not divulge such information to his brother, whose allegiances often differed from his. "Tykir, promise you will leave Britain and stay out of the fight to come."

Tykir refused to commit himself, and instead asked, "Do

you not ever tire of this double role you play, brother? You cannot always walk the middle road betwixt Saxon and Viking causes. Someday you will have to choose, and if these highborn guests here have their way, it will be soon. A battle approaches for control of Northumbria. On which side will you ride?"

"I truly do not know. But know this—I owed much to King Athelstan and I promised on his deathbed to support his brother Edmund, as well. I will not break my oath of loyalty to him, but I will not ever fight against you, my brother."

"Ah, Eirik, why do you always make life so complicated? 'Tis a simple choice, really. Are you Norseman or Saxon?"

"That is where you are wrong. I am both. And well you know that men of our time give loyalty to leaders, not countries." He stood then and squeezed his brother's hand warmly. "But no more of this. 'Tis my wedding, a night to rejoice," he said dryly. "Come stand with me whilst I raise a toast."

"Yea, but first let us have a personal toast atween the two of us," Tykir said solemnly, touching his goblet to his brother's. "Know that this wife you have chosen is indeed the Silver Jewel of Northumbria under all her tarnish. May you be the true Norseman I know you to be deep down, one who values women for their true worth, not the surface glitter."

Eirik arched his eyebrows in disbelief. "Words fine enough for a poet, my brother. Have you been traveling with that warrior-skald Egil Skallagrimmson again?"

Tykir shook his head and laughed.

"Why, then, do I find it hard to believe that the man known for bedding the most beautiful women in every land is suddenly a connoisseur of inner worth?"

"Nay," Tykir said, laughing, "you misread me. I did not say beauty was unimportant, just that ofttimes a man is, shall we say, *blind* to the beauty shining in his face."

"You speak in riddles, Tykir. Mayhap you have had too much mead to drink. I am not blind."

Tykir choked and sprayed Eirik with a shower of mead.

Brushing the wetness off his chest, Eirik shot him a look of disgust. "And speaking of beautiful women, Tykir, stay away from Britta. She is Wilfrid's leman."

They laughed together companionably, then stood as Eadyth approached, clasping on each side the hands of her son John and Eirik's daughter Larise.

Larise's blue eyes adored her father with childish worship. He felt guilty at his long neglect of his oldest child and was happy that Earl Orm had brought her home this morn—for good. Despite all his annoyance, he owed the earl much for his fine care of his daughter these many years.

His eyes turned to John. The seven-year-old boy was thin, like his mother, and would probably be as tall as he himself one day. In truth, Eadyth had been right. The boy's black hair and pale blue eyes matched his perfectly.

He should hate this son of his worst enemy, but somehow Eirik could not blame the boy for his father's sins. He held out a hand toward John, and the boy huddled closer to his mother's knees, turning frightened, questioning eyes up to her. She nodded gravely and shoved him gently forward.

Eirik put an arm comfortingly around John's shoulder and pulled Eadyth to his other side, and tucked her, as well, under his other arm.

Eirik motioned Tykir and Larise to stand on either side of John and Eadyth. Then they all turned to face the great hall, waiting for the silence of his retainers and guests.

When absolute quiet prevailed, Eirik said in a clear, authoritative voice that resounded across the length of the hall, "My friends and loyal supporters, I give you my wife, Eadyth of Ravenshire." He leaned down and kissed her cool lips in homage before she could jerk back in surprise. The crowd did not seem to notice her instinctive reaction. It cheered, raising goblets in a toast to the newly wedded couple.

Then Eirik raised an arm for silence and introduced his brother Tykir, who received a grudging welcome. After all,

Tykir had fought mightily against some of these very men the past few years.

His daughter Larise's turn came next. Eirik smiled as she preened like a peacock at the cheers of approval.

When silence prevailed again, Eirik waited for several long moments before lifting John by the waist and setting him on the table in front of him. With one hand on John's head and the other arm again holding fast the rigid shoulders of his new wife, Eirik announced, "My friends, I give you my true son, John of Hawks' Lair and Ravenshire. 'Tis with the deepest pleasure I am now able to claim the paternity I have been unable to recognize these many years."

A stunned silence greeted his words, then a low murmuring of surprise rippled through the crowd as understanding began to seep into their drink-muddled heads. Finally, Tykir overcame his amazement and raised his goblet, shouting, "To my nephew John, and my brother Eirik. May he be blessed with the family he has harvested thus far, and with the seeds he will plant in the fertile furrows of this new marriage." He winked at the pike-stiff Eadyth.

The assembly did react then and joined vocally in the toast with cheers and shouts of good wishes.

Eirik chuckled as he felt Eadyth cringe at his side, knowing full well she objected to his brother's words about seeds being planted in her fields.

Eirik squeezed her shoulder, just to see how she would react. He was not surprised when she jabbed him in the side with an elbow and hissed, "Mayhap I could put a few bees in your brother's braies. Fertile furrows, indeed!"

Eirik grinned.

"I had a docile wife at one time, Eadyth. 'Twas not a pleasant experience," he confided in a soft voice, leaning near her ear, liking the way the wispy fabric of her head-rail felt against his lips, feeling a sudden urge to taste her mouth again. " 'Twill be interesting to test your feisty nature in the marriage bed."

Discovering that he enjoyed teasing this new wife of his,

he was greatly pleased at her gasp of indignation. She was too sanctimonious by far.

In truth, the bedding might not be so bad, Eirik told himself silently, especially since he would not have to look at Eadyth's dour face or bony body in the dark of their bedchamber. If only he could put a gag in her mouth to halt her grating voice.

Her violet eyes flashed fiery sparks as if she divined his thoughts, and her chin jutted out angrily.

Eirik chuckled. Lord, he loved a good battle.

Actually, Eadyth was not truly upset over Tykir's lewd toast or Eirik's teasing ways.

When her new husband had acknowledged her son as his own in front of all the honored guests, Eirik had touched a spot deeply hidden in Eadyth's long-frozen emotions. She would be forever thankful, and, in her present mood, would forgive him much—even a little light amusement at her expense.

She forced herself to lay a hand on Eirik's arm when they sat back down at the table. In an emotion-choked voice, she told him, "Eirik, I thank you for your words regarding John. 'Twas more than I expected."

Eirik looked pointedly at her hand, then raised an eyebrow in question. "Grateful, are you? Just how grateful?"

"Not that appreciative, you lusty lout." Though she tried to frown, she could not prevent a small laugh from bubbling from her lips at his persistent teasing.

"Oh? And how do you know my meaning? Mayhap I was referring to an increase in your dowry—a few more coins, an extra ell of silk." He chuckled aloud and added, "Or more bees."

Eadyth shook her head disapprovingly. "Methinks your brother does not know you as well as he thinks."

"How so?" He smiled easily.

Eadyth cringed inwardly at the tugging attraction she felt toward Eirik. She had thought herself immune to a man's charm after her experience with Steven. And certainly she would not have expected herself to be drawn to a man as crude as the one she would now call husband.

Husband, she groaned silently. *Oh, Lord.*

She was having trouble even recalling the drift of their conversation. Oh, yes, now she remembered. "When I told your brother that he was just as frivolous as you, he told me I misspoke, that you have ever been the serious brother. To hear him tell it, you do not have a light-hearted bone in your body. But I know better. From the first we met, you have been teasing and making jest of me."

Eirik grinned. "Tykir speaks true. I have been accused of being too somber. Mayhap you bring out the lighter side in me," he offered silkily.

"Mayhap you play a pointless game if you hope to flatter me with sweet words. Save them for some lackwit maid."

Eirik smiled in a maddening fashion, as if he knew females well, and she was just like all the rest.

"And what would soften your hard shell, my wife?" he asked in a low, seductive voice, reaching forward to blow against the wispy edges of her head-rail, seemingly fascinated with the fluttery fabric.

Eadyth steeled herself not to pull away in fright at the sweet smell of his breath, a mixture of the honeyed mead which she had brought from Hawks' Lair and his own distinctive scent.

"A precious jewel? Would that tempt you?" Eirik went on, completely aware, no doubt, of his effect on her heightened senses. "Or fine silken robes? New tapestries to brighten the walls?" When she failed to react favorably to any of his suggestions, Eirik thought for a moment, then brightened. "How about a book of beekeeping notes from a Frankish monk? I seem to remember such in Athelstan's collection which he bequeathed to King Edmund."

At the rush of pleasure that must have shown on her face, Eirik threw back his head and laughed. "Ah, wife, will you really be so easy to please?"

"In truth, I am very easy to please. You could never give

me more than you have this eve in claiming John as your son. And I *am* grateful.''

She saw that Eirik was watching her closely, squinting slightly in the dim light, but she did not cower this time, and continued, ''I promise in return for your favor that I will be the best wife possible. I will make this keep into a home again. I will bring order to your staff. I will help you prosper with my beekeeping trade. I will care for your children as if they were my own. I will—''

Eirik covered her hand with his own much larger one, and Eadyth's eyes grew wide with alarm. She darted a quick look around the hall, but no one noticed his intimate touch.

Well, it was probably the husbandly sort of gesture expected at a wedding feast. But, Sweet Mother, the feel of his battle-callused palm was not repulsive to Eadyth. Far from it. Instead, an odd racing stirred her blood and fluttered in her chest.

Was this how she had felt with Steven, in the beginning? She tried hard to recall. No, these feelings were too strong, too primordial. Nothing like the sweet yearnings of the heart she had experienced with the Lord of Gravely before discovering his real nature.

She tried to pull her hand away, but Eirik chuckled and held her fast, turning her hand so it was palm to palm with his, fingers entwined. Only his thumb drew back, drawing tiny circles of sweet, sweet pleasure on the tender scar at her wrist.

A small smile played at the edges of Eirik's lips as he gazed at her, and the flutters in her chest increased and moved to the tips of her breasts. Involuntarily, she looked down, then quickly away. She knew he could not see the hardened peaks through the thick fabric of her gown, but, even so, her face warmed with an embarrassed blush.

Eadyth slanted a look his way, and her face burned even hotter. Eirik was grinning like a cat with a bowl of spilled milk. He knew exactly what effect he had on her, no doubt from long years of practice on dimwitted females. *Like her.*

"Argh!" Eadyth growled aloud and tried harder to pull from his grasp, but Eirik just laughed and pulled her even closer, tucking her arm at his side.

"Why do you try to deny your passionate nature, Eadyth?" Eirik asked in a husky whisper. "And do not speak to me of your age again as if it mattered in the bed sport. 'Tis obvious to me that hot coals glow under your cool skin just waiting for the right tinder."

"Tinder? Tinder? Best you keep your tinder in your braies, you lusty lout. And halt your wicked words. I have told you afore that I want none of your seductive words."

"Why? Are you fearful of what you might feel?"

"Nay! I feel naught, and you are wrong to expect otherwise of me. Oh, Eirik, please, do not try to make this marriage into anything other than what it is—a contract."

"And do you not think it would be wise to make the best of our . . . contract? Just a moment ago, you spoke of being the best wife possible. Did you mean in all ways except the true sense?"

Eadyth bristled. He was right. She had just promised to be the best wife possible, and now she argued with him again. Calming herself, she explained patiently, "I do not love you. You do not love me. We will never love each other."

"Who spoke of love? I want naught of that brain-letting emotion. But the nights get cold in these parts and—"

"Oh, you are a brute to tease me so. Bring your leman here if you must, but leave me be."

Eirik did not look pleased at her easy acquiescence to his mistress. Once again, she tried to pull from his hold, but to no avail. Instead, with his left hand, Eirik reached forward and touched the mole above her lip with the tip of his index finger. He smiled as if satisfied that the mark was still there. Then he traced the edges of her lips from one corner to the divot in the center where he stopped momentarily and sighed with pleasure, ever so softly, before moving his finger to the other corner and along the rim of the bottom lip.

"It would give me great pleasure, wife, to do the same

with the tip of my tongue,'' he whispered.

Eadyth's breasts swelled and ached, and an odd fullness lodged in the secret place at the joining of her thighs. Her lips parted involuntarily.

No one had ever said such a thing to her.

"I am old and uncomely," she protested weakly.

Eirik shrugged dismissively. "I had a woman twice my age in Frankland onct." He laughed appreciatively at the memory. "Rather, she had me—for a full sennight. I will ne'er forget that experience as long as I live. I cannot remember thinking then that her age made much difference to the marvelous things she could do in a bed. And on the floor. And on a horse."

Eirik looked at her, and his lips twitched with amusement. "Close your mouth, Eadyth."

Her jaw snapped shut with a click. "On a horse?" she choked out. "You jest."

Eirik smiled disarmingly.

Oh, what a nice smile! Eadyth thought. So dangerously nice.

"Wouldst like to try it sometime?" he suggested in a whisper.

"*Nay!* You are loathsome, speaking of such . . . perversions to a lady."

"To my wife," he corrected with a grin, not the least bit apologetic.

"Did I hear someone mention making love atop a horse?" Tykir interjected behind them with a gloating smile.

Eadyth shuddered with humiliation and finally pulled her hand out of Eirik's grasp.

Eirik just continued to grin.

"Hah! 'Tis too jolting a love ride, to my thinking," Tykir went on, ignoring her embarrassment. "Now, I had a woman onct on the prow of my ship, in the midst of a storm, and the swell of the waves, up and down, up and down, well, I tell you 'twas remarkable to—"

Enough was enough! Eadyth stood abruptly and glared at

them both before stomping off the dais, muttering, "Men! They are lecherous dolts with all their senses lodged betwixt their legs."

Eirik and Tykir's laughter followed in her wake, and she thought she heard Eirik say something to Tykir that sounded like, "Mayhap you were right about the swaying." She looked back and was horrified to see them staring at her hips.

Later, Eadyth was in the kitchen with Girta giving orders for the clean-up of the dinner and replenishing of drinks when she heard a loud commotion in the hall. When she emerged, she saw a number of men wearing the Golden Dragon crest of the House of Wessex on their shields.

Oh, not more guests! Eadyth thought, moving toward the entrance to the hall where they spoke to Eirik with great animation and seriousness. Earl Orm, Archbishop Wulfstan and Anlaf, even Tykir, watched intently from the dais.

"My lord?" Eadyth asked questioningly as she approached her new husband. "Shall I set places at the table for your guests?"

Eirik motioned her closer with a jerk of his hand and introduced her to the three well-dressed men standing at his side. "My lady wife, I would have you meet Earl Robert of Leicester, Earl Oswald of Hereford and Father Aelfhead, one of the chaplains to our good king."

"Greetings, my lords, and you, as well, Father Aelfhead," Eadyth murmured, bowing her head courteously. She turned and told Girta and Britta to prepare food and drink for the dozen heavily armed retainers who stood in the background, their weary faces and dust-covered armor bespeaking a long and hasty journey to reach Ravenshire. Why? Eadyth wondered uncomfortably.

The knowing glances exchanged by Eirik and the king's men told her that they did not wish to speak in her presence. She put her curiosity aside and asked Eirik if she should prepare bedchambers for the highborn guests.

"Nay," Father Aelfhead interjected quickly, "we must needs return to Gloucester as soon as possible." He cast a questioning look at Eirik as his bald head jerked nervously back and forth, scanning the assembly. Then he grunted with disgust as he saw Archbishop Wulfstan standing on the dais, obviously preparing to move toward them.

Noticing the Archbishop's intent, Eirik told Eadyth, "We will be in the private chamber off the great hall. Tell Wilfrid to make sure we are not disturbed." When Eadyth nodded without questioning his intent, she saw a look of grudging approval flash over Eirik's face before he added, "Dost think you could send us some food and drink? Especially the drink." He turned to the three new guests and said with seeming pride, "My wife brews the best mead in all Northumbria."

Eadyth was stunned speechless by his words of praise. Before she had a chance to step back, he leaned down and brushed his lips across hers in a feather-light caress, murmuring, " 'Tis sorry I am, wife, to abandon you alone to the wedding feast. I know 'tis not the husbandly attention you deserve on this night."

Amazed, Eadyth stared after him as he led his guests to the private room. Oh, she knew the kiss was just a gesture meant to perpetuate the charade of beloved bridegroom before the staring guests. But she could not help touching her lips in awe with the tips of her fingers, or imagining his taste still lingering.

More than that, she could not stop herself from wondering if the wedding night she had been dreading would be as bad as she had imagined. An odd thrill rushed through her, turning her face hot and her pulse racing as she thought of Eirik's bedchamber abovestairs and the night to come.

Chapter Six

Eirik and his guests sat around a small table in the private chamber, their empty trenchers put aside and more mead poured into their goblets.

"The king asks that you come immediately," Oswald said. "Even knowing of your wedding, he believes the situation of such urgency to demand desperate actions."

"I heard yestereve from a passing wayfarer that another attempt was made on Edmund's life," Eirik said, stroking his mustache thoughtfully. "Poison, this time."

The three men nodded gravely.

"And is his brother Edred—that misbegotten cur—responsible?"

"No doubt," Robert opined, "though it cannot be proven, of course." He shook his head woefully. "Our king could live one sennight or a hundred. No one knows for sure, except our Good Lord, but many say Edmund is doomed to a short life, the way the attacks have been increasing."

Eirik had heard as much but was still greatly saddened at the prospect of losing such a good man. As young as he was,

Edmund tried earnestly to follow in the footsteps of his brother Athelstan, the warrior-scholar, the first "King of All Britain."

"Already the vultures await Edmund's death to divide the kingdom," Robert went on, "and a devious lot they are, led by the likes of Steven of Gravely."

Eirik's back straightened at the mention of his hated enemy, but he said nothing.

"Even as he fights off his assassins, Edmund worries over the new influx of Norsemen from Ireland," Robert added, running his widespread fingers anxiously through his hair.

"And 'tis the very vipers who inhabit your hall that cause him so much distress," Oswald accused.

Eirik bristled. "Do you question my loyalty to my liege lord?" he asked hotly.

"Nay," Oswald said, backing down, red-faced at his hasty words. "But 'tis jarring to see the very men who would devour our king sitting about your hall in companionship."

"Oh, do not call it companionship. More like . . . what shall I call it? . . . let us say a fishing expedition."

"And you the whale?" Oswald asked with a chortle.

They all laughed, and Oswald's tense posture eased as he commented, "I wonder what other sea creatures they will snare as they troll the troubled waters of Northumbria."

"No doubt there will be many," Eirik admitted. "We all know Anlaf itches to regain the Norse kingship of Northumbria. And many there are who would follow him to shrug off the Saxon yoke."

"And the wily Wulfstan backs him, I wager," the cleric added from the corner where he had been sitting, quietly nursing his goblet of mead.

"Yea, he does," Eirik admitted. "Long has he supported the Norse cause from his pulpit in Jorvik, but even more so in his clandestine meetings throughout the shires."

"And Orm?" Oswald asked warily, knowing Earl Orm and Eirik shared a Norse heritage. "Does he join in their cause or will he play both sides of the coin, as usual, waiting to see which way the winds will blow?''

Eirik weighed his words carefully before answering. ''I know that Orm, and Wulfstan, as well, prefer my uncle Eric Bloodaxe to Anlaf. Eric flatters the Norse nobility in Northumbria, tantalizing them with the prospect of an independent Northumbria under a king of royal blood. So, yea, I think 'twould be accurate to say that Orm and Wulfstan support a Norse infiltration, whether from Dublin or the Orkneys.''

''The Orkneys—'tis where Eric Bloodaxe has been gathering forces since your other uncle, Haakon, expelled him from Norway, is it not?'' Oswald asked.

''Yea, and a bloodthirsty bastard Eric is. Even so, many see promise in him.''

''Will you come with us tonight? Will you answer your king's summons?'' Oswald finally asked.

''I still do not understand. What does the king think I can do to avert the Norse threat? Troops already gather throughout Northumbria, day by day, even from across the seas, just waiting for the king's death afore springing into action.''

'' 'Tis because you are both Saxon and Viking that the king thinks you may intervene. Even though he has Malcolm's pledge of loyalty, he mistrusts him mightily. Edmund would have you go to Malcolm and try to divine his true feelings, find out if he plans betrayal once again. In truth, the king wishes to avert fighting, and, with Malcolm behind him, that is still a possibility. If Malcolm reneges on his oath, a bloodbath will surely follow.''

Eirik saw the logic in their words but still he resisted being the emissary.

''Come back with us tonight and give Edmund a chance to plead his case,'' Oswald urged. ''Let him explain the details to you.''

The cleric stood then and walked wearily over to Eirik's side where he handed him a leather-wrapped article. ''Edmund sends you this gift,'' the priest said softly. ''He said you would know how much he needs your help when you see it.''

Eirik's shoulders sagged wearily when he recognized the crucifix inside. Ever the collector of relics, King Athelstan had cherished this one more than any other since it contained the eyelashes of his favorite saint, St. Cuthbert. He had bequeathed it to Edmund on his death. In giving it to Eirik, Edmund was telling Eirik of his high regard. But, more, Eirik knew Edmund would not part with this precious remembrance of his brother unless he felt his life or his kingdom depended on it.

In that moment, Eirik accepted that he had to obey his overlord's wishes. Even if it meant abandoning his new wife to celebrate their wedding feast alone.

God's Bones! he thought ruefully, smiling to himself, if the wench was shrewish before, she would be furious now. Mayhap he would ask his brother Tykir to break the news of his departure to her. Nay, he decided immediately, it was not a task he would push on any other.

He stood abruptly. "Please rest and help yourselves to more mead. By your leave, I go to prepare myself for our journey."

Outside the room, he told Wilfrid, "Send my squire to help me prepare for my departure. And tell Sigurd and Gunner they will accompany me with six other hesirs of their choice."

"And Lady Eadyth? What shall I tell her?"

Eirik rolled his eyes. "Tell her to come to my bedchamber."

Eadyth was decidedly uncomfortable in the great hall once Eirik had left. Oh, she knew that with the wedding she should now consider herself the Lady of Ravenshire, but the fine guests made it more than obvious that they did not regard her as such.

Eirik's knights and housecarls showed no disrespect. In fact, some appeared ready to jump to her defense if the noble guests offended her further. Apparently, Eirik had given orders after the disastrous betrothal feast that his retainers must treat her with the respect deserving of his lady wife.

His high-born visitors suffered under no such obligation. As she moved among them, replenishing their goblets of mead, attempting light conversation, Eadyth was shown too clearly that her scandalous past would never escape her.

"Lady Eadyth, will you be attending court now that you are wed?" Aldgyth, daughter of Earl Orm, asked snidely, looking at the other gentle ladies who sat next to her, snickering behind coy fingers. Her father was off to the side, talking animatedly with Anlaf and Archbishop Wulfstan, along with the knights who husbanded the visiting noblewomen.

Eadyth shrugged. "I have no particular inclination to participate in King Edmund's court, though 'tis said the scholars and artisans he gathers there from afar are very interesting."

One lady commented, "Yea, 'tis said you are fair bookish for a woman." The remark was not made in a kindly fashion, and several of the women giggled as if they shared a private jest.

"But, Lady Eadyth," Aldgyth continued, "are there not other reasons for attending court, aside from improving the mind? Such as . . ." She flicked her dainty hand airily as her words trailed off.

"Such as what?" Eadyth asked suspiciously in an icy voice.

"Oh, let us say . . . the renewal of old acquaintances."

Eadyth realized that Aldgyth was referring to the father of her child and rumors of her scandalous liaison with some unnamed nobleman. Would it never be forgotten? Or forgiven? Apparently, Eirik's claims of paternity did not convince everyone.

"Aldgyth, let us be perfectly candid with each other," Eadyth said with forced patience, much like a mother speaking to a dull-headed child. "I had the misfortune many years ago to succumb to the charms of a handsome man." Well, that was not entirely a falsehood. The fact that the man in question had been Steven, not Eirik, need not be mentioned. "My foolish heart led to the birth of my son John, whom I love dearly.

102

Now, you may choose to believe that I pine for another man, but I had hoped my marriage today would put those stories to rest. Apparently, my heart is still foolish in some ways, though, because it did not take into account the mean-spiritedness of some people."

Her eyes swept the ladies to let them know she referred to each of them in her condemnation. Aldgyth's face turned bright red and her chin lifted arrogantly as if she cared not how Eadyth regarded her, but the other ladies had the grace to drop their faces in shame. One even murmured softly, "My apologies, Lady Eadyth," as she swept by them and stepped off the dais.

Wilfrid approached her, worry creasing his handsome face. "Lady Eadyth, my lord asks that you come to his chamber immediately. He must speak to you. I will stay to entertain your guests."

Uneasily, she hastened up the enclosed stairway and through the torch-lit corridor to the bedchamber she knew to be her husband's. Eadyth sensed that his summons was related to King Edmund's representatives, and that it boded ill for her.

When she knocked, then entered Eirik's large chamber, she had to blink her eyes several times in the dimness. The few candles and smoking torches in wall brackets barely lit the large room, and no fire was laid in the hearth on this warm May night.

When her vision cleared, Eadyth stepped back with a gasp.

Eirik stood barefoot and bare-chested, wearing only his tight-fitting braies slung low at the waist. His broad shoulders and well-shaped chest, covered with silky black hair, tapered to a narrow waist and hips. The flat brown nipples in the midst of the finely molded muscles drew her attention, and Eadyth felt an odd pulling in her breasts.

Raised in a keep of fighting men, she had seen many men in various stages of nudity. But her new husband was a rare fine specimen, Eadyth had to admit.

Oh, Lord.

She forced herself to concentrate on other things. Eirik was talking to his brother while a squire laid out a padded under-tunic, a hauberk of flexible chain mail with an attached coif and matching mail chausses, cross-gartered leather boots, his helmet and shield with the embossed raven, and all the other trimmings of a warrior.

Before she had a chance to ask the significance of the battle gear, someone said, "Kiss me, dearling."

"What?" she choked out, looking questioningly at Eirik near the darkened alcove. He had just turned, noticing her arrival.

"Show me your legs."

"What did you say?" Eadyth asked him stonily, humiliated that he would request such a thing of her, especially in front of his squire and his brother. His true nature would come out now, it seemed.

"Kiss me, dearling."

"Kiss yourself, you bloody fool," Eadyth exclaimed, her face flaming hotly with embarrassment. Was he drunk? she wondered. His voice sounded oddly hoarse.

Eirik and Tykir burst out laughing as some sort of reali-zation seemed to pass between them. She shifted impatiently from foot to foot, unamused by their laughter.

When Eirik finally plopped down on the bed and Tykir wiped his eyes with the heel of his hand, Eadyth noticed a large gilded cage behind them containing a huge bird of many bright colors.

"Oh," she said with pleasure, moving closer. She had seen such exotic birds from the East in the marketplace of Jorvik, but never up close.

"Wicked wench!" the bird shrieked. "Would ye like to see me arse?"

Eadyth jumped back with a gasp at the vulgar words. She turned to the two brothers. "Whose coarse-tongued animal is this?"

"Yours," Tykir said with a laugh, patting her on the shoul-der. " 'Tis my wedding gift to you."

"Mine?" Eadyth asked hesitantly, not sure she was pleased with the gift, and reluctant to accept it. "What would I do with such a foul-mouthed bird? Did you teach it to speak?"

"Wicked wench!" the bird opined in what almost seemed a dry tone of human voice. It had a particular talent for mimicking the voices it heard, especially Eirik's.

She looked at the bird suspiciously. Surely, the feathered lump had no intelligence.

Tykir laughed. "The men on my ship passed the hours during a recent trading voyage teaching Abdul such words. Do not blame me. Leastways, I am sure you can persuade him to more genteel language. Do you accept my gift, sister?"

Eadyth eyed the bird warily, not so sure the animal could be refined. Abdul lifted its beak and stared back at her arrogantly. When she finally softened and nodded her head, the bird said roguishly, "Show me your legs."

Eadyth had to laugh then.

"Do I not at least deserve a sisterly kiss for my gift?" Tykir asked with mock shyness.

"Yea," Eadyth agreed, moving closer. " 'Tis a fine gift— a most unusual one, to be sure, but one I think I will grow to enjoy."

Before she had a chance to react, Tykir lifted her by the waist so she was at eye level and kissed her lightly on the lips. Then he hugged her so hard she could barely breathe.

"Enough," Eirik said finally, pulling his wife from Tykir's arms forcefully. "Go play your games elsewhere."

When Tykir grinned mischievously at his brother, Eirik told him to take the squire with him. "I wish to speak with my lady wife. Alone."

The instant the door closed, she turned to her husband, being careful to stay in the shadows, out of his range of vision. "What is the meaning of this?" She waved her hand to indicate all the battle raiment laid out for him.

"King Edmund summons me to his side."

Eadyth frowned. "This night?"

"Yea. He sends me on an important mission. 'Twould seem I cannot delay."

"Of course, you must go if you are needed."

Eirik frowned, obviously displeased by her easy acceptance of a separation on their wedding night.

"Will Tykir go with you?"

Eirik made a rude sound. "Not bloody likely. King Edmund would just as soon lop off his head as welcome him to his court."

"Then he will stay at Ravenshire?"

"Nay, I want him to return to Norway immediately. Anlaf and Orm and Wulfstan brew much trouble here, not to mention my uncle Eric Bloodaxe. The instant King Edmund dies—and it could be any day if his assassins persist—fighting is sure to erupt. I have urged Tykir to stay out of the battle this time."

"And you?" Eadyth asked, strangely concerned that Eirik might be placing himself in danger, as well. "Will you be able to stay out of the fray?"

"I doubt it," he admitted wearily.

"Is that why the king summons you?"

Eirik's face deliberately closed into a blank expression, betraying nothing. Eadyth realized then, sadly, that he did not trust her wholly.

"I do not wish to speak more on Edmund's plans. I have too many other things to tell you."

He went on to explain that he would take only a few men with him. "Wilfrid will stay to defend the keep in case of danger. Also, I have begun reconstruction of the castle walls. Let the stoneworker you brought from Hawks' Lair continue with that work. He will know how to proceed."

She nodded, listening carefully to all his instructions about the everyday running of the keep.

"How long will you be gone?"

"I cannot be sure. I hope no more than six sennights."

Eadyth nodded. "Mayhap, if the opportunity arises, you

may get Edmund's approval on our marriage, plant the seeds of your paternity for my son.''

"I had thought the same, and if the Witan is in session I will put the formal petition afore them. But I suggest you start referring to John as *our* son if you want people to believe the tale."

Eadyth thought of telling him that the noble ladies belowstairs did not believe his claim of paternity one whit, but decided he had enough to worry about now.

Eirik moved to the bed and picked up his *akerton*, the padded undertunic which would protect him from the chafing of the metal coils of his armor. She moved closer and offered, "Can I help you?"

Eirik looked at her thoughtfully, holding the garment in midair, as if he had just realized something.

"The marriage has not been consummated, Eadyth, and those who feast below must know that. It could be a danger."

Eadyth could not stop the flush of embarrassment that heated her neck and moved up her face.

Eirik laid his tunic back on the bed and moved closer. "We could do it quickly now."

"What?" Eadyth cried in a voice shrill with alarm. She needed time to prepare herself for *that* ordeal.

Eirik laid a hand on her arm and pulled her forcefully into his embrace. Eadyth twisted futilely, trying to escape his iron clasp and his close scrutiny. It was dark in this section of the room, but she could take no chances.

"Nay, I wouldst wait, my lord, 'til we have more time. The danger is not truly so great, in my opinion. I have been in your room alone for so long now that some, no doubt, believe the deed is already done."

Eirik regarded her with amusement before putting a palm to her chin, holding her face in place. His other arm wrapped around her waist. With a jerk, he pulled her forward into the cradle of his outspread thighs, and Eadyth inhaled sharply at the first touch of his manhood against the apex of her womanhood, at the caress of his bare chest against the thin silk fabric over her breasts.

Eirik chuckled softly and took advantage of her gasp of surprise, lowering his mouth to hers, using the tip of his tongue to do that intimate thing to which he had alluded earlier. First, he brushed the wet tip against her mole, than traced the edges of her parted lips with deliberate, lazy languor, sighing with seemingly exquisite pleasure.

Eadyth forgot to hunch her shoulders. She forgot to flinch at his touch. She forgot to scowl. She forgot to protest in a shrewish, cronelike voice.

In truth, Eadyth forgot everything except the sweet, sweet sensation of warm, firm lips moving over hers, shaping her lips to his satisfaction. When his mouth finally closed over hers in a mind-consuming kiss, Eadyth could not stop herself from arching against him. He sucked the very breath from her, but Eadyth could not care. She parted her lips wider, wanting more. Eirik groaned against her lips, then tested the new territory of her mouth with his tongue. Eadyth welcomed his entrance, unfamiliar with such tongue kissing, but liking it ever so much.

When Eirik's tongue plunged deep, then withdrew slowly, then entered once again, Eadyth's knees buckled, and Eirik released his hand from her chin, using both hands to hold her upright. He smiled against her lips, then pushed her back slightly. With his forehead pressed to hers, he waited for several long moments, eyes closed, breathing raspily. When he finally seemed to have calmed down, he moved away from her with a soft laugh, but not before brushing his fingertips across her cheek in a regretful caress.

"Ah, wife, I think we may be more suited than either of us ever thought."

The only sound in the room was the sputtering of a torch, which finally went out for lack of oil, throwing the room into even more shadows.

"You are right, Eadyth," Eirik continued in a low voice, " 'tis not the time for a hasty coupling. Be forewarned, though—on my return I intend to resume that kiss where we left off.''

Now that Eadyth's roiling passions had settled slightly, she felt vulnerable, standing alone in the middle of the room, facing Eirik's back. He stood near a small table, pouring a goblet of ale, which he downed in one long gulp before turning back to her. His eyes still blazed with passion, and the hard ridge between his thighs bespoke a raging arousal.

"Nay," Eadyth protested, remembering to add a shrill tone to her voice, "you are wrong. 'Tis just a contract atween us. Naught more. Do not expect lustful zest from me as a bed partner. 'Tis not my nature."

"How do you explain what just happened?" he asked with an eyebrow arched in amusement.

"I was merely surprised," she said weakly.

"Hah! Remind me to spring a few more surprises on you in the future, and you may burn me to a crisp with your inner heat."

"Oh, you are crude."

"Yea."

"I am not wanton," she cried.

"I never thought so. Why would you think responding to a husband's kiss is wanton?"

" 'Twas not as you think. It will not happen again, that I promise you."

"Oh?" Eirik said lazily, moving slowly, deliberately, toward her. "Shall we test the waters once again and see if you can bring them to a boil?"

Eadyth jumped back with a shriek of alarm and moved quickly toward the door.

"Yea, little beekeeper, best you buzz off now and send my squire to help me dress. Otherwise, I fear I will not be able to resist the temptation of your honey."

"Argh!" Eadyth exclaimed in frustrated rage. Slamming the door after her, she almost ran into Tykir, who was leaning against the corridor wall, examining his fingernails with nonchalance.

"What is wrong with your lips, my good sister?" Tykir asked with exaggerated concern. " 'Twould seem they have been bruised somehow. Mayhap you ran into a wall."

Eadyth shoved him aside in a most unladylike manner, muttering, "Loathsome louts. The whole lot of you are naught but loathsome louts. Probably descended from a line of louts. Runs in the blood, no doubt. *Lout blood.*"

She was not amused by his laughter, which followed her down the stairwell, nor the words he called after her: "Imagine the fierce sons he will breed on you, all *fine, loathsome louts.*"

A short time later, Eadyth stood in the torch-lit bailey amid the shifting horses, bidding Godspeed to her new husband. It was not the way she had envisioned her wedding night, but perhaps it was for the best, she decided. A reprieve. Their separation would give her time to prepare herself, and him, for the inevitable disclosure of her deception.

In truth, Eadyth was amazed, and alarmed, that what had started as a harmless ruse had escalated to such frightening proportions.

And the man before her now did frighten her.

This was not the laughing, playful Eirik she had observed thus far. Sitting astride his massive destrier, her husband was a formidable knight. Long-sleeved, flexible mail encased most of his massive body, a chain-mesh hood hanging loosely at his neck. A pale blue, sleeveless tunic of fine Yorkshire wool hung down to his knees, accenting the translucent beauty of his eyes, apparent even in the shadowy courtyard.

Pushing the noseguard of his helmet up so he could better speak, he leaned down toward Wilfrid, no doubt giving him last-minute instructions. When he finished, Eirik motioned his squire to hand him his heavy sword and the shield with the raven crest. Adjusting them with ease, Eirik then turned and noticed Eadyth.

With the same abrupt hand motion he had made toward his squire, Eirik called her forward. Eadyth thought about resisting such a peremptory command, but, instead, lifted her chin haughtily in a manner she knew irritated him and stepped to the side of the restlessly shifting horse. The stupid beast did not intimidate her, despite its size. Animals she could control. It was human beasts that caused her trepidation, at times. Like the scowling one before her now. She would surely have difficulty manipulating him.

Eirik raised an eyebrow at her feisty stance, but chose to ignore her insolence. Instead, he instructed her, "Wilfrid has authority to hire more hesirs to protect the keep. 'Twould be wise for you to stay inside the walls in my absence. Treachery abounds, and those who would harm me may attempt to work through you."

She nodded grudgingly.

"Also, keep a tight rein on Larise. Hold her to your side at all times. And John, as well. Keep in mind that Steven will not give up easily."

Now, *that* danger Eadyth could understand.

The snorting of horses precluded further conversation as King Edmund's men moved their destriers closer to Eirik, impatient to be gone. Hastily, Eirik concluded, "Need I remind you to stay within the keep to avoid further contact with Gravely?"

She shook her head, and Eirik gave her several more last-minute instructions. When he completed his directions and appeared about to lean down to kiss her in farewell, Eadyth hissed in a low undertone, "Do not dare think of embracing me in public. I will not abide it."

Truth be told, Eadyth did not want a repeat of the mind-shattering kiss that had taken place in his bedchamber a short time before. She needed time to get her confused emotions under firm control.

But her husband obviously did not care for commands from a new wife. He tilted his head and challenged, "Do you say me nay already, wife? I think not."

Before she had a chance to blink, he lifted her by the shoulders, set her on his lap atop the horse and kissed her deeply,

111

much more intimately than he had, no doubt, originally intended before her reckless defiance.

It was not a pleasant kiss, like the earlier one. His chain mail dug into her chest. His gauntleted hands bruised the sensitive skin of her shoulders. And his lips pressed hard and brutal against her teeth, drawing blood.

Eirik obviously meant the kiss to show his retainers and honored guests that he was lord and master. And to teach her not to challenge him again—in public or private.

Eadyth seethed.

When he set her down on the ground as quickly as he had picked her up, Eadyth rubbed the back of her hand angrily across her mouth.

"Have you naught to say, *wife*?"

"When a pig grunts, do you feel the need to oink?"

Eirik snapped his noseguard down with a resounding click, hiding half his face, but not before she saw a matching fury in his eyes.

"You will regret those hasty words, my lady. 'Twill be my pleasure when I return to teach you respect for your wedded husband."

Without another word, he rode off with the king's men and his small group of retainers.

The contest of wills had begun.

Chapter Seven

To her regret, Tykir prepared to leave the next day. Eadyth did not know how she would have survived the remainder of the wedding feast if it had not been for Tykir's help. Once Eirik had gone, most of the hostile guests had snubbed Eadyth openly, but not when Tykir had stood, glaring, at her side. Some had gone to bedchambers which had been prepared for them earlier, others had departed hastily, no doubt brewing their deceitful plots.

Eirik's behavior at their leave-taking still infuriated Eadyth, but her anger was tempered a bit when Tykir leaned down from his horse and handed her a linen-wrapped parcel.

"That had best not be the bloody shoe Eirik keeps trying to foist on me," she remarked shrewishly.

Tykir grinned. "Nay, my brother is saving that for another occasion. Eirik intended to give you this *morgen-gifu* this morn, after your wedding night . . . in appreciation of your pleasing him mightily in the bed sport, I wager." He moved his eyebrows comically. "But methinks you need softening up now, afore his return, lest there be no coupling at all."

Eadyth snorted with disgust at his continual reference to the marriage bed, but then she gasped with delight when she opened the package and saw the priceless beekeeping book Eirik had mentioned earlier. He must have sent to King Edmund for it. She realized, too, that the king must truly regard her husband as a friend to part with such a precious book from the renowned collection bequeathed him by his half-brother Athelstan. No wonder he called upon Eirik in his time of need.

She raised tear-filled eyes to his brother and said in a choked voice, "He could not have chosen better. In truth, I cannot remember anyone ever taking such care to choose a gift for me."

"Remember that, my sister, afore you snap his head off on his return," he advised, with a wink.

Tykir left then for his ship in Jorvik, gateway to all the world's busy trade routes—Ireland, the Shetlands, Rhineland, the Baltics and farther. His solitary departure saddened her greatly for she knew not when she would see her new brother again. Picturing the busy market town, she wondered if Tykir would go to some exotic land, or back to his Uncle Haakon in the Norse lands, as his brother had insisted.

" 'Tis odd," Girta said at her side, "that you readily accept Tykir as brother but cannot abide the idea of Eirik as husband."

"Humph!" Eadyth grumbled, walking back into the keep with her companion. " 'Tis because I always yearned for a brother, but I detest the need for a husband. Especially a loathsome lout like Eirik."

" 'Twas not always so."

Eadyth shot her a reprimanding look.

But Girta ignored her and plodded along. " 'Tis time you lightened up your countenance, girl," Girta called back over her shoulder. "In truth, you are becoming as sour as the crone you pretend to be. Start looking at the fate God hands you as a gift, instead of a bane."

"Gift? You call Eirik of Ravenshire a gift?"

"Mayhap," Girta replied, her gray eyes twinkling merrily.

Eadyth made a clucking sound of disgust. "For shame, Girta! You fall into the same trap as all the other feckless women, succumbing to a man's silky tongue and roguish looks."

Girta smiled knowingly, as if Eadyth, too, fell in that category.

"Is the Lord Eirik truly my father?" John asked later that day. He sat on a stool watching her put candles into wooden containers to be carried to her agent in Jorvik.

"Yea, he is," Eadyth lied unashamedly.

John's little face brightened. "He talked to me afore he left yestereve. He said I must needs take care of you, and he told me I could call him Father."

"Does that make you happy, dearling?"

Her son did not hesitate before nodding his head vigorously.

Eadyth was surprised and immensely pleased that Eirik had taken the time to speak with his new "son" in private. But her pleasure was short-lived.

"All the other boys at Hawks' Lair have fathers to teach them how to wield a sword, or snare a rabbit, or piss, or—"

"John!"

"Well, 'tis true. Lord Eirik . . . I mean, Father . . . showed me how to piss last night so I do not wet my braies. 'Twas just afore he rode off, out by the stables."

Eadyth's mouth dropped open in consternation.

"Men are different from women, you know, Mother," he informed her as if imparting some superior knowledge. "They have to shake their wicks after pissing. I did not know the proper method 'til Lord Eir . . . Father showed me. And did you know Uncle Tykir can whistle and piss at the same time?"

Eadyth barely stifled a grin.

"Do you think Father will teach me how to curse when he returns?"

115

"Certainly not! And I hope you will not be using such coarse words again in my presence."

"What words?" John asked innocently. "Piss or wick?"

"Both," Eadyth choked out. "And if you repeat them again, I swear I will soap your mouth."

"Will you do the same to Father? He says both words. And he knows a goodly number of curses. You should have heard the one he said when Master Wilfrid congratulated him on the wedding. And—"

"Enough!"

The next day Eadyth set to work. She gathered all the servants together, both free and thrall. Since her departure three sennights ago, their numbers had increased dramatically, no doubt due to the spreading word of the master's return and betrothal. In the castle ledger, which Wilfrid handed over to her, she listed all their names and particular talents so she could more efficiently assign them duties.

A much-changed Bertha would continue to rule over the kitchens with the aid of numerous scullery maids, kitchen boys and servers. Britta and two young thralls took over care of the bedchambers. Theodric, another longtime servant of Ravenshire, would rule the great hall with his underlings. Others were assigned to the laundry, dairy, buttery, brew house, poultry coops, stables, livestock, smithy and kitchen gardens.

Godric, the orphan child, would be her personal errand boy, not to mention a companion to her son John, who had already acclimated himself to his new home, and his new "sister" Larise. In fact, the three of them had quickly become fast friends, screeching with glee as they dashed through the keep, around the vast bailey and in the orchard with Prince barking happily at their heels. Because of the threat from Steven, they were heavily guarded at all times and never permitted beyond the inner castle walls or kitchen gardens.

The mood throughout the castle and surrounding keep seemed to lighten and expand under the influence of the children. Bertha grumbled, "The bloody buggers will no doubt curdle my fresh cream with their endless shrieking." But even she could not help but smile as the trio scampered through her kitchen, coming to a skidding halt as they stopped to swipe manchet bread or a slice of cheese, then resumed their squealing excursion.

Eadyth had to ban them from her bedchamber when they teased Abdul until his squawking could be heard all the way to the bailey. And yet, the foolish bird actually seemed downspirited when the children were not about.

Eirik's retainers cursed the youngsters when they approached the exercise yards, but were seen on one occasion teaching them how to shoot an arrow straight and true into a moving target. In a way, Eadyth thought, the carefree children represented hope and rebirth for Ravenshire, which many had considered doomed to abandonment.

By the end of the week, the castle was clean and running efficiently. Eadyth would have liked to launch many castle projects, but could not until she knew more about Eirik's financial situation. Having little to work with—no bright tapestries or fine furniture—she had to settle for clean.

Still, she envisioned a solar built next to the second-floor bedchambers for a family sitting area. And the timber chapel at the edge of the bailey, little more than a hovel, must be rebuilt. All the beds needed new linens and hangings. The now rustless battle weapons hanging from the walls had been polished to a fine sheen, but the few tapestries and banners which lined the walls drooped threadbare with age and neglect. The kitchen sorely lacked utensils—knives, spoons, ladles, even cauldrons. Apparently much had been pilfered over the years of Eirik's absence. And fabric must be purchased to sew new clothing for the servants, as well as for Eirik and his retainers.

When she had done all she could inside, Eadyth rode outside the keep with Wilfrid. It was not as pleasant an experience as it could have been, since she had to continue her disguise—hunching her shoulders, maneuvering her head-rail,

117

screeching her voice, cackling occasionally. She maintained her tiresome facade around all the servants, as well.

She saw an odd expression on Wilfrid's face occasionally when he did not think she noticed. It would not do for her husband's retainers to discover her duplicity before she had a chance to end this foolish masquerade on Eirik's return.

As they rode the vast estate, handing out seed to the free cotters who had begun to return, they discussed hopes for a bountiful spring crop of oats and barley.

"The farmland is rich," Wilfrid commented. "I followed your suggestion for plowing in narrow strips of three sections—the first for the spring sowing taking place now, the next for the fall crop of winter wheat, and the third to lie fallow for one year."

"And you will allow the few cattle left at Ravenshire to graze the fallow fields and the stubble after harvesting the spring crops?"

"Yea, my lady. You have reminded me three times now."

Eadyth smiled at Wilfrid's mild rebuke. "I do have a tendency to nag betimes."

Wilfrid rolled his eyes heavenward.

"The cotters' huts are in deplorable condition," Eadyth complained as they left the fields and traveled through the village.

Wilfrid shrugged. "The castle defenses and the planting come first."

Eadyth started to protest, then closed her lips. As before, she did not know if Eirik had the funds to undertake such renovations.

Eadyth was particularly saddened to see that the estate once known for its fine Yorkshire wool was now devoid of any sheep. "Do you think Eirik would object to our starting a new fold of sheep?" she asked tentatively. At Wilfrid's look of exasperation over all her plans, Eadyth added, "Of course, 'twould be a small fold at first."

Wilfrid shook his head and grinned. "Lady Eadyth, methinks naught you do is on a small scale. In the past three days, you have made me take notes on the purchase of additional cows, more oxen for the plows, renovations to the cotters' huts, pruning the orchard trees, digging a new well and two new cess pits, repairing the castle roof, enlarging the stables, transporting bees for a honey and candle business, and now a flock of smelly, bleating sheep.''

''Do not forget cleaning the garderobes.''

Wilfrid grumbled with disgust at that reminder.

''The garderobes *are* a top priority,'' Eadyth remarked with particular emphasis. The three garderobes were located just inside the outer curtain walls in the bailey, with their stone seats protruding outward so the excrement and fluids sank to the ditches below. To say the stench reached high heaven was an understatement. ''The moats have not been dredged in the two years of Eirik's absence, I warrant. Nor the cess pits under the two interior garderobes. When was the last time they were even limed?''

Wilfrid dipped his head sheepishly. '' 'Tis a distasteful task I have long put off.''

''Humph! Even worse, I noticed no clean straw or grape leaves in the servants' garderobes for wiping. What does that say for the cleanliness of Ravenshire's inhabitants? Small wonder Ignold and the others smell so bad.''

''My lady!'' Wilfrid groaned, his face flushed bright red with embarrassment. ''Must you discuss *all* the details? 'Tis enough that I know you want the damn pits cleaned.''

The next day she set Jeremy, the stoneworker she had brought from Hawks' Lair as part of her dowry, to work on the ventilation problem in the great hall. At one time, there had been a huge central hearth in the Viking style with a smoke hole in the roof, but Eirik's grandfather Dar had made many Saxon improvements, including two rare fireplaces at either end of the large room. Unfortunately, the chimneys were not large enough to accommodate the hall's size, thus the continual backdraft of smoke.

Jeremy's expert skills were much needed outside, as well, where she had pulled him from work on reconstruction of the castle walls. Like Hawks' Lair and many other keeps throughout Britain, Ravenshire was built on a high, flat-topped earthen motte, surrounded by a massive ditch.

"Dar replaced the wooden palisade fence and its guard towers with ones of stone," Wilfrid had explained, "both an outer and an inner curtain to enclose the bailey with its outbuildings and exercise yards. But the Saxon assaults on Ravenshire the last few decades have been unkind to its defenses."

"I noticed when I returned for the wedding that Eirik had already started repairing the walls. I am sure Jeremy will be able to speed the work along."

Wilfrid complained to her now about her priorities in taking away his new stone expert. "A little smoke in your eyes will not matter if our enemies break through the castle wall."

"Well, at least someone at Ravenshire appreciates a portion of my dowry. Eirik has made jest enough about my dower bees."

Wilfrid just smiled, accustomed by now to her complaints about Eirik.

"Come to think on it, the bees are the only part of my dowry I have not yet delivered to my husband, and I am anxious to transplant them to my new home."

Wilfrid muttered something vulgar under his breath.

"With all the work that needs to be done at Ravenshire, and not much evidence that Eirik has the means to pay for it, I want to get my beekeeping business established here so that the estate can be made to prosper."

"My lady," Wilfrid sputtered, " 'tis Lord Ravenshire's place to decide what he can or cannot afford to do with his keep. Besides, methought that was the purpose in the belated spring plantings."

"The sowing of the fields is, of course, a first step, but that would only bring self-sufficiency to the manor, at best. And the sheep and weaving operations could be profitable in time, but, for an immediate influx of coins, my honey and candles and mead are needed."

"You intend to trade your own products?" Wilfrid asked, horrified.

Eadyth cast a condescending glance his way. "Yea, I will. There is a huge demand for my wares, especially the unique timekeeping candles I fashion."

Wilfrid eyed her skeptically.

"The timekeeping candles were invented by King Alfred many years ago, but mine are of an especially high quality."

Wilfrid shook his head in despair, no doubt calculating how much more work she intended to make for him. But all Eadyth's plans hinged on her getting the bees to Ravenshire, which required that she patiently await her husband's return. And patience was not one of her virtues.

At the end of six sennights, Eadyth received a short message from her husband, which left her oddly hurt by its terseness and lack of sentiment.

My Lady Eadyth,
Forgive my delay. Am still in Scotland on my king's
business. I expect to be back at Ravenshire in two
more sennights. Take care.

Your husband,
Eirik

"God's Bones, I am tired of waiting for his return," Eadyth grumbled to Wilfrid, who was reading his own, much longer, message from his overlord. "Does he tell you why he is delayed?"

Wilfrid stared at her blankly, then shrugged, refusing to betray any secrets.

Looking at the date on her letter, Eadyth reckoned it would be at least another six days before Eirik returned. That would be plenty of time for her to go to Hawks' Lair, get her bees and the related equipment, and come back to Ravenshire before Eirik's arrival.

She was about to make that suggestion to Wilfrid, then

stopped herself. Eirik had told her to stay at Ravenshire and to guard the children well, with good cause, considering Steven's threats. But there was no reason why she could not go off by herself during the night and leave the children behind under the expert care of Girta and Eirik's retainers.

However, Wilfrid would never agree to her traveling alone. He would take Eirik's orders literally.

So she did not tell him of her plans. Instead, she left a message for Girta, telling her where she had gone and that she would return as soon as possible.

Eirik approached Ravenshire with his small band four nights later. He turned to Sigurd who rode at his side.

"Lord, 'tis good to be home. Sore tired and dirty I am, and sick to death of trying to persuade Scots and Norse and Welsh leaders to remain loyal to a Saxon king."

Sigurd laughed.

"I cajoled 'til my voice turned hoarse. I drank mead and wine in forced comradeship 'til my eyeballs felt like they could float. I bit my tongue bloody with diplomatic restraint."

"And we have all covered so much ground atop our horses that our arses have turned to leather," Sigurd added with a smile.

"Yea, we have done our overlord's work well, carrying King Edmund's message throughout Britain and beyond. But do you think we were successful?"

Sigurd shrugged. "To your face, they appeared loyal, but some of those border lords are so independent they might just as easily play our king false when the uprising begins."

"The only thing not in doubt is that a rebellion is in the offing. Everywhere we traveled, I saw evidence of more and more fighting men coming into the country. All drawn by rumors of the king's impending death," Eirik concluded, sighing wearily as they passed the last hill before Ravenshire.

As his hesir drew upwind of him, Eirik exclaimed, "Bloody Hell, you stink, Sigurd."

Sigurd chortled, "You do not smell like a rose yourself,

my lord. I saw a maid in Jorvik hold her nose as we passed by this morn. She remarked on the peculiar odor of heathen Norsemen.''

Eirik's lips tilted in a tired smile. In truth, he was too exhausted to laugh. ''Mayhap I should have let her smell my Saxon half. For comparison. I wager it would be a fair contest.''

All of his men laughed at his jest.

They should have stayed in Jorvik, at least overnight, Eirik thought. In fact, he had gone to the market town with the intention of seeking out his mistress, Asa. He had envisioned a hot bath, a short rest, and a long, hot night of lovemaking with his sweet jewelry maker. But he had encountered his brother at the harbor supervising some repairs on his longship which had delayed his departure. Tykir had reminded him of his new wife awaiting him at Ravenshire.

''The marriage has not been consummated, Eirik.''

''Hah! I think I know that better than you, brother. Stop your bloody meddling.''

Tykir had shrugged. ''Methought you had motives for marrying the old crone.'' He had grinned oddly, as if he enjoyed prodding his brother about Eadyth's age. ''Did you have any luck at Winchester with the king and his Witan regarding Steven's petition?''

''Somewhat. Edmund promises his support, and I filed a formal protest afore the Witan, claiming my own paternity of John.'' He shrugged, adding, ''You know that the Witan, in the end, will act as the political winds blow. But, most important, I spoke ofttimes and in public of my loving wife and son at Ravenshire. Hopefully, my words will anger Steven to careless action, and we can finally put an end to his perfidy.''

''You should return to Ravenshire then, Eirik. Wouldst you jeopardize your trap for Steven by dallying here in Jorvik? Afore the vows have even been formalized with the bedding?''

Eirik had narrowed his eyes suspiciously, studying his brother's concerned face. ''I am more interested in your motives for pushing me toward my shrewish wife. Do you know something I do not?''

''Me?'' Tykir had asked, slapping a palm to his chest in affront. '' 'Tis just that I softened the wench up for you with your bride gift. Oiled the way for your entry, so to speak. I would not want my brotherly efforts to go in vain.''

Eirik shook his head in remembrance of his sly brother's suddenly serious parting admonition: ''Remember my words, brother, when the time is right. Beauty is in the heart, not the eyes.''

Easy for him to say, Eirik thought, as he waved to Wilfrid and his other retainers atop the battlements. Tykir did not have to bed the scrawny crone.

He furrowed his forehead with annoyance as he remembered Eadyth's parting insult about pigs grunting and his threat to make her pay on his return.

Actually, other thoughts had been niggling at Eirik's mind since his departure. Eirik had been thinking much of late about that kiss he and Eadyth had shared in his bedchamber, and he wondered if the coupling might not be so abhorrent.

In truth, if Eadyth could only stop her cackling words, and the dark of his bedchamber could dim her gray hair and wrinkles, he might enjoy taming her feisty spirit amongst the bed linens. What was it Selik always said about all cats in the dark? With a laugh, he looked up at the battlements, searching for the object of his mirth.

Then he frowned.

Girta stood there, along with Larise and John, who were waving energetically. But no Eadyth. Where was his wife?

Perchance the bothersome wench hoped to punish him. He had infuriated her on his departure with his punishing kiss in front of all his retainers and guests. She no doubt hoped to retaliate. Well, he had had more than enough of her stubborn pride. His lips thinned with irritation. He would put an end to her defiant nature this night when she was flat on her back with her bony legs spread wide.

''Where is my wife?'' he demanded of Wilfrid the minute

124

he alighted from his horse in the courtyard, failing to stifle a groan of pain at his aching muscles. "Have her order me a hot bath immediately."

Wilfrid's face turned bright red. "Um . . . ah . . ."

"What?"

"She is gone."

"Gone? Where?"

"Back to Hawks' Lair."

"You cannot be serious," Eirik said incredulously, then stiffened with alarm. His lackwit wife endangered herself with her independent ways. "I ordered her not to leave the keep. And I told you to make sure she and the children were guarded every moment."

"The children have worn out a dozen guards whilst you have been gone," Wilfrid answered defensively; then he confessed shamefacedly, "but your lady left whilst everyone slept—four nights ago."

"And have we no guards?"

"Yea, but they thought she had permission to leave."

"Who rode with her?" Eirik asked stonily, his fists clenched angrily at his sides. By all the saints! He would strangle the wench for disobeying him. Best she hide her scrawny self for a good long time 'til his boiling temper cooled down.

Just then, Eirik heard a loud squealing ruckus accompanied by much loud barking. Three bodies, nay four, came barreling through the open door of the hall and down the steps to the bailey.

Larise screeched to a dust-raising halt before him, followed by John and the kitchen boy, Godric, who barely escaped colliding with Larise's back. All the while, the large dog that his missing wife had adopted yipped loudly at their heels.

"Father!" Larise screamed happily and hurled herself up into his arms, wrapping her arms around his neck in a stranglehold and her legs around his waist. His destrier pranced nervously behind him, snorting its displeasure, and Eirik, bone weary from his journey, almost fell backward from the force of Larise's embrace.

"God's Blood! Have I arrived home to a keep of senseless halfwits?" Eirik asked Wilfrid as he put Larise down on the ground. Her hair was wet and smelled of soap, and her shiny face bespoke a recent bath. The other two children had obviously been given baths, too, as had the squirming dog which John held in his arms as he stared wide-eyed up at him.

Girta stepped forward, shooing the children back into the keep. "To bed with you now."

"Where is your mistress?" Eirik asked her in a frigid tone.

"She went to Hawks' Lair on an errand. She did not think you would return so soon."

"What was so urgent she could not wait 'til my return?"

Girta shrugged, a closed look blanketing her face. She obviously knew Eadyth's mission and chose not to tell him. " 'Tis certain she will be back in the morn. Then she can explain herself."

"Oh, you can be sure she will explain," Eirik said icily, thinking he had little to thank his brother for this night. He could have been sharing a warm bed with Asa instead of rushing back to an absent wife.

Later that evening, after he had finally bathed and eaten, Eirik heard a soft knock at his bedchamber door.

"Enter."

Wilfrid walked in hesitantly, a somber expression clouding his usually jovial face.

"Come share some wine with me. 'Tis from Frankland, I believe. I bought it in Jorvik this morn."

Wilfrid shook his head and declined to sit in the chair opposite his master. Without any preamble, he blurted out, "My lord, Britta just showed me a missive she found this morn under the mattress in your lady wife's bedchamber."

He hesitated, then handed the folded parchment to Eirik. It was addressed to Lady Eadyth of Ravenshire.

"The seal was already broken when Britta found it," Wilfrid explained when he saw Eirik examining it closely.

Eirik opened the letter carefully, knowing from Wilfrid's demeanor that he was not going to like its contents.
And he did not.

My Dearest Eadyth,
I am told your wedding has taken place, as we
planned. My heart weeps for you and the sacrifice
you make for me, and our future. Pray God, the Beast
of Ravenshire does not learn of your pregnancy. I
work still on plans to end this fruitless marriage of
mine so that both *my children can bear the stamp of*
legitimacy. Hold on, my love, just a short while
longer until we can be together finally in our eternal
love.

Your heart's husband,
Steven

At first, rage choked him speechless. Then Eirik threw the letter onto the floor and ground it angrily into the rushes under his leather-clad foot.

"The lying, cod-sucking bitch," Eirik bellowed, wishing that Eadyth was standing before him, not Wilfrid, so that he could vent his fury on her deceitful flesh. Frustrated, he picked up his wine goblet and hurled it against the chamber wall. The other goblet, along with a silver linked belt, his battle helmet, a soapstone candle holder, even the pottery jug filled with wine soon followed suit. It was not enough.

"I should have known," Eirik gritted out. "By the Holy Rood, I should have known. All the signs were there. Her bastard child. Her repugnance at my touch. Her secretive ways."

"My lord, mayhap you should talk to the Lady Eadyth afore judging her too harshly," Wilfrid ventured hesitantly.

Eirik turned sharply on his friend. "Nay, you and my brother both advised me to give the lady some lead rope in her defiant ways. Hah! Defiant is too kind a word for her. Treacherous she has proven to be. I should have followed my instincts, which told me to trust no woman."

"But it does not make sense—"

"Sense! The only sense in this sorry mess is that of smell—the bloody, God-awful odor of a putrid, faithless woman." He ran his widespread fingers through his hair and pulled, shaking his head. "Holy Jude! How many times does a man need to be burned afore he learns not to trust the flame?"

"But I do not understand. What need would she have for marriage vows with you, unless she truly feared the Lord of Gravely?"

"Steven has ever wanted to ruin me. 'Tis certain he uses her in his devious plot. And who knows what Eadyth hoped to gain." He shrugged. "She fancies herself in love with the demon thane, no doubt."

"Somehow, she does not fit the picture," Wilfrid said with uncertainty.

"I know what you mean. I had thought her past the child-breeding years, too. And, more than that, Steven usually chooses more comely maids for his pursuits."

"Now, there you could be wrong. With all due respect, I have been riding about the estate with her in your absence. Like a burr in my backside, she has been, with all her demands. But I have a nagging suspicion she may not be what we originally thought."

Eirik waited for Wilfrid to explain himself, but his seneschal turned red-faced and stammered, "But 'tis not my place to reveal such things without proof. And you will think me wooly-headed if I say she is not *that* unattractive."

"Hah! More like your vision is starting to dim. Like mine. Or Britta has turned your manroot to mush."

Wilfrid ducked his head sheepishly.

Eirik picked up his wine goblet and searched the room for wine, then realized he had thrown it all against the wall and into the rushes. His lips curled with disgust at the mess surrounding him as rationality began to calm his emotions.

"Send me more wine," he directed Wilfrid. "And set a guard to watching John and Larise at all times. Do not let them so much as visit the garderobe without an escort.''

"Yea," Wilfrid responded with a nod, heading toward the door, then turned back. "Will you have me send out men to search for the Lady Eadyth tonight?"

Eirik's eyes met Wilfrid's in a steely gaze. "Nay, we will go on the morrow. And then, I swear afore God, she will pay dearly for her deceit."

Despite his exhaustion, Eirik did not sleep at all the entire night. He drank goblet after goblet of fine Frankish wine but could not reach the blessed numbness of drunkenness. Instead, his mind worked continually, weighing all the evidence, seeking answers, coming to conclusions. He kept coming back to two proven facts: Eadyth had made a bloody fool of him, at the least, and mayhap even helped to plot his death, at the most.

By the time dawn light crept through the arrow slit openings in his bedchamber walls, Eirik was rigid with fury, but he controlled his rage under a calm, self-contained facade. He went down to the great hall and headed toward the kitchen where his servants already worked industriously.

Despite his anger, he saw evidence everywhere of Eadyth's touch. The keep smelled fresh from its many scrubbings, and every wood surface sparkled with polish, or as much as it possibly could in its crumbling state. He noticed two new chimneys in the great hall, a project he had planned for years but had never stayed long enough to accomplish.

The crisp rushes sent up waves of sweet herbal scents as he crushed them in his walk through the hall. In the kitchen, Bertha worked before the hearth, wearing a clean tunic, having pulled her hair back under a white wimple and neat head-rail.

"My lord," she bowed deferentially, "would ye care fer a bowl of porridge, or sum bread 'n cheese to break yer fast?"

"Nay," he answered, open-mouthed with surprise at all the changes in the spotless kitchen. Long-stemmed, fragrant herbs and dried flowers hung upside down in clumps from the ceiling rafters. The rushes had been swept completely from the stone floor of the kitchen, which was being scrubbed with sand and soapy water by a thrall on hands and knees.

Godric, the orphan boy he had seen with John and Larise the night before, was snapping beans before the fire. He nodded shyly up at him.

And Britta came bustling in with an armful of bed linens, singing a bawdy song merrily. When she saw him, she slowed down and flushed with embarrassment at his perusal before rushing outside to give the items to the laundress.

Mumbling gruffly of work to be done, Eirik backtracked through the hall and out to the castle wall which neared completion under the direction of Jeremy, the stonemason Eadyth had brought as part of her dowry. Just how far did Eadyth's treachery extend? he wondered. Jeremy could be putting inferior sand in the mortar so it would crumble at the first assault. He would have to examine it closely.

Just as he was about to enter the stables and organize the hunt for his errant wife, the sentry atop the palisade rang the large tower bell which warned of visitors on the horizon. Wilfrid joined him on the ramparts. They watched with growing consternation as the Lady Eadyth, brazen as you please, rode a snow white palfrey over the rise to the castle motte. Behind her followed a caravan of pony carts filled to overflowing with the most ungodly assortment of objects—dozens of huge, conical baskets, large wooden boxes with finely latticed sides, hundreds of pottery containers and metal molds.

Worst of all, she and the young men who drove her carts were covered head to toe in the diaphanous veils she favored. Eirik's eyes narrowed intently. *Holy St. Sebastian!* Mayhap he would strangle her with one of the infernal wisps of fabric, cut her body into pieces to fit neatly into one of the large baskets, and send it to her lover at Gravely.

He grinned at the thought.

Eadyth was surprised, and oddly delighted, to see her new husband standing in the bailey with Wilfrid and some of his retainers when she pulled her carts into the courtyard. She had not expected him until the next day, but it was just as well. He could help her unload and place her beekeeping equipment beyond the orchard.

But then she noticed the challenging stance of his wide-spread legs. He was wearing skin-tight braies, covered with a black wool *shert*. He must have just awakened because the leather ties at the neck slit exposed an enticing expanse of sun-tanned skin and curly black chest hair. But Eadyth had no time to dwell on that as her attention riveted on his fists, which kept clenching and unclenching where they were braced on his hips.

Oh, Lord. She had known he would not like her leaving Ravenshire against his command, but she had not expected he would be this angry.

A squire stepped forward and helped her from her horse. The six carts halted behind her, the drivers waiting for her signal to alight.

Eirik did not move even a tiny bit from his spot at the top of the steps leading into the hall. Apparently, he expected her to walk to him in greeting. She grimaced but decided it was the least she could do after disobeying his orders.

When she climbed halfway up the stone stairway, she noticed the stone-cold fury in his blue eyes and paused momentarily. She saw his gaze sweep contemptuously over her beekeeping veils. *Sweet Mary!* Did he expect her to transport bees unprotected?

When she moved closer, he grabbed her by the upper arms and pulled her close enough to hear his snarling words. "My Lady Bitch, where in bloody hell have you been?"

Eadyth recoiled at his harsh words and tried to pull out of his grasp, to no avail.

"I have been to Hawks' Lair," she stammered out, confused by his blazing hostility.

"And who was there with you? Your lover?"

"My *what*?" she sputtered. "Are you daft? A lover is the last thing I want. Not you, nor any man, you bloody beast."

"Yea, your lover referred to me as the Beast of Ravenshire

131

in his letter, as I recall. Is it a pet name you two concocted for me?''

Alarm swept over Eadyth like brushfire. What was he talking about? What lover? What letter?

"Eirik, let us go inside and speak on this. There is a misunderstanding here that I can surely—''

"Nay, the only misunderstanding here is yours. I warned you afore the wedding that I would not tolerate falseness in a wife.''

Wilfrid stepped up then and put a hand on Eirik's arm. "My lord, 'tis unseemly to carry on this conversation in front of all your servants and retainers.''

Eirik looked around him and shook his head as if just coming to his senses. Still holding onto Eadyth's arm, he began to pull her into the keep.

"Wait," Eadyth said, digging in her heels. "I have to help unload the carts first.''

"Why?" Eirik asked suspiciously. "Are there gifts from Steven you wish to hide from me? Or mayhap a special poison you plan to put in my mead?''

"Steven?" Eadyth asked, stunned to realize that it was the Earl of Gravely he accused her of consorting with. In those few moments that she hesitated in amazement, Eirik had stormed down the steps and proceeded to throw the specially woven, conical beehives to the ground, cursing roundly as he searched for some hidden item to prove her guilt.

He was about to open one of the boxes when Eadyth screamed, "No!" But his eyes locked with hers contemptuously, and Eadyth realized that her protest only prodded him to do the opposite.

Then it was too late.

Eadyth moaned and rushed forward as he opened the first box and hundreds of angry bees burst free, swarming all over his face and neck, under his loose tunic, over his tight leggings.

"Oh, my God! Stand still, Eirik. For the love of heaven, I cannot help you when you jump around like this.''

Eirik cursed loudly and fluently in several languages, using words that turned her face bright red, as he tried to slap the stinging insects off his body. But there were too many of them, and his actions only agitated them more.

She called to Edgar and Oslac, two of the drivers of the carts, who were protected with beekeeping veils and leather gloves, to help her. Eadyth picked off several of the valuable queen bees, easily recognizable by their color and shape, and put them back in the bee cases. Then her two beekeeping assistants used smoking torches to chase the remaining bees off her husband's body and back into the box.

When they were finally back in the case or lying dead on the ground, Eadyth looked back at Eirik. Tears rolled down his face from the smoke, and tiny white marks covered his face and arms and undoubtedly all his skin under the tunic and hose.

Eadyth gave quick instructions to the men who had come with her about where to place the hives and bees, telling Girta, who had just come outside to investigate the commotion, to show them the way. She told Bertha to send up to Eirik's bedchamber a tub of hot water, several crocks of salt and a handful of raw onions.

"Eirik, hurry! I must remove the stingers as soon as possible afore the bites swell and perchance fester."

Eirik just stared at her, in shock. Then he said with dead seriousness, "Eadyth, I am going to kill you."

Chapter Eight

"Kiss me, dearling, Awk."

"Kiss my arse."

"Would ye like to see . . . awk . . . me arse?"

"Would ye like to have your feathers plucked and stuffed down your bloody throat?"

"Show me yer legs. Awk."

"Go bugger yourself."

"Kiss me, dearling. Kiss me, dearling. Kiss me, dearling."

Snorting with disgust, Eirik threw a wool cloak over the bird's cage, muttering something very foul. The squawking stopped immediately.

Eadyth stood stunned in Eirik's bedchamber doorway. She could not decide whether she was more amazed by the sound of her husband arguing in a vulgar fashion with a witless bird, or by the sight of Eirik standing in the middle of the room with his back to her—totally nude. The latter won out.

Truth be told, this devastatingly handsome man, *her husband*, stole her breath away.

Her eyes skimmed the sun-baked bronze of his skin from

the wide shoulders, to the supple back muscles, to his tapering waist and deliciously narrow hips. She licked her suddenly dry lips. Even his powerful thighs and sinewy calves were sun-darkened, she noted. Apparently, he must wear only a loincloth when exercising with his men or when on shipboard. The skin of his firm buttocks was the only part of his body that remained light.

Well, not quite, Eadyth amended quickly as Eirik turned. He had hidden another part of his body, as well. And, oh, Sweet Mother! It was a very nice part, indeed.

Eadyth put her hands to her hot cheeks and forced her eyes upward to meet Eirik's knowing, wintry smile. His cool regard chilled her to the bone, bringing her jarringly back to the present dilemma—Eirik's bee stings.

"Get out, Eadyth," he said with deliberate care. "I will deal with you and your treachery later. Leave me now to my misery."

"Eirik, I am truly sorry for what happened in the bailey. But 'tis not my fault. Bees sting when threatened, and—"

"Threatened? Best you have a caution, *wife*, and leave my presence afore I show you a real threat."

"Why are you so angry with me? 'Twas you who riled the bees. But that is the way of men, is it not? Always blaming women for their mistakes."

"Your biggest mistake, my lady, was in thinking you could play me false and escape the consequences." Nostrils flaring, Eirik moved toward her menacingly.

Baffled by his fierce fury, she backed up a few steps and protested, "You deliberately misunderstand me. Be reasonable. Leastwise, I need to tend to your . . . Oh, Sweet Mother of God . . ."

Eadyth's words trailed off as she noticed the dozens of white bites, already turning red, on his face, neck, chest, back, stomach, legs—in truth, every part of his body. And worst of all, Eirik was vigorously clawing at his flesh with his fingernails wherever he could reach.

"Nay, you must stop scratching," she ordered, slapping

135

his hands away from his body. "You lackbrain, do you not know better than to rub a bee bite? You must remove the stinger first."

Ignoring her words, Eirik moved closer to the window alcove so he could better see as he peered over his shoulder and tried to claw at the bites on his back.

Again, she shoved his hand aside and pulled out the small ivory-handled knife from the scabbard at her belt. "Here, let me help."

Eirik eyed the sharp blade in her hand and laughed mirthlessly. "Your solicitude comes too late, my lady wife. I am not half-witted enough to let you near my body with a weapon." With lightning swiftness, he grabbed the knife from her hand and laid it behind him on a table.

"How absurd! I just want to remove the stingers with the edge of the blade. When a bee bites, it leaves its stinger under the skin, then goes off to die, but—"

"Hah! Just as I thought! You are more concerned about your precious pests than my injuries."

"Oh, 'tis unfair of you to speak thus. And bees are not pests. I merely wanted to explain that the stinger must be removed with care, as soon as possible, or its poison will be pumped into the wound causing swelling or even fever."

"That would make you happy, would it not—you and your scheming lover?"

Eadyth stiffened at the barely bridled rage in his voice. "Lover? What lover?" Her brows drew together in confusion. But now was not the time for anger or explanations. Meeting his accusing eyes without flinching, she asked coolly, "Do you want my help or not?"

He glared at her for several long moments, then looked down at the angry welts already starting to form where he had rubbed. "No knife. Use your fingernails," he demanded finally.

Eadyth glanced skeptically at her blunt nails, but moved toward him, shaking her head in exasperation. Did he truly think she would kill him? She was not *that* angry about the rude kiss on his leavetaking. But then her sensitivity to his obvious pain won out over her growing chagrin.

"Sit down," she ordered, pointing to a low stool near the window. In order to see better, she removed her full-length beekeeping veil. She had neglected to put the usual ashes on her face this morn, thinking Eirik would not return to Ravenshire until the morrow. She hoped Eirik, with his watering eyes, was in too much misery right now to notice her appearance. In any case, it was a chance she had to take.

"Does it hurt?"

"Does a horse piss?"

"Tsk!" Eadyth clucked at his vulgarity and muttered, "You make it sore hard for a person to sympathize—"

"Save your sympathies for someone who cares. Mayhap your lover."

Eadyth bristled, angry herself now. "I do not know what you are talking about."

Eirik just scowled.

"Do you want my help or not?"

In response, Eirik hunched over on the stool, resting his arms on his widespread thighs. *The ingrate!* She reminded herself to bear with him. Like many fighting men, he could, no doubt, bear great battle wounds stoically but would whine like a child over the smaller ills of life, such as an aching tooth, or a small fever, or a bee sting.

First, Eadyth worked methodically on his back. One by one, she painstakingly scraped the edge of her index fingernail against the center of the bites until the stingers came out. It was not an easy task. Eadyth's fingers trembled at the first touch of her husband's pale gold skin as the smell of him enveloped her sensuously in a pleasant aura of soap and fresh sunlight and his own distinctive man scent.

She bit her bottom lip to stifle a soft groan of pleasure.

"What did you say?"

"Nothing. Keep your head down."

Eadyth moved lower to his waist and hips, pressing her fingertips in a testing fashion on his hot flesh. Sweet Mother, his body threw off heat like an oven. Was it fever, or just hot blood? And were all parts of his body so deliciously hot?

Scandalized by her wayward thoughts, Eadyth chastised herself silently. She had never had such lewd fantasies before, not even with Steven. In fact, her yearnings for Steven had always been pure of spirit. Until the one painful, joyless coupling, that is.

It must be her advancing age, she decided. She had heard that some women got these odd urgings as they grew older and their bodies matured. What other explanation could there be for this not unpleasant aching in her limbs? She studied Eirik's well-proportioned back for a long moment, refusing to believe that these new feelings stemmed from proximity to this man, and this one alone.

"God's Bones! What takes you so long? Do you deliberately malinger to prolong my agony?"

"Oh, hush," Eadyth said.

When she finished with his back and arms, she asked him to stand so she could work on his legs, both back and front. She studiously avoided *that* part of him, and instead found her senses teased by the inadvertent brush of his crisp leg hairs across her cheek as she moved about her work.

It seemed to take forever.

"Are you enjoying yourself, my lady wife?" Eirik said in a voice thick with sarcasm.

"Nay, are you?" she responded carelessly, and without thinking looked up to see his manhood standing out from his body, hard as polished marble. Immediately, she looked away, hating the blush which she felt sweep her face.

He laughed scornfully. "That part of a man's body cares not whether a woman is beautiful or ugly as a mole. Nor does it trouble itself whether she oozes treachery like a running sore."

Eadyth snapped her mouth shut, refusing to acknowledge his hurtful words. She straightened to begin working on his chest, taking care to keep her face averted. The room was dim, and he kept swiping at his half-closed eyes in misery, but she could not be too careful.

Even so, it was hard to still her hammering heart, which was unnerved by the lazy seductiveness of his stance. She found herself responding to his enticing nearness, despite her long history of disdain for the male touch, despite his cruel accusations, despite all that she sensed was dangerous to the self-control she so valued.

Forcing a shrill tone into her voice, she hunched her shoulders a bit and asked, "Why do you keep accusing me of treachery? I have done naught to cause your distrust."

He shot her a withering look but said nothing.

Moving through the wiry hairs that encircled his flat male nipples, she removed the last of the stingers there, then knelt to search out the stingers on his flat stomach. It was not a position she relished. Totally embarrassed, she studiously maintained a space between them and avoided looking down.

"Can you not don some small clothes?"

"Why?"

" 'Tis immodest of you to . . . to flaunt your body thus."

He laughed mockingly. " 'Tis naught you have not seen afore with your lover. Or is Steven's cock so different?"

Eadyth blanched at his vulgarity. Then shock quickly yielded to anger. She lifted her fisted hand and prepared to punch him in his stomach, but Eirik grabbed her wrist and held it in a painful grasp.

"Do not even think of striking me. In my present mood, I would not hesitate to hit you back."

"Your mother should have soaped your mouth as a child. You have a filthy tongue."

"I had no mother."

"Were you born under a rock?"

He twisted her wrist tighter and scrutinized her coldly, as if contemplating whether to break the bone or not. Finally, he dropped her hand with a snort of disgust.

Tears smarted her eyes, and she blinked to hold them back as she rubbed her sore wrist. "Why are you being so hateful? I have done naught to hurt you."

"You think not? Well, think again. The one thing I demanded of you afore signing the betrothal agreement was fidelity. Hah! The ink is barely dry, and you have spread your thighs for another. And our marriage not yet consummated!"

Eadyth stiffened and tilted her head questioningly. "You think I have lain with another man?"

"Yea, I do."

"Who?"

"The bloody bastard—Steven. Who else?"

"Are you daft? You know how I hate him."

"Nay, I realize now that I know naught of your true self. But know this, *my lady wife*, you will pay tenfold for your treachery, and I do not just refer to the bee stings."

Eirik's ludicrous accusation cut Eadyth deeply, and the hurt soon turned to blood-boiling anger. She spun around and proceeded to walk toward the door, needing to be by herself to understand the charges he leveled against her. Perhaps Girta could explain. But Eirik grabbed her by the forearm and hauled her back.

"Finish the work you started."

She lifted her chin defiantly. "You can do your neck and face yourself with the aid of a mirror." She pointed to the framed piece of polished metal on his wall.

"Nay. You will tend my bites—all of them. After all, 'tis you who caused them."

Eadyth opened her mouth to protest her innocence, then forced herself to remain silent. Until she understood what had happened in her absence, what prompted Eirik's ridiculous belief that she had taken a lover, her protests would be meaningless.

His eyes blazed blue fire at her, all-devouring in their intensity.

"Sit down again," she ordered icily. "And close your eyes." She did not want him looking at her face this close up.

Only a few stings remained on the sensitive skin of his neck, and those she easily removed. She was becoming quite adept at flicking her fingernail in just the right spot to pop out the stingers. Then she moved up to his face, which he lifted for her ministrations.

The crinkles of humor that had formerly webbed his eyes and lips had somehow turned into marks of cruelty. Eirik's long lashes lay like silky black fans against the shadowed underside of his eyes. He must not have slept much last night—no doubt, plotting ways to torture her on her return, she thought ruefully.

Carefully, she held his stubbornly jutting chin in place, unable to ignore the angry twitch beneath her probing fingers. She removed one stinger close to his right eye. It would probably swell shut before nightfall. She brushed back several strands of his long, tousled hair to get at the four bites on his forehead and thought irrelevantly that he needed a haircut. The straight ebony hair hung down to his shoulders in the Saxon style, but was much too long.

She was almost done. *Thank God!*

"You have several bites in your mustache. Mayhap you should shave it off in order to get the stingers out."

"Why is your skin so smooth?"

It took several moments for Eirik's words to register. She realized then that his eyes—brilliant blue, like glacial ice— were wide open, and that he had been watching her closely. *At close range.*

She frowned and hunched her shoulders, but it was too late.

Eirik gripped her chin tightly in one hand and tilted her face to the light. "Your skin does not have its usual grayish tint today. Nor is it as wrinkled or aged as I had thought it to be."

Eadyth could barely control the trembling of her lips under his intent scrutiny. "I have been out in the sun a great deal in your absence. The bronzing of the sun enhances the healthy appearance of all skin for a while, do you not think?"

He did not look convinced.

"Besides, good skin runs in my family. 'Tis said my grandmother had nary a wrinkle when she died after fifty-two years.''

Oh, Lord! Eadyth despaired. This should be the perfect opportunity for her to confess her masquerade, but in view of Eirik's present mood she feared his reaction. With the marriage not yet consummated, he could easily put her aside. Dare she take a chance with honesty? Nay, she decided to wait just a bit longer until she had cleared up the misunderstanding about Steven.

She needed to divert his attention. ''Well, if you refuse to shave your mustache, at least close your eyes again so I can dig amongst the spiny hairs.''

Eirik grumbled something, but the words were unintelligible with her left hand clamped over his mouth. Actually, the bristly hairs felt sensuously sleek under her probing fingers, and Eadyth could not help but remember how his mustache had felt during that one erotic, mind-jarring kiss in this very chamber.

Eirik seemed to have remembered, as well, for when she stepped away, his voice was husky. ''Are you done?''

''Yea, but turn around again. I need to apply something soothing to the wounds to prevent swelling.''

The servants had carried a tub full of steaming water into the room during her ministrations, as well as the salt and onions she had requested. She poured the entire crock full of salt into the bathwater, then turned to the table where her knife still lay. She sliced a large onion in half and began to rub it over Eirik's back in a sweeping motion.

''Aaah! That feels *so* good.''

''I thought it would. Now, stand so I can do your legs.''

As she knelt and worked briskly, Eadyth felt the powerful muscles of Eirik's legs stiffen suddenly.

''What is that ungodly smell?''

''Onion.''

With a curse, he reached down and pulled her to her feet. At first, he just stared incredulously at the white half-globe in her hand, then to the onion-induced tears which had begun to stream down her face.

"God's Bones! Do you truly dare to cover my body with smelly onion juice? 'Tis a jest you play whilst my body is in misery?"

"Nay, everyone knows that onion juice is the best thing to reduce the swelling of bee stings."

"Well, *everyone* can go to bloody hell." He grabbed her hand and pulled her along with him to the tub. He handed her a cloth and a bar of hard soap, ordering, "You will wash every drop of it off my skin or I will stuff onions down your throat 'til the juice comes out your ears."

He sank into the hot water, then immediately shot up, standing upright. "Ouch! That burns like hellfire. What is in the water?"

"Salt."

Stepping out of the tub, he grabbed her by the forearms and lifted her off the floor so that they eyed each other, nose to nose.

"You would rub salt in my wounds, as well? Truly, woman, you have passed the bounds of brashness and have now entered the arena of stupidity."

He shook her so hard she could not think clearly, then dropped her abruptly to her feet on the floor. She stared dumbly at him, his handsome face twisted into an ugly mask of fury.

"How would you like it if I rubbed your body raw with sand, then put you in a tub of salt water?"

"You cannot be serious."

"Oh, can I not?"

She backed away, stuttering in a rush of words, "You just do not understand . . . do not touch me . . . oh, now you got my gown wet . . . stop it . . . salt will stop the stings from swelling and prevent them from festering . . . truly, listen to me . . . oh, you loathsome lou . . ."

She could say no more because Eirik picked her up and dumped her, clothes and all, into the tub, then dunked her head under the water. She came up sputtering, only to hear him say, "Whilst you are in there, wash that vile grease from your hair. It stinks." Before she could answer, he pushed her head under again and held it there so long her nose began to burn.

When she finally emerged from the tub, livid, her hair hung limply under her soaking head-rail and her wool gown made a huge puddle on the rush-clad floor. "You . . . you . . . you . . . ," she stammered, unable to come up with the appropriate words to describe his odious self.

And Eirik just stood there in his naked magnificence, hands on hips, feet planted apart arrogantly, laughing his head off. When his fit of mirth finally passed, he said with dry amusement, "Well, I feel immensely better."

"You toad."

Still laughing, he threw her a linen cloth to dry herself and motioned her to the stool. Pulling on a pair of braies and a long-sleeved *shert*, he commented ominously, "*Now* we will discuss your treachery, and what to do about this ill-suited marriage we find ourselves in."

Eirik walked over to the small table near his bed and pulled a piece of crumpled parchment from the drawer. He smoothed it out on the tabletop, then turned and handed it to his wife, never speaking a word. Instead, he walked to the opposite side of the room and leaned against the wall, waiting for her to finish reading the incriminating words. His skin itched like hell, but he refused to scratch or apply her onion juice or salt water. He would wait until later and send Wilfrid to the local herbal woman for an ointment.

"Well?" he asked finally when she had pondered the letter for an inordinate amount of time. "Have you naught to say for yourself?"

"Where did you get this?"

"Britta found it under your mattress."

She lifted her eyes to him, horror covering her face. He shook his head in disbelief. She looked like a drowned rat with her greasy gray hair hanging in wet clumps under the sodden head-rail, onion-induced tears streaming down her face.

"Do you realize what this means, Eirik?" she said anxiously. "Steven, or one of his men, has been in this keep."

"Tell me something I do not already know," he remarked sarcastically, "like where the hell you have been the past four days. And with whom."

Eadyth waved his question aside as if it were of no importance. "At Hawks' Lair. You know that already. But what I meant was that we must take better precautions if Steven can enter this keep so easily. He could have taken . . . oh, my God, he could have taken John."

"Yea, he could have. Just as you planned."

Eadyth's brow furrowed in puzzlement. Blessed Lord, the traitorous bitch put on a good act. He could almost believe her innocence. "I never expected a maidenhead, *wife*, but neither did I expect to be cuckolded so soon after the vows were taken."

"What do you mean?" she asked stiffly. "Are you saying that you believe the lies in this letter? Do you imply I have been . . . involved with the man who tries to take my son from me?"

"All facts point that way. And I have only your word that he seeks to do you harm," he said, shrugging, as he walked up to her and removed the letter from her hands. "*Hold on, love, just a short while longer till we can be together finally . . . ,*" he read in a mimicking voice, then, "*Your heart's husband, Steven.*"

Eadyth stood abruptly, knocking the stool over. Angry pink spots dotted her cheeks as she snarled, "You think I am Steven's whore?" When he did not answer, Eadyth muttered under her breath, then exclaimed in a shrill, indignant voice, "You bastard! The only true statement in this missive is Steven's reference to you as the Beast of Ravenshire. Yea, you are a beast to think thus of me."

Tears filled her eyes, but Eirik remained untouched. She

145

had played him false with his hated enemy, and that he could not abide.

"Knowing how evil Steven is, why can you not see this letter for the ploy it is? 'Twas planted to divide us in our intentions to hold his son from him. And he succeeded, thanks to your gullibility, you bloody fool."

She turned and stumbled blindly toward the door, as fast as her legs could carry her, hampered by her sodden garment. For a moment, Eirik wondered if he had judged her unfairly, but then he remembered the other, the most important part of the letter.

"Are you breeding? With Steven's child . . . again?"

She gasped and her back stiffened. Then she turned slowly and her violet eyes flashed icily, remarkably beautiful eyes for an old crone, he thought irrelevantly.

"Nay, I am not carrying a babe. Not unless you believe me capable of an immaculate conception."

Eadyth's sarcasm irritated him. She had no cause to be affronted. *He* was the injured party.

"I will not harbor another of Steven's bastards," he informed her. "One is enough."

Her cheeks turned even redder, and he noticed her fists bunching at her sides. Then she reached toward the scabbard at her belt, forgetting that her small knife still lay on the far table. He was not so dim-sighted he could not see the speculation in her eyes as she measured the distance, wondering if she had time to get the blade and stab him.

"Do not even think it, or you will find yourself with a slit throat afore you can blink."

Giving up on that alternative, she lifted her chin defiantly, staring him down in silence. If she only knew how ridiculous she looked with her scowling countenance and her wet garments making a puddle in the rushes, he mused.

"This marriage will not be consummated 'til you get your monthly courses and I know for certain you carry no bad seed."

"And when you are proven wrong?" she sneered, disdain

giving a sharp edge to her voice.

"I will decide then whether I want to live with another false wife."

"Another?"

Eirik immediately realized his mistake, but refused to answer her question.

She scrutinized him haughtily, then repeated her earlier statement. "I am not breeding."

He just raised an eyebrow skeptically.

Her face turned crimson, but she met his eyes head on. "I am bleeding now."

That disclosure caught Eirik by surprise. Could he possibly have been wrong? But years of Steven's treachery had taught him to be ever suspicious. He could not stop himself from doggedly persisting, "How do I know you do not lie?"

Her lips curled scornfully. "What shall I do, my lord? Lift my robe and show you the bloody rag?"

Her contempt disarmed him. That and her demeanor of wounded pride.

"Yea, that would be a good start."

She backed toward the door, eyes wide with fear at his suggestion. "You . . . you would not ask that of me," she sputtered in a voice shaking with disbelief.

"Do not place a wager on it. Come here, Eadyth, and prove your innocence."

She gasped and turned quickly, hand on the door, but he moved even quicker and placed his body at the exit, barring her way. She jumped away from him in fright, like a bedraggled cat, and moved back to the center of the room, looking right and left for a weapon, to no avail.

"Oh, nay, oh, please, do not do this. You have misjudged me. I can expl—"

Eirik cut off her near hysterical words when he lifted her by the waist and threw her back onto his bed with a loud whooshing sound. He followed close after her, as her arms flailed out, hitting and scratching his already irritated skin.

Ignoring her enormous, doelike eyes, he straddled her body

147

with his knees, holding her body in place, and locked both her hands over her head in one fist. Despite the fear she tried to hold in check, her chin lifted defiantly like a martyr's.

Eirik hesitated. What if she was innocent?

"Tell me true, wife, have you ever, since we signed the betrothal agreement, deceived me?"

In the charged silence, Eadyth did not speak for a moment, averting her eyes guiltily. By the time she started to speak tentatively, "There is one small thing . . . ," it was too late, to his mind. Her hesitation spoke for itself.

Eirik snorted with disgust and pressed her tighter to the bed with his body.

"You beast, I will never forgive you for this. Worse, you will never forgive yourself when you discover the truth."

"Nay, I will never forgive myself if I do not find out for certain if you have betrayed me." Eirik, in a misty haze of utter fury, flipped her robe up to her waist, exposing long limbs.

And the bloody rag between her thighs.

Eirik looked up and saw the silent tears of humiliation seeping from her closed eyes. A nagging voice inside his head told him to release her, to be satisfied with the evidence he saw, but a berserk rage had overtaken his body. Blood roared in his ears as he passed the breaking point. He had been at the wrong end of Steven's perfidy for too long to be satisfied with less than the ultimate proof. Even the bloody rag could be a carefully concocted ruse.

Roughly, he reached down and tore the soiled cloth from her body and threw it onto the rushes. Then, swiftly, before she could comprehend what he was about, Eirik used his legs to maneuver her thighs apart and thrust his middle finger into her body.

She screamed then, loud and keening. He did not know if it was from the humiliation, or the pain, for her passage was dry and tight for even his lone finger.

Realization swept over him, even before he pulled the finger out and saw the bloody evidence. She did not carry Steven's child.

Eadyth lay stiffly, trying hard to control the racking sobs which shook her thin body. Her pale eyes stared lifelessly at the ceiling.

Eirik jumped up in horror and walked to the wall near the window. Angrily, he pounded his fist against the stone wall until he drew blood.

He had never, never been so ashamed of himself in all his life.

Chapter Nine

"Eadyth, we have to talk."

Eirik pulled a chair closer to the bed. For more than an hour, he had been pacing the bedchamber, watching his wife sleep restlessly, waiting for her to awaken.

After his gross assault on her person, Eadyth had refused to look at him or hear his words of apology. She had surprised him by hurling out a few surprisingly coarse curses that would make a Viking sailor blush, then curled herself into a pitiful ball. She had wept quietly for an ungodly length of time before falling into a fitful slumber.

He eyed the crumpled heap of clothing which hid Eadyth's slight frame as she came slowly awake and moved awkwardly into a sitting position in the middle of his large bed. He didn't know which Eadyth he misliked most—the shrewish, arrogant crone who had plagued him with complaints from the moment they first met, or the silent, humbled one who jabbed at his conscience now.

Hell's flames! He was sore tired from lack of sleep, and his skin itched unbearably from the bee stings. He needed to settle this matter between them. Then, he would like nothing better than to be off to Jorvik where Asa could minister to his needs—both the bee stings and that *other* long-unmet one.

"Eadyth, did you hear me? We have to talk," he snapped.

"We have absolutely naught to discuss," she replied icily as she eased herself off the bed and stood on the opposite side of the room from him. She adjusted her infernal headrail in her usual fashion so that it half-covered her face, but not before he noted her red nose, puffy eyelids and pink-blotched skin.

He hadn't thought it possible she could look any worse than before. She did.

He rubbed his index finger thoughtfully across his mustache, wondering how he had got himself into this mess of a marriage, then stopped in midstroke as he noticed something alarming. Suspiciously, he held the fingertips of both hands to his jaw bones, then moved them slowly upward to his eyes and over his forehead in an exploring fashion.

He groaned aloud at what he discovered.

His face had swollen, and one eyelid had puffed almost completely shut. He muttered something foul under his breath and rose and walked over to the wash table under the framed polished metal on the wall.

He had to restrain himself from jumping back in horror at his reflection.

"Damn!" he exploded. "I saw a leper once who looked better than I do now."

Eadyth laughed with a shrill cackle behind him. "There is some justice in the world then."

Eirik slanted her a warning look. "Do not be so cocky. I have seen corpses looking livelier than you."

She glared at him frostily with her violet eyes. Their beauty was surely wasted on such as her, he thought, not for the first time. Then she reached for the goblet near the bed, weighing it in her hands, glancing back at him as if contemplating him as a target.

Well, at least the old Eadyth was back again.

"Do not even think—"

A loud knocking at the door interrupted his words, and Eadyth put the goblet back on the table.

"M'lord, 'tis me, Bertha." The pounding continued.

Eirik shot Eadyth a meaningful glance that told her without words that their talk was only postponed.

"What is it now?" he grumbled as he pulled the door open suddenly, causing Bertha to pitch forward slightly. He caught her massive bulk, then held her upper arms to steady her upright.

"Jesus, Mary and Joseph!" Bertha exclaimed, craning her neck to look up at him. "You look like you been fighting with the devil."

"Nay, just my wife."

Eadyth gasped behind him.

Bertha tried unsuccessfully to peer past his large frame into the bedchamber.

"What do you want?"

"The mistress din't tell me what to prepare fer dinner this eve, and it be way past noon."

Bertha's complaint did not fool Eirik. After all, she had been operating her kitchen quite efficiently without her mistress's direction during Eadyth's absence. Curiosity, pure and simple, motivated the old cook—that and a well-known love of gossip.

"Do whatever you bloody well want."

"Well, 'tis no need to get on yer high horse with me. Jist 'cause you were lackwitted enuf to stick yer head in a basket of bees, 'tis no reason to take yer bad humors out on me."

"I did not—"

"You don't see me laughin' me bloody head off, do you? Nay, m'lord. Do you see me sittin' down in the kitchen with the scullery maids wonderin' if yer staff got bit by them bloody bees and whether it be swollen twice its size and whether you be up here givin' yer new wife twice the pleasure?"

Eirik choked back his laughter.

"Nay, I be up here jist tryin' to do me duty," she continued. "Even when I could be in the great hall listenin' to yer men makin' wagers on how many bee stings ye got on yer body. I got better things to do with me time. Yea, I do."

Eirik snorted with disgust. *God's Bones!* Now his wife had turned him into a laughingstock.

". . . 'cause I know there be no way you could have two hun'red stings on yer fine body," Bertha babbled on recklessly, failing to notice the stiffening of his back or his frowning face, "even if Master Wilfrid sez he picked up two hun'red dead bees in the bailey."

"Oh, nay, say 'tis not so, Bertha," Eadyth exclaimed with alarm. "So many of my precious bees dead? I must go at once to check the damage and see the remaining bees secure in their new hives. I cannot believe I was lying here wallowing in self-pity when so much needed to be done."

Eirik turned in surprise at Eadyth's words, which gave Bertha the opportunity to step past him into the bedchamber. Her mouth dropped open in amazement, displaying a half-dozen missing teeth.

Bertha looked at Eadyth's sodden clothing and tear-splotched face, then darted her beady eyes to Eirik, then back to Eadyth. Laughter rumbled from deep in her belly, erupted raucously, and continued until tears ran in rivulets down her bloated face.

"Oh, oh, I can barely credit the two of you. What a pair you make! Yer faces look like two bowls of day-old, lumpy porridge."

"Kiss my arse," a muffled voice said.

That stopped Bertha's laughter abruptly. "Wha . . . what did ye say, m'lord?"

"Show me yer legs."

The bloody bird displayed a real talent for bad timing and mimicking voices, Eirik thought.

"Well, I never thought to see the day, m'lord. Yer blessed grandmother mus' be rollin' in her grave to see you oglin' an old woman like me. Not that I have any trouble gettin' a

153

man into my bed even yet.'' Bertha sucked in her bulging stomach and thrust out her buxom breasts proudly.

Eirik's eyes widened in disbelief. The old hag actually thought he was attracted to her gross charms.

''Actually, now that I think on it, mayhap you have developed a taste fer older meat,'' Bertha added slyly, darting a meaningful look at Eadyth.

''That will be enough,'' Eadyth said stonily in her best lady-of-the-manor voice. ''Leave my presence at once if you value your misbegotten skin. I will come down to the kitchen as soon as I check my bees.''

Somewhat chastened, but still chuckling, Bertha headed toward the door.

''And make sure there are no weevils in the manchet bread like there were afore I left for Hawks' Lair. Nay, do not raise your chin at me, you lazy wench. I intend to check the flour closely, and every worm I find will be put on your loose tongue with my very own fingers.''

Bertha waddled away, muttering something about ungrateful mistresses.

''And make sure you do not gossip below stairs about what you have . . . seen here,'' Eadyth added.

Bertha clucked her tongue with disgust. ''As if anyone with eyes in their heads will not be able to see fer themselves fer days ter come what you two have been about.''

Eadyth prepared to follow Bertha through the door, but Eirik halted her progress with a raised arm and closed the door.

''We will talk now.''

Eadyth turned her nose up stubbornly. ''I do not wish to speak with you—now or ever.''

''That should make for a wonderful marriage.''

''No one ever promised you a wonderful marriage.''

''You pledged honesty.''

''And I have given it.''

''I asked you afore I did . . . what I did . . . ,'' Eirik said, searching lamely for a polite word for his vulgar act. ''I clearly asked whether you had ever deceived me, and you hesitated—''

''And you consider my mere hesitation a justification for such a vile response?''

''Nay, I do not. I am merely trying to explain.''

Eadyth's eyes flashed angrily as she challenged him, hands on hips, chin tilted upward. Suddenly, Eirik realized why she might have been considered a beauty in her youth. With that fiery nature, and just a little natural beauty, she must have been a woman worth her weight in gold. Nay, not gold, *silver*, Eirik reminded himself, recalling Wilfrid's reference to the Silver Jewel of Northumbria.

''Stop that,'' Eadyth demanded, stamping her small leather shoe petulantly in the rushes.

''What?''

''Looking at me . . . like that.''

''How?''

''Like I am one of your tarts.''

''Hardly.''

His wry observation did not sit well with her. ''You make me so *damned* angry I could spit.''

''So? Relax some of that self-righteous self-control of yours and do it.''

''Do what?''

''Spit.''

''Argh! Talking with you is useless. Why do you not go off to Jorvik and plague one of your mistresses?''

Eirik felt his face heat at her too accurate reading of his plans. And he misliked the fact that she accepted other women in his life so easily. Not that it was not a woman's role to be subservient to her husband, to turn her head at his sexual misdeeds. 'Twas the nature of men to seek many partners and had been through the ages. It just rankled that she practically pushed him into another woman's arms.

She glared at him fiercely, waiting for his reply. Armed to the teeth, no doubt, with another caustic remark, he thought. Then an odd thing happened. Her lips began to twitch, and she quickly covered them with both hands as if to hide something. Suspiciously, he leaned closer, thinking he heard a little twittering sound.

Then he knew.

The wench was laughing at him. She dared to laugh at her husband. She must have the brains of a flea to tempt his already overwrought temper thus.

"Oh, I cannot help myself," she confessed. "You look so funny, standing there like a raging bull, but looking like a puffy mass of red-speckled dough."

"So you think me amusing, do you?" Eirik said, advancing closer. "Have you any idea what your unwelcome bath and your blubbering have done to *your* appearance?"

Before she could protest, Eirik turned her toward the polished metal and forced her to look at herself.

"Oh, my."

"Oh, my, indeed."

"I guess Bertha was right. We look quite the pair."

Eadyth suddenly seemed to realize that she had dropped her anger toward Eirik too easily by laughing with him companionably. Forcing a scowl onto her mirthful face, she snorted with self-disgust and started to walk toward the door. Eirik figured he had best make his apologies quickly before she turned shrewish again.

"Come," he said, leading her to the chair and pushing her gently to sit. He pulled another chair closer so they sat facing each other, knee to knee. "I would have my say now."

Eadyth made as if to rise, but he halted her by shaking his head. "Nay, you will sit and listen. 'Twill not be easy for me to tell you of the reasons for my berserk behavior, but you deserve the explanation. It all revolves around that bloody demon, Steven of Gravely."

Eadyth's head shot up with interest, and she sat back, steepling her fingers in front of her tightly pressed lips. Studying him warily, she finally said, "I am listening."

Eadyth watched her husband as he shifted uncomfortably in the chair facing her. A soft white *shert* covered his taut body down to the wrists, and faded brown braies hugged his thick thigh and calf muscles down to the ankles, but Eadyth knew from his swollen face and the reddening bite wounds evident in the open neckline that he suffered terribly with the urge to scratch.

Good, she thought, remembering the vulgar thing he had done to her.

Until she had met Steven, she had been modest in her person, never allowing any man to touch her, not even for a chaste kiss. It had taken Steven months of seductive wooing to convince her of his love, and only then had she allowed that most intimate of all acts.

Since Steven's betrayal, she had learned her lesson well and kept all men beyond touching distance of her body. It had not always been an easy task once word of her child leaked out, for she had been deemed tarnished goods. In defense, she had avoided the royal court and any public places where she might have been vulnerable to men's advances, and she had made a concerted effort to downplay her attractiveness.

Mayhap that was why Eirik's vulgar action devastated her so. Like all the other men, he placed no value on her dignity. And, for some reason, his condemnation of her as an adulteress hurt deeply. Blessed Lord, she could not remember the last time she had allowed herself the indulgence of a good sob. Probably not since Steven's betrayal.

Eirik shifted noisily in his chair, breaking her reverie. ''I first met Steven when I went to King Athelstan's court as a boy for fostering.''

Despite her angry emotions, Eadyth could not curb her curiosity. ''Was it not odd for a Viking child to foster at a Saxon court?''

''Nay, 'twas not unusual. My cousin Haakon, as pure a Viking as there ever was long afore he became high-king of all Norway, fostered there with me. Not to mention an assortment of scholars and refugees from royal courts around the world.

"And I told you afore I am only half Viking." Eirik grinned in a ridiculous parody of a smile, considering the puffiness of his face. His lips tilted up only on one side. And, yea, Eadyth did remember all too well that earlier conversation when he had teased her, asking if she would like to see his Viking half. She curled her lips with distaste and made a clucking sound of disgust.

"Did your father force you to foster there?" she asked, choosing to ignore his insinuation about Viking parts.

"On the contrary, I coaxed my father into allowing me to be a Saxon fosterling."

"But why?"

He shrugged, scratching distractedly at his arms, then the back of his neck. Eadyth wanted to remind him that the onion juice would alleviate his discomfort but knew somehow that he would accept no help from her.

" 'Tis hard to explain, but even then times were changing for all Norsemen. Throughout Britain, you see evidence of how we Norsemen have assimilated, adopting Saxon customs, marrying their women. And 'tis not one-sided, this blending. Saxons have taken on many Norse ways, as well."

"Like Earl Orm?"

"Yea, and many others. It seemed to me, even as a child, that my future, and that of my fellow Norsemen, would be better served by learning the Saxon ways so both peoples could live together peacefully."

Eadyth bit her bottom lip thoughtfully and gazed at this husband of hers—a stranger, really—seeing him in a new light. She had heard of his military exploits, but this idealistic side of his nature intrigued her.

But mayhap his noble words were just a ploy to soften her anger. She would have to tread carefully.

"And Tykir? Did he foster there with you?"

"Hardly," Eirik scoffed. "He was more interested in the direct approach to settlement in Britain. Kill every Saxon in sight."

158

"What has all this to do with Steven and your disgusting behavior?"

Eirik stroked his mustache absently. Then he flexed his fingers nervously and combed them through his hair. His throat worked as he sought for the right words.

Eadyth studied him carefully. What could cause such distress in Eirik that he would have trouble expressing himself?

Eirik cleared his throat and began. "Steven was also a fosterling at King Athelstan's court. In fact, they were second cousins," he said. "When I arrived, I had seen only ten winters, and Steven five more than that. We should have been friends."

Eirik seemed drawn back in time, and a fierce anguish swept over his face in memory. A deep, deep pain misted his blue eyes.

"And?" she prompted when his silence went on and on.

At first, he did not seem to hear her as his thoughts turned inward.

"And?" she repeated.

"And we were *not* friends." Eirik sighed deeply, forcing himself back to the present. Then he looked her directly in the eye, determination turning his eyes dark blue. "Steven was evil even then. He delighted in torturing not only animals, but those humans unwise enough to cross his path—those younger or weaker than he."

Eadyth waited patiently for Steven to continue.

"I was only there a few sennights when he made arrangements with a notorious Norse outlaw, Ivar the Vicious, for my kidnapping. 'Twas intended as a trap to capture Sigtrygg, who was then the Viking king of Northumbria, but, instead, it led to my father's death."

Eirik held up his left hand, displaying his missing finger. "Ivar sent the finger to my father with a ransom note, but I blame Steven. 'Twas the first, and surely the least, of the injuries inflicted on me by the Earl of Gravely."

Eadyth was appalled.

"When I was back at King Athelstan's court, I knew

enough to steer clear of the brute. But one night I was careless. He and two of his friends trapped me in a remote corridor of the castle, and . . . and . . . they beat me viciously.''

Eadyth's heart went out to Eirik and all he must have suffered as a young boy. She wished she could do something to ease his pain, to wipe away all the bad memories. Forgetting her revulsion over a man's touch this once, Eadyth lay a sympathetic hand on Eirik's arm, willing him silently to raise his bowed head.

''Oh, Eirik, how sad for you,'' she said, reaching forward to place a comforting hand over his.

He shrugged her hand away. ''Your pity unmans me.''

''Pity! Eirik, you were only ten years old. Did King Athelstan punish Steven?''

''Nay, but I handled the matter myself several years later when my body's growth had caught up to Steven's. I beat Steven almost to death and would have suffered no qualms in snuffing the very breath from his body, but the king's retainers pulled me away. I was the one punished in the end with a wergild—and a hefty fine, it was—not to mention banishment from court for one year. 'Twas well worth the satisfaction it gave me.''

''I think I would have done the same.''

Eirik raised an inquiring brow. ''What a bloodthirsty wench you are. Let me tell you something else about the man. He and a group of his men raided a Viking homestead a few years later, and not only did they rape and kill the first wife of Selik, my father's best friend, but they carried the skull of his baby son on a pike for weeks to lure Selik out of hiding.''

''Oh, Eirik. So that is why you hate Steven so?''

''That, and much more.''

''I knew Steven was immoral after he betrayed me so callously, but I never suspected the extent of his wickedness. How could there be more?''

''Because I did not bend to his will, because I finally dared to fight him, Steven delighted in tormenting me through the years. Oh, never so openly again. He is a master at hiding his dirty tricks. My favorite destrier was found dead. My mistress was raped by masked attackers. Lying rumors were spread about my alleged cowardice and treasonous activities." He shrugged. "But I was not the only victim. Many men and boys suffered through the years to satisfy Steven's insatiable appetite for pain. And women, as well, of course. Like my wife."

"Your wife?" Eadyth barely squeaked out. "Elizabeth?"

"Yea." Eirik gazed at Eadyth accusingly. "Like you, she succumbed to Steven's *charms*."

Eadyth felt her face color at Eirik's reminder of her indiscretion. "Was she married to you at the time?"

"Yea, but that did not bother her overmuch. 'Twas more than ten years ago. We had been wed only a year, and we were very young." He shrugged. "Apparently I did not meet her . . . needs."

Eadyth stared at Eirik, dumbfounded. Even with his distorted features, she found him devastatingly attractive. Oh, 'twas true, Steven was godly handsome. Nay, she corrected herself, more like *devilishly* handsome.

"Do not dare to link me with your wife. Womanhood is our only bond. Oh, mayhap I was as blind as she in failing to see Steven's rotten core, but I have never betrayed you. And furthermore, I would never describe you as inferior to Steven in physical appearance. You win that contest without question."

"You think me attractive?"

Eirik's eyes flickered with interest, and his lips tilted in a lopsided smile. He looked ludicrous to Eadyth. And wonderful. She felt her heart tug oddly and expand, causing a rush of blood to all the extremities of her body, filling her with a wonderful warmth. "God's Bones! You turn a woman breathless and well you know it, you loathsome lout. But that will get you nowhere with me. I am immune to your blatant charms, you fool."

That caused his face to contort even more as he made a disastrous attempt to smile wider. For some reason, Eadyth felt absolutely no inclination to laugh. Instead, tears clouded her eyes.

"Do not cry for me, silly bird," Eirik said softly. "Weep for Elizabeth. Steven planted his seed in her, as well, but she chose not to carry it to fruition. Unfortunately, she waited too long to seek the midwife's cure, and she died along with Steven's unborn son."

Eadyth stared at Eirik in horror. No wonder he hated Steven so much. And mistrusted all women. Without thinking, she muttered, "Good Lord, the man may have bastards from one end of the country to the other. Why would he persist in seeking my son?"

"I think I know the answer. 'Tis rumored that he suffered from a massive bout of St. Anthony's Fire seven years past which has rendered him incapable of fathering any more children."

"Serves him right. 'Tis unfortunate the devil's disease did not burn off his very manhood."

"My thoughts exactly."

They sat in easy silence for several long moments, both lost in their own thoughts.

" 'Twas a foul thing you did to me, Eirik," Eadyth finally said.

"Yea, 'twas. I do not offer this explanation to justify myself. I just wanted you to understand why I went berserk when I saw the letter from Steven. I thought . . . well, I thought it was happening all over again. Like Elizabeth."

Eadyth knew that the perfect time had come to confess her masquerade, to lay all secrets out in the open between them. "Eirik, I have many faults, but dishonesty is not one of them. When I hesitated at your question about deceiving you, 'twas not because of adultery. Actually, 'tis just a tiny little secret I have. Of no real import."

Eirik laughed. "If 'tis naught to do with adultery, or with Steven, I do not want to know. Leastways, not now. Let us save that confession for later, my lady, especially since you say it is of no real import. Have you not heard that a man savors a bit of mystery in a woman?''

"But—"

"Besides, I find myself in need of a long draught of your good mead—the best in all Northumbria, did you not proclaim it on our first meeting?'' Eirik teased. "Go now and play with your bloody bees.''

She started to protest.

"Just one last thing, Eadyth. Do you accept my apology? Can we put this . . . incident . . . behind us?''

Eadyth nodded as they both stood. "But, Eirik, we must come up with a plan to safeguard Ravenshire. Do you not think it alarming that Steven, or one of his fiendish retainers, was able to enter the keep so easily and place that lying letter under my mattress? Is it possible one of your own people works against you?''

Eirik nodded gravely. "I go to meet with Wilfrid now. Ravenshire will be made secure against Steven, of that I assure you.''

"What can I do to help with—''

" 'Tis no longer your responsibility, wife. A man protects those under his shield.''

Eadyth did not care for the condescending tone of his words; they sounded too much like an order. "When I proposed marriage to you, I never asked for a knight in shining armor. All I wanted was to share your shield.''

Eirik patted her hand as if she were a child. "You are not to worry, wife. I will handle everything.''

Eadyth gritted her teeth. Later, she would have to explain to her husband that she did not intend to be a docile wife. But she let him think she was acceding to his superiority. For now.

The next day, Eirik discovered that he could not go to Jorvik, and Asa, as he had wished. He had to implement safeguards against Steven, as Eadyth had suggested. The castle wall needed completion. Letters were sent off to lowly knights in other keeps asking if they would like to serve the

Lord of Ravenshire. More and more of his grandfather's people—cotters, craftsmen, servants—were returning daily as news spread of Ravenshire's new life.

With dismay, Eirik realized that, without ever having made a real decision to stay at Ravenshire, he was digging himself deeper and deeper into a commitment to the land and the people.

And he was not sure it was what he wanted.

Besides taking extra measures to safeguard the keep, Eirik also tried hard to make amends to Eadyth for his despicable behavior. Over the next three days, while he slept in the hall in consideration of Eadyth's monthly flux, he allowed her to impose her silly rules: forcing the servants to bathe once a sennight; delousing all the mattresses, pallets and bed linens; decreeing that his men could no longer throw their bones and other refuse in the rushes of the hall after eating.

God's Blood! She even wanted to make a rule against belching and breaking wind in public, stating that his men had the manners of swine. "You have been raised in the king's court. You have a responsibility to teach those beneath you the polite ways of society," she had chided him.

That was where he had put a stop to her domineering ways. "Have you lost your senses? There are some things beyond my control," he balked. "My men would laugh me out of Britain. I refuse to discuss such piddling subjects with them. Nay, do not lift your stubborn nose to the roof. My word is final."

She had backed down on that demand, but then made many others. Plow new fields. Buy sheep. Clean garderobes. Dig wells. Repair weaving sheds. Erect new cottages. On and on she went in her shrewish, grating voice until she came to him with a new request.

"Wouldst you do me a tiny favor?"

"Bloody Hell! I think I hear those words in my sleep now."

"Could you please climb up on a ladder and dust some of the cobwebs in the upper beams of the great hall?"

"The servants can do that. Call Lambert."

"He has refused. They all have. 'Twould seem they are afraid of the height."

Eirik's eyes narrowed with suspicion. "Just where is this ladder?"

Eadyth pretended nonchalance, waving a hand airily. "Over there."

Eirik looked toward the end of the hall where she had placed a specially made ladder, one that extended up two stories to the highest beams in the ceiling. No wonder none of his servants wanted to climb the rickety thing.

"Holy hell, Eadyth!" he exclaimed, squinting upward. "How could you even see that far to tell whether there are cobwebs or gold dust?"

She sniffed haughtily. "Does that mean you will not do me the favor?"

"It means you are out of your mind. Hell's flames, this keep is so clean now it squeaks. Furthermore, you have bled my guilt dry these past three days. I consider our account paid in full. If you want favors from me, you had best start giving a few of your own. But, for now, go find some other lackwit to break his neck for you because I will not."

He stormed off to the practice fields to work out his frustrations in military exercises with his men, thinking once again that it was time to go to Jorvik and spend some time with his mistress. He needed the comfort of Asa's body and the peace of her undemanding silence.

Unfortunately, Eadyth soon intruded even into this all-male domain.

"M'lord, come quick," Bertha called out from the edge of the field.

"What is it? Are we being attacked?" Eirik shouted, rushing to her side. "Why did the sentries not sound the alarm?"

"Nay, 'tis yer wife, Lady Eadyth."

Eirik groaned.

"She be up a tree tryin' ter ketch bees and Godric sez she be stuck."

"Up a tree?"

Girta pushed her way through the crowd that was gathering. "I told Bertha not to bother you, m'lord. 'Tis naught to concern you. My lady has done this many a time in the past. She knows what she is about, I tell you."

"Is she stuck or not?"

"Yea," said Bertha.

"Nay," said Girta.

Girta explained with exaggerated patience, "Some bees left their hives and formed a new swarm in a nearby tree. My lady merely climbed the tree above the swarm. She is shaking the limb, and her beekeeper assistants will trap the swarm in a beecatcher box below her on the ground." Girta folded her arms across her chest and clamped her mouth shut, shooting Bertha an I-told-you-so look.

Eirik heard the people around him snickering. Actually, he had noticed a great deal of nudging, rolling eyes and odd whispers from his men the last few days, especially when he was in Eadyth's presence. No doubt, they considered him weak for allowing his new wife to order him about. Well, he had more than enough of her mannish ways. He would put her in her proper place this time.

Eirik pushed his way angrily through the crowd, stomping toward the orchard just beyond the outer bailey, then turned abruptly to the muttering mob which was following closely on his heels. "God's Bones! Have you naught else to do but mind my business? Go back to work. All of you."

When he reached the orchard, Eirik stopped abruptly in stunned disbelief.

Eadyth, wearing her beekeeping veil, was straddling a limb high above the ground, shaking it vigorously. The cluster of bees clung tenaciously to the end of the limb while two of her veil-clad assistants stood on the ground, holding a large screened box.

"Eadyth, come down from that damn tree at once."

Eadyth looked down, seeing him for the first time. "Eirik, I did not see you arrive. But do step back. You are only just

166

recovering from your last encounter with my bees. We do not want a repeat performance.''

"How nice of you to be concerned," he muttered, but moved away a short distance before informing her, "Eadyth, your behavior is unseemly beyond belief. I insist that you come down."

"Do not be ridiculous. I just need to shake the bees loose."

Her defiance angered Eirik. "Then I will bring you down." He stepped toward the base of the tree, preparing to climb up and rescue his wife, and give her a tongue-lashing she would not soon forget when they got back to the keep.

In the midst of trying to shake the limb and answer him and move a little farther out onto the branch, Eadyth lost her balance and began to fall. Reflexively, Eirik jumped onto the divided tree trunk and began to climb in hopes of rescuing the foolish woman. Eadyth managed to regain her balance, but in the process the hem of her robe and full-length veil got caught on a branch and pulled upward over one leg. At the same time, her head rail fell off, and a cascade of curly blonde hair escaped its confinement.

Curly!

Blonde!

His mouth dropped open in amazement as he gaped at his wife's exceedingly long leg exposed from trim, bare ankle, to slender calf to dimpled knee, all the way up to the top of her marvelously shaped thigh. And one fact became clear in that moment before Eadyth adjusted her clothing.

His wife was not old, or uncomely.

Bloody Hell! In one explosive instant, all the pieces of the puzzle came together in Eirik's mind.

He noted the smoothness of his wife's leg, unpuckered with age. Gentle curves and lean, youthful muscles molded her calves and thighs into a beautiful sculpture of visual delight. No bones protruded as he would have expected in an aging crone. Aging crone? Hah! The deceitful witch was younger than he, certainly no more than twenty-five.

Quickly, Eirik backed down from the tree and stepped

away a short distance, unwilling just then to let Eadyth realize that her masquerade was over. Thoughtfully, he rubbed his upper lip, forgetting that he had shaved his mustache the day before to alleviate the itching bee stings. His disoriented mind tried to assimilate the implications of his discovery.

"Eirik, are you still there?" she asked in a nervous voice.

"Yea, but I stepped away some distance to avoid your bloody bees," he lied.

He heard a rustling noise and knew she was arranging her garments. To continue her disguise. *Damn her!*

He smacked himself on the side of the head, suddenly understanding so many things: how she could have a child so young, why Steven would have been attracted to her in the first place. He squinted up at Eadyth, who had finally loosened the bees and was shouting instructions to her assistants on the ground. The Silver Jewel of Northumbria! The title referred to her hair, of course—not an aging gray under all that grease, as he had assumed, but that rare shade of silver blonde.

Eirik was not amused.

In fact, when he recalled his brother Tykir's words to him at the wedding banquet about a secret he and Eadyth shared, he realized that his brother had known of Eadyth's deceit. Yea, *deceit*. And Tykir had laughingly said he might have a skald put this secret into a saga. Eirik's temper rose another notch. If his brother dared, he might just wring his frivolous neck and save King Edmund the trouble.

And worse, Eirik suspected that the snickers and soft whispers he had overheard the last few days amongst his men meant they knew about Eadyth, as well. No doubt, they all laughed behind his back at Eadyth's grand jest, and his dim vision. He gritted his teeth angrily.

Eadyth dropped lithely to the ground and closed the lid on the damned bee box. Eirik started forward, but then he stopped himself. Nay, he needed more time to understand Eadyth's motives. And to think of the best possible punishment for this deceitful witch of a wife.

One thing was certain. She would regret the day she ever entered Ravenshire. But not before he peeled away the layers of her disguise and discovered exactly what he had in this mysterious wife of his. And not before he brought her to heel.

Eirik smiled with grim anticipation.

Chapter Ten

"Bloody Hell! Would you look at the way she walks," Eirik commented to Wilfrid as they watched Eadyth deliberately stoop her shoulders and limp a bit as she made her way through the hall toward the dais that evening.

Eirik had to restrain himself from leaping over the table and strangling her bony neck. No, not bony, more like gracefully slender, he reminded himself with self-derision.

"Damn her deceit! By the time I am done with her, she will hobble all right and with good cause."

Eirik had already discussed his discovery of Eadyth's charade with Wilfrid. While his good friend had suspected Eadyth was not as old or uncomely as they had originally thought, Wilfrid told him he had not been certain and, therefore, had hesitated to mention his seemingly farfetched impressions.

"My vision must be growing worse for the wily wench to have fooled me so," Eirik complained to his good friend. "Even though I was never sharp-sighted as a child, I never saw it as a real problem. Now I am not so sure."

"Nay, do not think such. Your lady wife fooled us all with her masquerade."

"I must admit my discovery of her charade today rattled me badly. What kind of future would I have as a blind soldier? Without eyes, a knight is but a shell, less than a man."

"Put it from your mind, Eirik. I truly believe you wanted to believe her old and, therefore, never recognized the signs of youth. Remember that first night when she blew into the hall like a winter storm and practically kicked the dog. Those were not the actions of a young, beautiful woman."

Eirik scrutinized Eadyth closely as she moved nearer, his lips curling with disgust as he saw how obvious her disguise was. He wondered just how big a hole she would dig for herself before confessing the truth.

"Do you still think she conspires with Steven?"

"I think not," Eirik answered, stroking his upper lip distractedly, missing his mustache sorely. That was her fault, too, he decided unreasonably. He wouldn't have had to shave it off if not for her bees. "I suspect she harbors a loathing for the lustful attentions of men and took advantage of the circumstances to keep me at bay."

"With all due respect, my lord, I have yet to meet the maid who could keep you at bay, or even wanted to."

Eirik shrugged. "Some women are born that way and ne'er change—always hating a man's touch." *And just my luck to wed one of the man haters!*

Wilfrid seemed to give the idea considerable thought, then nodded. "Will you confront Lady Eadyth about her deception now?"

"Nay."

"What will you do?"

"I will give her enough rope to hang herself."

Wilfrid laughed, no doubt anticipating an evening of entertainment at Eadyth's expense. Eirik did not intend to disappoint him. He, too, looked forward to making his lady wife squirm, but first he must bank his raging anger and force a bland expression to his tense face.

" 'Twill be interesting to see how far she will go in her foolery," Eirik continued, "and despite my doubts, I cannot be certain she has no devious intent. So, yea, I think 'tis best to watch her closely for a time. But you can be sure I will make her pay—both now, in my own special way, and later when I confront her with her deceit.''

Wilfrid just grinned.

Now that Eadyth had solved the smoke problem in the great hall with her new chimneys, Eirik could see the care she took with her disguise, pulling her head-rail forward slightly to cover her forehead and cheeks, frowning so hard her face muscles must ache, and cackling until her voice grew hoarse. She had even ashed her face a bit.

Lord, I must be a lackwit to have been so duped.

Throughout the meal, Eirik continued to study her with feral intensity as he downed cup after cup of her mead. It probably *was* the best in all Northumbria, as she had boasted. Mayhap he would drown her in a tun of her own brew.

Wanting to lull Eadyth into trapping herself, he reminded himself to squint occasionally and peer closely at objects on the table. *Let her think I am blind to her disguise. The witch!*

He played a mental game with himself, devising new, exotic methods he would use to torture her. Strangulation was too clean and quick, he decided. And he wanted to delay her punishment until he was sure of her motives. But what could he do now to prick her haughty countenance without betraying his knowledge of her game?

Aaah! ''Is that a bristly hair I see sprouting from your wart?'' he asked suddenly, looking at the enticing mole near her lips. ''I could pluck it out for you, if you wish. My grandmother used to get them on occasion after she had reached a certain . . . age.'' He watched with smug delight as Eadyth's hand shot to her mole, searching, even though she must know she had no such thing.

'' 'Tis a mole, not a wart,'' she protested indignantly and shot him a look of icy disdain.

Hell! How could I have thought her eyes rheumy with age? They are sinfully beautiful. ''Oh. Mayhap I was mistaken.''

Reaching out a hand, he touched a fingertip to the mole,

then trailed it gently over her finely sculpted upper lip with its deep center divot. An immediate jolt of awareness struck a part of his body he would as soon ignore right now. All the boiling blood in his body, which should have been directed at her in anger, rushed to that spot far removed from his brain, and he felt himself harden involuntarily.

When he pulled his hand back, a light coating of ashes covered the fingertip. *So this is why her complexion appeared gray. Does she consider me a half-wit? No doubt, she does,* he decided ruefully.

He rubbed his index finger and thumb together, then dusted the ashes off with exaggerated fastidiousness. Slanting her an assessing look, he commented, "You must have stood too close to the cook fires. You should be more careful."

Eadyth almost swallowed her tongue at his words.

"Are you angry with me?"

"Do I have cause to be angry with you, Eadyth?"

"Na..nay," she stammered. " 'Tis just that we seemed to be getting along so well lately, and now you seem . . . well, different."

"Yea, we have been living together congenially these past few days, now that you mention it, especially since I have been such a good, meek husband, following all your orders, doing all your assigned chores."

"You could have refused. I never insisted on your help."

"Nay, but you have milked my guilty conscience nigh dry. Admit the truth of my words." *If you ever ask me to clean another garderobe in all your life, dear lady, I may just turn you upside down and use your hair to mop up the filth. Better yet, I may bury you in the slops. That should bring your prideful nose down a notch or two.*

"Are you upset about my climbing the tree?"

Tree? Tree? She has been deceiving me for weeks and she speaks of trees! "Yea, I do object to my wife climbing trees. Do not do it again."

He could see his headstrong spouse start to protest, but then decide to hold her tongue for now, no doubt sensing his present bad humor. She probably had some other miserable favor she wished to ask of him. Hah! No more!

She sipped at a cup of mead, seeming to seek reinforcement for her faltering nerve. But no, he must be mistaken. His wife had the mettle of a seasoned warrior. When she had drunk every drop in three quick gulps, she looked up.

"Eirik, I have a confession to make. There is something I have been wanting to tell you for a long time."

Aaah, so now she chooses to make her disclosure. Well, my deceitful little witch, mayhap I do not choose to hear it just yet. "How long?"

"What?"

"How long have you been wanting to tell me ... this thing?" He eyed her lazily as he spoke, feeling much like a fat cat playing with a little mouse.

Suddenly, he realized with a grin of delicious anticipation that he might enjoy peeling away all the layers of his lady's deception to discover what "jewel" he had in this wife of his. Perhaps he would be pleasantly surprised.

"For several sennights. Actually, since our betrothal," she admitted, pale-faced and nervous.

Good. "Does it have aught to do with the letter you sent to your business agent in Jorvik yestermorn, even though I told you I would handle your affairs?"

He could see alarm shoot through her as she wondered how he knew of her dealings. Eadyth had exercised great care in sending her missive by way of a passing traveler, but he had been even more cautious of every stranger approaching or leaving Ravenshire since Steven had planted the letter within his keep. Especially because there had been more evidence of the demon earl's presence in the vicinity of late—a poisoned well, a burned-out cotter's hut, a village maiden raped by unknown marauding villains.

"Nay, 'tis not the letter to my agent I wish to discuss. Besides, I intended to tell you about *that*."

Eventually, mayhap. "Oh, then it must be the sheep you ordered without seeking my permission."

"I intend to pay for them myself," she protested, waving her hand dismissively, obviously chagrined that he refused to let her make her confession in her own manner. "I kept asking Wilfrid about the sheep, and when you were delayed for so long in the North, and summer was almost here, I decided . . ."

Her voice faltered when she looked up, no doubt noticing the scowl lines in his forehead and those deepening at the edges of his mouth.

"Then it must be your ban on allowing my dogs in the great hall."

Eadyth groaned with frustration. "I thought you would approve. I did not want to trouble you."

Trouble! You have been nothing but trouble from first we met, you shrew. "Actually, I know what distresses you then, my wife. 'Tis the words you have been teaching Abdul. Did you not realize that he would soon repeat your lessons to me?"

A pink blush hazed her throat and crept attractively up her face—the skin of which, he now realized, must be as deliciously white as new cream, not ashy gray.

She raised her chin brazenly, refusing to yield to his subtly cloaked accusations. "What words?"

"Loathsome lout! Bloody beast! Odious oaf! To name a few."

Fear flashed briefly across her rigid face, but she refused to back down. "How do you know 'twas me?"

"Because the damn bird has a talent for mimicking voices, as you well know. Because when the feathered half-wit called me a loathsome lout, his voice had a decided cackle to it. And there is only one person in this castle who cackles."

He had to admire her unwavering, unapologetic demeanor. In fact, the edges of her sinfully seductive lips twitched saucily with a smile. She would pay for that later. Eirik tilted his head questioningly as he realized that he had never heard his wife laugh aloud or even seen her smile spontaneously at any jest. She was too stiff-necked by far. *Hah! I will bend you to my will and relish the effort, my sly wife.*

"I do not know why you feel you cannot discuss these decisions with me aforehand, Eadyth. I am not an ogre." Eirik forced himself to speak with sweetness, and Eadyth eyed him suspiciously. "Oh, 'tis true, I mislike your 'managing' my life and household to your standards, but the only thing I demanded of you afore our wedding was honesty. As long as you do not play me false, *in any way*, I think we can abide together reasonably well." *Honesty! Hah!*

The blood drained from her face. Blessed Lord, if he were not so damned angry he would enjoy this game of cat and mouse. In fact, despite his anger, he *did* find himself vastly amused.

"So, this confession of yours—that is what you called it, is it not? Could it be the fact that you have finally decided you want to consummate our marriage, and you, shy bird that you are, just cannot find the words to tell me? Well, do not be embarrassed. I asked Bertha, and she told me your flux has ended."

Eadyth's expressive eyes widened with horror.

And his grin grew wider.

"I know it must be a worry to you . . . the lack of a consummation, that is. Especially since Saxon law specifically says a marriage is not truly valid 'til the *morgen gifu* is given the morning after the . . . well, for lack of better words . . . the satisfactory performance of the wife in the marriage bed." She need not know that the law was rarely enforced, Eirik decided.

Eadyth did choke then, and he solicitously handed her another cup of mead. When her bout of coughing ended, she sputtered out, "But Tykir gave me your 'morning gift' on your behalf, which I cherish, incidentally. The beekeeping book is the nicest gift I have ever received. I have not had a chance to thank you properly, but I assumed . . ."

Eirik peered at her in a squinty, questioning fashion. "Do not move about so much, Eadyth, I have trouble seeing you clearly." He clenched his fists tightly to control his temper.

Two could play this game of charades.

At first, she looked pleased with herself, no doubt congratulating herself for successfully making a fool of him. Then she returned to her earlier words. "I thought the gift Tykir gave me on your behalf would be sufficient to validate our marriage."

" 'Twas what I intended, of course, but the courts and the church could end our marriage, even now, without the consummation. There are those who know I was not here on my wedding night, and that I sleep alone. If Steven ever contested the marriage afore the Witan, we would have to swear that the deed was done."

He stared at her boldly, enjoying her discomfort immensely. "Is it a risk you wish to take?"

Eadyth hesitated only a moment before shaking her head.

"Good. Then you will not mind that I ordered the servants to move your belongings into my bedchamber."

"Already?" Although her face betrayed no panic—Lord, his wife was a consummate actress!—her slender fingers flexed nervously in her lap.

"Yea. Can you think of any reason for delay?"

Eadyth's mind seemed to go blank. His question had struck her dumb.

"Well, mayhap you are right," she conceded grudgingly. "After all, 'tis only one night. And, no doubt, 'tis best to get the bedding over and be done with the vile business so—"

"Vile business?" he asked incredulously. "That is the first time I have heard any woman refer to coupling with me as 'vile business.' You insult me, my lady."

"Oh, I am sure lustful play is not distasteful for some females, but I—"

"Eadyth, did you not enjoy making love with Steven?"

"Enjoy? What was there to enjoy—betwixt the blood and the pain?"

"But after you lost your maidenhead, did Steven not give you pleasure the other times?"

"Other times? Are you daft? Why would I participate in

such an odious act more than once?''

Eirik smiled then, and shook his head in wonderment. ''I thought—''

''You thought I had developed round heels and was spreading my thighs like a dockside trollop?'' she said with disgust. ''Oh, you are just like all men, especially the lecherous ones who approached me as fair game with their indecent proposals after John's birth.'' She glared at him hostilely, but he continued to grin like an idiot. ''Well, leastways, I will only have to do it this one more time, and be done with it.''

Eirik shook his head with amazement. Supremely informed in some areas, Eadyth was totally naive in others. He could not wait to hear what she said next. Truly, he was enjoying this new wife of his more and more.

''Wha . . . what?'' Eadyth asked suspiciously.

Eirik brushed his index finger back and forth over his upper lip, watching her closely, trying to imagine just how young and comely she really was under those voluminous garments and the ridiculous scowling wrinkles.

''I find I have grown fond of children now that John and Larise and Godric are about so much,'' he said softly. ''I have been thinking that mayhap I would like to have another child, perchance a son.''

In truth, it was the first time the thought had entered his head. Once the newness of the idea wore off, however, he found he was not so averse to having another babe. After Elizabeth's death and his determination never to remarry, he had grown used to the idea that he would never father legitimate children. And he had missed Larise and Emma sorely. Now that Larise was back at Ravenshire, he determined to bring Emma back, as well.

''A babe?'' Eadyth inhaled sharply in surprise. Then, she, too, seemed to consider the idea's merit. ''After Steven's betrayal, I had grown accustomed to the idea of bearing no more children. It is a tempting prospect, but . . .'' Cautiously, she asked, ''How many times do you think it would take? I quickened after only one time afore.''

Eirik smothered a chuckle at her apparent distaste for the bedding, but her obvious yearning for another child. " 'Tis hard to say," he replied, struggling to remain straight-faced. "The seed may not take so quickly at your advanced age." He barely stifled a laugh before continuing, "For some, once is enough. For others, it takes fifty or sixty tries, or more."

"Fifty?" she squeaked out, clearly horrified at such a repulsive prospect.

Eirik slanted a look of irritation her way when her body shuddered involuntarily with revulsion.

"Well, I am sure you are just as repulsed at the prospect of bedding an aged woman as I am by the prospect of bedding yo . . . any man."

"If the bedchamber is dark enough, I think I will be able to perform," Eirik commented dryly. "I can pretend the wrinkles on your face are smile lines. And I could fantasize that the legs wrapped 'round my waist are firm and well-curved, not bony and knob-kneed."

Eadyth gasped at his insulting, intimate words, but he just went on as if he did not sense her embarrassment. "Mayhap you could even pretend an enthusiasm for the bedding if my manhood needs any prodding to action. Do you think you could moan passionately on the odd occasion?"

Eadyth's mouth dropped open in amazement at his vulgarity. "Oh, you truly are a loathsome lout."

"Now, now, Eadyth. No need for shyness betwixt husband and wife. If you do not know how to make passionate love sounds, I can teach you." Then, in a falsely feminine voice, he moaned, "Oh, oh, yes, ah, that feels so-o-o good."

Eadyth stood indignantly, casting a look of horror at Wilfrid who chortled with laughter. Eirik had forgotten his seneschal was still there, hearing all his provoking words. He winked conspiratorially at his friend.

"How dare you speak thus to me?"

"Sit down, Eadyth," Eirik said, elbowing Wilfrid to behave himself. "I was merely making a jest."

"I am not laughing."

"Mayhap you should. It might loosen your stiff countenance. Most times you look like you have a pike up your arse."

Wilfrid chortled gleefully, but flame-hot anger turned Eadyth's face blood red, even through the ashes. She looked as if she would love to throttle him with her bare hands.

"You filthy-mouthed, wicked man!"

Eirik shrugged. "And you are a carping crone, my lady wife. Mayhap we make a good pair."

"Bloody beast!"

"Dour dowd!"

"Lecherous lackwit!"

"Shrill shrew!"

"Odious oaf!"

"Wench!"

"Wretch!"

Eirik smiled widely, enjoying their exchange and her anger to the fullest. He grabbed her arm, pulling her forcibly back to her seat.

Visibly fighting to control her roiling temper, Eadyth finally managed to speak in a level tone of voice, "I do not deserve to be treated in such a crude manner."

"Do you not? Ah, well, then I must be sorry, I suppose." He knew he did not look one bit apologetic. Eadyth turned to Wilfrid, glaring her distaste at his continuing mirth. Wilfrid had the grace to duck his head sheepishly.

"Here, wife. Methinks you could use a cup of your own mead."

Eirik reached in front of her for the tankard on her other side, accidentally brushing her left breast with his hand in the process. His eyes shot wide in response to the sensuous feeling it invoked. Testing, he surreptitiously repeated the stroke when bringing the tankard back in front of him.

He felt Eadyth's nipple peak against the hairs of his forearm, and a red-hot spear of sensation shot to his fingertips, which yearned to examine the shape and texture of her firm breasts. He licked his suddenly dry lips and tried to ignore the hardening evidence of his arousal beneath the constraint of his tight braies.

And he noted that Eadyth's body reacted involuntarily to his touch, as well, in a way she obviously could not comprehend. She stared at him in confusion before crossing her arms across her nipples, which were clearly outlined against the thin fabric of her gunna.

Despite Eirik's deplorable behavior, despite her aversion to the act men and women performed together, did her body ache for his caress? Was her blood thickening? Did her limbs grow heavy with longing?

"You are a perverted man," Eadyth exclaimed, jarring him from his sensuous reverie. "Do not mistake me for some lackwit maid who will spread her thighs for a mere whiff of your man scent."

"Ma . . . man scent?" Eirik sputtered out.

"Do not think you can bewitch me with your unholy ways."

" 'Tis naught unholy about the coupling betwixt a husband and wife."

Eadyth snorted in a very unfeminine fashion. "Go thee off to Jorvik and ease yourself on your mistress, but leave me alone."

Eirik smiled, realizing his new wife was finding it hard to resist his considerable charms. She would completely lose her sanctimonious self-control if he had any say in the matter.

She stood, preparing to leave the dais.

"Did you suckle your baby?"

"What did you say?" Eadyth asked, plopping back into her chair. Then she noticed, with consternation, that he was staring at her breasts.

Eirik loved it.

She folded her arms again, glaring violet fire at him.

"Did you suckle John as a babe?"

"Why?" she choked out through deliciously soft lips.

Eirik shrugged, finding it harder and harder to hold on to his anger in the face of her seductive allure. "I just wondered if your nipples were still pink, or a dusky rose as some women's are wont to be after bearing a child. And—''

''Argh! You are truly loathsome.'' Eadyth jumped to her feet, scowling equally at Eirik and Wilfrid, who both chortled gleefully at finally breaking the shell of her haughty composure. This time she would not allow Eirik to pull her back into her seat. The tune of their laughter followed her as she stomped down the dais steps and through the great hall.

Eirik realized that Tykir had been right about the sway of her hips. His eyes followed her form until she started to climb the stairway to the second floor and her bedchamber.

Several hours later, when Eirik entered the dark bedchamber, he lit a candle, then chuckled aloud when he looked toward the bed. His recalcitrant wife was lying under the bed linens, no doubt sweltering in the May heat. She hugged the edge of the bed frame, pretending to be asleep.

Eirik grinned.

First, he pissed noisily in a chamber pot behind a screen at the side of the room, certain that this intimate aspect of married life would annoy his prickly wife. After washing his face and arms in a bowl of water, he removed all of his garments and slipped naked into the huge bed which dominated the center of the room.

He slid a bare leg over to Eadyth's side of the bed, nudging her with his big toe. She jerked and almost fell off the bed. He smiled to himself, then exclaimed, ''By the Faith, Eadyth! Why are you wearing so many garments?''

''I got a chill,'' her weak, muffled voice said from beneath the bed covers now pulled up to her nose.

''Show me yer legs,'' another muffled voice, a mite more squawkish than Eadyth's, called out from the corner where a dark fabric had been thrown over its cage. Then, ''Would ye like to see me arse?''

Eadyth groaned and muttered something about making parrot porridge.

Eirik shook his head in wonder at the comedic turn his

somber life had taken of late. Then he grimaced with self-disdain when he remembered that he was the target of the biggest jest of all—his lady wife's grand charade.

"Take the damn shroud off, Eadyth. You will make the bed too hot for me to sleep with your body heat."

She grumbled something under her breath, and Eirik could have sworn he heard Abdul snicker.

"At least, snuff the candle. 'Tis immodest," she demanded shrilly. When he did not immediately do her bidding, she turned in chagrin, no doubt intending to land him a good clout to the head. She inhaled sharply when she saw his nude body reclining indolently alongside her, with hands folded behind his head. Quickly, she turned her face away in embarrassment.

"Ah, well, I can understand a bride's shyness with a new husband," he said in a voice oozing with solicitude before rising to do her bidding. When the room was in total darkness, he returned to the bed, realizing that Eadyth had removed her gown in record time and was naked but already covered once again by the bed linens.

Oh, Eadyth, you are sadly mistaken if you think you can hide from me. You are going to pay for your deceit. In good time. In my own way.

She lay on her side with her back to him, stiff as a cold poker. Slowly, he slid his leg closer to hers, testing her reaction. At just the slightest caress of his furred leg against her smoother calf, she jolted. Eirik felt a jolt, as well, but his was of raw desire shooting up his leg and ricocheting to all the important sensual spots on his body—especially those centered in his aching staff.

Suddenly, he wished he had not snuffed the candle. He would like to better see this new wife of his. And that long, curly hair he had barely glimpsed this afternoon. How would it look spread out against the white bed linens?

Eirik reached blindly toward the vicinity of her pillow but felt no strands of silky hair. Feeling his way closer, he eventually found her head, but the wily witch had braided her hair and wound it into a tight coronet around her head. And even worse, it was covered with a thick coating of grease. He sniffed his fingers. *Lard. So, that is why her silvery-blonde hair appears to be gray with age. Eadyth has gone to much trouble to dupe me. Why?*

Suddenly, Eadyth shoved his hands away with a sound of disgust and sat up in the bed, making sure the linens were pulled up, hiding her breasts from his scrutiny. Not that he could see them in the dimness anyway.

"Listen, I do not believe in delaying the inevitable, no matter how distasteful. I have much to do on the morrow. 'Tis time to gather honey from some of my hives. Bertha and I intend to strain it all and put it in containers for market. Let us get this . . . this bedding over with so that I can get some sleep."

"Huh?"

"Just do . . . it."

Good Lord! The shrew thinks she can "manage" the coupling betwixt man and wife, as well.

He heard a rustling of cloth and moved closer to see what she was about. By the moonlight coming through the two arrow slits in the near wall, he could see, just barely, that his dutiful wife was lying on her back, arms frozen stiff at her sides, eyes squeezed shut and her legs spread wide like some sacrificial victim. And she was bare-arsed naked!

Despite the lack of sensuality in Eadyth's martyr-like pose, Eirik felt his heartbeat accelerate. His fingertips yearned to examine all the mysterious places that his wife had been hiding so long. His lips ached to shape her finely defined lips with his kisses. His tongue thirsted for the suckling of her mouth and for the taste of her supple skin, and, oh, Lord, even the nectar between her legs.

And his staff! His rock-hard staff wanted nothing more than to plunge deep into her virgin-like body and be caressed by the inner folds of her femininity.

Eirik inhaled deeply to slow the raging fire that threatened to consume him, then knelt between her legs. The only sounds in the room were his heavy breathing and the occasional flutter of Abdul's wings as he shifted in sleep. Eadyth appeared to have stopped breathing altogether.

Placing his hands on each of her widespread ankles, Eirik slowly brushed his fingertips up her calves, trying to learn the shape and texture of her body by touch alone in the near-darkness.

He had no intention of consummating their marriage tonight, not until he was absolutely certain of her motives in deceiving him. But he could still enjoy teasing her, though he was beginning to suspect that he might not emerge from the night's play unscathed.

When his roaming fingers had examined the curves of her shapely knees and began to move upward on the muscled contours of her thighs, Eadyth made a strangled sound of protest, then clamped a hand over her mouth.

His hands moved higher toward the apex of her thighs. He wished he had left the candle lit so he could see if any moisture glistened there. Not likely! Icicles would be more probable. Next time, he would be prepared. He would fill the chamber with dozens of her precious beeswax candles and be damned with her false modesty.

When his fingertips just barely skimmed the silken hairs, Eadyth whimpered, "Stop it."

"What?" he asked innocently.

"Touching me."

"Why?"

"I do not like being touched."

"Does it make you nervous?"

She made a soft sound of surprise at his question. "Yea . . . I mean, nay . . . oh, for the love of God, just get on with it and be done so I can go to sleep."

"I must touch you," he whispered huskily.

"Nay."

"Yea."

She slapped at his exploring fingers, but Eirik just laughed low in his chest, ignoring her protests as his hands moved like butterfly wings up her body. They traced the curve of her slim hips and the womanly indentation of her waist, over her abdomen, then under her breasts where he could feel the wild beating of her heart. For just a moment, he let his hands rest under the firm mounds. When he cupped the small breasts in his hands, testing their weight and shape, Eadyth stiffened even more, seeming to hold her breath. Still cradling her breasts in his palms from the underside, he flicked both tips with the callused pads of his thumbs, bringing her nipples instantly erect.

Although her breasts were not particularly big, the nipples were large and hard as pebbles. He liked that.

She moaned, fists clenched tightly in the bed linens at her side, and tried to buck him off. "Oh, you are vile. Take your perversities and leave me be."

Eirik wanted to know all of her. His fingertips became his eyes, exploring her flat stomach, her armpits, the high arch of her feet, her spidery eyelashes—yea, her eyes were still squeezed tightly shut—her knees, the small of her back. By the time he blew softly in her ear and traced the delicate whorls with the tip of his tongue, Eadyth was tossing her head back and forth, her body rigid with tension.

Eirik discovered a liking for the taste of his wife's skin, even the salt of her perspiration. He licked the smooth skin of her neck which smelled faintly of beeswax and her own woman scent—and fear.

Actually, Eirik had carried this bed sport much farther than he had intended for tonight. If he did not soon put a halt to the love play, he would be unable to stop.

But there was just one thing he wanted—nay, needed—to do. Leaning down, he took her left nipple between his lips and flicked it with his tongue, then suckled it wetly against the roof of his mouth. He held her nipple in his mouth only a moment. It was all he could stand.

But he was almost undone when she sighed and instinctively arched upward for more. Blood roared in his ears, and Eirik felt his control slipping fast at her involuntary response.

"Oh," she whispered.

"Oh?"

"It was ne'er like this with Steven."

Steven! Mention of his hated enemy drew Eirik jarringly back to his present dilemma. Could he risk making love to Eadyth and possibly planting his seed in her womb when there was even the remotest possibility that her charade these past few sennights connected somehow with Steven of Gravely? Nay, he decided, forcing himself to ignore the pulsing hardness between his thighs and the churning of his blood which ached for the satisfaction that only her body could provide. With determination, he rolled over to his side of the bed.

"Wha . . . what?" Eadyth asked.

Eirik yawned loudly and tried to appear unaffected as he lied, "I find I am not really up to all this bed sport tonight. Mayhap another night." Then he turned his back to her and pretended to fall asleep.

For once, he had stunned his shrewish wife speechless. She probably thought her age and uncomeliness repelled him. Hah! If he were any more attracted, the bed might burst aflame. Smiling, he considered, then discarded, the notion of relieving himself with his own hands to ease the ache of his powerful erection. He had given Eadyth enough shocks for one day.

Eadyth lay on her back, frozen in the same position for a good long while, stunned by Eirik's rebuff. Oh, it was humiliating beyond belief. Finally she had yielded to a man's lustful advances, and he had found her . . . deficient.

Eirik let out a loud snore. Her lips curled with disgust as she turned to view her husband's naked back. The brute! How could a person fall into such a sound sleep so quickly? She was sorely tempted to kick his bare bottom.

But Eadyth was not sure she wanted him awake. She felt her carefully guarded self-control unraveling, and she did not like the prospect one bit. Acutely conscious of her sensitized body, she needed to understand the odd pleasures Eirik's touch had ignited just moments ago. Slanting a look his way to make sure he could not see, Eadyth brushed her fingertips over her thighs, across her flat stomach and up over the still turgid nipples of her breasts. She felt nothing nigh approaching the delicious sensations Eirik's fingers had evoked.

Why did it feel so different, so achingly wonderful, when it had been Eirik's hateful fingers doing the caressing? What would it have been like if he had kept doing those wicked things with his lips and tongue on her nipple? Her breasts swelled and ached oddly at the image. And if he had kissed her lips, especially if he had kissed her with his tongue as he had done that one time in this very room, and if he had been touching her body with those feathery caresses at the same time . . . well, Eadyth did not know if she would have been able to hide her response.

The puzzle nagged at her for hours before she finally fell into a troubled sleep.

Eirik was already up and gone when Eadyth awakened the next morning. *Thank God!* She recalled that he and his retainers intended to travel to the far reaches of his estate to investigate reports of strangers on horseback trampling a new field of wheat. Eadyth shuddered, knowing that Steven was, no doubt, behind this latest trouble that plagued Ravenshire.

The demonic Earl of Gravely played with them—a macabre game designed to set their nerves on edge as they waited for his final action. What that would be, she could not guess, but she swore it would not involve her son John.

Eadyth also resolved not to let Eirik put her off again today. She *must* confess her ludicrous masquerade before it went any farther. Especially since he had put such emphasis on honesty in their talk yestereve. *Oh, Lord!*

Later that morning, she sat at the kitchen table helping Bertha and Britta shell a basket of early peas. She wanted to clear the large table for the dozens of honeycombs she had gathered that morning. She intended to prepare them for market in small pottery containers she had designed. Kettles of hot water and special straining devices lay at the ready.

"I heard how our Lord Raven teased you at the great table yestereve," Britta commented companionably. "Men are such vulgar beasties sumtimes."

Eadyth popped several sweet peas in her mouth and crunched as she raised an eyebrow in question.

"You know, about the color of your nipples and such."

Eadyth choked and the peas went down the wrong passage. She coughed and coughed until Bertha finally fetched her a cup of water.

"You know what Eirik said to me?" Eadyth finally asked the artlessly blunt maid, not sure if she was more incredulous or angry at her private talk being repeated about the keep. But then, that was ever the way with servants, she supposed.

"Yea, Wilfrid . . . I mean, Master Wilfrid . . . sumtimes tells me things."

I bet he does. The wretch!

"Do not be embarrassed, my lady. All men are like that on the odd occasion, 'specially when they are drinking or when they are 'specially . . . uh . . .'specially lustful." She blushed prettily at her last word.

Oh, Good Lord! How did I get involved in such a conversation?

" 'Tis the tits what will do it every time," Bertha offered sagely. "Men do love a good bosom, 'specially if it wobbles."

"Wobbles?" Eadyth and Britta both asked, turning to her in surprise.

Bertha threw back her shoulders, thrusting her massive breasts forward with pride. Then she put her beefy hands under the two udders, lifting them higher and jiggling them in a ridiculous fashion.

"See. Mine wobble. 'Tis why the men's tongues hang out when I pass by."

Eadyth's mouth dropped open in amazement at the thought of any man being interested in Bertha's overblown form, but, come to think on it, the bawdy cook did seem to have a continuous supply of bedmates. Britta's eyes widened with interest, as well, and then they both looked down at their own bosoms. While Britta's lush breasts might wobble if she walked with an exaggerated sway, Eadyth knew her smallish breasts would never develop the slightest wobble, even if she jumped up and down.

One side of Eadyth's mind told her that Bertha was just an ignorant old hag who knew nothing of the world or its men, but another side whispered slyly that perhaps that was why Eirik had not consummated their marriage yestereve. He found her woman parts lacking.

She looked over at Britta, who was still studying her own chest. Then their eyes made contact with sudden understanding, and they burst into giggles like young children.

Wobbling breasts! What next?

Chapter Eleven

For the rest of the day, Eadyth enlisted every servant inside the keep to help with her honey gathering. The spring blossom harvest always netted the most bountiful and best quality honey, but honey production was, at best, an arduous, sometimes messy process.

Basking in this work which she adored most of all a chatelaine's chores, Eadyth forced everyone who entered her kitchen to scrub their hands with strong soap and to wear clean overtunics. She even examined the honeycombs for cleanliness and removed all particles of dirt or insects with meticulous care.

She cut some of the honeycombs into sections and placed them in special pottery containers for those customers who preferred their honey still in the comb. But mostly Eadyth preferred to keep the waxy combs for her own use and sell only the nectar.

She insisted on performing some chores herself, those requiring expertise. With a critical eye, she first examined the color of the honey in the combs, and sorted them accordingly.

"What difference does it make? Honey is honey," Bertha complained, wanting all the workers gone as soon as possible from her cooking domain. Now that Eadyth had forced rules of cleanliness on the castle, Bertha took proprietary pride in her sparkling kitchen.

"It makes a great deal of difference, Bertha. See that bright yellow honey? 'Tis from the dandelion flower. The whitish yellow comes from clover. Fruit blossoms, like the cherry trees, produce a light, golden yellow. I like to label my pots so people who purchase my honey know what kind they are getting."

Bertha grumbled, "Seems to me sum people are too perticya-ler."

Eadyth just smiled as she sliced the caps off the honeycombs with a fire-heated, sharp knife. The process had to be carried out quickly and with a deft touch to avoid losing any of the precious honey or making a sticky mess in the work area.

She immediately handed the honeycombs to Britta, who placed them in loosely woven cloths hanging over huge earthenware crocks near the warmth of the cook fire so the sweet nectar would strain through, leaving only the wax combs behind. Later, Bertha would mash the drained honeycombs in a massive bowl. Then they, too, would be placed in another clean straining cloth over a second crock near the fire. This second extract would be of poorer quality, but suitable for kitchen use, never for selling in the market stalls of Jorvik.

Eadyth placed the comb fragments and the wax caps she had cut off previously in warm water to clean them thoroughly, then set them out to dry. They would be saved for autumn when she made her beeswax candles.

Finally, she cut the straining cloths into strips and gave them to John and Larise and Godric to suck on for a special treat, shooing them out to the courtyard. The children, always in the company of at least two of Eirik's guards, had been hovering all morning in the kitchen, ostensibly to help, but more often causing mischief.

"Can we play with Prince in the orchard?" John asked as Eadyth wiped his sticky fingers with a damp cloth.

"Nay, sweetling. Your father wants you all to stay inside the keep today." Eadyth had made a conscious effort to refer to Eirik as John's father since the wedding feast, and her little boy surprised her by accepting him so readily.

John gazed up at her through eyes as blue and captivating as Eirik's and whined, "But nobody wants us about. They all tell us to stop bothering them. We make too much noise. Father said he would show us how to spit off the ramparts when he returns, but it may be too dark by then."

Eadyth made a clucking sound of disgust at John's words about spitting, then advised, "Listen, dearling, why do you not ask 'Uncle' Wilfrid to teach you to play that board game? *Hnefatafl*, I think the Norsemen call it."

His doleful face brightened and he shouted to Larise and Godric, even though they were only a few steps away, informing them of the new plans. They ran, shrieking, from the kitchen.

Wilfrid would, no doubt, have much to say later about the favor she did him. But everyone in the kitchen breathed a sigh of relief at the blessed quiet.

"Gawd, I ne'er heard so much squawkin' 'n squealin' in all me life," Bertha commented with a smile.

"That Godric never said more than two words afore John and Larise arrived," Britta added with a rueful shake of her head. "Now the halfling babbles endlessly."

Eadyth remained silent, knowing that both women, despite their complaints, cherished the warmth the young children brought to the forlorn castle. Even with the threat of Steven hovering over her head, Eadyth, too, found herself relaxing under Eirik's protection and enjoying the seductive lure of family life.

By late afternoon, when they had finally cleaned up the kitchen, Eadyth looked with pride at the long line of pottery containers—twenty pots with the combs, and fifty of the strained honey, each with a special mark on the container to denote its variety.

"What is that God-awful smell?"

Eadyth looked up to see Eirik filling the doorway of the kitchen with his large frame. He tunneled his fingers through his overlong hair. His clothing was filthy. And she could swear she heard his stomach growl with hunger from across the room.

Her husband had been gone since early morning on his ride to the far northern reaches of his estate to investigate the new misdeeds. She anxiously waited to learn what he had found, but his scowling expression spoke of bone-weary exhaustion. She decided to wait until later to ask her questions.

In the meantime, she motioned several kitchen maids to begin preparing the tables in the great hall for the evening meal. Then she turned back to her loudly sniffing husband.

" 'Tis my honey," she said defensively, trying to still her fast-beating heart. It was the first time she had seen her husband since sharing his bed the night before, since he had touched her naked body so intimately. She pulled her head-rail forward, hoping to hide the blush which no doubt heated her face. "Do you not like honey?"

"I love honey, but too much of a sweet can gag a person. The whole keep reeks of it. Even the outer bailey. There are so many flies out there, I swear some have come from as far as Jorvik."

Eadyth stiffened at his mocking words. "At Hawks' Lair, I have a separate shed for processing my honey, away from the keep. In any case, the flies will go away in a day or so."

"Oh, I dare say they will be gone sooner than that," he remarked lazily, "especially since the flies have drawn every crow from all the shires in Northumbria. There are so many bird droppings in the courtyard, I could barely see the dirt." Then he looked pointedly at his white-speckled boots which were dirtying her newly scrubbed kitchen floor and smiled wickedly. "Mayhap you should get your broom brigade out there. The lackwit birds have not yet heard of your strict code of cleanliness.''

Eadyth bristled at his taunting criticism. Did he jest? Or did he truly mislike her pristine ways?

Meanwhile, Eirik moved closer to where Eadyth stood at the table, as Bertha and Britta began to move the pottery containers to the scullery. Peering over her shoulder, he placed a palm familiarly over her right buttock, and let it rest there.

Eadyth almost shot off the floor. ''Unhand me, you lecherous brute,'' she hissed.

''Oh, forgive me, wife,'' Eirik said, his blue eyes blinking innocently. ''I thought it was the table edge I was holding.''

She glared at him, disbelieving.

''I had not thought to mention it afore, but I have a problem seeing some things up close.'' He squinted at her, emphasizing the defect.

Eadyth slanted a suspicious look his way, not sure whether to believe he had grasped her backside accidentally. When she looked at Bertha, though, who was gathering the last of the pots at her side, the bawdy cook rolled her eyes and whispered in an undertone, ''What did I say 'bout lustful men? First wobbling tits, then the arse.''

Eadyth stifled a giggle. *A giggle! God's Bones! The man is turning me barmy.*

But Eadyth soon forgot about Eirik's violation of her person when she saw what he was doing to her honey. First, he inserted a long finger into the pot of her best clover honey and licked the finger clean. He was about to test another pot when she slapped his hand away.

''Are you daft, man? Those are for my customers in Jorvik. Who would want to purchase them after you have stuck your dirty fingers inside?''

Eirik just grinned and pretended not to hear her, sticking a finger in the next pot, drizzling honey carelessly across the clean table on the way to her mouth, where he offered the sweet nectar to her on his fingertip. ''Here, have a taste, my lady. 'Tis always best to sample your own wares. Besides, you need sweetening up.''

''I have tasted enough for today,'' she protested, backing away. But he persisted in following her, waving his honey-laden finger in front of her lips, drizzling some accidentally over her bosom. To her horror, Eirik looked as if he might lick it up, but, instead, he pressed his fingertip against her lips.

''Try it.''

''Nay. Oh, Good Lord, at least use a spoon. Have you no manners at all?''

''Apparently not.'' He was still grinning, and Eadyth's heart slammed against her chest at his enticing closeness. He smelled of horse and sweat and wood smoke and man. Instead of being repulsed, Eadyth was drawn inexplicably by his particular scent. The man discomfited her mightily, and she did not like it one bit. And now that he had shaved his mustache, he looked younger, less hard, too enticingly handsome.

She was backed against the far wall by then and did not want to create more of a scene, so she flicked the tip of her tongue against the end of his finger. It was a big mistake.

Be careful, she admonished herself silently as every hitherto unknown erotic spot in her body came to full attention. *One devilishly handsome man tricked you afore. This one could toss you aside just as Steven did.*

But Eadyth could not ignore the delicious sensation of her tongue rasping against the rough skin of his forefinger. It heightened and brought to the forefront her own softer femininity. It made her feel wicked. And wonderful. She wanted to taste his skin again.

She should not.

She did.

''Umm,'' she moaned. '' 'Tis the cherry blossom honey.'' *Now, go away, you fiendish wretch, afore I do something foolish. Like brush the hair off your forehead. Or run my hands over your muscled chest. Or, Sweet Mother of God,*

*give over to my baser self and reach up to taste the honey
on your lips.*

"Try more," he urged in a husky voice. The finger still
lingered in front of her mouth enticingly.

"Eirik, I do not—"

He rested his other hand on the wall above her head, leaning sinfully close. Brazenly, he stuck his finger in her mouth,
and she had no choice but to lick and suck on it, especially
when he pushed it in and out several times. For some reason
she could not explain, she thought suddenly of that novel
tongue kiss he had given her in his bedchamber on their wedding night. The one she had liked so shamelessly.

Soon she forgot about the honey altogether as Eirik's moving finger created an odd reaction in other parts of Eadyth's
body. Her breasts suddenly felt fuller. Her blood seemed to
thicken and lodge heavily in her arms and legs, and, oh dear,
in that secret place between her legs. She wanted to put her
arms about his neck and pull him even closer. Restraining
herself forcefully, she drew on that small part of her self that
had not turned totally wanton.

The only saving grace was that Eirik did not grin anymore.
Instead, his blue eyes darkened, and his lips parted, moving
closer. He was staring at her mouth like a starving man suddenly offered a feast.

Fighting the pull of his gaze, Eadyth tried to resist this
devious charmer of a man who could turn her senses inside
out with a mere finger. She must be turning into a lewd
woman. Oh, surely he would not kiss her here in the kitchen
in front of everyone. But Eadyth did not care. For some reason she could not understand, against all her better instincts,
she leaned closer, hungering for his lips, wanting something
she could not name, but knew would bring her immense satisfaction.

Bertha's lewd chuckle from the other side of the room
jarred them both back to awareness, but not before Eirik
pulled her closer and nipped at her ear through her head-rail,
whispering silkily, "And would you suckle the honey from

my tongue, as well, sweet wife, if I bring a pot to our bed-chamber tonight?''

Eadyth's heart skipped a beat in alarm, and a breathless thrill of pleasure rushed through her.

"Mayhap I will not be so tired this time," he said in a raw undertone of promise as he pushed her in front of him, away from the wall, giving her backside a crude pinch in the process. Before she could chastise him, he asked, "Have you practiced those love moans I taught you yestereve?"

Eadyth stopped mutinously, refusing to budge any farther. Turning indignantly, she put both palms to his chest, giving him a mighty shove to show her displeasure. He did not move a hairsbreadth.

Instead, linking his hand in hers, he pulled her out of the kitchen through the corridor to the keep, then looked back at her over his shoulder, "Best you close your teeth, Eadyth, especially with all these flies about. And you smelling like a honey pot."

She snapped her mouth shut in self-disgust, promising to get her rioting emotions under control. If only she could stop herself from rising to his continual baiting. The charming rogue was getting under her skin and would soon dominate her with his seductive ways. That she could not allow.

But then she forgot her annoyance when Eirik explained, "I must talk to you in private about Steven and our findings today."

"Steven! Oh, Holy Mother!" Eadyth chastised herself for momentarily forgetting the danger that had brought her to Ravenshire in the first place. How foolish she had been to relax her defenses! What had the evil Steven done now? By Eirik's somber demeanor, she knew it must be very bad.

When they were in the private chamber off the great hall, Eirik slumped into a chair and waved for her to sit, as well. For the first time, Eadyth noted Eirik's condition. He had removed his chain mail but still wore the padded undertunic over his heavy wool braies. Scratches and bruises and soot covered his face and arms. *Soot?* Eadyth pondered.

"There has been a fire, has there not?"

He nodded.

"The cotters' huts in the north end of your estate?"

He shook his head wearily and poured mead into two large goblets, handing one to her.

"Nay," she declined, feeling sick. The honey smell of the keep, in combination with Eirik's news, was turning her nauseous.

But he shoved it into her hands. "Drink."

His blue eyes studied her closely, but Eadyth was no longer concerned about whether he discovered her ruse. She felt a sour, sinking sensation low in her belly—guilt that she might have brought misery to Eirik's people. And that guilt far outweighed her silly masquerade.

Eirik's grim expression frightened her, and his insistence that she drink . . . well, there could be only one explanation. She took a long swallow, barely tasting the liquid as it passed the fast-forming lump in her throat, then quickly drank the remainder in her cup.

"Hawks' Lair?"

"Yea."

"How could that be?" she cried. "I left it well-protected."

Eirik shook his head. " 'Twas not the keep. The castle and its walls are still secure."

Eadyth frowned in puzzlement, waiting for her husband's explanation.

Suddenly Eirik pulled his chair closer to hers so they were sitting almost knee to knee. Gently, he took both her hands in his. Instead of comforting her, Eirik's concern filled her with dread. Then he surprised her by changing the subject. "Tell me, Eadyth, how many of those bees do you have in my orchard?"

"Wha—what?"

"The bees—they seem to have increased an ungodly amount already. Do you have any idea how many you have?"

She lifted her shoulders as if to guess. "Mayhap a hundred thousand."

"A hundred thousand bees!" Eirik's sweet consideration vanished under his consternation. "Have you lost your senses, woman? They will overrun the entire estate."

Eadyth smiled. "Nay, a hundred thousand is not that great an amount. In just one colony, with one queen, there can be more than fifty thousand workers and two thousand drones. And I have dozens of colonies thriving."

Eirik's eyes widened in amazement.

This was the first time Eirik had exhibited any interest in her business, and it pleased her greatly. She did not even feel the need, in the glow of her pride, to pull away her hands which he still grasped warmly in his. Not even when he distractedly caressed the betrothal scar at her wrist with the callused pad of his thumb, sending subtle tingles of sweet pleasure up her arm which started her heart to racing.

"After all, Eirik," she continued in a surprisingly level voice, trying to ignore her heightened senses, "the queen bee lays up to two thousand eggs every day from March 'til October."

He shook his head from side to side in disbelief. "What will we do with all those bees? Turn the keep into one giant hive?"

"You did not let me finish. 'Tis not an endlessly increasing supply. For example, the male drone bees die after they . . ." Eadyth's words trailed off when she realized where her words had taken her.

"After they . . . what?" he prodded.

"Mate," she said in a small voice.

Eirik hooted with laughter. "Ah, Eadyth, is that not the way of the world? Men fornicating themselves to death. And women, well, women just buzzing off to another . . . flower." He winked at her.

Eadyth tried not to smile, but she could not help herself, even sensing there was more bad news to come. Eirik released one of her hands and reached up to touch her lips with his fingertips. "You should smile more often. You are not so barley-faced when you do."

Barley-faced! Eadyth stiffened at his backhanded compliment, then narrowed her eyes suspiciously when she noticed the mischievous glint in his blue eyes.

"Mayhap you take life too lightly, you brute. Methinks you smile too much."

"Well, I give you credit, wife. A few hours ago, I did not think I would be able to smile again for a long, long while."

She slapped his hand away from her lips then and forcefully pulled her other hand from his grasp, demanding, "Spare me your mysterious words. What happened today?"

"Steven burned all your beehives at Hawks' Lair," he disclosed bluntly. "There is not a bee betwixt there and Ravenshire."

Eadyth gasped and tears sprang to her eyes. "Was anyone hurt?" she whispered.

"Nay, but it was a horrid mess—putting out the fires and cleaning up the debris. The fires spread over at least one hide of land."

"Why would Steven be so cruel? I have never hurt him. 'Tis obvious this latest act was aimed at me."

Eirik shook his head. "Nay, not just you. He means it as a warning to us all, but do not fear, my lady. I promise I will protect you and your son."

Eadyth was touched by his words, expressed with such heartfelt sincerity, and was about to tell him so when he continued, "And I will help you replace every one of the damn bees, even if I have to wear one of your bloody veils to do it."

Eadyth swiped at her eyes and tried to smile. "Now, that would be a sight to set the servants ashivering—the two of us walking through these gloomy halls in gossamer veils."

"Especially if we were wearing nothing beneath," he added, flashing her a devastatingly seductive grin of deviltry.

Too stunned to rebuke him, Eadyth lingered even after he had gone to his bedchamber to bathe. Did married couples do such perverted things? It was perverted, was it not?

* * *

Eirik lay soaking his weary muscles in the huge wooden tub long after the water had cooled. *Blessed Christ!* He wished he could just meet Steven face to face and end his evil misdeeds. Surely God would not condemn him for such. Surely the world would thank him for it.

And Eadyth? What of his lying wife? Should he allow her to confess her duplicity, as she so obviously chafed to do now? Or should he continue his own deceit a short while longer in hopes of discovering her true motives?

Eirik did not doubt that she was surprised and sorely grieved by Steven's burning her bees today. *Unless* . . .

In some ways, it was too convenient that Eadyth had given him a goodly number of her precious stock for dowry and that she had just happened to remove them from Hawks' Lair before the fire. The puzzle nagged at Eirik and he saw no ready answers. But he was determined to clear up the mystery. And soon.

While he lay in the tub, he sent Wilfrid to fetch Sigurd. His trusted friend from the Norse lands listened carefully to his instructions. Eirik instructed Sigurd to go to Hawks' Lair, the surrounding villages, even Jorvik, and learn everything he could about Eadyth and her associations with Steven of Gravely over the past years. If anyone could discover whether Eadyth was in collusion with Steven, it was his crafty retainer. He directed Sigurd to return as soon as possible.

Aside from the danger, Eirik had another reason for wanting an answer with all haste. Of a sudden, he ached to consummate this marriage with his wedded wife. He had not bedded a woman for many, many sennights, and his body craved satisfaction between a woman's thighs. But not just any woman, he realized with chagrin. He wanted to make love with the feisty Eadyth. Who would have ever believed it possible that The Raven, infamous for his woman-luck, lusted after his own true wife? Not the drab sparrow she pretended to be, but the sleek bird he suspected he would find under all her dowdy raiment.

Throughout the day Eirik kept remembering her nude body

in his bed the night before, wondering exactly how she would look without the ashes and drab garments, with the grease washed from her hair. Under his body in the throes of passion.

Like a blind man the night before, he had begun to learn the womanly shape of her. Beneath that cold facade she liked to portray, he suspected there lay banked the embers of a hot sensuality, just waiting for the right man to blow them to life.

Could he be that man? Did he want to be?

Hell, yes!

Eirik shook his head in self-derision, then lathered his hair and slid under the water to rinse. When he came up for air, Eadyth stood frozen in the middle of the room carrying a bundle of folded linens. She gawked at him in amazement, as if he were a whale blowing water through its breathing hole.

He used both hands to slick the wet hair back off his face. And stood.

Her jaw dropped like an iron weight.

Eirik barely stifled a grin. "Would you hand me one of those drying cloths?"

Eadyth was staring at a part of his body that liked to be stared at. Very much. He felt an immediate reaction, and his wife's eyes shot upward in embarrassment.

"What did you say?" she squeaked out.

"When?"

"Just now."

"Would you hand me one of those cloths in your hands?" he asked with amusement.

"Oh." She stepped closer, making an obvious attempt to keep her straying eyes above his chest as he stepped out of the tub.

Quickly, she laid the rest of the cloths on a chest and turned to leave.

"Could you dry my back?" he asked, trying to delay her departure.

He thought he heard a choking sound.

"Please?"

She returned to his side, practically dragging her feet. Reluctantly, she reached for a cloth and began to dry his back, starting with the shoulders.

"You have a bad bruise on your shoulder. Does it hurt?"

She pressed her fingertips inward, and he jerked. "God's Bones! Of course it hurts."

"How did it happen?"

He shrugged. "We were putting out the fires, and a smoldering tree limb fell on me. I have more than a few scratches, too, I warrant."

"The orchard trees burned, as well?" she asked in a small voice.

"Yea, but many of them can be saved with careful pruning. Knowing your expertise in just about everything in the world, I have no doubt you will be able to revive them."

She ignored his taunting words. "You need to put some ointment on the bruise. The skin is broken."

"How about some of that lard from your hair?" he offered dryly.

He felt her fingers hesitate, as if questioning whether he jested or was serious.

"You did say it worked well on horses, did you not?"

"Yea, I did, and you certainly fall in the same category, though more like a mule." She laughed, and the tenseness left her fingertips as she continued drying him with gentle, sweeping strokes that left his senses uncommonly agitated.

"Why is your skin always so hot?" she blurted out.

"What?"

He looked back over his shoulder. Eadyth was biting her bottom lip and blushing through that infernal gray film on her face.

"Your body throws off heat like an oven."

"It does?" Eirik smiled. "Mayhap 'tis just you and your intoxicating nearness that warms me," he teased.

"Hah! Me and every other maid from here to Jorvik."

Eirik disregarded her insult and asked huskily, "I wonder, my lady wife, what would it take to turn you hot?"

Eadyth's face drained bloodless, making the ash even more uncomely. She threw the drying cloth aside with disgust and stepped away from him. "Stop muddling my senses all the time."

Eirik grinned. "I muddle your senses?" *I would like to muddle a lot more than your senses right now, sweet witch. Why do you not come a little closer? Come, Eadyth, let us play a little game of... muddling.*

Her senses were not the only ones muddled, Eirik realized, as he looked down ruefully at his burgeoning arousal. He started to turn, then hesitated, lest he give her another shock.

Shock be damned, he finally decided with a roguish grin, and turned anyway.

Eadyth looked down, blushed again, then looked him directly in the eye, obviously realizing that he was teasing her. "Best you don some garments, my lord, or some of those crows you mentioned below stairs may find a new roosting spot."

It was Eirik's turn to choke. He had to admire his wife's quick wit, even when she turned it on him. Chuckling, he donned small clothes and a pair of faded braies, all the time watching her graceful movements as she put the cloths in a chest at the foot of the bed and proceeded to pick up his dirty garments and wet drying cloths, mopping the damp rushes near the tub into a pile for discard.

"You need to be trimmed," she remarked behind him as he ran an ivory comb through his shoulder-length hair.

"Yea, I do," he agreed, looking at himself in the polished metal above the washstand. "You can do it for me."

"I am not very good at hair cutting," she balked.

"God's Breath, Eadyth! Have we finally uncovered something at which you are not the master?"

She did not smile at his jibe.

"Lighten up your countenance, wife. Life is too short to frown all the time."

"Cut your own hair, lackwit. I have no time for your foolery." She started toward the door with her bundle of laundry.

"Nay, stay and cut my hair. I cannot reach the back," he cajoled. "Besides, I want to talk to you about Steven."

She returned reluctantly and laid the laundry down. When he was seated on a low stool, his back to her, he handed Eadyth a pair of shears.

"How short do you want it?"

He shrugged and drew an imaginary line across the back of his neck with a forefinger. "Short enough. Just do not nip my ears." *Or any other body part.*

She remained silent at his back as she held clumps of his hair together and clipped the ends off with the shears.

"Eadyth, do you never laugh?"

"Yea, I do, when I hear something laugh-provoking. Mostly, though, the things you consider amusing are just vulgar jests at my expense."

Well, that was mostly true, he supposed. "What would make you laugh?"

"You tripping over that appendage betwixt your legs that you prize so highly," she retorted quickly. He could feel the immediate regret for her hasty words in her fingertips which stilled in their work.

Eirik chuckled. "You overestimate my powers of . . . enlargement," he replied quickly, finding that he liked this lighter, less prim side of his wife.

Wife!

Eirik recalled his earlier thoughts about Eadyth and his yearning for consummation of their marriage vows. And the reason why he hesitated to do that which his body ached for—Steven of Gravely.

Mayhap he should just toss her on the bed right now and be done with all the games. A day in bed with a willing woman was a damned good idea. He looked over his shoulder to find Eadyth scowling at his last words of humor.

Maybe not, he decided wisely.

Finished with the cutting, Eadyth ran a comb through his hair to check the evenness of her efforts. "'Tis good enough," she declared, putting her implements aside, and tossing his hair clippings on the pile of damp rushes to be removed.

She stood in the center of the room, as if pondering some weighty subject.

"Eirik, I have wanted to discuss something important with you for a long time," she said hesitantly.

He sat down and motioned her to the chair beside him.

"I am not proud of what I have done, but I would have you know why 'twas necessary to my way of thinking."

Eirik's body became alert, knowing she planned to confess her masquerade. Now that he was aware of her ruse, Eirik saw clearly that Eadyth was an uncommonly handsome woman. What he had previously considered wrinkles were nothing more than temporary scowl lines. And that mouth of hers with its disarming mole, well, he looked forward to exploring it and many other parts of her body she had kept well hidden.

But did he want her to confess before Sigurd returned with his report? One part of him needed to have the confession over with so that he could take her to bed and work out this fever of wanting in his blood. It was the part below the waist, for a certainty. The other, more logical part warned that he risked planting his seed in yet another woman who might be conspiring with Steven for his demise. No, he must wait a few more days until Sigurd's return.

Eirik tried to think of a way to forestall her confession. His senses came to full alert on one blossoming, tantalizing idea.

"Eadyth, tell me more about those timekeeping candles of yours?"

"Huh?"

"You told me you specialize in timekeeping candles. What are they? Did you invent them yourself?"

"Nay, King Alfred designed them first, many years ago. But I have experimented and refined mine so they are near perfect."

"Would they dare be any less?"

"Do you want to know, or just make sarcastic remarks?"

"I *really* want to know."

Eadyth looked at him warily but then explained, "The good Alfred devised candles of seventy-two pennyweights of wax that would burn for four hours, thus six candles per day in succession to mark the time. I developed one extra-large candle, with hour markings, that would burn for twenty-four hours, thus—"

"Thus eliminating the need for someone to remember to light the subsequent candles," he finished for her, impressed, despite himself, with her ingenuity. "They must needs be huge."

"Exactly. And very expensive, but still people buy as many as I can make." She studied him quizzically for several moments before asking, "Why did you want to know about my candles?"

So, she does not accept my sudden interest in her wonderful talents. Clever lady! "You do not want to know."

"Yea, I do."

"Well, if you insist." *Before I am done with you, you will learn never to lie to me again. You will regret your masquerade much more than you could possibly guess.* "I was wondering—could you make me a five-hour candle?" he asked meekly.

She raised an eyebrow, her suspicions definitely aroused now. "For what purpose?"

I thought you would never ask, my prim and proper little wife. Let me see if I can muddle your senses a bit more. "Have you ever heard of the five-petaled lotus?" *Not in a thousand years, I wager, especially since I just conjured it up in my mind.*

"Nay." She frowned, obviously trying to connect his question about timekeeping candles with a lotus flower. "Does the flower have aught to do with the type of candle wax produced when bees gather petal dust from it?"

Eirik could barely keep from rubbing his hands together with relish before saying casually, "Nay, it has more to do with what is done during the five hours the candle is burning."

"Oh?"

"I am sure you would not be interested." He examined his fingernails in a bored fashion. *Ask me. Ask me. Ask me.*

"You have piqued my interest."

Peak! That is the key word here, my trusting little pigeon. And you stepped very nicely into my word trap, thank you very much. "Well, if you *really* want to know, there was a caliph in one of those eastern harems—"

"Oh, nay, not another one of those harem tales of yours!"

He raised his eyebrows innocently. "Have I told you this saga afore?"

"Remember, you mentioned once that sheer fabrics, like my beekeeping veils, are used for a different purpose in the eastern harems."

"I had forgotten. Nay, 'tis another tale." He wagged his fingers impatiently in the air in front of his face. "This one involves time, and mayhap your candles."

She eyed him skeptically with the most beautiful violet eyes he had ever seen, finally prodding, "Go on."

Oh, I love it, I love it. "As I was saying, there was a caliph in an eastern harem who bought a slave girl who did not appreciate the honor of sharing his bed."

"Humph!"

"Even when he agreed to make her his eleventh wife, she refused to let him ease himself with her bodily charms."

"Eleventh! Hah! He was probably too tired to do more than breathe."

Eirik grinned, satisfied that he had snared her interest, looking forward to trapping her in the web of her own curiosity. "He tried gifts, aphrodisiacs—"

"Aphro . . . what?"

Eadyth's question stopped Eirik short for a moment, setting all kinds of indecent fantasies in motion in his head. When he regained his composure, he said gruffly, "Let us save that explanation for another time. Are you going to keep interrupting me? If so, mayhap we will miss dinner, and I am mightily hungry.''

"Go on, I promise not to interrupt again.''

I doubt that sincerely. "In any case, the caliph tried everything, but to no avail. Finally, he consulted a wise old man who told him of the five-petaled lotus.''

He looked over to Eadyth who was leaning forward with interest. *That is a good trusting bird, Eadyth. Just a little longer.*

"The wise man advised the caliph to set aside five hours to peel the petals of the lotus flower. For the first hour, there was to be absolutely no touching. Both the man and woman were to remove their clothing and just talk. They could share a glass of wine, mayhap, to relax, and the man could tell the woman what he was going to do. Of course, the woman could tell the man what she would do, as well, but if she was shy, mayhap she would just discuss what she liked having done to her. And if she was *really* timid, perchance she would just nod when he hit on something particularly tantalizing.''

"Oh, you truly are beyond belief, Eirik, telling me such ridiculous tales. I think 'tis beyond time you went to visit your mistress in Jorvik. Mayhap Asa could cure you of your lecherous delusions.''

Eirik stiffened. He did not like the idea of Eadyth dismissing him so easily. And, oddly, he did not like the way Eadyth accepted his mistress. 'Twas unnatural.

"I do not want to make love with Asa right now. Actually, I am thinking more these days of you in my bed.''

Eadyth was stunned speechless. In fact, he was stunned himself at his disclosing so much of his secret inclination. But he took advantage of Eadyth's momentary silence and hurried on with his imaginary tale before she regained her shrewish tongue.

"During the second hour, they would only kiss, but then there are many kinds of kisses, as you undoubtedly know. Involving *all* parts of the body.''

Eadyth gasped with indignation and stood as if to leave his

abominable presence. "You . . . you—"

He pushed her back in her chair and continued, "By then, of course, she would have already had one of her . . . uh, peaks, and then—"

"Peaks?" Eadyth sputtered.

Now Eirik was at a loss for words. His naive wife, even though she had lain with a man and birthed a child, did not know what it meant for a woman to climb the mountain of sexual arousal and explode with erotic pleasure. He searched carefully for the right words before saying, "You are no doubt aware that a man becomes mindless with pleasure during the bed sport when the coupling comes to a, well, a peak. The same can be true for a woman."

"Mindless! And that is a pleasure to be sought? I do not think so."

Eirik grinned, rushing to finish before she throttled him, or something worse. "During the third hour, they caress each other's bodies, learning all the secret places that heighten sensations. The woman would, of course, peak another time. Or two." *Are you listening, Eadyth? Or just trying to catch flies with your open mouth. God's Breath, I can think of a better occupation for those luscious lips.*

She finally regained her senses and snorted with disbelief. But she did not rise from her chair. Apparently, his story had caught her interest.

"During the fourth hour," he went on blithely, "she must lie perfectly still while the man explores her breasts and the womanly folds between her legs."

"Oh, you are a horrid, horrid man," Eadyth cried, her face flaming bright red. "How could you say such perverted things to me, a lady?"

"Not a lady. *My wife*," he corrected, "and 'tis not perverted, what goes on atween a husband and wife. Nay, do not leave 'til I have finished."

She stood, glaring down her condescending nose at him. Well, he would finally bring her haughty chin down a notch or two. "During the fifth hour, the man would finally bury himself in her welcoming sheath, and she would no doubt peak and shudder into mindlessness another few times.''

Eadyth was scowling mightily, obviously no longer believing his tale. At that moment, her face had turned so purple with rage and crinkled with frown lines that he could almost believe she was as old and ugly as she pretended.

''And just how many times would the man be 'shuddering' and 'peaking' during all this excessive bed play?''

''Oh, ten or twelve times,'' he lied with a straight face.

Her eyes widened in surprise. Eirik was amazed that his usually bright wife did not recognize the absurdity of his exaggeration. *Best you be careful, man*, he chided himself, *or she will expect more of you than you can deliver.*

Eadyth was staring at him, open-mouthed with astonishment.

''So now you know the story of the caliph and the five-petaled lotus,'' he concluded with a flourish.

Forcing her composure back to its usual iron self-control, Eadyth mumbled something about loathsome louts as she picked up the soiled garments again and sailed indignantly toward the door.

''So will you make me a five-hour candle?'' he called out to her rigid back.

''When hell freezes over and angels wear ice skates,'' she replied frostily, never bothering to turn. She slammed the door loudly behind her.

Well, at least he had forestalled her confession. For the time being. But he knew he could not put her off forever.

So what could he do next to prevent her from telling all her secrets before Sigurd returned? And, of course, prickle her infuriating, so-sure-of-herself pride, at the same time?

Eirik smiled at a particularly delicious idea.

Chapter Twelve

Eirik was driving her mad.

"I have to talk to you," Eadyth insisted as she crawled into his bed that night. She desperately wanted to confess her foolish masquerade. In fact, hour by hour, she was becoming increasingly fearful of her fate if she did not.

But concentration came hard when her husband's nude body lay only a hairsbreadth from hers, and he showed absolutely no interest in consummating their wedding vows. If he yawned, open-mouthed and loudly, one more time, she might just shove their marriage agreement down his throat.

"Eirik, stop that rude yawning and look at me."

"Yawning is rude? I did not know that. See, you are good for me, Eadyth. You teach me so many *significant* things."

Eadyth slanted a suspicious look at him. Was he mocking her? "Eirik! Stop changing the subject. I want to tell you something important."

"Nay, 'tis too hot to talk. I can scarce breathe with all these bed linens." He looked pointedly at the one covering her naked body. "And every time you have 'something important' to tell me, it involves more work. You make my blood boil when you nag at me, and 'tis already too stifling in here.''

"Mayhap 'tis all these candles you have lit." She looked about the bedchamber where a dozen candles burned wastefully at his insistence. Eirik claimed a sudden need for light in the event he needed to use the chamber pot during the night.

"In any event, I was not going to nag." Eadyth studiously tried to avert her eyes from his naked body as she continued talking. "I just . . ."

She failed.

Her words trailed off as she inadvertently glanced at him in the midst of her reply, and, oh, Lord, he lay with his arms folded behind his head, his long legs crossed at the ankles, and *that* part of him standing straight up in the air like a steel-firm pike.

She gasped and forced her eyes upward toward his face.

"Eadyth, you *always* nag."

Thankfully, Eirik did not seem to have noticed her perusal or subsequent embarrassment. He stared back at her blithely, his blue eyes distastefully scanning the bed linen she had pulled up to her chin.

"It feels like an oven in here," he grumbled again.

"What do you want me to do about it?" she snapped and immediately regretted her impulsive question.

"Get rid of the bed linens. All of them."

Eadyth gulped.

Eirik slid downward and rolled back and forth, trying to get comfortable. Once, he flung an arm out, accidentally brushing her left breast through the coarse linen. When she turned her back on him, his knee nudged her buttocks, ever so briefly.

She stiffened. However, she soon relaxed, realizing that his touch must have been accidental. He had told her often enough how her form and face and mannerisms repelled him. In fact, the only part of her body that seemed to hold any attraction for the insufferable man was the mole above her lip. Blessed Saint Bridget! The man was perverted. If he mentioned one more time what he'd like to do to her mole with his tongue, she just might strangle him.

And yet he failed to consummate their wedding vows. *Hmmm.*

Suddenly, Eadyth realized that she had allowed the man to divert her attention once again from the matter at hand—her confession. She sat up abruptly in the bed, barely catching the bed linen from its quick descent to her breasts.

Eirik's eyes widened and almost popped from his head. 'Twould seem he could see well enough for some things!

"Eirik, I insist on telling you something important. Stop fidgeting and listen—"

"Mayhap we should consummate our marriage," he interrupted smoothly. "*Now.*"

"Now?" she squeaked out. Lord, the man did run hot and cold from one moment to the next.

"Yea. If you would just do a few things to help, I might be able to rise to the occasion," he offered solicitously. Eadyth could swear she saw a grin twitching at the edge of his firm lips, but the movement stopped before she had a chance to study him more closely.

"Seems to me your dough has more than leavened," she remarked dryly, remembering too well how *it* had looked just moments ago. She waved a hand in the direction of his man part, but refused to look at *it* again. "A limp lily you are not."

"Ah, so you noticed. But, as you can see, the bread has fallen again. Look for yourself."

Not even if my life depended upon it! Eadyth lifted her chin and looked, instead, toward the opposite wall, her face flushing as she tried to wipe the mental picture from her mind.

He made an odd chuckling sound. "Of course, if you tried some . . . *things* . . . we might be able to get it to rise again."

"Things? What things?" she asked suspiciously, turning onto her back to look at him.

"Well, I knew this man once—"

"Not that bloody caliph again!"

"Eadyth! Your language! Tsk tsk. Nay, 'twas another man, not the caliph. A silk merchant from Micklegaard, methinks it was," he said, waving a hand airily. "This man's dough had a 'leavening' problem, as well. No doubt because his wife's face looked like the back end of a mule." He gazed at Eadyth with soulful compassion.

Eadyth cringed inwardly at her husband's appraisal of her physical attributes...or lack of them.

"But his wife did try hard, I give her that," he went on. "He said she ofttimes would stand on her head at the foot of the bed to entice him. Nude, of course. With her long hair hanging down to cover her homely face. The man said it always worked. And, of course, they had ten children. I do not suppose—"

"Never!" Eadyth snapped her gaping mouth shut, rolling over on her side away from the insufferable wretch. Of course, he lied. Women did not do things like that. Eadyth just knew they did not.

Did they?

He infuriated her then by rolling over and ignoring her once again. Not that she wanted Eirik to want her. Really, it was better this way, she told herself.

So why did she feel oddly bereft?

The next morning, she awakened to hear Abdul squawking to high heaven. Eirik was standing before the bird's cage, fully dressed in black braies and boots and his padded undertunic, obviously preparing to go to the exercise fields with his men. He held out a morsel of bread for the hungry bird.

"Loathsome lout! Awk!" the bird squawked in a voice a lot like Eadyth's. "Bothersome brute! Witless wretch! Lord Lackwit! Awk!"

Eirik glanced toward her, arching a brow accusingly. "Mayhap you have too much time on your hands, Eadyth."

"Wouldst ye like to kiss me tail feathers?"

"I did not teach him *that*," Eadyth asserted when he raised another mocking brow in question.

"Limp lily. Limp lily. Limp lily."

Eirik's eyes narrowed menacingly as the bird repeated Eadyth's words of the night before.

Eadyth felt her cheeks flame with embarrassment.

"Hmmm. Mayhap you need a *lesson*, my lady wife," Eirik said in a silky voice and reached into the cage, picking up a long green feather that the bird had molted. He slanted a look at her speculatively as he walked toward the bed, then sat down on the edge, his hip warm against hers, despite the cloth barrier.

Touching the edge of the feather to her mole, he said huskily, "Someday . . . someday, Eadyth, we are going to do some fascinating things with this feather."

She stared at him, entranced by the rapid pulse that beat in his neck, the fiery sparkle of sensuality in his pale eyes, the fullness of his marvelous lips. How could the man go from complete lack of interest to flaming passion from one moment to the next? And there was no question in Eadyth's mind that, at this moment, he wanted her, in the way a man wants a woman. She would warrant he was having no trouble with leavening under his tight braies now.

Holding her eyes, he began brushing the feather over her lips, along her jawline, over her bare shoulder, and, oh, Sweet Mary, over the tips of her still-covered breasts. Through the thin linen, they could both see her nipples peak.

Eirik inhaled sharply.

Eadyth closed her eyes on a soft groan as a new and wondrous pleasure flooded her body.

But her eyes shot open when she felt the feather trace a light line down between her breasts, past her waist, over her belly to the juncture of her thighs. The worn linen offered no protection at all. Her precious self-control crumbling, Eadyth wanted desperately to part her legs and arch into the feathery caress. It took all her determination to stop herself.

Oh, I am becoming a shameless wanton, Eadyth berated herself. *And I like it.*

Her skin turned hot everywhere he touched, even through the fabric—over her knees, down her legs, to her ankles. Blood rushed to her ears, and her breath came out in ragged gasps. Her body craved some sinful sustenance she could not understand. Before she realized what he was about, Eirik flipped up the bottom edge of her bed linen, and teased the arches of her feet with the silky feather.

She keened aloud at the pure ecstasy of his torture. Or was it the pure torture of his ecstasy? Her befuddled mind could not distinguish one from the other.

Eirik stood with a grim look of satisfaction on his face as an intense physical awareness crackled between them, like summer lightning. He seemed to hesitate, then turn away from her with reluctance, before walking toward the door.

"You are going to leave me here in this . . . condition?"

He stopped and turned slowly, flashing a heart-stopping smile at her. Eadyth could see that his emotions raged as much as hers. Softly, he asked, "What condition?"

"By the faith, I do not know, but I warrant that you do. Stop it, I tell you."

"Stop what?"

Eadyth could tell that her discomfort amused him. "These games you play with me."

"Games? Nay, wife, 'tis not I who play games." He tucked the feather into the clasp of his dragon shoulder brooch and patted it. "I will save the feather for another time, Eadyth. I promise we will play the game to completion then."

"What game?" she cried out after him, but he was already gone.

And her body thrummed with an appetite he had whetted for . . . *feathers*.

Yea, the man was driving her mad.

Eadyth was driving him mad.

Eirik forced his body and the bodies of his men to the limit

218

of their endurance on the exercise fields that day, but he could not erase the image of his wife lying in his bed that morn, her body quivering with the need for consummation. A need he shared mightily.

Not only had he been mistaken about his wife's true appearance. But, apparently, she was not the cold man-hater he had thought her to be, either. Cold? Hah! If she were any hotter, he might burst into flames.

Indeed, Eirik had a problem. He was a healthy man with a man's healthy appetites. And he had been without a woman since before his betrothal, ten sennights ago. He knew he would not be able to resist her allure one more night in the intimacy of his bedchamber. But he could not risk impregnating her whilst still unsure of her loyalty.

No, he had to form a barrier between them until Sigurd returned from his spying mission. But how could he do that when he knew he was about to succumb? It was up to Eadyth. He must do something to make his wife turn cold toward him, for a while; something to make her angry enough to halt her unconsciously seductive invitation to bed her. He must make her stone-cold angry.

That should not be too difficult.

Eirik wiped a forearm across his sweaty brow and glanced distractedly to his side where one of his new men, Aaron, was greeting his young wife, a beautiful Moorish woman of tiny stature with slanted eyes and olive skin. With a smile of sudden inspiration, Eirik approached the young couple with a quickly concocted scheme. At first, they protested, skeptical of his unusual proposal, but soon, with the warmth of a few coins crossing palms, they agreed to cooperate.

Eadyth would have a fit, Eirik thought with a grin. He only hoped it would last until Sigurd's return.

Eadyth dropped her beekeeping veil onto the kitchen bench and brushed the raindrops from her mantle and gown. Thunder cracked loudly outdoors presaging an early-summer storm that promised to be turbulent but brief.

"Have the men returned?" she asked Bertha, who was cracking eggs in a pottery bowl for a sweet custard.

The cook nodded, but her eyes shifted secretively.

"What is amiss?"

"Naught."

"You are lying. I can tell. Where is Eirik?"

Bertha's pudgy face turned beet red. "How would I be knowin'?"

"You know everything else."

"Hah! Find him yerself then."

"Best you mind your manners, or you will find yourself assigned to scrubbing the garderobes," Eadyth rebuked Bertha, but not unkindly. She had grown fond of the outspoken cook.

Grabbing a chunk of cheese from the table, she walked away, nibbling thoughtfully. Eadyth decided to search for Eirik. She sensed that she and her husband would be consummating their marriage soon, and she wanted no guilty secrets between them. She determined to tell Eirik about her charade, *now*, even if she had to tie him down and gag him to do so. She smiled, with an unaccustomed thrum of pleasure in the pit of her stomach, at that oddly tantalizing prospect.

Rain drummed loudly on the rooftop, and Eadyth examined the ceiling of the hall for moisture as she passed through. Apparently her workmen had finally repaired all the leaks, she thought with satisfaction. Next, she would set them to the chapel renovations.

Eadyth was about to mount the stairs to Eirik's bedchamber when Britta called out, "Mistress, I would not be going up there now."

"Why not?"

" 'Twould not be wise," Britta muttered, turning away sheepishly, just like Bertha.

Something was amiss. Something she would not like. And it involved Eirik. Her eyes narrowed and she started up the steps again, determined to put an end to the mystery.

"Oh, Lord," she heard Britta mutter ominously behind her.

"Now the goose feathers are gonna fly."

Eadyth did not bother to knock on Eirik's bedchamber door—*their* bedchamber door, she amended. Instead, she turned the handle and opened the door with a flourish. Then gasped with outrage at the sight before her.

Eirik was lying on the bed, propped on his elbows. He wore only a loincloth, and his body and slicked-back hair gleamed with moisture from a recent bath.

He was not alone.

A young woman—a young, *beautiful* woman—knelt on the bed with him, his foot on her lap.

Eadyth's eyes widened in disbelief.

The Moorish woman was paring Eirik's toenails, and he lay practically naked. In her lap.

"Eadyth, I did not know you were there. Come in," Eirik said with seeming innocence. His slumberous eyes spoke of some other emotion.

Oh, the humiliation of it! Eirik had actually brought a mistress into her home in front of everyone. She would kill him! Perchance with that little paring knife the woman wielded. Mayhap she would kill them both.

In the midst of her anger, Eadyth's eyes swam with tears of disillusionment. She had not realized until then how much she had grown to trust this man, her husband, and to look forward to their union. Oh, 'twas unfair. First Steven, and now this womanizing wretch.

What a foolish maid she had been, walking into this marriage with her heart wide open. Raising her chin angrily, she tried to hide her misery from Eirik's probing stare. She was a strong woman, well accustomed to the harsh reality of loneliness. She would survive yet another man's betrayal. Yea, she would.

Without thinking, she grabbed a bucket sitting next to his dirty bathwater and dumped the contents onto his still-reclining body. It soaked him and the bed linens and splattered the gown of the slut who sat back on her haunches on the bed staring at her in horror.

"Holy damnation, Eadyth! That water was ice cold," Eirik exclaimed, reaching for a drying cloth. "Do you take exception to a man practicing good bodily habits?"

"Bodily habits?" she barely choked out and filled the bucket with dirty bathwater, approaching the bed again. The young woman screeched with alarm and jumped off the bed, darting around her and out the door.

Eirik stood and eyed her challengingly. "Do not dare to throw that filthy water at me, or you will suffer the consequences."

Despite her fury, Eadyth had to admit that the man looked glorious standing there, bare-chested and bare-limbed. The light from the arrow slit played on the fine muscles that sculpted his shoulders and arms, highlighting the bunching sinews of long legs which had been honed by years of horseback riding. He threw the linen cloth onto the bed and put both hands on his hips with supreme arrogance. Amusement twitched at his enticing lips, and his pale blue eyes sparkled with some perverted pleasure.

A red haze of fury blinded Eadyth then. The man was laughing at her. He amused himself with another woman and found humor in her anger. He had promised her loyalty in the betrothal agreement and then committed adultery even before their marriage was consummated. Worst of all, he found that ignorant peasant attractive, and her . . . and her, his true wife, he could not even bear to bed.

She threw the bucket of water in Eirik's face. Soapy water dripped from his hair and eyelashes and chin. Stunned with surprise that she had actually disobeyed his command, Eirik's mouth dropped open. But only for a moment. His surprise swiftly turned to anger and he promised ominously, "You will regret, wife, that you did not heed my warning."

Eadyth realized then that she had perchance been hasty in her method of showing her displeasure to Eirik. She should have waited until she had contained her roiling fury and discussed the situation with him rationally. God's Bones! Where was the cool-headed, logical woman she had been before coming to Ravenshire? She did not recognize this hot-tempered termagant she had become.

Eirik started toward her, a predatory gleam in his eyes.

Eadyth spun on her heels and ran down the steps and through the hall, ignoring the knights who had come in out of the rain and sat about dicing at the long tables. She raced blindly out the courtyard door, unsure of her destination, just knowing she had to escape the pounding footsteps she heard following her.

She had barely reached the courtyard when she heard Eirik's bare feet slip on the outside steps. He slid, swearing loudly, before falling to the muddy ground of the bailey.

Eadyth looked over her shoulder with concern and considered going back to see if he was all right. One look at Eirik changed her mind. He was sitting in the mud, still wearing only the brief loincloth, glowering at her, and she decided she had best find a hiding place until his anger cooled.

She made it almost to the kitchen garden when Eirik lunged at her from behind, grabbing her waist. She landed flat on her stomach, her face pressed into the mud, Eirik atop her. The rain pounded down on them both, creating a pool of mud.

Eadyth pressed her palms into the soggy ground and tried to raise her head and shoulders, but she could not move. Eirik covered her from neck to toes with his own much larger body, and she was having difficulty breathing.

"Get off me, you big oaf."

Eirik rolled Eadyth onto her back but continued to press her to the ground with his body. Despite the rain, which was lessening now as sunlight peeked through the clouds, despite the fact that his lady wife looked like a drowned, muddy rat, despite his formidable anger, Eirik felt a keen pleasure in the pressure of his hard body against her womanly curves. Yes, curves, he realized, not without pleasure; his wife definitely was not the bony creature he had once imagined.

With deliberate care, he adjusted his body atop hers and ground his burgeoning manhood against her center.

She gasped and gazed up at him with questioning innocence. Rivulets of rain made tracks in the mud plastering her face, and her sodden hair escaped her wimple in ugly gray clumps.

But somehow Eirik was not repulsed.

With a deft movement of both legs, he entwined his ankles with hers and spread her legs. Then, through her thin, rain-sodden gown, he expertly touched himself to her center of pleasure—at least, it was a pleasure point on other women he had known. But then, mayhap his wife was different.

Eadyth's mouth parted on a soft sigh of enchantment. "Oh."

Eirik smiled. She was no different, after all. And in that he found great cause for satisfaction . . . and anticipation. "Oh?"

"Oh, you are a brute!" Eadyth exclaimed in her usual prickly tone of voice, trying to shove him off as she came to her senses.

"A brute, am I?" he asked. "My lady, you do not know, *yet*, what a brute I can be." He reached his right hand out and gathered a fistful of mud. Then, with a chuckle of glee, he smeared it onto her face. "That is for throwing dirty bath-water in my face."

She sputtered and spat, spraying his face with mud, and tried to claw at him. But he pulled both wrists above her head with one hand. Then he dished up another handful of mud and smeared it onto each of her breasts, rubbing his palm seductively over the slick surface he created. Fascinated, he watched her nipples blossom through her thin gunna.

And he grew even harder against her.

"Why are you doing this?" she moaned.

"Because I like to."

Carefully, he rotated his hips back and forth against her, experimenting, watching closely for her reaction. She did not disappoint him.

Instinctively, her legs widened and she arched up for more. Closing her eyes languorously, she parted her lips to accommodate her short, ragged breaths. Her body told him what her prideful tongue could not: she wanted him. As much as he wanted her.

"Ahem. Ahem."

Eirik groaned aloud at the slight coughing sound and he knew his opportunity was lost, even before he looked up and saw Britta and Bertha and several of his knights near the kitchen door.

Eadyth instantly overcame her passionate response and chastised him in a mortified voice, "Oh, you are the world's worst husband. To think of consummating our marriage afore an audience. In the mud. In daylight."

"Is that what we were doing?" he asked with amusement. "Well, I must admit this is a first for me. You must be a bad influence on me. What other deviant paths will you lead me on, wife?"

"Me? Me?" she shrieked and tried to buck him off.

He laughed and would not move.

She bit his shoulder.

"Ouch!"

He bit her shoulder.

She shrieked even louder.

Meanwhile, their audience continued to stare open-mouthed at the spectacle they made. Eirik figured it was time to move indoors before they really did consummate their wedding in public. The rain had stopped, and already bright sunlight peeped through the clouds, causing steam to rise from the damp earth. Thinking quickly, Eirik looked up and ordered, "Britta, get me some soap, a comb and several drying cloths. And some clean garments for me and my lady wife. Take them to the spring."

"What?" Eadyth croaked out.

"We are going to bathe . . . in the pond."

"*We?*"

Eirik recognized the panic in Eadyth's voice, but he did not care. She had pushed him too far. He had waited too long to bed his wife, and he would wait no longer. In truth, he *could not* wait any longer.

"Is this a private game, or can anyone join in?" a deep voice inquired above him.

Eirik peered over his shoulder to see Sigurd sitting astride his destrier. He had ridden the animal right into the kitchen courtyard. Eadyth would go into a rage if he trampled her precious herbs.

But then Eirik realized the significance of Sigurd's appearance, and he stood, releasing Eadyth from his body's pressure. He allowed her to rise but held onto her wrist, refusing to let her pull away.

"What did you find?" he demanded anxiously as Sigurd alighted and handed the reins of his horse to a stable boy. "Does she spy or not?"

Amazed, Sigurd glanced from him to Eadyth and back again, then looked pointedly at the still-raging arousal at the juncture of Eirik's thighs. With a laugh, Sigurd shook his head in exaggerated despair. "Methinks the waiting has been sore *hard* on you, my lord."

"Methinks you had best spit out the news or join us in a mud bath."

Sigurd grinned widely, prolonging the suspense. Finally, he disclosed, "She is innocent as a newborn babe."

It was Eirik then who grinned from ear to ear. "Are you certain? Where did you check?"

"Hawks' Lair. Jorvik. Even two of Gravely's estates. Yea, I am sure. She hates the man. Those closest to her know of it. And there had been no contact betwixt them 'til he came seeking his son this past year."

"You set spies on me?" Eadyth asked incredulously, pulling out of Eirik's grasp. Her face turned stormy with rage. "How dare you? Oh, how dare you?" Winding her arm back, she swung in a wide circle and punched him in the stomach.

"Oomph!" Taken off guard, Eirik slipped and fell back into the mud, taking Eadyth with him.

She flailed and fought furiously against his restraint as they slopped about in the mud, covering themselves from head to toe once again.

"You arrogant ass!" She slapped his face and tried to crawl away.

"You willful wench!" He grabbed her ankle and pulled her forcibly back toward him.

Her body went stiff then and her face froze into a mask of hurt as she suddenly seemed to remember something painful. "You betrayed me with another woman," she accused, coming to her knees before him.

"I did?" At first, Eirik forgot what had prompted their rolling about in the mud—the ruse he had concocted with Aaron's young wife. Had he really been so lackwitted as to think he could rile his wife by pretending to be with another woman and not suffer the consequences? "Oh, that was just a charade to provoke you," he confessed unashamedly.

"Why?" she asked, her forehead furrowing with puzzlement.

"So you would not tempt me into consummating our marriage 'til . . ." Eirik's words trailed off as he saw the fury boiling in her luminous violet eyes. Perchance he had revealed too much too soon. Some women were quick to temper and needed to be "handled" carefully. In his anger, he had forgotten to employ tact.

"Tempt you? Tempt you?" Eadyth sputtered. Then that iron-willed chin of hers raised to the heavens and she turned the tables on him. Raising two fistfuls of mud that he had not seen her gather, she hurled them into his face. Momentarily blinded, he sat back on his haunches and released her, trying to wipe the oozing mud from his eyes. When he could finally see again, Eadyth stood before him, hands on hips, glaring at him with affront. "You truly are an arrogant bastard."

"I do not like your choice of words, wife, nor your tone." Realizing they still had an audience, Eirik barked out to all the spectators at the kitchen door, "Depart! All of you. I would be alone with my lady wife."

Britta snickered and said something about them looking like two sows in a sty. Bertha laughed lasciviously and made an odd remark about even the flattest breasts appearing to wobble when covered with mud. Sigurd and Wilfrid merely chuckled.

When they were finally alone and stood facing each other, panting for breath, Eadyth reproached him, "You set spies on me even when I gave my word that I was true. You believed I conspired with your most hated enemy—*my* most hated enemy. And you planned to bed another woman just to avoid the odious prospect of my touch."

"Odious?" he choked out. "My lady, you are suffering from delusions if you cannot see that I crave your body . . . and your touch."

"You do?" The pleasure that flickered momentarily on her face disappeared as she realized the implications of his words. "Are you saying that you deliberately staged that scene in your bedchamber with the Moorish woman?"

"I repeat, it was a ruse. I did not intend to couple with the maid. She is married to one of my men."

"How deceitful of you!"

He raised a brow mockingly.

Eadyth blinked to keep the tears welling in her violet eyes from overflowing.

He felt a momentary twinge of guilt. "I had to know for sure," he said defensively.

"Why could you not ask me? I would have told you the truth."

"Would you?" he asked softly.

He knew.

In that moment, Eadyth saw the light of recognition in Eirik's pale blue eyes, and she realized that he knew of her masquerade. Suddenly, she understood his odd behavior these past few days.

"How long?" she asked, backing away defensively. "How long have you known?"

He shrugged. "Long enough."

"Are you . . . angry with me?"

He nodded, taking one step closer to her.

She took one step backward.

"Well, I am angry with you, too."

"Oh?" He took one more step.

This time, she took two steps backward. "You spied on me."

"With good reason."

"Mayhap I had good reason for my . . . my innocent little harmless masquerade."

Eirik grinned at her choice of words, and Eadyth realized that he taken two more steps closer to her while she talked. She stepped backward five paces, just to give herself more distance, and he smiled at her in a predatory fashion that she did not like one bit. She felt like a helpless bird being stalked by a wise old cat.

"Mayhap you would like to enlighten me as to your motivations," he asked, rubbing his muddy upper lip thoughtfully.

"You look ridiculous standing there practically naked, covered with mud," Eadyth snapped without thinking. Actually, he looked remarkably virile and alarmingly handsome, Eadyth admitted to herself. She would never tell him that, though.

Eirik's wonderfully clear eyes sparkled mischievously. "Ah, then, 'tis only fair that we should even things up."

Eadyth's brow furrowed in puzzlement. She had said he looked ridiculous, standing *naked* and covered with *mud*. Looking down, she saw that she, too, was completely covered with mud. That only left . . .

Her mouth dropped open. He would not!

Eirik lunged for her.

Apparently, he would.

Throwing Eadyth over his shoulder, Eirik ignored her squeals of protest and flailing arms and legs. By the time they reached the pond, he was shaking his head at her unladylike language.

Lord, he loved a good battle, and this stubborn, domineering, stiff-backed wife of his was going to provide him with good sport. Without any hesitation, Eirik waded knee-deep into the ice-cold water of the spring-fed pond. Despite the hot

229

sun, their baths would be coldly invigorating because of the recent rain. He smiled widely and dumped Eadyth, clothes and all, into the watery depths.

She came up sputtering, calling out every epithet she could name. "Loathsome lout! Odious oaf! Bloody bastard! Lusty Lackwit!"

Shamelessly, Eirik removed his loincloth and approached her. "Let us see just what I have bought in this marriage bargain, wife."

"Bought? Bought? You have not *bought* me, you wretch. If anything, I have bought you with my dowry," she shrieked, trying to walk past him to the shore with as much dignity as possible in her water-heavy garments. She had already lost her head-rail and wimple in the dunking, and the rest of her garments molded her body with enticing promise.

Eirik raised an amused brow at her feisty words, tearing his eyes from the clear outline of her breasts and hips and long legs. "Well, then, we shall both examine our purchases."

As he stepped after her into the shallow water, she glanced downward and inhaled sharply, noticing that he'd discarded his loincloth. "Have you no shame?"

"None whatsoever."

He proceeded to remove her clothing. And it was no small feat, with her kicking and scratching and swearing vengeance on him the entire time.

"Do not dare touch me . . . oh, you have torn my gown, you clumsy brute."

"Stop twisting so. You are as slippery as an eel. Ouch! You scratched me. You drew blood with your claws," he exclaimed incredulously and dunked her under the water.

She came up sputtering, "You bastard!" and launched herself at his chest, knocking him over, attempting to kneel on his chest. His nose burned, and he barely escaped emasculation when she tried to knee him in the groin.

"Eadyth! 'Tis time you behaved like a wife, not a fish-wife."

"Hah! 'Tis time you behaved like a chivalrous knight, not a rude troll."

"A troll!" he gasped out. "We shall see who is the troll here. I have had enough of your obstinance and unwomanly ways." Forgoing tenderness then, he roughly ripped her gown and undergarments from her body.

"Look what you have done to my shoes. Oh, you will pay for all this damage to my belongings."

Grinning at her soft leather slippers which floated by ignominiously, he yanked her stockings from her legs.

Once naked, Eadyth gave him no opportunity to view her bodily charms. Slipping out of his grasp, she dove into the water and swam away from him, giving him only a momentary glimpse of her bare buttocks and deliciously long legs.

He smiled.

Grasping the soap Britta had left on the bank, he took off after her, overtaking her in a few strokes. Grabbing hold of her hair, he pulled her back toward the shore and sat down on the bank, pushing her into a sitting position in the water between his knees. Her screams could, no doubt, be heard in Jorvik.

"Do not turn your back on me from this day forth, you heathen Viking beast, for I will pay you back tenfold."

"I quiver with fright, my lady." Quickly, before she had a chance to turn and truly render him impotent, Eirik soaped her long hair, then dunked her head under the water. Three times he repeated the procedure, ignoring her shrieks of outrage at his brutish treatment.

When he was satisfied that he had finally removed all the lard from her hair, he let Eadyth stand. Angrily, she flicked her long, wet hair over her shoulder and stormed away from him before he had a chance to truly study her body. Ah, well, he would have plenty of time for that later.

He began his own ablutions, going off to the deeper water. He washed his hair and body, diving underwater again and again to remove all the mud. When he finally emerged from the water, Eadyth was standing on the shore, fully clothed in a belted gunna of soft lavender silk, combing her waist-length hair.

And she was beautiful.

Britta must not have brought undergarments for his lady wife, thank the gods, for the thin fabric of her gown molded her womanly curves. She was slender as he had originally thought, but not uncomely so. Once again, he berated himself for being such a dim-sighted fool.

His lips twitched with a grin of anticipation. He reached for a drying cloth and slowly, languorously blotted the moisture from his body, watching her the entire time.

And she was watching him, too. Warily.

He felt himself grow hard under her steady scrutiny.

She blushed and looked away.

"We are finally going to consummate our marriage. You know that, Eadyth, do you not?"

She hesitated, biting her bottom lip, then nodded grudgingly. "But do not think I will be standing on my head for you."

Eirik's eyes widened. "Well, mayhap it will not be necessary now that I see you do not look *quite* like the back end of a mule."

Eadyth shot him a look that said clearly he was the one most resembling a mule's arse. "And do not think I am going to give you one of those five-hour candles for your lusty purposes," she added shrewishly.

"Huh?"

She waved a hand dismissively. "You know . . . that five-petaled lotus thing you boasted about. Oh, I know that I cannot escape the marriage bed now, but do not think you will get me to cooperate in your perversions."

Understanding began to dawn on Eirik then, and he laughed aloud. Good Lord, Eadyth believed his outrageous tale of five-hour sexual bouts, and no doubt she expected such a performance from him on this their wedding night.

"Ah . . . refresh my memory, Eadyth . . . how many times did I say the woman in that tale *peaked* in one evening?"

"I disremember," she said, her face flushing prettily. "Seven or eight times, methinks."

"Sev . . . seven or eight?" he said, amazed at his own fantastic stories. Then he thought of something else. "And how many times did I say the man *peaked* during that five-hour session?"

"Twelve," she said without hesitation.

Eirik made a small, choking sound deep in his throat and stepped closer. He took the comb from her hand and threw it to the ground. Then, putting his hands on her waist, which fit rather nicely into his palms, he lifted her off the ground so their bodies met—thigh to thigh, belly to belly, breast to chest.

Lowering his head, he murmured huskily against her lips, "Eadyth, I fear I will not last five minutes, let alone five hours."

"Ah, I should have known. Men ever boast of prowess they have not."

He put the tip of his tongue to the mole above her lips, then traced the edges of her finely sculpted mouth with mindsplintering pleasure. "Do you challenge me already, wife?"

"Nay, we are in agreement on that, at least. I care naught for any extended periods of love play. I would just as well get it over with and be done," she said in an unconvincingly defensive tone as she leaned her head backward, trying to escape his lips. Her movement only gave him access to her smooth neck.

"Ah, that is where you are wrong, wife. We will light your blasted five-hour candle," he said, nuzzling the warm skin, "and I promise to make your pleasure last . . . even if we both have to peak over and over and over 'til we get it right."

For once, Eadyth had nothing to say. But the wildly beating pulse in her neck jumped traitorously against his lips.

233

Chapter Thirteen

As they walked back toward the keep, Eirik draped an arm casually over her shoulder.

She glared at him.

He winked.

What kind of husband winks at his wife?

Eadyth ducked and moved away defensively. "Stop teasing me," she demanded and started to walk ahead of him at a brisk pace.

The brute called after her with seeming innocence. "Me? Teasing? I was just behaving as a husband should. By the way, Tykir was right about your hips."

She looked back over her shoulder and saw his eyes riveted outrageously on her backside. Holy Saint Hilary, the man's mind ran on one path only. She stopped and waited for him to catch up. She was not going to display her posterior for him in her flimsy silk gown, especially since Britta had failed to bring her a chemise or any undergarments.

"You really should accustom yourself to my touching, Eadyth," he remarked offhandedly as he tried to entwine his fingers with hers.

She swatted his hand away. "Why?"

"Because I intend to do a goodly amount."

She frowned, not understanding his words at first. When she realized that he meant he would be touching her excessively, a hot flush worked itself up from her suddenly full breasts to her undoubtedly red face. "You . . . you . . . libertine," she sputtered, trying to find the words to tell him of her lack of appreciation for his playful ways. He surely did not mean them. He only goaded her to raise her ire. At least, that's what she thought until she noticed his eyes gazing appreciatively at her chest.

She looked down and almost groaned aloud. Her nipples had grown hard. *Oh, Lord.* "Are you perchance a pervert?"

Eirik laughed, and the tiny crinkles around his eyes deepened in a most delightful way. He had slicked his thick, black hair off his face, but already the sun was drying it and the vast amount of skin revealed by his short-sleeved, open-necked tunic. His freshly scrubbed, sun-bronzed skin shone with good health, vitality and raw maleness. Really, her husband was sinfully attractive. And a danger to her hard-won independence.

"Nay, Eadyth, I am not a pervert."

"Then why do you talk so much of touching and fornication?"

"Mayhap because it has been so long since I have done either."

That surprised her. She wanted to ask how long, having assumed he had visited his mistress between the time of their betrothal and his return to Ravenshire several days ago, but she could not. Asking would indicate she cared. And she did not care for him, or any man. She could not. *Oh, Lord.*

"Three months," he said, as if answering her silent question.

Her eyes widened, and, against her wishes, a little flutter of gladness rippled through her. Fighting to regain her cool demeanor, she commented in as uninterested a voice as she could manage, "Well, I suppose that is a long time for a man, but surely you place far too much significance on the coupling betwixt a man and woman.''

''A husband and a wife,'' he corrected her with a slight grin.

She waved a hand dismissively. ''Man, woman. Husband, wife. 'Tis just an overvalued physical act in the end. Like eating. Or yawning. Of too short a duration to merit such importance. Oh, I warrant it is pleasurable for a man. At least, they boast of it often enough, but I misdoubt it is more than a nuisance for very many women.''

Eirik gave her a sidelong look of amazement and shook his head slowly from side to side. ''Yawning? Ah, Eadyth, 'twill be a joy to teach you otherwise.''

''I want none of your sinful lessons.''

''There is naught sinful about *good* lovemaking betwixt a husband and wife.''

''Good. Bad. Little difference it makes to me.''

''It will.''

''Hah!''

Eirik reached forward and took a long lock of her curly hair in his fingers. Sensuously, he rubbed it between his thumb and forefinger, then, holding her eyes, he lifted the strand to his lips. ''I suspect, my prim and proper lady, that you harbor a misconception about lovemaking. If you had your way, I wager, 'twould be quick and quiet, clean and cool. You would manage it very efficiently, like your household.''

She lifted her chin, stubbornly refusing to rise to his bait this time.

He chuckled softly and continued, ''Well, let me tell you, dearling, *good* lovesport is long . . . and wet . . . and messy . . . and noisy . . . and very, very hot.''

Hot? Wet? Oh, Lord. Eadyth could not stop her mouth from opening with incredulity. ''See what I mean?'' she scoffed finally. ''You are constantly taunting me. All I wanted was a husband to protect my son, a legal arrangement.'' She closed her eyes with exasperation and gritted her teeth.

"And I want more."

Eirik's softly spoken words startled Eadyth, and she opened her eyes to meet the hungry fire of his burning scrutiny. *Hungry? For what? Oh, nay, it cannot be ... oh, surely not for me.*

She stumbled, and Eirik grasped her by the waist to help her stay aright. The mere graze of his hands against her silk-clad skin was enough to set her heart thumping and blood pounding to all her extremities. And, Sweet Mary, his touch felt so uncommonly wonderful, she wanted to catch the moment and hold it in her palm forever.

This was the sweetness she had dreamed of as a young girl, before Steven of Gravely had shattered her illusions. Her mouth parted on a soft moan of despair at her crumbling resistance to Eirik's lure.

Eirik inhaled sharply, apparently understanding too well her unwilling response to him.

Before she could turn and run, as she surely should, before he burned her alive with his smoldering eyes, Eirik pulled her sharply against his hard chest. Then, wrapping his arms tightly around her waist, he lifted her body upward so her bare toes dangled in the soft grass, and he walked her to a nearby tree.

With her back braced against the rough bark and her feet still barely touching the ground, he pressed his hips against her belly and proceeded to show her exactly what he had meant by a great deal of touching.

"Lovely ... so lovely," he murmured against her neck as his hands played havoc with her body, moving the slippery fabric of her silk gown along her thighs, across her back.

"Do not ... oh, please stop, you lusty goat," she gasped out, trying to catch his wrists, but he was too quick for her. His hands were everywhere at once.

"I cannot stop, Eadyth ... I cannot," he rasped out huskily and nipped playfully at her ear.

"I feel shameless."

"A shameless wife," he said pensively. "Hmmm. I think

237

I like that prospect, Eadyth. Very much.''

Then, like a bursting dam, his caresses moved over her in waves, out of control, without direction or concern for her cries about the unseemliness of the intimate places he claimed. When he moved his wool-clad chest lightly, from side to side, against her silk-covered bosom, Eadyth shuddered with the pure, exquisite sensation of her breasts being abraded so enticingly.

"I did not know," Eadyth said, with wonder.

"I know," he said with maddening arrogance.

She wanted to say more, but she was too overcome with the erotic tingles that were spreading like wildfire across her body.

"I do not want to feel like this," she groaned.

"Yea, you do," he asserted and moved his warm lips closer to hers. At the same time, his large palms cupped her buttocks in a scandalous manner she should have found repulsive, but did not, and pulled her even closer against his hardness.

"Do you want me to kiss you, Eadyth?" he whispered against her lips.

"Nay," she lied, still trying to fight the raging fire which threatened to consume her and all that she had held dear.

"Why, then, are you trembling so?"

"With revulsion."

He chuckled softly at her resistance and moved his right hand to her left breast. With the heel of his palm on the underside, he flicked a callused thumb back and forth across the pebbled tip until her breast felt heavy and ached for some fulfillment she could not understand. Then he did the same with his left hand and her right breast.

She was drowning in a pool of ecstasy.

"Does that feel good?" he asked in a thickened voice.

She could not speak, just shook her head stubbornly.

"You lie, Eadyth," he said with a knowing grin. "Your lips swell in invitation. Your eyes, your beautiful violet eyes, are hazed with passion. And your legs have parted of their own volition for our joining.''

Horrified, Eadyth looked down to see that she had, indeed, spread her legs to accommodate the cradle of his hips.

''Oh . . . oh . . . see what you do to me. I have become a sinful wanton.''

''Nay, not a wanton. My wife,'' he said thickly, with satisfaction, brushing his warm lips across hers lightly—tempting, teasing, tantalizing her hunger for more. ''Tell me what you want, *wife* . . . tell me . . . tell me,'' he coaxed.

''I want your kiss, and you well know it,'' she cried out finally in surrender, then pressed her lips against his.

The surprised hiss of Eirik's breath mingled with hers. Then he turned his head slightly, shaping his firm lips to better fit against her mouth. Oh, the sheer pleasure of his deepening kiss! When his tongue slipped between her lips, she wrapped her arms around his powerful shoulders and whimpered incoherently, wanting what he gave her and so much more.

Eadyth never knew a kiss could be so erotic, stripping away a woman's resistance petal by petal. Her mind whirled with all the delicious sensations accosting her, surrounding her, enveloping her—the taste of Eirik's mouth, a breeze carrying the scent of sweet clover, the raspy sound of their ragged breaths, the buzzing of a hornet, the feel of Eirik's long fingers tunneling in her hair, the delicious odor of her husband's sun-warmed skin, the snorting of a horse—

The snorting of a horse! Eadyth tore her mouth from his, and her eyes fluttered open. Glancing over Eirik's shoulder, she saw, to her horror, Wilfrid and several of Eirik's men sitting astride their horses a short distance away, watching with amusement the degenerate display she and Eirik had been putting on for them.

Mortified, she tried to shove her husband away from her, informing him in a strangled hiss, ''We have company.''

Eirik's misty blue eyes had turned slumberous with desire, and his lips looked sensually swollen from their deep kiss.

Oh, Sweet Mary, what must she look like? A trollop, that was what, she thought, cringing.

"What?" Eirik asked, a violent shiver of restraint passing over him as he gently brushed some strands of hair off her face. His eyes remained unfocused with passion.

"Your men are here, and they are ogling us," she informed him in a suffocated whisper.

Suddenly alert, Eirik glanced over his shoulder and nodded to the men companionably, as if embracing his wife openly were an everyday happenstance. As if they were not there for some special reason.

"I must seem a wanton in your men's eyes. Oh, I will never forgive you for embarrassing me so!"

"Really?" he asked silkily. "Well, best you get used to being embarrassed then because I find I like the idea of a wanton wife." He winked at her and pinched her backside outrageously before starting to turn toward his men.

She pulled him back.

He raised his right eyebrow inquiringly. "Changed your mind already, have you?"

"Nay, 'tis not that, you dolt. Do not turn around, or you will humiliate us both, more than you already have."

He looked down at his braies unashamedly. "You are right."

He pushed her along in front of him, over to where Wilfrid and the others sat atop their horses, idly flicking their reins back and forth, smirking from ear to ear.

" 'Twould seem you have taught the bee how to make honey, after all," Sigurd, the Viking soldier, commented crudely. Another man in the background made a soft buzzing sound.

And Eadyth wished she could sink into the very earth.

But Eirik and his men soon forgot about her as Wilfrid informed Eirik anxiously that a cotter had just arrived to tell of more cattle being slaughtered, this time at a farmstead near Ravenshire. Eadyth noticed Eirik's saddled destrier then, which they had brought for him.

"I thought you would want to know immediately," Wilfrid finished explaining, looking apologetically toward Eadyth.

"Yea, you did right in coming to me. We will go now to investigate."

"Well, then, I will just return to the keep," Eadyth interjected with deliberate casualness, thankful to have this respite from Eirik's intoxicating presence, an opportunity to rebuild her shattered defenses.

But her husband had different plans.

Eirik walked back to her, leading his horse by the reins. A small, mysterious smile lifted the edges of his lips. "Nay."

"Nay? What do you mean, 'nay'?" Her voice betrayed her by rising shrilly with dismay.

"You will not escape me so easily from now on, *wife*. You will come with us. 'Twill make for a pleasant ride, in any case. But do not fear for your safety. I will protect you from any villains."

Hah! And who will protect me from you? "I cannot ride with you," she protested, then lowered her voice so the others could not overhear. "I am wearing no undergarments."

"I know," he said and smiled wickedly.

He knows? Well, of course he knows with all that touching and feeling he has been doing. "I do not know how Britta could have been so careless in bringing only my outer gunna. And it is my best silk gown!"

He grinned as if he knew exactly what Britta's intent had been. The lout! Her upper lip curled with disgust. "'Tis scandalous."

"I know."

Say that again, husband, and I am going to tie your tongue in knots. "Do you not care that others will know?"

"No one can tell you are naked beneath this wisp of fabric but me," he said smoothly, fingering the sleeve of her gown. "Do you not see? That is what is so tantalizing—knowing you are naked, just for me."

Oh, Lord. He is doing it again. Making me feel all hot and fluttery. "I refuse."

"I do not recall giving you a choice."

Eadyth recognized an impasse when it hit her smack in the face. This was not the time or place to argue with her husband. He would not budge in front of his men. "Well, get my horse then," she conceded grudgingly.

"There is no time," Eirik said, smiling ominously as he folded his arms across his chest, daring her to challenge him.

What are you up to now, my husband?

When she did not snap back as she sorely wanted to do, he added, "You will ride with me."

"In a silk dress? Are you bloody daft?"

"Tsk tsk! Such language. I will have to teach you better ways, wife."

Yea, I definitely think he would look good with a knot in his tongue.

Then, before she could blink, he bent down to the ground, pulled the back hem of her gown forward and upward, handing it to her at waist level. She looked down, aghast, at the billowy leggings that were formed, like a laundress' gown. Once again, before she could protest, he picked her up by the waist and lifted her astride the horse, then mounted behind her.

Her legs were spread wide atop the huge destrier and her bare, shoeless and stockingless legs were exposed up to the calves. The horse started to move then, and Eirik wrapped his left arm tightly around her waist to hold her steady. The reins were in his right hand.

"Oh, how could you? Everyone can see my bare skin."

"Sigurd, get my long mantle. 'Tis hanging from a peg in the hall. My lady has taken a sudden chill." In a lower voice, he whispered in her ear, "See, Eadyth, how accommodating I can be? I think I am going to be an exemplary husband. Truly, I do."

Mayhap two knots would be better. Eadyth started to tell him exactly what she thought of him, but she was stunned speechless by the hard ridge of his manhood pressing at her derriere and the rocking of her most private woman parts against the saddle as the massive horse ambled along.

And once Eirik had gathered his long mantle over his shoulders and hers, covering them both from neck to ankle, she knew what a lowly ant felt like when enticed into the spider's web.

Wilfrid guided his horse to Eirik's right and Sigurd to his left, the five soldiers following behind them.

When Wilfrid commented, "This is the fifth case of cattle being slaughtered, without the carcasses being taken for food, in the past three months," Eirik's left hand moved to her right breast, under cover of the mantle.

Eirik nodded, commenting, " 'Tis Steven of Gravely's work, no doubt." Meanwhile his long fingers were tantalizing her breast with expert manipulations—weighing it with his palm from the underside, making large moving circles over its whole, taking the tip between his thumb and forefinger and twisting gently. *Oh, Lord.*

She glanced back at Eirik over her shoulder, but he was looking at Sigurd, listening intently as Sigurd told him, "I think we must needs implement your plan to set guards at intervals throughout your lands, for the time being."

"Yea, you are right, Sigurd," Eirik said calmly, seemingly unaware of the havoc he was wreaking under the cloak. "I fear he will start the burnings in my lands, as he did at Hawks' Lair, and then we may have dead bodies of people to deal with, not just cattle." Meanwhile, he moved the reins to his left hand and was giving equal, seductive treatment to her right breast.

Wilfrid and Sigurd were totally unaware of Eirik's actions.

"Can the king or the Witan do naught?"

"I tried when I met with Edmund, but he says I need proof of Gravely's misdeeds—not just the word of a peasant—if I want the Witan to act against him."

"And Gravely never leaves evidence," Sigurd finished for him.

"I have sent for some Jomsviking knights, old comrades of my father's, to help us guard the keep 'til we catch Steven.

They will not arrive for several sennights, however; so the men we have now must be extra diligent."

"And the additional men you hired in Jorvik as part of your permanent hird?"

"They will be here in a few days, along with the Viking fighters my cousin King Haakon sends from his Norse lands."

Eadyth was surprised by his news. He had failed to tell her of sending for troops. But she was even more surprised by the large hand now pressing against her flat belly, its long fingers creeping downward to the apex of her femininity. When he cupped her intimately, she made a small squeaking sound of protest.

"Did you say something, my lady?" Wilfrid asked politely.

"Nay," she choked out, " 'twas just a bothersome gnat."

She turned and glared at Eirik over her shoulder.

He smiled innocently back at her. And began to rub the heel of his hand against her. Heat rushed to her face and swept over her body. She felt open and vulnerable with her legs widespread on the horse's large back. And then an odd, swelling ache began to thrum there under his gentle, rhythmic touch.

"I hate you," she hissed softly.

"Mayhap I can correct that," he whispered back, and she knew he had been aware of what he was doing to her the entire time.

"Let us see how good an actress you can be now, my lady of the charades." He turned back to Wilfrid. "I see all the western fields are planted with new wheat." And his hand lay on her thigh, gathering her gown, bunch by bunch, until its hem lay in her lap, exposing her bare skin.

" 'Tis the work of your lady wife," Wilfrid informed Eirik. "Ask her how she badgered me into getting a spring crop in whilst you were away on the king's business."

Eirik's long fingers skimmed the smooth skin of her thighs, then inserted themselves in the hot liquid that pooled embarrassingly between her legs. She would have shot upward off the horse then if Eirik's left hand, holding the reins, was not pressed firmly against her waist, holding her in place.

"Is that true, wife?" he asked silkily.

She could not speak, just nodded.

All the other men kept glancing surreptitiously at her now that her disguise had been unmasked.

"Why, Eirik, your lady turns crimson with modesty. Did you know your wife had such a humble side to her disposition?" Wilfrid teased.

"Nay, I did not," Eirik said with a chuckle. "She usually tells me what a dunderhead I am and how there is naught I can teach her about anything. Is that not so, wife?" His middle finger found a spot on her body then that she had never known existed, and he proved she did not know everything.

A red haze blurred her vision as a sweet, almost painful, need began to build from that bud of sensation he was touching so gently. A new and unexpected warmth spiraled throughout her body. She groaned aloud.

"My lady," both Wilfrid and Sigurd exclaimed at once. "What is amiss? Are you ailing?"

Eirik removed his hand, and she felt as if she were hanging on a cliff of anticipation. She rejoiced that he had removed his torturing fingers. She wanted to pull them back.

" 'Tis her monthly time," he lied unabashedly.

Eadyth sputtered indignantly and ducked her head self-consciously. If she ever survived this ordeal, she would take great delight in killing her husband, very slowly.

"Why do you two not go on ahead with the other men? 'Tis only a short distance yet," Eirik offered solicitously. "I will take my lady over to that stream there. Mayhap a drink will refresh her sensibilities afore we follow you."

Uh oh. Eadyth was not too besotted with Eirik's lustful touch to know she would be in even bigger trouble if they were left alone. "Nay, I am all right now. 'Twas just a . . . a stomach cramp," she said quickly.

But the men were already moving ahead of them, and Eirik was smiling down at her with supreme satisfaction as he guided the horse toward the stream. But he did not stop there. Instead, he crossed the stream, moving the horse into a secluded spot on the other side. Deftly, he dismounted and tied the horse's reins to a small tree near the water's edge.

She started to pull the hem of her gown down now that Eirik was no longer at her back with the protective cover of the mantle, but Eirik reached up a hand, restraining her.

"Nay, I want to look at you," he demanded huskily, and Eadyth saw now that he was not as cool and composed from all his fondling as she had thought. His pale eyes glimmered with passion, and his firm lips were turgid and parted with longing.

Oh, Lord.

Forcibly he pushed her hands to her sides, then lifted the hem of her gown to her waist. Silently he stared at her most intimate woman parts, glistening with a strange, dewy moisture. He inhaled sharply, probably in shock at her vulgar display.

Eadyth bent her head in shame, and a hot tear slid down her cheek and onto his hand which lay on her exposed thigh.

"Eadyth! Why do you weep?" he exclaimed softly, picking her up off the horse by the waist and standing her in front of him. Putting a fingertip under her chin, he lifted her face and asked again in a puzzled tone, "Why are you crying?"

Tears were streaming from her eyes now. "Because I am ashamed."

"Of what?" he asked with surprise. "The way I touched you?"

"Yea, but more than that . . ." Her words trailed off. She could not finish her shameful confession.

Eirik cocked his head quizzically, and then his face brightened with understanding. "Oh, Eadyth, there is no shame in a woman's passion, especially with her wedded mate. Look how my body shows its need for you, and I am not at all ashamed."

"Anything so pleasurable must be a sin. And I am as perverted as you, for surely women would be shouting the news to the world if they were getting as much ... as much ... delight from a man's touch. Sweet Mother of God, you turn me mindless with your devilish fingers. Mindless! Oh, I will never be a good chatelaine again, or manage my business affairs wisely, knowing I am as weak as any other woman.''

"It pleases me immensely to know that my touch makes you mindless," Eirik said softly, and for once he was not laughing at her in boast. "And somehow I think you will manage to be as strong-willed as ever."

He pulled her toward a flat, grassy plot away from the stream and threw his wide mantle onto the ground. Then he removed his silver belt and sat down, slipping off his short leather boots.

"What are you doing?" she asked, wiping the last of her tears with the sleeve of her gown.

He drew his tunic over his head and stood before her, bare-chested and barefoot. "Taking off my garments."

He undid the laces of his braies and was about to pull them down when she cried out in alarm, "Why?"

"So I can make love to my wife, good and proper," he said matter-of-factly and dropped his leggings to the ground.

"Here?" she squeaked out. "Outdoors? In the daylight?"

He just grinned and nodded, then stood before her with maddening boldness, totally naked. She saw more bare skin than she had ever seen on a male, from his wide shoulders to his tapering waist and slim hips, past a staff so erect she thought he might burst, to long muscled legs and narrow feet. He held out his arms to her in invitation, and Eadyth thought she might just die.

The man was outrageously handsome. And he was her husband. And her body thrummed with the hot fires he had ignited with his flaming touch. And she wanted him. And she didn't want him. And, oh, Lord.

He smiled enticingly and crooked a finger, coaxing her closer.

The intense physical awareness building between them resonated in the stillness of the silent glen.

How could she surrender?

How could she not?

Hesitantly, Eadyth moved one step closer. "You have ensorcelled me," she whispered.

"Yea, but 'tis a sweet enchantment." He gave her a soft smile that set her pulses racing, and she stepped a little closer.

She loved the fact that he was not forcing her to mate with him, that he gave her the choice. Not that she had any choice now, really. A new inner excitement filled her with wonder. "You make me . . . uninhibited, out of control."

Eirik's lips quirked with humor. "Ah, Eadyth, do not lay that sin at my door. You were uninhibited long afore we met. You just channeled your passion in other directions."

"Oh."

" 'Tis naught to be shamefaced about, my lady. A woman's lack of inhibition is a man's pleasure."

"Really?"

"Really."

Eirik gazed at his wife and knew the time for talking was over. His patience and his self-control were wearing thin. "Come, Eadyth, 'tis past time." He reached out a hand to bridge the gap between them, and she allowed him to pull her forward into his arms, finally. He sighed deeply with satisfaction.

"I feel as if a million butterflies have jolted to life in my stomach and are threatening to break through my skin," she confessed shakily, her warm breath caressing his neck.

Eirik felt a jolt of his own, between his legs. He chuckled against her hair, her wild mane of silver blonde curls, and wondered how he could have ever been so blind to her beauty. "Butterflies are good," he said, pulling back to gaze at her. "Let us see what we can do about freeing them."

He removed her gown slowly and forced her to stand still while he feasted on her beauty. Her hair tumbled carelessly about her shoulders and down the smooth skin of her straight back, matching the tight curls of her nether mound. Eadyth was tall and long-legged, with a narrow waist and breasts just big enough to fill a man's hand. She pressed her finely defined lips together nervously, calling attention to the delightful mole.

"You are so beautiful," Eirik said in wonder, "and you are mine."

"I have marks on my stomach from giving birth," Eadyth said shyly, trying to be honest about her defects, under his intense scrutiny.

"Yea, but your breasts are glorious."

"The nipples are too large."

Eirik almost choked on his tongue. "Nay, I do not think they are too large," he told her when he calmed his senses to the point where he might not spill his seed upon the ground.

"Truly?"

"Truly. They are just right to fill a babe's mouth for suckling. Or a man's."

Her eyes lit up at that, but then she bit her bottom lip in hesitation before adding with misery, "But my breasts do not wobble."

"Wobble?" He burst out laughing then. "What do you mean, wobble?"

"Bertha says men like women with wobbling breasts."

"And you suddenly take advice from Bertha? Ah, Eadyth, I think I am going to enjoy having you for a wife."

"Mayhap I will not hate having you for a husband, either," she added with sudden impishness.

He reached forward and touched the enticing mole above her full mouth, then traced her parted lips with the pad of his thumb. All humor ended as he lowered his lips to hers.

At first, his kiss was gentle, persuasive, but when she accommodated him with open, eager curiosity, his lips turned hard and searching. Eadyth returned his kiss with reckless abandon, even when he plunged his tongue into her moist depths. Pleasure, pure and explosive, burst through his body, and Eirik sank to the mantle on the ground, taking Eadyth with him.

She lay on her back, looking up at him expectantly, and Eirik felt a long-dead part of his heart begin to stir. "Oh, Eadyth, do you realize how much I want you?"

Her mouth curved into an unconscious smile of age-old femininity.

"You like that, do you, having me under your thumb?" he asked with a growl, skimming the smooth skin of her belly with an open palm. Then his hand moved lower, toward her hidden depths.

She gasped. " 'Tis more like you having the controlling thumb, methinks."

He smiled. "Open your legs for me, sweetling."

When he knelt between her legs, looking at the honeyed folds of her womanhood, Eadyth blushed and turned her head aside. "You make me ache."

"I do?"

She nodded, then gasped as his fingers found the swelling bud in her center.

"And does it hurt, this ache?"

Shaking her head in silent negation, she tried to close her legs. " 'Tis too much," she cried when he refused to stop the fluttering of his fingertips against the blossoming nub.

"Nay, 'tis not nearly enough," he said rawly, not sure how much more of the "ache" he could stand himself. "Sweet Lord, you are like warm honey flowing over my fingertips."

When he inserted a long finger into the slick tightness of her sheath, he could feel the tremors of her building arousal. Desire roared in his ears as her hips arched upward, seeking the fulfillment he knew she craved but did not understand.

He took his hardened staff in his hand and placed himself at her entry. With his other hand under her buttocks, he lifted her for his penetration.

The head of his staff had no sooner entered her gates than Eadyth shuddered with her own driving need. Small spasms clasped him hungrily and almost unmanned him before he even began.

"Come with me, dearling," he coaxed. "Let us make the journey together."

She gazed up at him with passion-glazed eyes, not fully understanding until he covered her mouth hungrily and embedded himself in her tight sheath with one long stroke.

"Oh ... oh ... o-o-h." Her hot, silky inner folds welcomed him with rhythmic convulsions that grew stronger and stronger as she reached her first peak of satisfaction, tossing her head from side to side. She whimpered helplessly in her need.

When the shudders finally faded into little ripples, she opened her eyes and seemed to notice him for the first time. She smiled shyly up at him, then tilted her head questioningly. "Why do you look as if you are in pain?"

"Because I am," he grunted out, still hard as a pike and embedded in her to the hilt, but not for long if she kept squirming.

He knew the moment realization of his problem hit Eadyth. "This is about that peaking business, is it not?"

He nodded. "Do not move ... yet."

The contrary witch made a low purring sound and arched her breasts upward, like the cat she was.

With a groan, he pulled himself out of her almost completely, and her mouth dropped open in amazement. When he plunged back in, she exhaled on a loud whoosh of disbelief. With each deliciously tortured stoke of his manhood into her heat, he slowly awakened the dormant sexuality in his siren of a wife.

"Tell me," he gasped out.

"I want ..."

"Tell me."

"I want ... oh, Eirik, you make me feel ..."

His strokes turned harder and shorter, and the extent of his prim wife's responsiveness stunned him. Thrashing her head from side to side, she whispered brokenly of her need. A floodtide of the most overwhelming pleasure he had ever experienced washed over him then, and he pummeled his wife with a hardness which would not be sated.

"Please," she begged.

"Soon," he promised.

"Will you come with me?"

"For a certainty. Ah, Eadyth, you are burning me with your woman heat."

"You set the flame, my love."

My love? Eirik exploded then with a roar of primal male satisfaction, his neck arching back as his manhood spilled its life seed into Eadyth's convulsing body.

At first, Eadyth could not move, so stunned was she by the new and marvelous waves of pleasures that continued to ripple over her.

"Eadyth . . . oh, Eadyth . . . you were wonderful," Eirik rasped out against her neck. "You take all I have to give and make me want to give you more. Everything."

"I was . . . I was satisfactory then?" she asked tentatively, remembering Steven's harsh appraisal of her lovemaking.

Eirik raised his head slightly. "How can you ask? You are everything a man could want, and more."

"Truly?" she asked, inordinately pleased.

"Truly." He lowered his head and laid his lips against her neck. Soon she felt the warm breath of his sleep against her skin. She was not offended. She felt oddly lethargic herself after all that "peaking" and allowed herself to doze for a moment.

Moments later, Eadyth awakened, still feeling wonderfully replete, still on her back with her husband's weight pressing her to the ground, his half-limp man part embedded in her.

She should have been repulsed now that the lovemaking had ended and her senses were returning to normal. She was not.

She should have felt crushed by the boorish weight of a man she did not want in her life. She did not. Instead, she felt oddly cherished in the cradle of his arms which held her fast.

She should have been appalled at her wanton responsiveness to the lusty lout who had bedded her. She was not.

So this is what it is like to be loved, Eadyth thought. For the first time in her life, she knew the power women wielded when they yielded. She smiled, arching her hips up sensuously.

'Twas time to awaken the lusty lout, and his wonderful lusty male part.

Chapter Fourteen

My wife.

Eirik flicked the reins of his horse and looked down with wonder at the woman sitting across his lap, her head resting against his chest. She had been fast asleep for the past half hour, almost as soon as the horse started moving.

Eadyth cuddled closer—God's Bones, the waspish woman was actually *cuddling*—and made a soft, purring sound of satisfaction. Well, she should be satisfied, after draining him nigh dry that second time. No doubt he had grass stains on his arse and claw marks on his back.

He was having trouble reconciling the prim and proper lady he had wed with the siren who had just proven more than a match for him in the love sport. Her innocent enthusiasm would be a joy to watch as it unfolded in this marriage he had resisted, but now looked at in a different light.

Leaning his head back, he tried to see her better. Her hair fell like skeins of spun silver about her head in wild disarray. Her lips, her finely defined lips, were swollen and bruised from his many kisses. And a pink, sexual flush hazed her creamy cheeks. The overmodest Eadyth would shudder with mortification if she could see herself, he thought with a chuckle, but he liked knowing his wife looked well-satisfied and carried the marks of his loving.

My wife. Eirik smiled to himself—unable to believe his good fortune. 'Twas like falling in a dung heap and realizing it was really gold. He doubted Eadyth would appreciate the comparison. Mayhap he would tell her anyway, he decided with a contrary chuckle.

Then he turned more serious. The Eadyth he had glimpsed today was the kind of wife he had longed for years ago—one who would provide a home and family for him, at the same time she was a sensuous and willing bed partner. Eirik tried to restrain his optimism. After all, this was how he had felt before he married Elizabeth. And she had proven a sore disappointment. 'Twas not good to raise one's hopes too high. Yea, he must tread carefully.

Eadyth awakened slowly to the rhythm of the horse beneath her legs and of Eirik's thudding heartbeat against her ear. She did not open her eyes at first, wanting to relish this sweet moment out of time.

'Twas not good to raise one's hopes too high. She knew that better than most women. But, oh, Sweet Mary, she had never dreamed the mating between a man and woman could be so glorious. *A husband and a wife*, she corrected herself immediately, with a contented smile.

My husband.

Eadyth wanted to sing aloud with joy at all the new, wonderful feelings rippling through her. And, at the same time, she wanted to hold them close, in private, to examine and cherish them, lest they prove fragile and unreal.

She wriggled her bare toes against the horse's side and knew she would have to get her emotions and her appearance under control before they returned to Ravenshire. The servants would never respect her if she failed to uphold a certain level of conduct appropriate for the chatelaine of a keep, even one in such poor condition as Ravenshire. But it was pleasant to be free of those restraints for now.

Failing to stifle a yawn of contentment, Eadyth drew Eirik's attention. " 'Tis about time you awakened. My men await us just ahead."

Eadyth straightened immediately and tried to whisk the wrinkles out of her gunna and pull her hair back into a coil as best she could atop the horse. "How do I look? I mean, do I look like—"

"You look fine," Eirik said warmly, brushing some pieces of grass off her shoulder. A small, self-satisfied smile tipped the edges of his firm lips. Lips which looked erotically bruised from her many kisses.

Eadyth put her fingertips to her own lips, realizing that she probably looked the same, or worse. She felt a hot blush rise in her cheeks.

Oh, Lord.

Eirik grinned triumphantly.

"My shame pleases you, does it?"

"Nay, but you do." He gave her a quick kiss and seemed about to say more, but the horse had stopped and Wilfrid was approaching on foot.

Eirik dismounted. "Stay here," he ordered tersely, already walking over to Wilfrid, who began talking animatedly to him in low whispers which she could not overhear.

When Wilfrid finished, worry etched Eirik's features. And alarm swept over Eadyth in foreboding. Eirik turned to her once again. "Stay here, Eadyth. I will return shortly." He started to walk away.

"Nay, I will come with you."

He spun on his heels and snapped impatiently, "I said to stay here, and I mean what I say." He was soon gone from sight.

Just like that, he dismissed her, ordering her about like one of his chattel. Eadyth fumed. Because he had breached her and drawn a sigh or two from her lips, he now thought her besotted and lackbrained with lust for him. Like all his other wanton women.

"Not bloody likely," she muttered, dismounting awkwardly from the huge beast which stood contentedly grazing on a lush patch of grass. She made her way over to a small group of cotters' wives with two small children and an infant, huddling near one of the huts. Like her, they were all barefoot.

"I am Lady Eadyth of Ravenshire. What is amiss?" she asked an older woman with graying hair beneath a neat cap. The woman began to weep, something she had been doing for some time already if her red-rimmed eyes were any indication.

"The demons killed all our cattle. Oh, surely, Satan sent his very own. 'Twas inhuman the way they tortured the animals so."

Eadyth shuddered with apprehension. The despicable affair smacked of Steven's hand. "Did you see it happen?"

"Yea, we did, and a more horrible sight I have ne'er seen in all me days."

"They plucked the animals' innards out whilst they were still alive," a young boy spoke up, "and they threw the bloody parts to their vicious dogs. Like wolves they were, the men and the dogs. And they held ol' Bess down and let one rabid beast feast on her afore she even died." The boy's big brown eyes glistened with tears.

"Hush, Howag," the older woman said, not unkindly.

"How will we survive the winter?" a young woman wailed. "The master sez we cannot even eat the flesh, fer it be tainted by the dogs."

"Your master will take care of you. He will replace the cattle and repair your damaged property," Eadyth assured them, lifting the crying infant from the woman's arms. It smelled of soiled swaddling cloths and sour milk, but she did not mind. She had not held a babe in her arms since John was young, and it felt uncommonly good. "The best thing we can do is start to clear up the mess here whilst the men take care of the dead animals."

"But will the master agree to what ye say?" the old

woman asked. "He has ne'er taken such interest in us afore."

"I say that it will be done," Eadyth said in a clipped voice, "and my word is enough."

The woman looked skeptical at Eadyth's assuming so much command but said nothing more.

Eadyth surveyed the clearing, clucking with disgust at the broken plows and overturned wagons that the vandals had destroyed wantonly in their retreat. Already she could smell the acrid odor of burning flesh as Eirik and his men set afire the slaughtered animals. Such a waste!

She gave the babe back to its mother, telling her to care for the infant's needs first. Then she ordered the women and children to help her set the small cluster of homes to rights. She sent Howag to Ravenshire, warning him to take the open road for safety, and told him to instruct Bertha to send a cow and a wagonload of feed and food supplies.

When the men returned an hour later, all the debris had been swept into two piles—one containing reparable items, and one which would need the men's work. A huge cauldron of rabbit bones and vegetables stewed in a savory broth, and flat, unleavened manchet bread baked in the hot coals of the open fire.

Eirik washed his bloody hands at a bucket near the well, then splashed water in huge handfuls onto his face, combing his hair back with his fingers. Suddenly, his eyes widened with surprise as he took note of Eadyth's presence across the clearing. His surprise soon turned to displeasure, however, when the old woman approached him, speaking hurriedly. Eirik glanced Eadyth's way intermittently as the woman talked to him.

When the woman left, Eirik regarded her questioningly. Then he walked over to Eadyth lazily, only the flare of his nostrils betraying his anger. He put an arm around her shoulder and pulled her to his side, whispering against her hair, "You did not obey my order to stay with the horse."

"You have been gone more than an hour. Did you expect me to grow hooves and nibble on the grass all that time?"

"You miss the point. You disobey my orders at will, and that I cannot abide."

"I do not take orders well," she conceded, not wanting to argue with Eirik, especially after their recent lovemaking.

"That is an understatement," he growled. "Didst you make promises on my behalf to the cotters' wives?" Apparently, that was what the woman had been discussing with Eirik.

"Yea, I did," she admitted, suddenly realizing how inappropriate that would seem to Eirik, "but I assure you, I pledged naught that you would object to, my lord."

"Oh? So now you read my mind, as well?"

Eadyth tried to shrug off Eirik's arm which held her fast to his side. "Do not be so testy. I did what had to be done. You are just too stubborn to recognize that a woman can think for herself."

Eirik's eyes scanned the clearing, seeming to notice the good work she had done in his absence. "Even though you disobeyed my orders, I thank you for helping with the women."

Eadyth felt an uncommon satisfaction in knowing she had pleased him in this small way, despite the grudging manner in which he thanked her.

"Was it Steven who enacted this bloody crime?"

He nodded.

"He gets more bold in his exploits, coming so close to Ravenshire. 'Tis a challenge to us, do you not think?"

"Yea. Methinks this festering battle betwixt Gravely and me will come to a head soon."

" 'Tis not just your battle, Eirik. Remember, he wants *my* child. He wants me to drop my appeal afore the Witan."

"Yea, but I am responsible for your protection now. Best you remember that, my wife." Eirik pulled her closer, his large palm caressing her shoulder intimately as he spoke. And Eadyth realized suddenly that everyone was watching them in amazement, no doubt because she was not the shrewish old crone they had thought her to be, but also because their stiff-backed lady was allowing herself to be held so possessively by the master.

Did Eirik do it deliberately, to show his mastery over her? Eadyth narrowed her eyes suspiciously, casting a sidelong glance at him. He smiled down at her arrogantly. The cad!

Should she clout him on the head, as was her wont with an unruly servant? Oh, she would like to clout him, for sure, for taking such liberties in public, but not here, she decided. He was just as likely to clout her back. Or kiss her.

Oh, Lord.

Later. Later, she would get back at him.

Eirik's men and the villagers were beginning to serve themselves from the cauldron, no longer paying attention to them.

"Release me, you brute," she hissed, squirming out of his hold.

He laughed mirthlessly. "You will come home with me now, wife," Eirik said silkily and held out a hand to her. "I prefer to sup in my own hall."

"Are you ordering me . . . again?" she asked testily, trying hard to ignore the tempting hand he offered to her.

"And if I am?"

His lips twitched with a condescending smile, and Eadyth was equally torn between wanting to wipe it away with a slap, or a kiss.

Oh, Lord.

"Then my answer is 'nay,' " she declared, lifting her chin in defiance.

"A wife should obey her husband," he noted in a cool voice, no longer amused. His hand was still extended to her.

"Says who?"

"The Holy Church, for one."

"Which is made up of men," Eadyth scoffed.

"Why do you fight that which is natural for a woman?"

"Woman surrendering to man is not my idea of natural."

"All I did was ask you to come home with me," he said, shaking his head wearily from side to side.

"Nay, you did not. You ordered me."

"Will it always be a contest of wills betwixt us?"

" 'Tis up to you."

Eirik studied her intently for a moment, rubbing his upper lip thoughtfully. "Will you come home with me?" he asked finally in concession.

"Of course," she answered brightly and entwined her fingers with his.

She thought she heard him mutter under his breath, "Blessed Lord, spare me from a contrary woman."

Eirik went to the pond to bathe with his men after dinner that evening, but Eadyth had a tub brought up to her chamber. She was just finishing her bath when he returned. With a small squeak of embarrassment, she sank deeper into the soapy water.

Eirik had not spoken with his wife since their return, other than small pleasantries during the evening meal. But he had much to say to her now, and she would not like the actions he felt compelled to take with her.

"Come," he said to the two male housecarls who followed behind him.

Eadyth cried out with dismay, "Get those men out of here! Get yourself out of here, as well, you lackbrain. Can I not even bathe in private now?"

Eirik ignored her screeching protests and began to pile all of Eadyth's garments onto the outstretched arms of the servants—her gunnas, undertunics, hose, mantles, every item of clothing he could find. Then he handed the men all of his own apparel and the bed linens. After telling the men to store the items in the adjacent bedchamber, he locked the door and deposited the key in a loop at his belt.

"Have you lost your bloody mind?" Eadyth shouted when they were alone.

"Nay," Eirik said, drawing a low stool close to the tub. Putting his hands to his chin and elbows on his knees, he gazed at his wife, trying hard to ignore the sight of Eadyth's damp curls cascading over the edge of the tub, and the curve of her breasts barely hidden by the murky water. Finally, he explained, "I am merely ensuring that you do not leave this room 'til we have come to an agreement, even if it takes a sennight. Or more."

"A sennight!"

Eadyth scowled at him in disbelief. He saw the moment her confusion turned to hurt, then rage, at his domineering act. In that moment, Eirik saw the new, wonderful relationship that he had envisioned flowering between them being nipped in the bud.

"Do not do this, Eirik," she pleaded softly, closing her eyes as if on a sudden wrenching pain. "I will never be able to forgive you, and I crave . . . harmony."

"I must, Eadyth. You force me into this position," he said, trying to make her understand. "From the day we met, you have challenged me, both in private and in front of my people. Your masquerade is just one example. Your flaunting my orders today and making decisions for me were just part of a series of acts I can no longer tolerate."

And there was another reason, one which he could not disclose to Eadyth. One of his cotters had overheard Steven of Gravely this morn as he boasted of a plan to kidnap the Lady of Ravenshire and hold her hostage for his son. Even now, Eirik's blood boiled and his fists clenched at the unspeakable acts Gravely had planned for Eadyth whilst in his snare.

Eirik could not chance Steven getting his depraved hands on Eadyth, and he knew his stubborn wife would never willingly restrict herself to the inside of the keep. When it came to her own safety, she was too lax. Oh, she would promise to take care, but the first time a new lamb birthed, or her bees swarmed, or she heard of a bargain to be had on some piddling product in Jorvik, she would leave the defenses of Ravenshire without a thought for her well-being.

"You make too much of my willful ways," she argued, interrupting his thoughts. She continued to lie immersed in the cooling bathwater, and he wanted so much to tell her that her willful ways were part of her charm. He wanted to pull her from the tub, into his arms, and resume where they had left off earlier that day in the glen.

But he could not. Not yet. "Willful! You underestimate your temperament, my lady. If I am to stay at Ravenshire, I must have the respect of my men and my people."

"But—"

Eirik held up a hand to stop her next words. "There can be only one master of a keep. And I am it, my lady."

She eyed him warily. "So I am to be punished for my headstrong ways. Is that what this prison is about?" she asked, waving her hand to indicate the locked room.

" 'Tis a prison only if you want it to be."

She raised an eyebrow skeptically. "Exactly what is it you ask of me?"

"We can discuss the details later," he said, reaching for a drying towel. "You are turning blue with cold."

She knocked the towel he handed her to the floor. "Tell me." Her eyes glittered furiously, and she panted through parted lips. Deliciously parted lips.

Could he tell her the truth about Steven and his fears for her? Nay, he decided, 'twas too dangerous a risk to take until he had more time to ensure her obedience. He must protect her at all costs. Steeling himself, he continued, "I will make all decisions related to Ravenshire—its defenses, its farms and crops, its cotters and thralls. 'Twill not be necessary for you to leave the walls of the keep. If you have aught to suggest about the management of Ravenshire, I will listen, of course, but the final decision will be mine, as it should be."

"And in your absence?"

"Really, Eadyth, you make too much of this."

"And in your absence?" she demanded icily.

This conversation was not going at all the way Eirik had planned. Oh, he had known Eadyth would protest his new rules, but he had not expected to feel so guilty. "You will confer with Wilfrid in my absence."

"Confer or defer?"

Eirik felt his face turn hot, and he refused to answer.

"And my beekeeping **business?** Will you take that away from me, too?"

"Eadyth, I am taking **naught away** from you. You should be glad I remove these burdens from your shoulders." Even he realized how weak his arguments sounded as he floundered for the right words. "You will be free to—"

"I asked you a question, husband. Please give me the courtesy of an answer," she sneered. "What about my beekeeping business?"

"You may continue to tend your bees and make your honey and mead and candles, but I do not want you going into Jorvik to conduct your business. 'Tis too dangerous. And unseemly."

"You bastard!"

Furious, she stood in the tub, swishing water over the sides, uncaring of her nudity. For one brief moment, Eirik's blood rushed to all his vital parts and his heart slammed against his rib cage as he glimpsed Eadyth's statuesque beauty.

But then she grabbed the small drying cloth, holding it in front of her body, and said in a calm, icy voice, "Get out. Get out of this chamber afore I kill you with my bare hands. I do not care if you lock me in this chamber for the rest of my life. I will never agree to those terms. Never."

Tears filled her luminous eyes, but she blinked repeatedly, stubbornly refusing to allow them to flow. Eirik felt as if he had been kicked in the stomach.

"I never wanted this marriage. I told you the first time we met that women lose their independence when they wed. I thought you were different, damn you." Then she added, more softly, "I thought you were different."

He reached out a hand to her.

She swatted it away.

"Eadyth, trust me, please. It may only be for a short time, and then—"

"Why should I trust you?" she shrieked. "And why for only a short time? Do you mean if I prove biddable, like a cow-eyed maiden? Or if I bow whenever you enter a room?

Or simper at every word of wisdom that oozes from your mouth?''

Eirik gritted his teeth, no longer feeling so conciliatory. "Let us go to bed, Eadyth. It has been a long day. We can discuss this more in the morn, when you are more calm."

"God above! You must have porridge for brains if you think I will sleep next to you this night . . ." A sudden thought occurred to her then and her face turned bright red before she continued, ". . . or spread my thighs for you, you miserable wretch."

"We will sleep together, wife," Eirik assured her, stepping toward her as she backed away, still clutching the ridiculously small cloth to her body, leaving her long legs and so much more exposed. He had a sudden inclination to feel those legs wrapped around his waist and that mouth moaning under his kisses. "Yea, we will sleep together. Furthermore, you will wear the one garment I have left for you."

"Garment? What garment?" She scanned the room and saw nothing except the beekeeping veil hanging on a peg. When understanding dawned on her, she choked out, "You cannot mean—"

"Yea, I can." He took the veil in one hand and a pair of shears in the other, deftly cutting a rough neckline in the fabric. He handed it to her. "Either you put it on, or I will."

Eadyth watched her husband as he turned away from her. Her eyes darted about the room, searching for an escape. Or a weapon. There was neither.

Reluctantly, she donned the wispy gown, which was worse than no garment at all. It covered her from neck to ankle and wrist, but its sheerness made her feel more naked than bare skin.

Eirik proceeded to light at least three dozen of her costly beeswax candles. Her lips curling ferally, Eadyth made a mental account of the number he wasted and decided to bill him for them in a few days. Hah! He probably considered them his property now. *Just like me.* She bit her bottom lip to stop the tears from welling in her eyes at that horrid thought.

Laying the tinder on a table, Eirik turned, and his mouth dropped open. He gaped at her in open appreciation as his eyes traveled from the top to the bottom of the revealing garment.

To Eadyth's satisfaction, Eirik did not look so cool and angry now. A wistful smile tugged at his lips. "I have been dreaming of you in that garment for a long time, afore I even knew of your beauty."

"Keep on dreaming, lackbrain, because 'tis all you will do."

"Do you think so?" he challenged, moving closer.

"I do not want you, Eirik."

"You wanted me earlier today . . . with a passion," he reminded her.

To her chagrin, Eadyth felt a blush heat her face. "I was besotted with lust then. Now that I know your true intent, it will not happen again."

"I say it will."

"So rape *and* imprisonment are to be my punishment."

"I have never forced a woman in my life and have no intention of starting now," he snarled, clenching his fists at his sides. "But, God's Bones, you tempt a man to violence with your shrewish tongue."

"You did not mind my shrewish tongue earlier today."

Eirik shook his head in amazement at her quick words. "Ah, but then your tongue was engaged in more pleasant duties. In truth, I had planned on teaching you a novel exercise for your tongue this eve." And he proceeded to tell her a most scandalous thing that men and women could do to each other with their tongues.

"Oh . . . oh . . . you really are a wicked man. When did you last attend confession? Surely, the priests must wring their hands with glee when you arrive in the confessional. No doubt, you are weighed down for weeks afterward with heavy penances."

"Always," he replied, unabashed.

Eadyth stared at him, speechless, trying hard not to imagine the scandalous sins he might have to confess.

Eirik raked his hands through his hair, seeming to search for the proper words. Finally, he stared at her levelly. "Eadyth, I would like to make love with you. Very much. Will you let me?" he asked in a low, raspy voice.

"Nay." *Dear Blessed Mother, keep me from being tempted. Dear Blessed Mother, keep me from being tempted. Dear Blessed . . .*

"Please."

Eadyth bit her lower lip and dug her nails into the palms of her fisted hands, trying desperately not to remember the way this wicked man had made her feel earlier that day.

Eirik stepped a little closer, and she almost moaned aloud at the sweet need she saw in his parted lips. His pale blue eyes swept her almost nude body like a delicious, sensuous caress. And every spot they touched turned warm and yearning. Eadyth felt herself weakening and tried even harder to resist his charms.

"Not even if you stand on your head, totally naked, and wag that tail that stands to attention betwixt your legs," she asserted brazenly, hoping to shock him away with her crudity.

Instead, he laughed appreciatively. "You will never let me forget that tale I told of the caliph and his mud ugly wife, will you?"

"That was not the caliph story, you dimwit. That was the merchant from Micklegaard, and his wife looked like the back end of a mule," she corrected him.

Eirik raised both brows. "The brilliance of your memory stuns me."

"I would like to stun you, all right. You and all the ridiculous stories you told me. Twelve times! You must have been laughing yourself into Kingdom Come at my gullibility."

"Twelve what?" he asked, puzzled, and moved a little closer.

Eadyth sidled to the left, uncomfortable with his nearness,

even though he had promised not to force her in the bedding. "Yea, twelve times, you dolt. You told me a man could . . . you know . . . that peak thing . . . twelve times. Hah! Two times was an ordeal for you."

"Oh, so now you taunt me about my manly capabilities, do you? A dangerous game, Eadyth. Very dangerous. Mayhap I planned to complete the 'peaking' thing when we returned to Ravenshire. After all, there are twenty-four hours in the day, and we only spent one hour in that glen."

Eadyth frowned, unsure if he was serious or teasing her again. He was rubbing his hairless upper lip in his usual manner, still missing his mustache, and she could not see the expression on his lips. Twelve times! Was that really possible? "Well, little difference it makes to me if you grunt and groan once or fifty times, it will not happen again with me."

"Grunt and groan! Really, Eadyth, you have a way with words that is not seemly for a woman."

"You knew my language was unseemly afore you married me."

"But I did not know how beautiful you are, and now that I do, I want to make love with you."

Eadyth's heart skipped a beat at his enticing words. "Will you take away your lackwit rules?"

Eadyth thought she heard the grinding of Eirik's teeth.

"Nay, my 'lackwit rules' stand . . . for now. Will you trust me, Eadyth, that I know what is best . . . for now?"

"You ask too much," she said on a soft groan

He threw his hands out in resignation. "I will not beg." He turned then and walked away from her toward the bed.

Her eyes widened, but she could not turn away when he sat down and removed his leather boots, then drew the wool tunic over his head. He held her eyes the whole time as he stood and unlaced his braies, letting them drop at his feet.

Eadyth gave a quick intake of breath at his wonderful body, with all its hard surfaces of muscle and sinew, silky hair and masculine curves . . . and hard, hard manhood standing out in invitation to her. She should close her eyes to shut out the temptation. She did not.

"I know how Eve felt in the Garden of Eden," she admitted ruefully, despite her better judgment.

"Tempted are you, Eadyth?" he asked huskily. "Are you likening me to Adam?"

She came to her senses immediately. "Nay, the snake."

He chuckled softly and lay down on the soft mattress, watching her.

"I cannot sleep next to you."

" 'Tis your choice. Sleep on the stool, or on the floor, or in the bed. I already promised not to touch you against your will."

Eadyth moved closer to the bed and removed her veil-gown. Then she edged herself onto the mattress on the far side, complaining, "There are no bed linens. What will I use if it turns cold?" She immediately regretted her words.

"Mayhap you can seek my body heat. I swear my skin is hotter than Hades right now."

"I would rather grow icicles on my nose," she declared stubbornly. "And best you keep that icicle of yours on your own side of the bed."

He laughed. " 'Tis more like a hot poker right now."

She made a sound of disgust and turned onto her stomach, burrowing into the mattress as she tried to get comfortable. "I cannot sleep without a bed linen covering me."

"I could cover your cold body with my 'hot poker'."

"You are as vulgar as a hog in heat."

"Do hogs go into heat? Or is it sows? Hmmm. I did not know that. But then you know so much more about these domestic matters."

"How would I know if hogs go into heat?" she exclaimed sharply, her nervousness gaining the better of her emotions.

He chuckled.

The boor.

"Did you know that hogs have a cock shaped like a

twisted, spiral bore, and that it grows to be as long as a man's arm when it is erect?''

"Liar."

"I swear, 'tis the truth. Ask any farmer. And then there are turtles, of course. Did you know that their male parts turn inside out in the mating? And Tykir told me once that he met a man who had two, but I do not know if I believe that.''

"Oh, you are outrageous! I am not listening to you anymore. So go to sleep," she said, putting her hands over her ears. "Go and snore your head off.''

"Mayhap I will pleasure myself, instead.''

She gasped and turned angrily on him, revealing that she could hear his words even with her hands over her ears.

He lay with his hands folded behind his head, grinning arrogantly back at her, his manhood standing up in the air. "Did you want to watch?''

Her mouth dropped open. In truth, she did not really know what he meant, but she was sure it was perverted. "You look . . . foolish," she declared, waving a hand at his nether parts, but refusing to look again.

"Do you think so? Some women do not share your opinion.''

Eadyth turned away from him again, an odd tearing sensation pulling at her heart. He spoke of other women so easily. Would he go to Asa, his mistress, now that she'd turned him away? Or find another closer to home? Eadyth tried not to care. But she did.

Reluctantly, Eadyth recalled the sweet lovemaking Eirik had initiated that afternoon. The brute had taught her body how to respond to passion, something she had never thought possible. And she had allowed herself to hope that they could have a true marriage, one like she had dreamed of as a young girl.

"Eirik?" she asked softly.

"Yea," he answered, his tone equally soft.

"Can you not compromise? Cannot you allow for equality in this marriage? Would it be so bad to have a wife with a

270

mind of her own? I would not want to usurp your authority, just share it. Can you not agree to that?''

A long silence followed.

Finally, Eirik exhaled loudly. "Nay, not now. Mayhap someday, but not now, Eadyth. Not now.''

Eadyth's heart dropped. Clinging to her edge of the bed, she allowed the silent tears to stream down her face. So this was what the rest of her life would be like.

Eadyth did not allow herself to wallow in self-pity for long. In truth, her fate—a loveless marriage—was no worse than that of most women she knew, and better than some. Resigning herself, she tried to sleep, but could not. She tossed. She turned. Finally, she rolled over on her side and looked at her husband whose even breaths bespoke a deep sleep. Her lips curled into a sneer. How like a man! They riled a woman, made her angry and upset, then, in the midst of an argument, walked away or fell into a snoring slumber. Well, Eirik was not snoring yet, but he probably would. The mule!

And this coupling thing, Eadyth thought with chagrin, having thought about little else all day. Why was it a man's choice to make love or not make love? Why must men be the ones to initiate the loveplay and the women docilely await their whims? Those pleasures Eirik had made her feel that day . . . well, men, no doubt, kept this a secret from their wives so they would not demand more from them. It was one further way in which men controlled women, Eadyth decided.

But what if . . . hmmm.

Nay, I could not.

Well, why not?

He might awaken.

I could be very careful.

So Eadyth, ever the managing person, took matters into her own hands.

Chapter Fifteen

With supreme care, Eadyth edged closer to Eirik, who slept on his back, one arm thrown over his head. Through the light of the burning candles, Eadyth watched, fascinated, as he breathed deeply through parted lips. Even his breathing was enticing, sexual, Eadyth acknowledged with a rueful shake of her head.

Leaning her head on one elbow, Eadyth studied her husband's face. Fine laugh lines crinkled the edges of his eyes and the corners of his firm lips. She liked them. Yea, she did. The wrinkles added character to his face.

Now that she had become accustomed to Eirik's lack of a mustache, she decided she liked that, too. Some men looked better with a mustache because it hid thin, weak lips. Eirik's lips were full and sensuous, definitely not weak. Could she touch them without awakening him? Well, mayhap, very lightly. With the tip of her forefinger, she traced the sculpted edges and wished, very much, that she could press her lips against his. Not because she wanted to kiss the brute, she told herself, just to satisfy her curiosity about their firmness.

With reluctant admiration, Eadyth assessed the rest of Eirik's body, from his lightly furred chest to his big, narrow feet. With all its myriad scars, it was a soldier's body, finely honed with thick muscles and manly curves. Very nice. But then the loathsome lout no doubt knew that too well. 'Twas why he had such wordfame with women, she supposed. That and his talent for the "peaking" thing.

Just examining her husband's body had turned Eadyth's blood thick and her limbs heavy and aching. She looked down at her breasts, then over to Eirik's flat male nipples. How different they were, and yet the same. Tentatively, Eadyth touched a fingertip to one of his nipples. One touch was not enough. Checking to make sure he was still asleep, she leaned forward and enclosed one of the hard buds with the wetness of her lips. Then she stabbed it lightly with the tip of her tongue. She pulled away immediately when she thought she heard him groan. But, checking quickly, she saw that he slept evenly, though his parted lips had closed, and he now breathed evenly through his nose.

Carefully, Eadyth sat up, then knelt on her haunches. There was a part of Eirik's body she wanted to look at a bit more closely. Making sure he had not awakened, she leaned forward and looked at "it" curiously. Nestled over his male sacs, the limp man-thing certainly looked different than it did when standing at attention.

She touched it with her fingertips and immediately drew her hand back, as if burned. She almost giggled aloud. It felt so soft and squishy, like a giant worm.

Getting more daring, she reached forward and this time wrapped her fingers gently around it. *Oh, the skin is loose . . . and movable. How odd!*

Then "it" started to grow under her fingers. Eadyth gasped and released "it" carefully. Slanting a look sideways, she saw that Eirik continued to sleep soundly. He must have drunk a great amount of her mead at dinner. Then she turned her attention back down and saw that his man part continued to grow, thicker and longer. Now the skin tightened like smooth

273

marble and glistened. 'Twas like magic.

Well, not magic, really. Eadyth had lived in a household of rough men for too many years not to have heard of "morning lust" or "piss hard" male parts. Apparently, "it" grew for many reasons, not necessarily just for mating.

This coupling business was all a puzzle to Eadyth, a wondrous puzzle, one she could not yet fathom. Even looking at Eirik's body made her feel strange, rather restless. Wanton. She wanted to touch all of his body, learn his secret places, what brought him pleasure. And she wanted him to do the same to her.

Why did he have to ruin everything with his silly rules?

With a deep sigh of regret, Eadyth knelt upright and was about to lie down and try to sleep again when she glanced at Eirik's face and saw his eyes, wide open and staring at her.

Their gazes held for a long, interminable moment. He said nothing, but his glazed eyes and parted lips told her of his desire. Still, he did not reach for her or ask her to make love with him. Then she remembered. He had told her he would not beg.

"I do not want to make love with you," she said defensively, then realized she was kneeling before him, naked. She sat and drew her knees up to her chest, wrapping her arms around her calves.

Eirik said nothing, but his ragged breathing spoke for him.

She slanted a look at him. "Men make such a pother about their bodies. I just wanted to see what all the fuss was about."

He snickered softly in disbelief.

"Well, 'tis true. Besides, men are always assaulting women, forcing their favors on them, making them submit. I wanted to see how it would be to reverse the order, to be in control."

"So why stop now?" he asked thickly, as if he had trouble speaking.

"Huh?"

"Making love is not about control, Eadyth. But if you think

274

you would enjoy being the aggressor, please ... *please*, be my guest.''

She blinked at him, not understanding. Then he leaned forward and lifted her over his body, high up, with her knees on either side of his hips. Before she could protest, he lowered her onto his hard staff, filling her, causing the walls of her womanhood to shift and expand to accommodate him. By then, Eadyth could not have protested if her life depended on it.

A light sleeper, Eirik had known the moment Eadyth moved to his side of the bed. With rigid self-control, he had forced his breathing to an even rhythm, his eyes to remain shut.

Eirik had counted to one hundred in his mind, trying desperately not to react to his wife's light touch. *Easy, easy*, he had told himself, and had been forced to start his counting over three times.

When Eadyth had taken his staff into her hand, Eirik had gritted his teeth. Surely, his eyes had been rolling in circles behind his closed lids. He had willed his body to stay motionless, but his staff had a mind of its own.

Eirik had lain with so many women he had lost count years ago, but he did not know how to handle this wife of his. She sat astraddle him, the hot sheath of her womanhood clasping him in welcome, her passion dew flowing over him like warm honey, but her pale violet eyes were wide with fear and confusion.

''I suppose you think you have won,'' she said.

''Won what?'' he asked on a groan, having difficulty reining in his body's raging need.

''This war betwixt us. This need you have to control me.''

''Eadyth, you have me pinned to the bed with your woman heat. My bones are melting for need of you. If I do not touch you soon, or taste you, I fear my mind will splinter apart. Now, I ask you, who is controlling whom here?''

She smiled in satisfaction. The minx! Then she turned more serious. ''I do not understand what you are doing to me. You twist my passions 'til I can barely think.''

Good. "Eadyth, come here," he coaxed, pulling her down onto his chest. "Kiss me, Eadyth . . . do you hear me, just a kiss, that is all.''

"Hah! Just a kiss! I am not so besotted yet that I do not recognize a hot poker quivering in my belly.''

Taking advantage of the momentary lull in her hostility, Eirik rocked his hips against her moistness.

She made a small whimpering sound.

He grinned. *So far, so good.*

Putting his hands on her waist, Eirik lifted her slowly upward, then down again, showing her the rhythm.

"Oh.''

He inserted a finger between their bodies, playing a rhythmic tune with her slickness.

"I . . . do . . . not . . . want . . . this," she gritted out, but opened her legs wider for his ministrations.

He removed his hands and forced them to his sides. "Then take yourself off me. I will not force you," he reminded her.

"If I agree this once, do not think it sets a pattern. It would be just this once. No more.''

Once! Hah! Well, once at a time, mayhap. Once an hour. Once an hour, every hour, 'til I get my fill of you. "Whatever you say, Eadyth," he said meekly, smiling inwardly.

She inclined her head in compliance.

And he let her have her way with him.

Eadyth proved to be a quick learner, and she taught him a few lessons, as well. Once she mastered the rhythm, she rode him with wild abandon. Her eagerness excited him immensely. Her lack of inhibition was a marvel to behold. And Eirik felt blessed by the gods.

When he lay depleted and immensely satisfied under her, Eadyth asked softly, while she nibbled contentedly on his ear, "Did I hurt you?''

And Eirik laughed, and laughed, and laughed . . . until Eadyth bit him on the shoulder. Which set him to thinking of other things she could do with her teeth.

Cradled in each other's arms, they finally slept. During the night, Eirik sought his wife again. This time, they came together slowly, with gentle strokes and soft words. They climbed the mountain of passion at a leisurely pace, prolonging the anticipation with sweet torture. Then they both tumbled mindlessly into a whirlpool of intense convulsions.

At the end, he cried triumphantly, "You are mine." And, of course, Eadyth disagreed, claiming, "Nay, you are mine."

Eirik awakened before dawn with a smile on his face. He looked down at the woman sleeping in his arms, cuddled against his warmth. He kissed the top of her silky hair, gently, and thought about rousing her with a kiss of her "other" hair. That was a delight to which he had not yet introduced his new wife. Nay, he would wait until she was awake and he could see her reaction to that deliciously scandalous exercise.

Besides, another hunger pulled at him, as well. Eirik decided to go down to the kitchen and bring up some food to share with his wife. Then they would talk. Nay, he corrected himself with a smile. They would make love again, and then they would talk and come to an understanding.

He pulled on a pair of braies and walked barefoot through the dark, silent halls. When he entered the kitchen, he put a taper to a wall torch, ignoring Bertha's loud snores from her pallet in the corner. He placed some bread and hard cheese and several slices of cold venison onto a wooden trencher and poured a large goblet of mead. Then he headed through the closed corridor toward the great hall.

"So your new wife does not satisfy all your hungers, my brother."

Eirik jumped and almost dropped his platter.

"Bloody Hell, Tykir, what are you doing, skulking about these dark halls? I thought you left for Haakon's court long ago."

"I was delayed in Jorvik," he said, rolling his eyes, as he lit a wall torch. "I come with urgent news from Rain's House, the orphanage in Jorvik."

"Rain's House? Oh, nay, say it is not Emma! Does my

277

daughter ail? Is there trouble?''

Tykir nodded. ''Urgent trouble. There is spreading fever at the orphanage—mayhap the bloody pox. Rain and Selik have sent Emma and the other children to Gyda's house, awaiting your word.''

''Does Emma have the pox, as well?'' Eirik asked with a shudder of fear.

''Nay. At least, not yet. I did not know if you would want her here at Ravenshire. You have not indicated an interest in having the child here afore. But, my brother, 'tis unfair to leave her in Gyda's home, good friend that she has been to our family. You must go to her at once.''

''Yea. Gyda must be sorely overtaxed having all those children about. Should I bring the orphans here?''

''Nay, you cannot,'' Tykir advised quickly, ''not with the threat of Steven abounding. And another thing, Eirik. Rain says Emma is beginning to regain her voice, and her memory. There may be hard times ahead for her when she recalls all that happened to her and her mother.''

Eirik inhaled deeply with understanding. ''Will you return with me to Jorvik, Tykir?''

Tykir nodded. ''I will ready the horses. Can we depart within the hour?''

''Yea.''

Eirik went back to the kitchen and awakened Bertha, giving her instructions, telling her he expected to be back by nightfall. Then Eirik returned to his bedchamber where Eadyth still slept deeply. He laid the trencher on a table and dressed quietly.

He considered waking his wife and telling her about his daughter and his concerns. But he knew Eadyth would want to travel with him, or leave this bedchamber in his absence. They needed to talk before he could allow either, and there was no time for that. So he kissed her lightly on the lips, and locked the bedchamber door after him.

Eadyth awakened later that morning, stretching lazily. She was not surprised that Eirik no longer lay at her side. She could tell by the slant of sun through the arrow slits that it was already well past dawn. Blessed Lord, she had not slept this late since her childhood, Eadyth thought, yawning widely.

She donned the beekeeper veil, grimacing at her only choice of garment. Well, she would get her other clothing back soon, after she broke her fast. She noticed the trencher of food on the table then, and smiled at Eirik's consideration.

After she ate, reliving in her mind the wondrous events of the night before in Eirik's arms, Eadyth walked to the door, hoping to slip to the next room unseen and gather her garments. The door did not open. She turned the handle again, to no avail.

Realization dawned slowly on her. The bastard had locked her in his bedchamber.

She would kill him. She would throttle him with this damn beekeeping gown. Oh, the humiliation of it all! After all she had ''surrendered'' willingly to her husband yestereve, he still intended to enforce his loathsome rules.

She began banging on the door, shouting shrilly. When the door finally opened, Bertha stood there, hands on hips. A guard stood behind her in the hall, barring Eadyth's exit.

Eadyth scooted behind the door to hide her sheer gown. Then she peered around at Bertha. ''Where . . . is . . . my . . . husband?'' she demanded, spacing her words evenly. Rancor gave a sharp edge to her voice.

''He went to Jorvik,'' Bertha informed her.

''Jorvik?'' Eadyth had not expected that. ''Why?''

Bertha shrugged. ''How would I be knowin'? He said he would be back by nightfall, and he said to keep you locked in his bedchamber 'til he has a chance to talk to you. Said ye should rest a mite.'' Bertha leered with her last words.

''Tell me what you know about Eirik leaving so suddenly for Jorvik,'' she ordered sternly.

''I already told you, I know naught of his intentions.'' Her eyes widened with sudden insight, though, and she ducked her head sheepishly.

''What? What is it you have thought of?''

''Well,'' Bertha said reluctantly, ''his mistress Asa does live there. Mayhap he felt a sudden inclination to visit with her.''

Like ice water dashed in her face, sudden and devastating realization swept over Eadyth. She shook with the impact.

Closing the door on Bertha and the guard, she listened, uncaring, as the key turned in the lock. A raw and overwhelming grief flooded her, and her throat ached with defeat.

Betrayal! Again! When will I ever learn? First he puts me under his thumb with his lustful sorcery. Then he tosses me aside like yesterday's porridge. How will I bear the pain?

And, most important, how will I escape?

Eadyth spent exactly two hours feeling sorry for herself. She knew because one of her costly 24-hour candles that Eirik had lit the night before was still burning, wastefully.

She wept.

She berated herself for being a fool.

She despaired that her shattered heart would ever be the same again.

She was starting to love Eirik. *The lout!* She was starting to hate Eirik. *The lout!*

She cried at her conflicting emotions. She pulled at her hair when she could not stop thinking about the sweet life she had envisioned. A fleeting gift—cherished for a moment, then lost.

Then Eadyth got angry.

She called Eirik every foul name she could think of, and then had to listen to Abdul repeat each word, with infuriating precision, back to her.

She threw the wood trencher and all its remaining food against the wall. Then, failing to find anything else to throw, she tore apart the mattress and threw the straw stuffing about the room.

When she finally calmed down, hours later, Eadyth was her old self again. Cool. Sensible. A little wiser. And fit to kill.

Late afternoon shadows danced through the arrow slits as she plopped down with a whoosh of flying straw onto the remains of Eirik's bed. And she began to plan.

*Well, I have fallen for the soft words of a deceitful man
once again. So that just means I am weaker than I thought.
But now that I know my weakness, I must strengthen my defenses. How do I do that? Hmmm. I will have to get away—
for a time, at least—from Eirik and his seductive
tongue . . . and lips . . . and hands . . . and . . . oh, Lord!*

*Mayhap I could go back to Hawks' Lair. 'Twould not be
unsafe if I took enough guards with me. Then, when I am
stronger—when my bones do not melt at his mere glance,
when my heart does not leap at his slightest touch—then I
can confront Eirik with new terms for this marriage of ours,
which is not really a marriage, after all. First, I will have to
escape Eirik's prison. But, Sweet Mary, how will I ever escape the pain of my breaking heart?*

With renewed determination, she picked up one of the
heavy side supports which had splintered off Eirik's bedstead
in her tirade and walked to the door.

"Brian . . . Brian, is that you out there?" she called
sweetly.

"Yea, mistress," the guard answered tentatively. "Did ye
get the message I slipped under yer door? Ye were makin'
so much noise I did not know if ye heard me."

"Message? What message?" Eadyth looked down and saw
a piece of parchment on the floor, half buried in the scrambled
rushes. Unsealing it, she read the note Eirik had sent to her
from Jorvik.

> *Eadyth,*
> *I have been delayed. Expect my return tomorrow
> afternoon. I bring with me a beautiful girl. I know the
> maid will captivate you, as she has me. I will explain
> all, Eadyth, and we will talk of those other matters
> we left unresolved. Trust me, dearling.*
>
> > *Your husband,*
> > *Eirik*

Eadyth leaned back against the door, closing her eyes on
the cruel pain which shattered her heart. *A beautiful girl! Cap-*

tivated! The brute did not even hide his indiscretions. A suffocating sensation constricted Eadyth's chest as she crumbled the note in her hands and tears slipped once again from her eyes.

Trust him? How could she do that? He wanted to rut with his mistress and, at the same time, have a wife waiting meekly here at Ravenshire for him, as well. Even worse, he would bring his leman to Ravenshire.

And how dare he call her "dearling" after betraying her so? She wiped her eyes with the back of a hand and wondered, with a catch of breath, what endearments he used for Asa.

Girding herself with resolve, Eadyth pushed herself away from the door.

"Brian, would you send Bertha up here with a broom and some cleaning cloths?" she called through the closed door. "I need to sweep up a slight mess in my bedchamber."

He muttered something, but then she heard him stomping off.

"Here comes trouble," Abdul squawked, and Eadyth shot him a glare. The parrot lifted his arrogant nose, ignoring her growling admonition. "Here comes *big* trouble."

Eadyth narrowed her eyes menacingly. She would have to do something about the rude, far-too-insightful bird. But not now.

Tapping her foot impatiently, Eadyth awaited Bertha's arrival. Very soon, the key turned in the lock. Bertha held the door open with her wide rump and edged inside, carrying the cleaning supplies. The door swung shut after her with a loud bang.

Bertha's mouth dropped open and her eyes grew as wide as cow pies when she turned, gaping at Eadyth's nude body bedecked in the transparent gown. "Oh, my Gawd! Wait 'til the others below stairs hear what the master has done to you! The wily devil! Not only does he lock his stiff-backed lady in his bedchamber fer his own pleasures, but he dresses her skinny body up like a harem slave." She burst into ribald laughter.

"Of course," she choked out, "if yer breasts wobbled more, he probably would have stayed at home with you, 'stead of traipsing off to his mistress. I wager *her* breasts wobble like a sweet custard." Bertha was bending over with infuriating mirth.

Eadyth felt no compunction then about pulling the board from behind her back and whomping the prattling wench on top of her head. The blow was soft enough to do no real damage, but hard enough to cause the robust woman to slide to the floor in a dead faint.

Grunting with exertion, Eadyth managed to pull Bertha's huge body over to the corner, where she quickly removed her drab gown. Taking off the ridiculous beekeeper gown, Eadyth tore it into strips and bound the cook's arms and legs and gagged her mouth. With haste, she donned Bertha's gown, not wanting to take a chance of being seen naked in the halls.

Then she cleverly lured Brian into the room by asking him to help her and Bertha move a chest. She dealt him the same fate as Bertha.

"Big, big trouble," Abdul opined.

Eadyth turned on the pesky bird, hands on hips. "How do you feel about cats, my fine feathered friend? Seems to me I saw a huge mousecatcher out in the stable, with a decided fondness for tasty wings and tiny tongues."

Abdul apparently knew when to shut his beak.

Satisfied with her work thus far, Eadyth whisked her hands together efficiently, then left the room, locking the door behind her.

Late the next day, Eirik and his weary guard rode into the courtyard at Ravenshire. Emma slept soundly, nestled against him in the saddle. In truth, she had not allowed him out of her sight since first she laid eyes on him in Gyda's house, whimpering alternately, "Father" and "home"—two more words than she had spoken in the past three years. A good sign, he supposed.

Luckily, it was not the pox which had afflicted the orphanage, but a much less serious fever. Eirik had helped Selik and Rain move the children back to their homestead outside the city before returning with his daughter.

Wilfrid approached him on foot and started to speak. "My lord, I would tell—"

"Shush," Eirik cautioned softly, putting a finger to his lips as he dismounted carefully. He did not want Emma to awaken in strange surroundings until he had a chance to forewarn Eadyth. He looked eagerly toward the castle and hastened up the steps with Emma in his arms.

"Please, my lord, I must needs inform—"

"Later, Wilfrid, let me put the child to bed first." And see my wife. *My wife!* Eirik was worried about his daughter and wanted to seek Eadyth's advice. In addition, he had thought much about Eadyth and their budding relationship during the past two days. He had so many things to tell her, and, most important, he found that he missed his wife fiercely, much more than he would have expected. He was too mistrustful of all women yet to call these new feelings love, but he was beginning to care deeply for his new wife. In time, mayhap . . .

After tucking his daughter into a bed in the guest room on the second floor, Eirik went to his own adjacent bedchamber.

"Eadyth," he called out softly as he unlocked the door. She was probably asleep, since it was barely past dawn.

There was no answer, and the room loomed blacker than Hades. Taking a torch from a hall sconce, he entered.

It was a shambles. Strewn about the floor were food, mattress stuffing, broken pottery, and pieces of his shattered bed.

But no wife.

"EADYTH!"

His roar could be heard all the way out to the bailey and beyond. And Emma began to cry loudly in fright.

Abdul began squawking, "Big trouble, big trouble, big trouble. Awk. Oh, Lord. Awk. Big trouble, big trouble . . ."

Eirik said a foul word and went to his daughter. After comforting her back to sleep, he sought out Wilfrid, who was fortifying himself with vast quantities of mead in the great hall.

"Well?" he demanded icily.

"She went back to Hawks' Lair and took her son with her," Wilfrid said all in one breath, as if he had rehearsed the words.

"And how did she escape my locked bedchamber? Fly through the window?"

Wilfrid groaned and put his head in his hands. "Nay, she cracked the skulls of Bertha and Brian."

Eirik's eyes widened in surprise. "She what? Never mind. I do not think I want to know . . . just yet. And where were you when all this skull cracking was taking place?"

"I was patrolling with a guard near Peatshire. Some strange men were seen skulking about." At the questioning rise of Eirik's brows, Wilfrid shook his head. "They were gone by the time we arrived."

"And Eadyth risked her life and that of John to leave Ravenshire? Why?"

"Well, she did order a goodly number of men to accompany her. So, to be fair, she did take precautions against Gravely. As to why she left . . . well, Bertha did hint that, mayhap, she might have led the mistress to believe . . ."

"What?" he asked impatiently.

". . . that you went to Jorvik to be with Asa."

"Bloody Hell! Whyever would Eadyth believe that?"

Wilfrid shrugged. "Who understands the turn of a woman's mind? But you left with no explanation to Bertha for your hasty departure, and I was not here to explain, and, well, you did hasten to Jorvik, and Asa does reside there, and—"

"I thought I told Bertha why . . . hmmm . . . mayhap in my haste I neglected to mention . . ." His words trailed off as he stroked his upper lip thoughtfully, deciding he might have neglected to inform Bertha exactly why he needed to rush to Jorvik. "Still, Eadyth should not have left Ravenshire against my orders."

"For a certainty," Wilfrid agreed, slamming his goblet down on the table for emphasis.

"Will ye lock her in yer bedchamber again with naught but a harem veil ter cover her bare arse?" Bertha asked hopefully behind him.

Eirik almost jumped from his seat with surprise at his cook's shrewish voice. "God's Bones, Bertha! Must you creep up behind a man without warning?"

"Ye mean like yer vicious wife with the heavy hand? Do you see what she did to me? Do you?"

Bertha's head was covered by a huge swath of linen, large enough to bandage an elephant Eirik had seen once in his travels.

"Gawd! All I did was laugh at her garment!" Bertha complained.

Eirik gaped at his outspoken cook. "Bertha, 'tis not your place to mock your lady."

"Well, you would think the lady would appreciate some helpful advice. Jist 'cause I remarked on her breasts not wobblin', as a woman's should, even in that scandalous garment, was no reason to split me head open."

"Wobbling?" Eirik and Wilfrid both sputtered out.

"Yea, wobblin'. Men like a little jiggle in the tits, you know," she informed them sagely. "And I have told yer lady wife so on more than one occasion."

Wilfrid rolled his eyes at Eirik, and they both grinned.

After listening to more of Bertha's complaints, Eirik dispatched her to start cleaning his bedchamber. "And stop repeating those tales about Eadyth's attire. She will not be pleased."

"Hah! Everyone already knows, anyway. We are all jist waitin' fer yer next move. I think puttin' her in a cage out in the bailey might be a nice touch."

Eirik ignored Bertha's unwanted advice and turned back to Wilfrid, more serious now. "I cannot leave Emma. She starts screaming at the least little start as memory of her mother's death comes back in bits and spurts. Take twenty of my men and go after Eadyth.''

''Now?''

''Yea, I want her back here tonight, even if you have to tie her to a horse to accomplish the deed.''

Wilfrid stood reluctantly, obviously not looking forward to the task. ''What will I tell her?''

''Tell her naught but that her husband demands her return. I can do my own explaining.''

''I will no doubt have to gag her,'' Wilfrid muttered as he walked off to do his master's bidding. ''And she will have my hide, in one way or another, in her own good time. No doubt set me to cleaning the garderobes. Again.''

Eadyth was, in fact, gagged and tied to the saddle of her horse when they arrived back at Ravenshire near dawn. As Wilfrid began to undo her bindings, she glared at him icily. She would deal with the oaf later. Right now, she had a knave to kill. A black-haired, blue-eyed knave. And he was nowhere in sight.

'Twas bad enough that Eirik demanded her return so peremptorily, but he had not cared enough to come for her himself. Truly he considered her mere chattel, Eadyth thought, trying hard to squelch a groan of despair. She must remain angry, not let the loathsome lout see how much he had hurt her with his betrayal and lack of caring.

Eadyth stomped up the steps as the new sun rose on the horizon, painting the sky a brilliant red. Servants gathered to watch her ascent, wide-eyed with curiosity, many of them giggling. She heard some mention veils and wobbling and knew Bertha's tongue had been at its usual work.

She entered Eirik's bedchamber without knocking. The empty room had been tidied, and a plump mattress and coverlet graced the newly repaired bed. All of the spent candles had been taken away and new, unlit ones—dozens of them—had been placed in their holders. Well, she would have something to say to someone about this waste of her hard-earned wares.

Turning on her heels, Eadyth was about to go back down the stairs and look for her loathsome lout of a husband when she heard a soft, mewling sound, like a wounded cat. It seemed to be coming from the guest chamber. Backtracking, Eadyth laid a hand on the door and opened it gently.

Eirik was sitting in a high-backed chair, cradling a beautiful, golden-haired child who wept softly in her near-sleep as she snuggled against his chest. Her vicious, loathsome lout of a husband was crooning tenderly, "Hush, sweet Emma. No one can hurt you now. Hush, now. Hush."

Eadyth realized, in that instant, that the "beautiful girl" Eirik had referred to in his missive was his precious little daughter. Eadyth put the back of her hand to her mouth in horror at her mistake.

Eirik looked up then, his furious eyes holding hers steadily. And Eadyth knew she would pay dearly.

Silently, without saying a word, Eadyth closed the door after her and went back to Eirik's bedchamber. Sitting on the side of the bed, she awaited her punishment, which was sure to come. She had challenged his authority one time too many.

Eirik entered their bedchamber a short time later, closing and locking the door, then leaning back against it lazily. The whole time, he held her eyes, his rigid face betraying none of his emotion, or intent. But Eadyth knew he was angry. Very angry.

Into the silence, Abdul decided to contribute his sage wisdom. "Lecherous lout. Awk. Seducer of virgins. Awk. Traitorous troll. Awk. Weak-willed son of Satan. Awk. Silk-tongued liar. Awk." All were delivered in a perfectly delivered imitation of Eadyth's voice.

She groaned.

"Huge cat. Huge cat. Awk. Comin' soon. Comin' soon. Awk. Dead bird. Dead bird. Awk. Awk. Awk."

Eirik's face remained rigid with fury.

"Eirik, let me explain—"

"Yea, that would be a start," he said with stony dryness and moved away from the door. He poured two goblets of wine and handed one to her. Despite the hour, Eadyth accepted the drink, feeling a tightening in her throat.

He propped a shoulder against the wall near the bed and waited, twirling the stem of the goblet in his hands with frightening casualness.

Eadyth drank the remainder of her wine in three quick gulps, then set the goblet on the floor at her feet. "I was angry that you locked me in your bedchamber after . . ."

She gulped.

He waited.

". . . after we made love," she said weakly.

"So you thought that if you seduced me in the night you could buy your freedom?"

Eadyth snapped to attention indignantly. "I did *not* seduce you. I mean . . . oh, why bother!" She shrugged. "Who started what is not the issue. I am trying to explain why I left this room—"

"—and cracked the skulls of two of my loyal servants," he offered icily, "leaving them for dead."

"I never did! I barely tapped them on their wooden heads, and they both know it. If they say differently, they are lying."

"So continue with your tale. You were angry . . . and?"

"I was angry that you locked me in, and then Bertha said that mayhap . . . mayhap . . ."

"Why do you hesitate to speak your mind now, wife? 'Tis not in character. Speak up in your usual shrewish manner and accuse me of my sins. Because, for a certainty, I have more than a few sins to lay on you."

She sneered at his condemning tone. "I thought you were fornicating with your mistress," she snapped.

"But, Eadyth," he said with mock sweetness, sitting down beside her in a predatory fashion, "you told me on more than one occasion to take my lecherous self off to Jorvik and my mistress. Do you suddenly care whether I make love with other women?''

She closed her eyes against the tears that began to well hotly and dug her fingernails into her clenched fists. *Sweet Mary*, she prayed, *do not let me break down in front of him*. She could not speak over the huge lump in her throat.

Eirik's fingertip traced the edges of her quivering lips, questioningly, and caught a fat tear that escaped her eyes. Then another.

"Do you? Do you care if I am with another woman?'' he murmured.

Was his voice soft with gentleness or suppressed anger? Eadyth wondered. She opened her eyes and nodded.

"Why?''

"I do not know,'' she wailed faintly, wringing her hands with dismay. "I wish I did. I loathe this weakness that turns me mewling and weepy-eyed.''

"I did see Asa whilst I was in Jorvik,'' Eirik admitted unashamedly, twining her one hand with his and pressing hard.

She stiffened at his words and tried to pull away. "You let me sit here sputtering an apology, when you were guilty the entire time. Oh, you are a brute!'' she charged, trying to slap him with her free hand.

Eirik took both her hands in his, forcing her to turn toward him. Conflicting emotions tore at him. He wanted to shake Eadyth for her willfulness. At the same time, he wanted to kiss her endlessly and forget all the problems that weighed him down.

"Do you want to know why I met with Asa? Would you hear the important message I had to give her?''

"Nay,'' she said stubbornly.

He dropped her hands suddenly. '' 'Tis just as well. I do not wish to tell you now. You do not deserve an explanation.''

"I don't deserve an explanation! Why, you—''

With a jerk, Eirik jumped up from the bed and began to

pace back and forth. He must maintain his distance from this sorry wench. Her nearness disconcerted him, the sweet mole near her luscious lips tantalized him, the smell of her lavender-scented soap drew him closer and closer.

"I am still angry with you, Eadyth." *Despite a part of my body that has forgotten why.*

"Well, I am still angry with you, too."

"Oh?" *Would you like to sit on my lap and "control" me again, Eadyth?*

"You imprisoned me."

"With good reason." *Perhaps that tongue that wags at me so could be put to better use. How about . . .*

"I can think of no good reason for imprisoning a wife, especially after . . . well, you know."

He barely stifled a grin. *I can.* She noticed his grin, and her face suddenly flushed. Apparently, her imagination was painting the same erotic mind pictures as his. Then his mood changed as he remembered what she had done. He decided to put a stop to her harsh recriminations.

"Steven is planning to kidnap you as ransom for his son," he announced bluntly. "And what he plans for your entertainment whilst under his 'care' does not bear repeating."

Eadyth gasped. "How do you know?"

"He was overheard boasting during his cattle-slaughtering spree."

As the implications of Eirik's words began to seep into Eadyth's dulled senses, she stiffened, then pulled her hands from his grasp and shoved her palms against his chest. "You thick-headed, dull-witted, lackbrained . . . oh, there are no words to describe you! You chose to imprison me rather than talk to me sensibly?"

When Eirik did not move or respond to her taunts, she raised a hand to slap him, but he caught both wrists and held her firm.

"You were 'imprisoned,' if you could call it that, for your own protection."

"Argh! How dare you lock me up like a timid, wooly-brained maid rather than tell me the truth?''

"I knew you would not obey my orders to stay inside the keep. And your leaving for Hawks' Lair, at the least provocation, just proves me right."

"The least provocation! I would hardly call infidelity 'the least provocation.' ''

He shrugged, and was pleased to see her face turn almost purple with rage at his seeming lack of concern.

"How would you react if your wife . . . if I . . . went off to be with another man? And locked you in a bedchamber to await my every whim?''

He did not even try to stifle his grin then. "Now, that poses some interesting possibilities."

His thumbs were tracing sensual circles on the soft inner skin of Eadyth's wrists as they talked. He felt the traitorous increase in her pulse under his fingertips as he spoke. And the flush that swept her face now was undoubtedly caused by his proximity, not her continued anger. He pulled her closer, against his chest, and wrapped his arms around her waist.

She tried to turn her expressive face away from him, but he cupped her chin in one hand and turned her back to him.

"You cannot continue to make decisions for me," she protested weakly. "I am not a child. Nor an untrustworthy wife."

"You cannot continue to ignore every decision I make," he countered, "as if I have no ability to run my own estates, or care for those under my shield."

They glared at each other.

"You will have to be punished."

She raised her chin haughtily. "I will not display myself for your pleasure in that wispy veil again."

He grinned. "That was not a punishment."

"It was to me. You have already made me a laughingstock with the servants. Will you lock me in this bedchamber again?"

"Not unless I am in here with you," he said with velvet promise. He considered the possibilities of such a shared confinement and felt an immediate thickening in his loins. "In truth, that is not a bad idea," he conceded silkily. "See, Eadyth, I do listen to your advice sometimes."

"I did *not* recommend our being locked together in a bedchamber," she asserted indignantly.

He laughed softly. "But, you must admit, it has definite possibilities. Hmmm. I will have to think on it more."

"I have to tend my bees, and see what havoc Bertha has wreaked in the kitchen in my absence, and—"

"I did not mean just yet, Eadyth. Tsk, tsk. Do not be overanxious. I know you seek a means to relieve that itch you have developed, but—"

"Overanxious? You are vile to say that of me! And what itch?"

He grinned widely from ear to ear.

Puzzled, Eadyth stared at Eirik's smile, which did not reach his angry eyes. Then her lips parted with astonishment and her face turned hot with understanding. "Oh . . . never mind. I see you are just teasing me about punishment."

"Nay, I am not. You will pay, and pay well, according to my terms, Eadyth. But I need your help with Emma first. Once I lock the door on this bedchamber—and I have decided that poses many opportunities for your 'punishment'—I do not want to be disturbed for days, not even by my needful daughter."

For days! A delicious tingle swept over Eadyth. *What could two people do for days?* But then his other words seeped in. "What is wrong with Emma?" she asked.

He proceeded to tell her of the six-year-old's muteness since the fire that had taken her mother's life three years before. "Her memory is coming back, no doubt prompted by the fever at the orphanage and the burning of tainted clothing and bed linens. She has even started to speak some words. But she screams and cries out at all hours of the day and night."

Eadyth forgot about her own troubles then and Eirik's continued anger toward her. "Tell me how I can help."

When Eirik was done, she nodded and moved toward the

door with him. Just before they went to Emma, he turned to Eadyth and said, "You and I have much unfinished business betwixt us, wife. Do not think I will forget what you have done. I have a long, long memory, and your tally sheet grows day by day."

Chapter Sixteen

That afternoon, Eirik returned from the exercise field with his men. Sweaty and exhausted from the physical punishment, as well as the mental anguish of the past days over both Emma and Eadyth, not to mention the lack of news from the Witan, Eirik proceeded slowly up the steps.

He stopped at the open doorway of his bedchamber, stunned at the domestic tableau. Eadyth was sitting on his bed with her back propped against the headboard. One arm was wrapped around Emma and the other around John. Larise and Godric sat cross-legged at the foot of the bed, facing his wife. And the mangy dog, Prince, lay spread-eagled on the floor, gazing up at Eadyth adoringly.

The children were listening raptly to a tale Eadyth was telling about his grandfather Harald Fairhair, once king of all Norway. "And Harald fell madly in love with Gyda, the daughter of the king of Hordaland. But Gyda refused to marry him unless he conquered all of Norway, a feat no man had ever accomplished afore."

"And my grandfather Thork was Harald's son?" Larise asked in awe.

"Yea, one of many, many sons. Some say he had twenty-six sons, and as many daughters."

Emma tugged on Eadyth's sleeve. "More," she prodded, urging Eadyth to continue the story. And Eirik realized there was yet another word his mute daughter had spoken, without thinking. He saw the light in Eadyth's eyes and knew she recognized the progress, too. Eadyth gave Emma a quick squeeze and continued.

"And Harald loved the fair Gyda so much that he pledged never to cut his hair or wash his body 'til he ruled all Norway and gained Gyda for his wife. So for years he roamed on his exploits, growing hairier and dirtier. Some called him Harald Mop-Hair then."

"He must have smelled like a bloody pig," John chortled.

"John! Watch your foul tongue."

"Can I forsake bathing and cutting my hair for years and years and years?"

"Nay, you may not."

"Tell us more," Larise pleaded. She and Emma were clearly enthralled.

Eirik shook his head in wonder. How could Eadyth have known it would please his daughters to hear of their family, especially when they had never had any family life to speak of? And where had his wife learned these stories of brave deeds and romantic entanglements involving one of his ancestors?

"And Tykir told me that your great-grandfather never cut his hair 'til the beautiful princess agreed to marry him," she exclaimed, finishing her tale with a flourish. "And that is how he got the name Harald Fair-Hair."

My brother! I should have known Tykir would weave a fanciful saga about our bloodthirsty grandfather. Eadyth neglects to mention how many wives and mistresses Harald mounted to beget so many babes. Babes who grew into vicious men who killed each other to gain the throne.

But Eirik did not break the mood for the children, or Eadyth. Instead, he leaned against the door frame, enchanted by this new side of his shrewish wife.

And inside his chest Eirik felt his heart expand and shift, and a yearning so intense it was almost painful rippled through his body. He had never had a home, even as a child. Always, he and Tykir were guests in the homes of others while his father pursued his Jomsviking duties and tried to protect them from their vengeful uncles.

Oh, to have a wife and children to care for! Who cared for him in return! What a wonder that would be!

A war of emotions raged within him. He did not crave wealth, and, in truth, had plenty. He did not covet vast lands and titles, just security and peace on his own small plot. How could he have plodded through these 31 years without realizing that the warm scene he saw in front of him right now was what he had been searching for all his life? Tears misted his eyes, and he started to turn away before he was discovered.

But John saw him and called out, "Father."

His heart lurched at the boy's easy acceptance of him, and Eirik was forced to hold out his arms when John rushed with a flying leap into his embrace, wrapping his skinny legs around Eirik's waist and his arms around his neck. Emma and Larise jumped off the bed, as well, and ran over, twining their arms around his legs. Godric, the orphan boy, stood to the side shyly, holding back Prince who was yipping and yapping, tail wagging like a fan.

His throat constricted, and at first he could not speak.

"Are you gonna teach us how to have a spitting contest now, Father? Huh? Huh?" John prodded. "You promised."

He remembered, with a chuckle, his playful boast days ago that, when he was a boy John's age, he could spit the straightest stream from the castle tower to the motte.

"Oh, John, you and your spitting!" Larise exclaimed condescendingly. His oldest daughter loved to lord it over John, though she was only one year older than he. "Father is going to show me how to dance."

Eadyth quirked her eyebrows in question. "Dance?" she mouthed silently.

He had no opportunity to answer her as the children demanded his attention. Soon he was laughing heartily as their youthful mirth blended around him in a warm cocoon.

"Larise does not believe you can pick up a piece of straw with your toes," John informed him, casting a scornful look down his nose at Larise. He looked a lot like Eadyth just then. Haughtiness, no doubt, ran in their blood, Eirik decided.

He glanced up and caught the amused eyes of his willful wife, who was moving off the bed, shaking her head at his foolishness. Their eyes connected and held. And, for a moment, he forgot that he was supposed to be angry with her for running off to Hawks' Lair. He just wanted to shoo the children from the chamber and lay his wife upon their bed. The fragile thread that held them in thrall grew taut with tension, then changed shape and grew stronger, pulling and binding them in a strange, new, compelling way.

"Or else we could have a pissing contest," John offered.

And Eirik's dulled senses jarred back to life.

"John!" Eadyth cried out. "How could you?"

Larise and Emma and Godric giggled.

"That is not proper language to use in front of ladies," Eirik said sternly, fighting to control his twitching lips.

John hung his head shamefacedly.

Abdul decided to contribute his wisdom then by shrieking, "Pissing. Awk. Pissing. Awk. Pissing. Awk." And Eirik realized, to his chagrin, that the word would no doubt be a permanent addition to the barmy bird's coarse vocabulary.

" 'Twould not be a fair contest anyway," Larise informed Emma authoritatively, in a sisterly fashion, "because boys have their barrel taps outside the body. Gives an unfair advantage."

Eirik looked at his daughter, then Eadyth, with stunned amazement.

Then they all burst out laughing.

*   *   *

A sennight later, Eadyth sat with Eirik at the high table, following the midday meal. "Thank you for your help with Emma these past days," he said, placing a hand over hers. "I see more improvement every day." He glanced at his daughter, who nestled in his lap, half asleep.

Eadyth looked down with alarm at Eirik's hand which lay casually over hers. His mere touch set her pulse racing, despite her continuing anger over the visit he had made to his mistress Asa. She tried to ignore the warm yearnings which grew stronger and hotter, day by day, especially considering the fact that they had not shared a bed since the night Eadyth had seduced her wretch of a husband.

She should pull her hand away. She should fight this mounting attraction. For the moment, she did nothing.

"Do you think Emma will ever completely recover?" she asked.

Eirik traced his upper lip distractedly, and Eadyth wished she could do the same. His lips were full and firm, masculine. And Eadyth knew too well how they felt when they moved expertly against hers, shifting, shaping, coaxing . . .

"What are you thinking?"

"Huh?"

"You asked me if I thought Emma would recover, and I said I see more and more progress everyday. Then I asked what you thought, but your eyes were glazed and you were staring at me oddly."

Eadyth shook her head to clear her muddled mind. "I am just tired. We both are. Taking turns sleeping with Emma in her bed. Waking every few hours when she screams out in her dreams. Having her cling to one or the other of us every moment of the day. It does take a toll. And, yea, she talks more now, and she seems happy, most times. Still . . ."

". . . still, she continues to cling to us, and the nightmares continue," Eirik finished for her.

She nodded. "If only we could get her to talk about the fire."

"I have tried, but every time I mention her mother or the

299

raid which destroyed her village, she puts her hands over her ears and refuses to listen.''

"Just imagine what horrors she must have witnessed, Eirik. Seeing her home, with her mother and grandparents inside, go up in flames. And she so young and unable to help.''

"Well, thank God she was able to hide in the trees 'til the villains left. She will get better, Eadyth, and then we can get back to normal business. And do not forget, my wife,'' he added, squeezing her hand and leaning closer to whisper in her ear, "we have unfinished business betwixt us.''

Her heart skipped a beat and she looked at him questioningly.

He winked.

The lout! "Of course, you are talking of Asa and why you felt the need to go to her.''

He laughed. "I am not. I refer to your punishment.''

"Oh, that.'' Eadyth waved her free hand, as if that were no longer of any concern.

"Do not think I have forgotten, wife. And do not think you will escape my wrath. I am planning a most sweet torture.''

Eadyth wet her lips nervously and saw his eyes follow the movement of her tongue, hungrily. She could imagine what he meant by "sweet torture." "Do not think you can hop back and forth between your mistress's bed and mine. Like a horny toad.''

"Horny toad! Now, that poses some interesting mind pictures. But tell me, dear wife, what will you do to hold me in your bed?''

She gave him a sidelong look of utter disbelief and tried to pull her hand from his grasp, to no avail.

"Will you 'attack' me again?'' he teased.

"I did not attack you.''

"You are right. 'Twas seduction.'' And he did not look displeased.

She felt her face color with heat, unable to deny his claim, and fought to control the swirling images in her mind of the scandalous things she had done. "It will not happen again, now that I know you left my bed for Asa's. I would not make love with you now, even if . . . even if . . ."

". . . even if I stood on my head, bare-arsed naked?" he finished for her, reminding her of his story once again.

"Even then," she said stubbornly.

An easy smile played at the corners of Eirik's mouth. "And if I told you that I did not?"

She stared at him, confused. "Did not what?"

"Make love with Asa."

Eadyth's heart lurched painfully at Eirik's putting into words her heart's torment. "Well, I am glad you brought the subject up, Eirik. I have been thinking that I treated you unfairly."

"Oh?"

"Before we wed, I told you that I would not mind your mistresses, as long as you were discreet. I should not have changed the rules now. If you really feel the need to—"

"Stick out your tongue," Eirik demanded sharply.

"Why?" she asked, shifting backward in her seat, away from him.

"So I can pull it from your prattling mouth, you lackwit wench."

"Well! Here I am being extremely generous with you, and do you appreciate my bigheartedness? Nay. You just—"

"Shut up, Eadyth."

"I beg your pardon."

"You should."

"Humph!"

"I told Asa I could not see her anymore. If you would stop wagging your tongue long enough to listen, you would know that."

Eadyth's heart leapt in her breast with hope. "Before or after you bedded her?"

He grinned and shook his head ruefully at her question. "Neither. I settled a sum of money with her to buy her own business and maintain her home. And I did not touch her enticing body, not even once." He leaned forward and

301

brushed his lips lightly across hers, teasing, tantalizing her senses.

Eadyth's heart began to pump wildly. Eirik's thumb drew erotic circles on her wrist where he continued to hold her hand. Surely he could feel her racing pulse.

"Do you object?"

She shook her head and cleared her throat. "No doubt I will have to sell a great many more candles and honey and mead to cover the expense," she said, trying hard not to succumb to the seductive magic of his fingers and imploring eyes.

He chuckled softly. "Ever the shrew, Eadyth! Nay, those coins came from my own pocket."

Then another part of Eirik's words came back to her, painfully. "So Asa has an enticing body, does she?" *No doubt her breasts wobble like cows' udders.*

The brute grinned, and despite her elation over his good news, Eadyth felt an uncommon urge to wipe the grin off with a slap.

"Well?" he said finally with a self-satisfied smirk. "Do you not want to know why I severed my ties with Asa?"

The magnetic pull of Eirik's pale eyes drew her to him, but she fought mightily, feeling her defenses crumble. "Because you found another mistress?" she offered weakly.

"Nay," he said, the edges of his lips tilting upward.

"Because Asa has grown fat and slovenly . . . and . . . and her breasts no longer wobble?"

Eirik's mouth dropped open in disbelief at her crude words. Then he recovered himself. "Nay, Asa is gloriously beautiful."

The idea of a slap to his mouth became increasingly more attractive. "Then why?"

"Because I have a wife who pleases me greatly, in the bed and out. When she is not disobeying my orders, that is, or masquerading as an old crone, or attacking me with bees, or nagging at me shrewishly, or demanding I do her bidding, or usurping my authority, or calling me foul names, or—"

Eadyth pulled her hand out of his grasp and put her fingertips to his lips, halting his words. "But that is all the time," she said on a groan.

He held her fingers at his lips, then nipped and suckled on the tips, one at a time, causing her to inhale softly with delight.

"Yea, 'tis," he agreed, "but I have decided to allow you time to change your waspish ways if—"

"If?"

"—if you will continue to please me in all other ways," he said smoothly.

And Eadyth thought *that* would not be such a sore fate.

John and Larise and Godric ran up the steps of the dais then, all speaking at once. Barefoot and covered with grime, they smelled like the stables. Normally, Eadyth would have chastised them. Today, it did not seem so important.

Emma straightened in Eirik's lap and brightened with pleasure, clearly wanting to be with the other children, but fearing to leave the safety of her father's arms. But then, all of a sudden, Emma jumped off Eirik's lap and ran to the figure following behind the children. It was Tykir.

Dressed in fine wool braies and a short-sleeved, knee-length tunic of a soft brown color, Tykir looked the fierce Viking warrior. His long blond hair hung down to his shoulders, but it had been braided off to one side to highlight a rakish gold loop earring. Wide metal armlets encircled the huge muscles of his upper arms. He walked toward them jauntily, knowing full well the handsome image he portrayed.

"Blessed Lord, I had best lock up all the maids in the keep," Eadyth muttered.

"And you call me a lusty lout!" Eirik responded, but with an affectionate regard for his brother.

"Uncle Tykir!" Emma yelled happily and threw herself into Tykir's open arms. Wrapping her thin arms around his neck as he twirled her in a circle, Emma giggled like any normal child. Her laughter rippled merrily around them, sweeter than a harpist's music. And Eadyth began to believe, finally, that Emma really might recover.

Eadyth and Eirik exchanged grateful looks.

Eadyth rose and gave Tykir a kiss of welcome, then slapped his hand away when he tried to pinch her backside.

"I thought you were coming back here days ago," Eirik grumbled. "I could have used your help training the new men and patrolling the northern reaches of Ravenshire."

Tykir shrugged. "We had a fiercesome storm in Jorvik and my workers could not complete the work on my ship 'til today."

"Does that mean you will be leaving us once again, now that your ship is seaworthy?" Eadyth asked. She liked her brother-by-marriage and, with all the problems she and Eirik had been having with Emma, not to mention their own disagreements and her agonizing over the ominous silence from the Witan, they could all use a little of Tykir's levity in their lives.

Tykir grinned in his usual rascally fashion. "Well, if I had known I was missed so much, I would have returned long ago. Apparently, I have not taught Eirik well enough how to keep a woman . . . happy." He jiggled his eyebrows at his frowning brother.

"Sit down, Tykir," Eirik muttered, "lest I teach you a few lessons in brotherly respect."

"Hah!" Tykir said, trying to ease into the chair next to them. It was difficult with Emma wrapped around his body— arms circling his neck, legs locked around his waist.

Eadyth stood and held out her arms for Emma, but the little girl shook her head vigorously and held on even tighter, whimpering, "Uncle Tykir."

"Women love me no matter their age," Tykir boasted unashamedly. "But listen, sweetling," he added gently, stroking the little girl's bony shoulders, "I must needs visit the garderobe. Let go, for now."

She refused.

And Eirik looked at Eadyth, offering her a quick, arresting smile, as if suddenly enlightened. He stood and snaked his arm around her waist, looking down at Tykir. "You know how you hate to sleep alone, my brother," Eirik said smoothly. "Well, you have a new *lady* to share your bed linens." He pointed at Emma, who smiled brightly, apparently understanding perfectly and having no objection to her Uncle Tykir taking the place of her father or stepmother.

"And, you, my lady wife," Eirik said, turning to Eadyth. "I have something for you." Searching the various folds of his surcoat and tunic, he finally retrieved a bedraggled green feather.

"What?" Eadyth asked, tilting her head questioningly as Eirik laid the parrot feather in the palm of her hand.

Eirik's eyes twinkled mischievously. "Since I abandoned you on the night of our marriage, and since we have had no time to ourselves since then," he said in a low, husky voice close to her ear, "you have my permission to consider this our wedding night."

"Permission?" Eadyth choked out, then looked down at the feather. "And this?"

" 'Tis your bride gift."

"A bride gift?" Tykir chortled. "What kind of bride gift is that? You have become tight-fisted in your old age, my brother."

Eirik ignored his brother's taunts and put his hand over Eadyth's. His eyes smoldered with some hidden message. "Remember the feather I demonstrated for you one day in our bedchamber and my promise that the exercise would continue?" he said smoothly, running the quill across her lips as a reminder of what he had done once before. " 'Tis time, Eadyth. Past time."

Then he scooped her up in his arms before she had a chance to protest and started to carry her off the dais. She squirmed and protested shrilly as Tykir and his men cheered and offered lewd suggestions.

"You are truly a loathsome lout."

"Yea, I am."

"And an odious oaf."

305

"Yea."

"A lecherous libertine."

"Most definitely."

"And a . . . a . . ."

"Do not forget horny toad."

Eadyth tried to push out of his embrace, but he held her arms firmly in his embrace. Then he called out over his shoulder, "Good eventide, everyone. We will see you on the morrow."

"The morrow!" Eadyth squeaked, giving up on her struggles and burying her hot face in his neck. " 'Tis only past noon now."

"Yea," he said, smiling with supreme male satisfaction. Then he added in a voice of silky promise, "I have twelve 'peaks' to climb afore then, and I want to get an early start."

"Twel . . . twelve! Oh, you are outrageous."

"Yea. That is one of the things women love about me."

Once they were in his bedchamber, Abdul began squawking, "Loathsome lout. Awk. Big trouble. Awk. Kiss my arse. Awk." Without hesitation, Eirik picked up the cage and deposited it in the hall, ignoring the bird's angry protests.

Then, with the door locked behind them, Eirik began to light the many beeswax candles scattered around the room. Eadyth's heart was beating so loudly, she was sure he could hear it across the room. She leaned against the closed door, almost light-headed from her thickened blood and heavy limbs.

Oh, Lord.

"You do not need candles now. 'Tis daylight outside," she remarked nervously, still propped against the door.

"Yea, but you know I have a vision problem. And I want to make sure I see *everything* today." He flashed her another of his bone-melting smiles.

Oh, Lord.

"You can see well enough when you want to. Do you know how much those candles cost?" she said, weakly searching for conversation, hating the sudden reticence that had overcome her once the door closed.

"Do you know how much I do not care?"

She started to reprimand Eirik for his spendthrift ways, then stopped when she saw him hop about on one foot, then the other, as he removed his boots. Then he lifted his tunic over his head. His eyes glowed with a savage inner fire as they held hers captive. Unable to look away, she watched as he released the ties on his braies and dropped them to the rushes, stepping out of them easily.

Boldly, he took his hardened manhood in his hand and said in low, strangled voice, "Do you see how much I want you, wife? Do you want me half as much?"

Twice as much, Eadyth thought as she felt a hot liquid pool at her center. The tips of her breasts ruched and ached. And he had not even touched her yet.

Oh, Lord.

"Disrobe for me, Eadyth," he entreated in a low, throaty voice. "Take off your garments whilst I watch."

And Eadyth surprised herself by doing as he bid. Shyly, she moved away from the door a few steps and undid the belt of her gunna, letting it drop to the floor. With the edges of her toes, she removed her leather slippers, then removed her overtunic and chemise.

She should have been embarrassed to stand naked before a man, but she was not. Eirik was not just a man. He was her husband. And the pleasure she saw on his face as his eyes scanned her body gladdened her.

"You are beautiful, Eadyth," he whispered rawly. And Eadyth did feel beautiful then, for the first time in many, many years.

"Touch the tips of your breasts with your fingertips, Eadyth," he coaxed, still standing a short distance from her. "I want to see your pleasure as you imagine they are my hands on you."

"Oh," she said on a soft whisper, but did as he asked, and almost swooned with the intense yearning that radiated, almost painfully, from her nipples.

"Now leave one hand on your breast and place the other at your nether hair. And tell me what you feel."

Eadyth felt a hot flush sweep her face and shoulders. "Desire," she whispered in embarrassment.

" 'Tis your body readying itself for me, Eadyth," he barely choked out, and closed the distance between them.

She tried to put her arms around his neck and draw him into her embrace, but he would not allow it yet. "Nay, sweetling, we are going to go slowly this time . . . very slowly." He kissed her lips lightly and took her hand, leading her over to the window well. "Stand here," he directed. Then placing her against the wall, near the light of the window, he positioned her arms so that her fingers were clasped behind her neck.

"Oh, I do not know if I like this," she protested. "Let us lie on the bed, Eirik."

"Nay, not quite yet. We are going to play a game first."

"A game?" she choked out.

"Yea, the feather game."

"I do not understand."

"You will. You will."

"And what do I get if I win?"

"Me."

She laughed scoffingly. "And what do you get if you win?"

"You."

Her brow furrowed in puzzlement. " 'Tis the same thing, is it not?"

"Oh, nay, there is a vast difference. 'Tis all in playing the game. Now, first off, you must not remove your hands from behind your neck. Not even a bit. Or you lose. And I may not touch you with anything other than a feather, not my hands or lips, or I lose."

"And how will I know if I have won?"

"When you 'peak'." He smiled widely as if he were the most brilliant man in the world.

"Peak?" she squeaked out. "With feathers? Are you sure? Have you done this afore?"

"Never, but I am absolutely sure."

Then he picked up the feather which she had dropped on the floor and began to trace her eyebrows, the lines of her nose, her mole, the edges of her lips. She closed her eyes with a sigh as the delicious caresses progressed.

"Nay, you must keep your eyes open," he said. "That is another one of the rules."

"Oh," she said suspiciously. "Do the rules change as we go along?"

"Mayhap." He moved on to the undersides of her upraised arms, down her sides, circling her breast. She held her breath, waiting. The circles got smaller and smaller as he edged the feather closer to the center of her breast.

"Do you want me to touch you there?" he whispered seductively.

"I will die if you do not."

"Well, we cannot have a dead bride on a wedding night, now can we?" he chuckled, and flicked the feathery edges back and forth over her pebbled nipple. Her hands almost slipped from behind her neck with the overwhelming pleasure that flooded her.

"Tell me," he urged in a passion-thick voice as he began to do the same to her other breast. "Tell me how it feels."

"I ache. I throb. I yearn for . . ."

"For what, sweetling?"

"Your mouth on me . . . suckling, I think . . . oh, I do not know."

"Soon, Eadyth, soon. Nay, do not close your eyes. Remember the rules."

She forced her eyes open and looked downward where his feathery torture had moved to her belly and inner thighs. "Why are those blue veins standing out on your man-thing? Does it hurt?"

Eirik made an odd strangling sound deep in his throat and leaned an arm against the wall, closing his eyes for a moment, as if to gain strength. When he opened them again, Eadyth asked with a knowing smile, "Do the rules say you can close your eyes whilst I cannot?"

"Yea, you minx," he said with a shake of his head.

Eadyth had no mind to tease him after that when Eirik employed his feather on her woman hair. Kneeling before her, he asked her to separate her legs, and Eadyth complied, mindless with yearning now as all the boiling blood in her body seemed to lodge in one tiny nub of sensation. Using the feather, he separated her folds and told her how she looked to him.

As his game progressed, Eadyth began to whimper helplessly, especially when he set the feather to fluttering, like birds' wings. The ache in her breasts and her woman folds grew and grew, almost to bursting, and Eadyth arched her hips outward, her legs stiffening. Eirik increased the pace of the flickering feather, rapidly, rapidly.

Eadyth wrenched her hands from behind her neck and put them on Eirik's shoulder for support as her knees grew weak and tiny spasms of pleasure rippled outward from her core. Bright lights exploded behind her closed eyes, and she moaned, "No more, Eirik. No more. 'Tis too much."

He dropped the feather and put his face against her taut belly. When he finally stood, Eadyth saw through her passion-glazed eyes that his manhood had grown enormous and a small bead of his seed stood out on its end. His eyes raked her body hungrily and ragged breaths came from her parted lips.

He wanted her, Eadyth could see, and she was pleased.

"Did I lose?" she asked self-consciously as he moved closer.

He flashed her a dazzling smile and lifted her into his arms. "I would say that we both won, sweetling. But now it is my time for the prize."

He threw her onto the bed and followed immediately after her. Putting his hands on either of her ankles, he pushed upward and outward. He looked down at her appreciatively for one moment only, then plunged into her depths with one long stroke. Eadyth keened with the intense pleasure of being filled by her husband, as they melded together as one.

"You are so hot," Eirik ground out as he leaned over her on straightened arms, his neck arching with his painful control. "Your womanheat is burning me alive. I want to kiss you and suckle your breasts and whisper sweet words to you, but I cannot wait . . . I cannot wai.."

He pummeled her body then with long strokes that grew increasingly shorter and harder. She braced her upraised palms against the headboard and tried to match his strokes. When the quivering flutters began again in her woman parts, she spread her legs wider and arched her hips up off the bed. The flutters became spasms, then full-blown convulsions, as Eadyth flailed her head from side to side, reaching, reaching, reaching. . . . When she reached her "peak" and splintered into a thousand shards of pleasure, Eirik arched his neck back and slammed into her one last time, crying out with a raw, masculine groan of triumph.

Eirik fell heavily across her, his chest heaving from his efforts, his ragged breaths tickling her neck. Eadyth felt a wetness between her legs—his seed and her woman's moisture. His limp man part still nestled inside her.

And a warmth like spring sunshine flowed through Eadyth. She brushed her fingertips lightly across his shoulders and down his back. In the aftermath of their fierce lovemaking, Eadyth felt peace and a sense of rightness.

"I love you, Eirik," she whispered, stroking his hair.

Silence reigned for a few moments. Then he raised his head, grinning. "I do have a talent for the bed sport, do I not?"

"I said I *love* you, Eirik," she said, shoving him affectionately. "I do not ask that you return the sentiment, but do not make light of my affections, either."

"I would not do that. Ah, Eadyth, I do not know if I believe in love anymore. It takes more trust than I have for womankind. I have grown fond of you, and I am pleased that

311

we are wed, but I cannot promise more than that. For now.''

Disappointment tugged at Eadyth's senses, but he was being honest with her, and that counted for much. "Well, then, I will just have to teach you to trust me." But what she really meant was love.

He smiled and kissed her mole. "Ever the managing woman, are you?" Then he slipped lower and blew against her breast. "What were you saying earlier about suckling?"

Eadyth could not "manage" a word right then.

Later, Eadyth asked Eirik if the feather game could be played with her wielding the "weapon," and he said, "Oh, for a certainty. 'Tis the best way."

By morning, they had torn the mattress in several places. The stool had a broken leg. Rushes were scattered in clumps all over the room.

Eirik's knees were brush-burned and his shoulders had teeth marks in them. Eadyth's face and breasts smarted from Eirik's whiskers.

She cracked one eye open to peer at Eirik where he stood drinking deeply from a goblet of mead. He winked at her and she saw an invitation there. Again!

"Nay, no more. I could not do it again. Not even if . . ." She yawned widely and closed her eyes sleepily.

"Ead-yth," Eirik called out a short time later in an odd tone of voice. When she ignored him, he cajoled, "Ead-yth, look here what I have for you."

She scrunched her eyes closed tighter. "I already know what you have for me and I have had enough."

"I know, I know, not even if I stand on my head barearsed naked. But have pity on me. You will not believe this. Truly."

And he was right.

Eadyth's mouth dropped open when she unshuttered her eyes, which grew increasingly wider with disbelief.

Eirik was standing on his head. And he was bare-arsed naked.

After she stopped laughing and he had dropped back to his feet, she said, holding out her arms to him, "Well, mayhap I have changed my mind. A little manly exercise deserves its reward."

Chapter Seventeen

They awakened later to a loud pounding on the door.

"Go away," Eirik growled and pulled Eadyth more closely into the cradle of his arms. Her head lay on his chest and one leg was thrown wantonly over both of his. Eirik shook his head in wonder at the implausible picture . . . and his good fortune.

"Not again, Eirik, I am too weary," Eadyth mumbled sleepily.

Eirik's lips turned up with immense satisfaction, knowing he had done a superior job of tiring her out.

"Eir-rik," Tykir whined, knocking on the door again, "open up. 'Tis past dawn, and I have four bothersome children in my bed making so much noise my head hurts. 'Tis time for you and Eadyth to take over."

"Begone, Tykir. And do not come back unless the keep is under attack."

Eirik heard Tykir mutter several swear words, then stomp off. He put a hand on Eadyth's satin-smooth buttock, relishing the idea that he had a husband's right to do so. New, wonderful feelings washed over him as he gazed at his wife, and he feared examining them too closely, lest they be ethereal and fade away, like dreams. He closed his eyes, preparing to fall asleep again.

But Eadyth had other plans, soon evident when she shifted and rubbed her breasts across his furred chest, then placed a hand possessively over his exhausted man part, purring, " 'Twould seem you need a bit of leavening in your life, dearling.''

And it was Eirik then who protested with a groan, "Not now, Eadyth, I am too tired.''

But he soon changed his mind when she asked saucily, "Not even if I stand on my head, bare—''

"You would not!'' he said with shock, his eyes shooting open. "Would you?'' He could not hide the gleam of interest in his eyes.

"Nay, you brute, I would not.'' But then she swung her body atop his, challenging, "Are you done 'peaking' so soon? You promised me twelve 'peaks,' and you are only up to six so far.''

Eirik found he was no longer quite so tired.

An hour later, Tykir was back at their door, pounding insistently. "Eirik, you push the bounds of brotherly love. Get your arse out here and take these whelps off my hands. John has challenged me to a pissing contest. Larise has my feet aching from dancing so much. *Dancing! For the love of Thor, who ever heard of a Norse warrior dancing?* Emma has honey in her hair. Godric is shooting arrows into Bertha's butter churn. Abdul has begun to molt. And your damn dog shit on my bed.''

Eirik and Eadyth exchanged looks of amusement before both exclaiming at the same time, "Go away!'' and then they burst into laughter.

"Are you laughing at me?'' Tykir demanded, affront turning his voice churlish.

"Why do you not teach the children some of your magic tricks?'' Eirik finally choked out when Tykir continued to mutter loudly outside in the corridor. Tykir told him exactly what he could do with his "magic tricks" and stalked away.

Since they were already awake, Eirik decided to teach Eadyth a few "magic tricks."

"Have you ever heard of the famous Viking 'S' spot?" he asked his wife, grinning against the cleavage of her breasts, and moving lower with a trail of kisses.

"Nay. Is this another one of those caliph stories?"

"Of course not," he said, affronted. "My 'Uncle' Selik told me about the 'S' spot. The tricky thing about it is that it can only be found with—"

"With what?" Eadyth asked with a gasp as Eirik knelt between her legs and raised her knees over his shoulders.

"—the tongue," he answered smoothly, with a wink.

And Eadyth told him later, much later, that he could practice his magic tricks on her anytime he wanted.

The third time Tykir came banging on their door, about mid-day, he demanded, "Eirik, come quickly. Britta is missing, and we fear Steven may have her."

Eadyth gathered the frightened children about her while she watched Eirik and his men ride off in full battle gear to search for the missing maid. She tried to hide her terror, both for Eirik and Tykir, and especially for the helpless Britta, who had been pulled into their battle with Steven.

Before he had mounted his horse, Eirik had drawn Eadyth into his arms and whispered against her lips, "I am well pleased with you, wife. I had hoped to have more time to show you my joy."

"I, too, am happy in this marriage," she had admitted huskily as she ran her fingertips caressingly across his cheek. "Take care, my husband. Take care."

She and Bertha took the children in hand, forcing them to wash all the grime from their bodies, then seating them around the kitchen table where Eadyth proceeded to teach them their lessons. Though they shifted restlessly from time to time, they were all eager students, even Godric, and much was accomplished in the three hours before they heard the horses returning in the bailey. Eadyth ordered the children to stay with Bertha, then rushed through the hall with foreboding.

Wilfrid was carrying Britta's limp and battered body up the steps when Eadyth opened the door. Eirik and his men were already riding off again in search of the evil Gravely and his conspirators in crime.

"Is she alive?" Eadyth asked Wilfrid.

"Just barely," he said through gritted teeth.

"Bring her to the guest chamber," she said, leading the way, and called out to Girta, "Tell Bertha to send hot water and cloths."

When Britta lay on the bed, and they had removed her shredded garments, Eadyth and Wilfrid both cried out with alarm at the horrendous cuts and bruises which marred almost all her skin from forehead to feet. Blood and man-seed had dried on her thighs. Her one eye was already swollen shut and her bottom lip cracked open. Her left arm appeared broken at the wrist.

Wilfrid exclaimed, "The bloody bastard. I will kill him for this, I swear."

"Leave, Wilfrid," Eadyth pleaded finally, putting a gentle hand on his arm. "'Twould be best to let me cleanse her body in private. Find the herbal woman in the village, if you will, and send her to me with healing draughts."

"Will she live?" he asked brokenly.

Eadyth shrugged. "I hope so. I will do my best. 'Tis all I can promise."

By the time she was done cleaning Britta, the maid had gained consciousness, moaning, "Oh, mistress, the beasts . . . the things they did to me . . . I hurt so bad . . ."

"Hush, Britta, you are safe now." But she had to ask, "Was it Steven of Gravely?"

Britta looked up at her, wide-eyed with horror. "Yea. He and five of his men took turns . . . oh, the perversions . . . the horrid things they made me do . . . I will never forget . . . and he gave me a message for you."

317

Eadyth stiffened with apprehension.

"He said . . . he said . . . to tell you that you are next. And he said he would not be so gentle with you."

Eadyth brushed Britta's lank red hair, once as lustrous as spun gold, off her battered face. Then she took the young servant in her arms and rocked her like a child, knowing full well that Britta had lost any remnant of innocence she still held that day. And her tears blended with the sweet maid's.

By the time Eirik and his retinue returned that evening, Britta was sleeping restlessly, thanks to the herbs the village woman had brought. Eadyth was optimistic that the maid would recover, in time—at least in body, if not in spirit.

Her first glance at Eirik's stormy features told her he had not found Steven. Once again, the devilish earl had eluded capture.

Quickly, she ordered servants to prepare baths for Tykir and her husband and to begin setting the tables for the evening meal. "And bring out several tuns of mead," she told Lambert. "Methinks the men will have a mighty thirst."

By the time Eadyth finally got upstairs, Eirik and Tykir had both completed their baths and were sitting in Eirik's bedchamber, discussing the day's events. She told them of Britta's injuries and her hopes for recovery.

Eadyth's heart went out to her husband as he sat with wide shoulders slumped in weariness and disillusionment. His handsome profile was rigid with tension. He had not shaved that day and a dark stubble shadowed his face. He was a strong man . . . he truly was . . . but he had been pushed sorely that day.

Eadyth hesitated, then put her hand familiarly on her husband's shoulder. He looked up at her, in surprise at first, then laid a hand over hers. Eadyth thrilled at this small show of affection outside the fever of bedlust.

"We can no longer wait for a decision from the Witan on the custody petition," Eirik said.

She nodded, knowing the danger grew day by day as Steven grew more bold in his misdeeds.

"I still say we could lure the bastard into the open if we used Eadyth or John," Tykir grumbled.

"Tykir, I warned you not to broach this subject around Eadyth." Eirik stood, towering over his brother menacingly.

Eadyth pushed Eirik gently back down into his chair. "Now, Eirik, let Tykir speak his mind. For once, treat me as a woman, not a child."

"A child!" Despite the seriousness of their situation, Eirik grinned at her. Eadyth blushed, knowing he was thinking of all the ways in which he had treated her in a very womanly way, all night long.

"The answer is 'nay,' and we will not discuss it again, Tykir," Eirik stated flatly. "We will find another way. On the morrow, I intend to travel to Gravely's estates in Essex, and I will hide out there 'til he returns, no matter how long it takes."

But the solution was taken out of their hands the next morning when Earl Orm came to give them the news. "King Edmund was murdered at Gloucestershire. 'Twas on the feast of St. Augustine. He and his court were feasting at Pucklechurch when the villain Leofa stabbed the king in the heart."

Eadyth and Eirik exchanged startled glances. What could it mean?

"The king's men tore Leofa limb from limb after the assault, but 'twas too late. Edmund was already dead," Orm said, gulping down deep draughts of mead.

"He was so young," Eadyth murmured with dismay. "He could not have seen more than twenty-four winters."

"Yea," Eirik agreed, "and his sons Edwy and Edgar are barely out of swaddling clothes, being but four and two years old. His brother Edred will, no doubt, succeed him now, and him not much younger than Edmund was . . . only twenty-two, methinks."

Tykir stood and paced uneasily. "But unlike Edmund, who compensated for his youth by surrounding himself with wise advisors, Edred thrives on evil companions such as Gravely. An ill wind blows over Britain, I say."

"Was Edred responsible for his brother's death?" Eadyth asked the earl.

Orm shrugged. "He is suspect, but there is no proof thus far. His supporters sweep down on Wessex even now, presumably for the funeral, but more likely seeking their spoils."

"And the Witan?" Eirik asked uneasily, voicing Eadyth's silent concern over Steven's custody petition now that the king was dead.

"The Witan cannot be changed 'til after the funeral and a short mourning period. At least one month," Orm advised. "Rumor has it, though, that the present members will meet in three days at Gloucestershire to plan strategy. But already Edred demands acceptance by the Mercians and the Danes of the Danelaw. Next will be the Northumbrians, and there is no question, Eirik, that you and I will be forced to swear fealty. From there he goes to Tadden's Cliff where he expects homage from all the northern kings."

"He wastes no time," Eirik said scornfully, "but 'tis what we all expected. Yea, we will swear allegiance to him, Orm. What other choice have we? But mayhap we can work with the present Witan to forestall sweeping changes in his governing body."

"My thoughts exactly. Can you meet me in two days so we can travel together to Gloucestershire?"

Eirik nodded.

Later, after Orm left, Eirik and Tykir sat discussing this new development with Eadyth.

Eadyth laid her hand over Eirik's to get his attention. "I will not allow John to be used in any way, but 'twould seem you have no choice but to use me as a lure for Steven," she told her husband. "'Tis more dangerous now to delay. Once Edred gets his own men on the Witan, I fear Steven's custody petition will be granted."

Eirik glared at her stubbornly, but finally he nodded his agreement. "We will do it my way, though, Eadyth, and you will do naught to endanger yourself. Do you hear?"

"I promise. But I tell you this, husband. I would kill myself and my son afore I would allow that son of Satan to get his hands on John. Putting a child in his care would be like casting it into the pits of hell.''

Eirik put his arm around her shoulder and drew her protectively against his side. For now, she felt safe. But who knew what the morrow would bring.

Later that day, Eirik took her into the underground level of the castle to show her a secret exit from the keep, one they might use in the plan against Steven of Gravely. She had never realized there was a secret entrance to the below-ground level from behind a panel in the great hall.

Mainly, the rooms held old weapons and discarded furniture. Eadyth eyed the broken chairs and tables and bedsteads closely, thinking some might be salvaged for the cotters' huts.

"What is in that locked chamber?" she asked.

"Treasures," Eirik said offhandedly. He was squinting in the dim light as he gingerly picked up a rusted sword and put it out of harm's way.

"Treasures? What treasures?"

Eirik looked at her and shrugged. "Coins. Jewels. Fabrics."

A ripple of annoyance passed over Eadyth. "May I see?" she asked sweetly.

Eirik's head shot up at her oozing tone, but he drew a large key from the ring at his waist and opened the creaking door. Then, taking a torch from where he had placed it in a wall sconce, he led the way.

Eadyth gasped. She could not believe her eyes. Everywhere she looked, she saw incredible riches—chests overflowing with jewels and gold coins, fine silks and rich wools, several ivory tusks, casks of wine, scented oils, tapestries, heavy plates and silver cutlery.

She turned on her husband and shoved his chest with the palms of both hands. "You tightfisted troll! How could you?"

"Wha-at?" he said, backing away.

"You must have been laughing heartily at my meager

321

dowry. You let me think you were impoverished, you lout.''

"Well, I did laugh. But only a little.''

She was not amused and glowered her displeasure at him. He was leaning against the wall, grinning at her, totally without remorse. *The boor.*

"Now, Eadyth, do not get your hackles up. You told me you did not care about riches and such.''

"Do not play me for a lackwit, husband. You know good and well, 'tis one thing to not care about riches, and another to have to slave to make ends meet.''

"Slave? You exaggerate.''

"How would you know? Oh, when I think how you made me feel guilty for ordering a few piddling sheep, and—''

"Twenty.''

"What?''

"You ordered twenty sheep, Eadyth, not a few.''

"Oh.'' She had not been aware that Eirik kept such a close eye on her management of his keep.

"And the cow! There was one mere cow to serve this keep when I arrived.''

"There are eight now. I wonder how they got here,'' he remarked dryly, raising a brow pointedly. And Eadyth was amazed once again that Eirik had been more observant than she had realized.

Then he ducked his head sheepishly. "I was going to get more cows myself. I just never got around to it.''

Her upper lip curled contemptuously. "Tell me, Eirik, why do you live so penuriously?''

"'Tis not wise for a Norseman—even a half-Viking, such as myself—to provoke the envy of his Saxon neighbors.''

Eadyth understood then, but that did not explain Eirik's failure to tell her, his wife.

"How did you think I was paying all the new soldiers I have brought to Ravenshire?'' He tugged playfully on one of the curly strands of her hair while he spoke, wrapping it around his finger.

Eadyth felt her face grow hot. "I had not considered that.

No doubt, you were muddling my thoughts at the time.''

"Yea, I am rather good at . . . muddling. Am I not?" He grinned at her and forced her closer by pulling on the lock of hair still wrapped around his finger. She tried to ignore the sweet heat he was stoking with his mere closeness.

"Oh, you are outrageous! And Asa, your mistress—this is how you paid her, is it not?" Eadyth waved her hand at the room's contents, and her throat tightened at the thought. Fool that she was, she had even expected Eirik to use some of her profits to pay off his mistress. Instead, he had, no doubt, laid vast riches at her feet. Mayhap he had not even ended his relationship with her.

"Wipe that nasty thought from your head immediately," Eirik snapped. "If you dare to accuse me of infidelity after wearing my cock nigh down to a nub, I swear I will pull out your tongue and nail it to your frowning forehead."

Eadyth inhaled sharply. "You are *so* vulgar."

"Yea, I am." Then he grinned mischievously. "Would you like to lie down on one of these lengths of silk and get vulgar with me?"

She shot him a look of disgust, but could not help the smile which crept over her lips. He looked so engaging, standing there like an overgrown boy, grinning happily. "Nay, I would not ruin good samite by rolling around on the ground with you."

"Ah, ever the sensible wife!" He gazed at her fondly, then added, his eyes twinkling, "Wouldst you consider good wool?"

She laughed despite herself.

He held out his arms to her and she stepped into his embrace. She pinched his belly, though, just to show she had not lost all her anger with him.

Later, when they exited arm in arm from the secret tunnel which led to a cotter's hut just outside the castle walls, Eadyth said, more serious now, "Eirik, I am fearful for John's fate now that Edred is king, but I just wanted you to know . . ." Her voice broke with emotion.

"What, dearling?" he asked, tilting her chin up with a forefinger.

"I just wanted you to know that I am happier at this moment than I have ever been in all my life."

He tried to make light of her serious tone by teasing, "Yea, I am rather good at making you happy, am I not?"

But she would not allow him to trivialize her sentiments. "I love you, Eirik. Nay, do not shift your eyes and look downward. I am not asking you to return my sentiments." *At least not yet.* "Mayhap women are different. All I know is that I could not yield myself the way I have with you unless I gave my heart, as well."

" 'Tis hard for me to talk of these things, Eadyth. Trust comes hard for me, and without it, I do not think I could love anyone. Give me time."

"I will," she said, smiling up at him. "'Tis just that I fear hard times are coming, and I wanted you to know how I feel." She looked about then, wanting to change the subject, and said, "Look at that green pasture over there. I have never seen it afore. Do you think . . . hmmm . . . I was wondering if we might purchase a few . . . just a few, mind you . . . goats?"

"Goats?" he choked out.

Then he laughed when he saw the teasing expression on her face. "You are beautiful when you smile, Eadyth. If you had smiled once or twice when you were pretending to be old and ugly, your charade would have been over in a trice."

"You think so, do you?"

"I know so, dearling. Even with my damned eyes, I would not be able to miss the beauty of your smile."

"Oh, Eirik, do not speak so of your eyes. I love your eyes." After all, it was those pale blue eyes that had drawn her to Ravenshire in the first instance.

"You do? Ah, well, they are my weakness, but—"

She put her fingertips to his lips. "There is nothing weak about you, my husband. I recognized your vision problem almost from the start, because my father experienced the same, and it never made him less a man."

"Well . . . ," he said, seeming to shrug off her words of confidence, but Eadyth could tell that he was pleased. His dim sight—his one weakness, or so he perceived it to be—was a sensitive point with her husband. And she had rankled his pride by playing on that foible with her foolish masquerade.

She gazed at him adoringly, recognizing her good fortune in having gained this man for her husband.

"What? Why are you looking at me so?"

"How?"

"Like your bloody dog, Prince."

Eadyth chuckled softly. What an apt description!

"I do not suppose, Eadyth, that you would . . . oh, never mind . . ." He let his words trail off deliberately, arousing her curiosity. He stroked his upper lip, scrutinizing her the whole time. His eyes twinkled with mischief.

Putting both hands on her hips, Eadyth tilted her head in question.

". . . wag your tail," he finished with a chortle of laughter.

"You have better parts to wag than I do," she retorted, shoving him playfully in the chest. He fell backward, pulling her with him to the ground.

Taking her face in both his hands, Eirik kissed her deeply. In truth, Eadyth could never seem to get enough of his lips and teeth and tongue. Why had she never known that kissing could be such a pleasure?

"You are looking dreamy-eyed again, Eadyth," he said, blowing softly on the wetness of her lips.

"And no wonder! You turn a maid's mind inside out with your kisses, and well you know it."

"Just yours, Eadyth. Just yours. Now, will you tell me why you were looking at me like Prince looks at a juicy bone?"

"I just wondered how I could have grown to love you so quickly."

"No doubt it is my manly prowess," he boasted immodestly.

"I think I loved you long afore you ever touched me."

"Really?" His eyes sparkled with interest.

She nodded. "Yea, 'twas when you acknowledged John as your son at our wedding feast, no doubt. And then when you gave me that tongue kiss in your bedchamber the same night, I suspected I would not be able to resist your charms for long."

"Yea, my charms are formidable."

She nipped at his shoulder and continued, "And then there was the time you were stung by my bees and did not beat me."

"I was tempted."

"But you did not."

There was a long moment of silence as their eyes locked, and Eadyth cried inwardly that Eirik did not tell her that he loved her, as well. She told herself it did not matter, but, of course, it did.

"I am trying, Eadyth," he said softly.

"I know," she whispered, trying to hide her pain, and leaned up into his gentle kiss.

"Are you two at it again?" They looked up to see Tykir emerging from the tunnel entrance. "Hell, Eirik, every time I turn around, you are counting Eadyth's teeth with your tongue."

"Thirty-two," Eirik said without a blink of his eyes.

"Huh?" Tykir said.

"Eadyth has thirty-two teeth."

They all burst out laughing then.

Tykir dropped down to the ground next to them once their merriment ended.

"Where are the children?" Eadyth asked.

"I tied them to posts in the great hall."

"How could you!" Eadyth exclaimed, horrified at his cruelty, and started to stand.

"Do not get your dander up, sister. Sit back down. They think it is a game. I am the mighty Viking warrior and they are my captives. At least it gives me a moment to breathe." He grimaced comically. "I promised that when I return I will be their captive. Hell's flames, I think I may go a-Viking when I leave Ravenshire just to get a rest."

They all turned more serious then as they discussed the plan to lure Steven into their trap.

"I will leave with a large contingent of men on the morrow," Eirik said. "If Earl Orm has not already done so, I will spread the word that I go to Gloucestershire to speak with the Witan."

"Surely Steven will watch you carefully," Eadyth said worriedly.

"Yea, but I will leave in full battle gear, including a helmet which covers my hair. When I get a few hides from Ravenshire, there is a wooded area where Sigurd will be waiting for me. Sigurd is much the same size as me. He and I will exchange garments. After the troops move on, I will backtrack to Ravenshire and enter through the secret tunnel."

Eadyth bit her bottom lip anxiously.

"I know you are concerned about John. I am sending him under heavy guard, along with Larise and Emma, to Hawks' Lair. They will leave tonight through the tunnel. I do not want them inside the keep, in the event something should go wrong with our plan."

Eadyth put a hand to her mouth apprehensively. "And Tykir?"

"Will sail out tonight from Jorvik, along the Humber to the North Sea. Then he will travel back here by land. He will be the one to stay with the children at Hawks' Lair. I do not think Emma will be manageable for long without one of us there."

"It all sounds so . . . sensible . . . but you know that Steven does not think as a normal man does. I fear his treachery."

"We will be careful, Eadyth. I protect what is mine." He put an arm around her shoulders for emphasis.

Eirik's gesture warmed Eadyth, even more than his words. He did not love her . . . yet, Eadyth could see that. But she believed that he did care about her. That was something. A start.

"One last thing, Eadyth. 'Tis possible we have a spy within the keep. So we must not discuss this plan with any of the servants, and I must not come abovestairs once I leave Ravenshire. We will prepare the rooms underground with bedding and food and drink for me and some of my men. Even the horses will have to be kept with us."

At her look of distaste, he added, "It should only be for one night or two. I am certain Steven will be lured to the prospect of you and John in a seemingly ill-protected keep."

Two days went by, and still there was no contact from Steven. Eadyth paced her bedchamber, and the kitchen, where Bertha complained, "Gawd! Yer wearing a groove in the floor, and yer makin' the milk curdle in me custard with yer constant complainin'."

Eirik had warned Eadyth not to step outside the keep under any circumstances, and only Wilfrid and Jeremy, her trusted stoneworker from Hawks' Lair, were aware of the plan. At the first sign of Steven's, or any stranger's, presence inside the keep, Eirik was to be contacted. To outward appearances, the keep must look understaffed and poorly guarded.

"When Steven contacts you, you must be within range of Wilfrid or Jeremy so they may signal me and my men. You must obey my orders totally, do you hear me, Eadyth?" Eirik had told her over and over before he left.

On the third day, Eadyth was so jittery and frustrated she decided she had to do something to keep busy. "We will work on my honey today," she told Bertha and Girta.

The cook muttered something about the mess she would make of her kitchen, but was silenced by a quick glare from Eadyth. Britta would be unable to help since she was still bedridden, though recovering slowly from her battering. Eadyth instructed Oslac, one of the beekeeping assistants she had brought from Hawks' Lair, to gather as many honeycombs as were ready from her hives. Eirik had forbidden her to go even to the orchard where her hives were located, lest Steven be lurking about.

When Oslac returned a short time later, pushing his bee-keeping veils back off his face, he brought with him three dozen honeycombs and said there were at least that many more for him to fetch. "It has been way too long, mistress, since we have harvested the honey, though the bees have enjoyed the feast mightily."

Eadyth nodded, realizing that she had been busy with other things the past few days. She sent Oslac off for more of the honeycombs and made sure the fire was hot enough and all her utensils were set out on the table.

Girta went to get more pottery containers from the scullery. Bertha wiped the sweat from her forehead with a forearm and grumbled, "Well, best we get this over with."

A short time later, Eadyth already had the three dozen honeycombs decapped, dripping nectar through the straining cloths near the fire, and Oslac had not yet returned. She fidgeted and glanced impatiently about the kitchen, wanting to complete her work.

"Wash all the empty combs for me, Bertha," she said and stepped to the doorway leading to the kitchen courtyard.

Oslac was approaching, carrying a huge armful of the honeycombs in one of her beecatcher boxes—at least six dozen. There must have been many more than he had originally thought. He stopped near the well and laid his box down. At first, Eadyth was puzzled by his behavior, but then she saw him sit down on a boulder and remove his shoe, then shake out several loose stones.

Smiling, she stepped out into the courtyard, lifting her face to the warmth of the midday sun. She missed being outdoors, working with her bees, being free to ride her horse through the cotters' fields, or go into the markets of Jorvik. She ambled closer to Oslac and remarked, "'Twould seem our bees have been industrious. We will have a great supply of wax for my candles this year, do you not think?"

He nodded as he rubbed the bottom of his bruised foot,

then replaced his shoe and stood.

An odd tingling prickled Eadyth's scalp, then raised the fine hair on the back of her neck. It was Oslac's height. She had not realized he was so tall, or that—

Before she had a chance to assimilate the warning signals, Oslac threw off his beekeeping veils and grabbed her arm in a pincerlike grip. She started to scream, but he pulled her back against his body, one arm wrapped across her chest like an iron bar, the other clamped over her mouth.

It was Steven of Gravely.

"You bloody bitch! Where have you hidden John? Oslac says he has not seen him in the keep for days."

Eadyth twisted her head to peer at Steven's face over her shoulder. He was dragging her toward some bushes where they would be hidden from view.

Her blood ran cold at the tremendous change in his appearance since they had last met. Although still a handsome man, he had lost much weight and his cheeks were sunken. Illness cast a grayish pallor over his once healthy skin. His bloodshot eyes raked her feverishly, darting about the kitchen courtyard searchingly. There was madness, too, in his wild eyes, and Eadyth suspected that the disease of his male parts had moved to his brain.

"I asked you a question, bitch," he said and tore a length of fabric off her sleeve, using it to tie a gag around her mouth. He did the same with her other sleeve and bound her hands behind her back and her ankles together. Then he shoved her to her knees and slapped her mightily across the face. "I am going to remove your gag for a moment, and if you dare to cry out, I swear I will slit your bloody throat." He pulled a dagger from his belt and held it to her neck while he untied her gag with the other hand.

"Where is John?" he asked once again.

Apparently he already knew that John was not within the keep, thanks to Oslac's treachery. Oslac must be the spy in their midst.

"In Jorvik," she lied.

"You cannot hide my son from me, you know. Already Edred has promised him to me in return for my past loyalties. 'Tis only a matter of time."

"Then why are you here?"

She saw her mistake when Steven's eyes flashed angrily and he backhanded her across the other cheek. She reeled under the impact and almost fell over, but Steven grabbed her painfully by the neck and held her upright.

"My grandsire is dying of the wasting disease in Frankland as we speak, Eadyth. He has an aversion to me, for some unfathomable reason, but has agreed to pass his estates on to my heir. If I do not bring my son to him afore his death, all his lands will go to the church. I cannot allow that."

"Go to your own wife, Steven. Breed sons on her," Eadyth said, unsure if Eirik's tale of Steven's sterility were true.

At first he appeared about to strike her again, but then lowered his hand. "Did you not know my wife died two sennights ago?" he asked, slitting his red-rimmed eyes slyly. " 'Twas a fearsome stomach ailment . . . came on Eneda of a sudden . . . the poor soul." He chortled most unsympathetically and pulled a small vial from his robe, holding it in her face. "She did not suffer much in the end, thanks to this sleeping draught I gave her."

Eadyth felt a suffocating, squeezing sensation in her chest, and a ripple of fear passed over her body. She knew without being told that the vial held poison which he had administered to his wife. But why?

He soon answered her question.

" 'Tis the exact same potion you will be giving to your husband."

Eadyth inhaled sharply. The man had truly lost his senses. "Why would I do that?"

"Now that I am free to marry, you must be the same."

Stark fear, black and deadly as a tidal wave, washed over her, and Eadyth could barely control her tremors. "But you said the Witan will grant you custody. Why would you need me as wife?"

He sneered at her question but answered anyway. "There are a few on the Witan who will not heed the new king's orders. They believe your husband's claims of paternity . . . or seek his good favors. In the end, the Witan will grant me custody, you can be sure of that, but time is of the essence. I cannot wait. Quite simply, Eirik must die, and you will perform the deed."

He jerked her to her feet then. "But first, we go to Jorvik to gather my son."

"I think not," a steely voice said behind them.

Eadyth looked back to see Eirik emerging from the kitchen, sword raised, and a dozen men coming behind him. Others came from the bailey and even more from beyond the orchard.

Steven tightened his hold on her bound body and held the dagger harder against her throat, drawing blood. Eadyth saw Eirik's eyes rivet angrily on her neck and feared he would act precipitously.

"John is not here, or in Jorvik. You will never see him again, Gravely. In truth, you will not live to see another day," Eirik said in a hard, ruthless tone as he advanced slowly.

Steven laughed harshly. "I think not, you bastard, unless you wish your sweet wife to go to her reward with me." He pressed the knife deeper, and Eadyth felt wet rivulets running down her neck and under her tunic.

Eirik's thinned lips twitched with tension, and he halted in his progress toward them.

"A trade then," Eirik offered with obvious reluctance. "Your escape for Eadyth's freedom."

"You have no bartering power. The bitch goes with me. Methinks you would not risk Eadyth's life, though I fail to see its worth."

" 'Tis worth much to me," Eirik said huskily, holding Eadyth's eyes significantly for a moment. Then he looked back to Steven. "But I would kill you, and endanger her life as well, afore I would allow you to take her from my keeping. Take your loathsome hands from my wife's body."

Heedless of the danger, Steven cackled demonically and pressed the knife tighter, placing his other hand familiarly over her breast and squeezing. Eadyth moaned with the pain and saw Eirik's hands clench tightly at his sides as he tried desperately to restrain his temper.

Steven started to back up, taking her with him. With each step backward he took, Eirik and his men moved forward, carefully.

"I give you my oath," Eirik said finally, when they were almost at the point where Steven's horse was tethered to a tree, "if you will release Eadyth now, I will not follow you for at least one hour. Nor will any of my men."

Steven hesitated, seeming to consider Eirik's vow.

"You know I honor my oaths, Steven. Give over, for now."

Finally, Steven nodded and leapt up into his saddle, viciously kicking Eadyth to the ground in the process. Eadyth could not fail to hear his alarming message to her as he rode off.

"I will be back, Eadyth."

Chapter Eighteen

Eirik insisted on carrying her back to the keep and up to their bedchamber, where he wiped the blood off her neck with gentle care and tried to wrap a linen around the wound. He shooed a clucking Girta away, declining her offers to minister to Eadyth. "I am capable of caring for my own wife," he said huskily. "Go off and tend to Britta. She is sore distraught."

Eadyth kept telling Eirik it was just a deep scratch and refused to have it bound. "Blessed Saint Beatrice!" she finally snapped, swatting his fussing hands away. "You will have me looking like Bertha with her elephant dressing. Besides, air will heal the cut best."

"Lie quietly for a while, Eadyth, and stop trying to 'manage' everything. You have suffered a great shock today," he rebuked her with a soft smile. Sitting on the edge of the bed next to her, he brushed the curly strands of hair off her face as he spoke and kissed the tips of her fingers. Eadyth could not fail to see the concern in his rigid jaw and stormy eyes. His gentle ministration bespoke more than husbandly duty, and she was hopeful that he was growing to care for her more.

"Tykir and Sigurd are readying my retainers for departure," he continued, "but we must talk on my return . . . of other matters. When I saw Steven holding that knife to your throat today, I . . . I . . ." His words trailed off as he clearly fought for composure.

He does care for me, Eadyth thought joyously.

"You are going after Steven then?"

He nodded. "I will give him his promised hour, but not one minute more."

Eadyth took pride in her husband's honor and reached up to caress his whisker-stubbled jaw with her knuckles. He had been living in that dismal underground room for three days now and could use a bath and warm food and a soft bed. But there was no time for that now. Not yet.

"The bastard will, no doubt, have escaped by now," he grumbled, standing abruptly.

"There will be another time."

"For a certainty." His pale eyes glittered like shards of blue ice as he gritted out the words.

He lay down next to her on the bed for a time, just holding her as if she were a fragile piece of fine glass, not the hard rock she had been forced to be these past few years. And love swelled her soul with hope for a better life they might have together.

He kissed her softly as he finally arose with reluctance. Pressing his fingertips to her lips, he halted the love words he must know she was about to utter. Warm tears of regret welled in her eyes.

After he left, Eadyth surprised herself by dozing off. She awakened hours later when she heard the tower bell ringing, announcing visitors to the keep.

She quickly whisked the wrinkles from her garment with her hands, and splashed cool water on her face. Ignoring Girta's pleas that she stay abed and rest, Eadyth drew on a soft, white wimple, then a head-rail, which hid the thin, blood-encrusted line across her throat.

When she emerged from the great hall onto the steep stone steps leading to the bailey, she saw Earl Orm and his retainers entering the gates, with Eirik and his men close behind.

"We met up on the road," Eirik explained when he dismounted, glancing with distaste at her wimple and head-rail. He had told her on more than one occasion how he hated for her to cover her beautiful hair. "Am I married to a nun now?" he whispered near her ear.

"Did it feel like a nun with her legs wrapped 'round your waist yestereve, husband?" she retorted boldly.

Eirik hooted with laughter and put an arm around her shoulder with an easy familiarity that would have been unthinkable to Eadyth a few short sennights ago. Then he drew her along with their company into the hall.

Suddenly, Eadyth noticed the concern on Eirik's face and the stiffness with which he held his body. She stopped and put a palm to her chest in dismay. "What? What is it now? Has Steven done something more? Oh, will his evil never end?"

Eirik shook his head. " 'Tis not Steven. Earl Orm has just returned from Gloucestershire, and he brings us . . . news," he said grimly. "But let us discuss this new matter in private."

Alarm rippled over Eadyth's skin like butterfly wings, and her heart began to race wildly. *Gloucestershire? 'Tis where the Witan has been meeting. Has it made a decision regarding John? Oh, Blessed Mother, please . . . please help us.*

Girta followed them into the private chamber off the hall, carrying several trenchers of manchet bread, slices of cold meats and hard cheeses. A servant followed behind her with goblets of mead.

Eadyth sat down with trepidation next to Eirik at the trestle table, wringing her hands nervously in her lap, while Orm, Tykir and Wilfrid sat across the table from them. Even Tykir, who usually had a flippant, teasing word for her, was ominously silent.

She refused the drink Eirik placed in front of her, and he

did not insist. Another ominous sign.

Wasting no time, Eirik soothed her. "Now, do not be frightened, Eadyth. 'Tis not as bad as it will sound."

She gazed at him questioningly, unable to speak.

"The Witan demands that John attend Edmund's funeral at Glastonbury Abbey with me. Then John will travel to Winchester where the king will appoint a temporary guardian for him."

"A guardian! Oh, Sweet Mother of God!" Then she choked out, "Temporary?"

" 'Til the new Witan meets officially next month."

"Oh, Eirik, how can you say this news is not as bad as it sounds? 'Tis the worst possible news."

He reached out his hands and took both of her trembling ones in his. "Trust me, Eadyth. I will not let John come to harm."

"How?"

Earl Orm took a deep swallow of mead and wiped his forearm across his mouth. "I have already spoken with several members of the Witan—Ealdormen Byrhtnoth of Essex and Elfhere of Mercia. They are sure to stay on the Witan, even with Edred as king, along with Ealdormen Elfheah of Hampshire and Ethelwold of East Anglia. All are powerful nobles who see the danger in the new king allying himself with Steven of Gravely. They promised their support."

Eadyth saw the wisdom in Eirik's words, and she knew some of these men herself—good men of honest intention. Mayhap they would help her and Eirik in the custody battle.

"Despite his youth, Edred has to know the political tightrope he walks," Wilfrid remarked. "His brother Edmund managed to bring all of Britain under his domain. One slip and Edred could lose power with the dissenting kings."

"And Edred needs to watch his back in his own territory, as well," Tykir noted. "His nobles have become so wealthy and influential in these times of prosperity. Their own self-interest weighs heavier than their loyalty to their liege lord. And Edred is not as popular as his brother Edmund was. He will have to work harder to win their favor.''

"Yea, all you say is true," Eirik said, looking at each of the men in turn. Then he gave his full attention to Eadyth. "More important to our concerns—I will travel to Glastonbury Abbey and then to Winchester with John. I will ask Edred to appoint me as the boy's temporary guardian," Eirik assured her. "Archbishop Dunstan, Edred's cousin, will be there, and he, more than any other, can influence the king. Long has Dunstan been a favorite advisor of the rulers of the House of Wessex. Furthermore, Dunstan owes me for a favor I did him once in Frankland. An *immense* favor. I will call in my marker now.''

"Would we take Larise and Emma with us, as well?"

"Nay, Eadyth, you must stay here at Ravenshire with them. I have already sent Sigurd to fetch them home."

She started to rise indignantly, but Eirik pushed her gently back into her chair. " 'Tis best that you not show yourself at court. No matter how you may mislike the bias, the Witan would resent the interference of a woman. And you do have a tendency to lose your temper and turn shrewish on the odd occasion." He said the last with a slight smile. "You will have to let me handle this."

Eadyth knew she must trust in her husband's judgement, have faith in his abilities to solve her problems. Even so, it was hard to place her concerns in another's hands.

But she nodded in silent agreement.

A sennight later, Eirik had not returned, and Eadyth missed him and her son desperately. Eirik sent daily missives, however, telling of his progress, or lack thereof. The ealdormen that Earl Orm had mentioned appeared supportive to their cause, but they were a small part of the king's larger council.

Eirik laid his hopes more with Archbishop Dunstan, but the wily cleric was negotiating a harsh deal with Eirik for the favor. Among other things, Dunstan was demanding that Eirik agree to serve as ealdorman himself on the king's advisory council, a political position Eirik had long disdained. Dunstan hoped to have more bishops appointed, as well—men who would do his bidding.

Unfortunately, Eirik had been unable to speak directly with King Edred since he was suffering mightily from a physical ailment that ran in the blood of his family—a debilitating and most painful swelling of the joints. With all the wet weather of late, he had been bedridden for days following his brother's pompous funeral at Glastonbury.

And Steven of Gravely was absent.

Another sennight passed and Eadyth's nerves were strung so tight she feared she might explode. Seeking the numbness of hard physical labor, she worked industriously from dawn to dusk each day, forcing her disgruntled servants to follow suit.

Tapestries from Eirik's treasure room now lined the great hall and private chambers. She moved all the fabrics out of the damp lower level and up to a second-floor storage room. Then she oversaw the cutting and sewing of the fine wool into garments for Eirik and Tykir and Wilfrid, not to mention the children.

Although she usually waited until autumn for her candle-making, she, Bertha, Girta, and a slowly recovering Britta produced six dozen tapers and ten timekeeping candles the day before. Today she planned to set Gilbert to helping her build a still for making mead. Because she had promised Eirik not to venture beyond the kitchen courtyard and the front bailey, she would have to build a temporary facility near the keep.

She was watching Gilbert lay the stones for the shed's foundation when Emma tugged on her gown. "Godric," Emma said, her wide blue eyes pleading with Eadyth. "Help Godric."

Eadyth went down to her haunches beside the child. "What is it, sweetling? Do you want me to help you find Godric? Is he hiding from you again?"

Emma shook her head briskly. "Nay. Godric is gone."

Alarm swept over Eadyth with sudden foreboding. "Come," she said, taking Emma's hand. She sought out Larise, who was helping Britta shell peas in the kitchen. "Where is Godric?"

Larise and Britta looked up at her with surprise.

"I have not seen the boy since yestereve," Britta said. Then her eyes, no longer swollen shut as they had been after her attack, widened with concern. "Now that you mention it, he failed to come to the kitchen this morn to light the fires."

"He has been sulking ever since John left," Larise added, unconcerned. "No doubt he plays with Prince in one of the empty bedchambers.

"Stay here, Emma," Eadyth admonished. Then she searched the keep, from scullery to second-floor bedchambers, from bailey to kitchen courtyard. Godric was nowhere to be found.

Eadyth found Wilfrid in the bailey where he was taking a packet from a messenger who had just arrived. He handed her a sealed parchment, which she immediately opened. Quickly, she scanned Eirik's words.

Eadyth,
Glad tidings. John and I leave for Ravenshire on the
morrow. I finally had an audience with Edred. Dun-
stan's power is formidable. Edred agreed to my tem-
porary guardianship of John. He expects much in
return, but will discuss all with you. Have not seen
Steven, but he is reportedly livid. Take care, heart-
ling.

Your husband,
Eirik

Heartling! Eadyth smiled joyously and shared her news with Wilfrid. Then she turned their discussion back to the missing Godric.

"He could have gone into the village," Wilfrid advised and went with several men to search for the lost boy. After he left, Eadyth headed back toward the kitchen. She met Emma in the hall.

"Apples," Emma said with seeming irrelevance.

"What? You want an apple? Now?"

"Nay. Godric likes apples," Emma said hesitantly, then beamed up at Eadyth, proud of her achievement in having made her thoughts clear in spoken words.

Eadyth suddenly remembered Godric's passion for apples, especially the tart early variety. Eadyth bent down to the tiny girl. Putting both hands on her shoulders, she asked earnestly, "Emma, dearling, are you saying Godric might have gone outside the castle to pick some apples?"

Emma nodded vigorously.

Sending Emma back to the kitchen to help Larise with the peas, Eadyth stood, staring off into space pensively, one leather slipper tapping impatiently. Surely, Godric would have been seen if he had left the castle. Guards were posted at all gates and at marked intervals of the castle wall.

Thinking deeply, she tried to picture every apple tree she had seen near Ravenshire, then shook her head as she eliminated one after the other as his destination. There were guards everywhere along the way.

Except . . .

Eadyth smiled, suddenly enlightened. Except for the tree just outside the exit of the underground tunnel, near the abandoned cotter's hut. And, now she thought on it, those apples were especially sour and to Godric's taste.

She looked about the empty hall for someone to send after Godric. Well, she could wait until Wilfrid returned, but . . . hmmm. Moving hesitantly toward the door to the lower level, she thought that mayhap she would just go below and see if there was any evidence of Godric's having been there.

Lighting a torch, she made her way through the damp corridor and grinned with satisfaction when she saw an apple core near the outside entrance. She smiled even wider when she saw that the door was shut. The little imp must have gone outside, and when the door swung shut behind him, he'd had no way to return except around the keep and through the main entrance. He no doubt feared a beating from Wilfrid for having disobeyed his orders.

Well, she could easily forestall such a severe punishment for the little boy. Easing the door open, she peeked outside and immediately realized her mistake.

Steven of Gravely stood there in full armor with six fierce-looking men. He was leaning lazily against a tree, chomping on an apple. Godric was nowhere in sight.

"Well, what a pleasure meeting up with the Silver Whore of Northumbria!" He grabbed her before she could scream and put a blindfold over her eyes and a gag in her mouth, binding her wrists and ankles. Then he threw her over a horse in front of him and galloped off.

Eadyth's first thought was of Eirik and how angry he would be that she had disobeyed his orders once again. But, immediately, she realized she had more urgent concerns—her safety and that of Godric.

They rode for what seemed like an hour to Eadyth. When they finally stopped, Steven pulled her roughly off the horse and removed her ankle restraints. She fell to her knees. His fingers bit into her upper arm and he pushed her ahead of him up a set of stone steps and through a long corridor. Only when they were well inside did he remove her blindfold. Then Eadyth saw that they were in a small manor house, one she did not recognize.

Still pushing her ahead of him, Steven took her to a gallery which overlooked a small room below, well lit with torches. Eadyth jerked back with horror at what she saw and tried to break free from Steven's grip on her forearms, to no avail. She screamed silently behind her gag as tears welled in her eyes and overflowed.

A whimpering Godric stood in the center of the room, his arms raised above his head and tied to a loop of rope over an exposed beam, his thin body exposed to the coolness of the chamber. A guard sat indolently in a nearby chair, a sword laid over his lap. Eadyth saw no wounds on the precious child, just a few bruises, but his eyes were wide with fright and his body trembled.

When Steven felt she had seen enough, he turned her with a shove toward another corridor, then led her into a small chamber. Eadyth saw no servants about. The manor appeared to be abandoned. When they were inside, Steven put a torch to several hanging soapstone candles. He motioned for her to sit. Then he removed her gag, but did not release her wrists, which were still tied behind her back. He dropped into a chair opposite her and glared at her malevolently.

Steven's appearance had deteriorated even more the past few sennights since he had escaped from Ravenshire. Once godly handsome, his leanly muscled body had wasted away to a sickly gauntness. A gray pallor had erased the bronze that had colored his healthy skin. Even his hair, which had been thick and glossy like black silk, hung lankly about his face.

"You are unwell," she remarked without thinking.

"Yea, but do not think I will be leaving this life anytime in the near future. I have many years ahead of me, bitch, and once I secure my inheritance, through *our* son, I will make for the Holy Lands. There is a Saracen doctor who promises a cure for my . . . ailment."

Eadyth shrugged. "Steven, release Godric. The boy has done you no harm."

"Nay, I have plans for the child." He cackled evilly, then broke into a fit of coughing, finally spitting bloody phlegm into a linen cloth.

"What kind of plans?" she asked, trying hard to hide her fear from Steven, sensing he would gain pleasure from her pain.

He leaned forward, and Eadyth almost reeled from the foul breath that swept her way.

"I told you, Eadyth, to kill your husband and make way for our marriage. Instead, you set your bastard spouse on me. Tsk, tsk! I cannot abide such disobedience of my orders. Really, Eadyth, what shall I do to punish you for your transgressions?'' He tapped a forefinger to the side of his head, as if suddenly enlightened. ''Ah, the boy!''

''Nay, you cannot kill Godric to get back at me,'' she cried, jumping to her feet.

Steven leaned forward and shoved her back into her chair. ''I said naught of killing,'' he said calmly, his cold blue eyes knifing her contemptuously. ''Leastways, not yet.''

Eadyth shifted uneasily in her chair under Steven's mirthless smile. Finally, he said in a deadly cold voice, ''This is how it will be, *my future wife*. I will give you another vial of the poison, like the one you failed to use afore. You will give it to your husband. This particular poison leaves no trace, and you will be pleased to know that the passing is painless, almost like a deep sleep. Then, when a suitable time passes . . . say, four sennights, we will be wed. And live happily ever after.'' He grinned with evil satisfaction.

''Whyever would I do that?''

''Because, you troublesome bitch, you have no choice. If you dare to tell anyone of our plans, especially your husband, the boy will suffer unthinkable pain, tortures you could never imagine.''

She gasped and shook her head.

''If Eirik is not dead within three days, I intend to deliver a special package to you at Ravenshire. You do like surprises, like most women, do you not?'' he asked. He waited several long moments before informing her, ''His head will be delivered to your door.''

Tears were streaming down Eadyth's face as she stared at Steven in horror. She had never believed in demonic possession; she did now.

Steven stood and pointed to a small pallet in the corner. ''You may sleep here tonight, or for as many nights as it takes to make up your mind. In the end, I am sure you will agree there is no other way.''

He locked the door after himself, but she could hear his evil laugh as he walked away.

For the rest of that day and then the sleepless night, Eadyth considered all the alternatives, and tossed most away as unworkable.

She wanted desperately to tell Eirik, but decided she could not. How could she risk Godric's life, not knowing if Steven still had a spy in Ravenshire? Eirik's rage would be evident to all in the keep.

But, of course, she would not kill Eirik. She would kill no man, but certainly not the husband she had grown to love. However, Steven did not know that. As far as he could see, theirs was a marriage of convenience, arranged to suit her need for husbandly protection and Eirik's need for lands and wealth.

She thought about going away herself, perhaps even seeking the asylum of the Church. But that would mean leaving John with Eirik. Even that painful separation she could bear if it would ensure John's safety. But it would not. Steven would merely intensify his efforts to kill Eirik to reach his son.

If she could kill Steven herself, she would. But not once in her contacts with him could she think of any time he had left himself open to attack. If Eirik had been unsuccessful thus far in killing the demon, how could she hope to succeed?

Back and forth, Eadyth debated the dilemma in her head. Over and over, she recalled her words to Eirik that she would never, ever deliver herself and her sons into Steven's filthy hands. She had sworn she would die first.

In the end, that was precisely what Eadyth decided that she and John would do—die.

The next morning when Steven returned to unlock her chamber, Eadyth had her emotions under control. She had become quite the actress while fooling Eirik over her appearance. She drew on that expertise now.

"I agree," she told Steven woodenly.

"I knew you would," he said with a self-satisfied smirk. He drew the vial of poison from his tunic and handed it to her. Eadyth noticed that he had bathed and shaved. He almost looked like his old self. And Eadyth knew that if he chose to wield his old charm he could probably still lure some trusting women into his seductive traps. Or fool the nobles of Edred's Witan.

" 'Tis best if you return to Ravenshire as soon as possible," he advised. "Eirik has not yet returned with John, my informants tell me. I suggest you do not tell him you have been here with me. Say you were lost in the forest, or some such thing. You will think of something. Women are good at lying."

And men, too. You deceitful wretch. "You must release Godric to come back with me."

He shook his head emphatically. "He will stay 'til I have proof of Eirik's death."

Eadyth's heart sank with dismay. "But I cannot leave the poor child here to be tortured."

"He has not been tortured, nor will he be, unless you fail in your mission."

"Why should I believe you?" she cried out impulsively.

A muscle twitched near Steven's thinned lips, but he did not strike her, as Eadyth would have expected. "I was tor . . . treated badly when I was of the same age," Steven revealed, to her surprise. "You may find this hard to believe, but I have no taste for inflicting the same . . . pain on another child. Yea, I know Eirik has told you how I beat him as a child, but I knew even then that I got no joy from torturing children. An adult . . . now that is a different matter."

Eadyth saw a searing pain in Steven's bloodshot eyes as he momentarily forgot himself and stared off in space, remembering some events in his far distant past. What could have happened to him as a child to have twisted his mind so?

"You have an odd sense of morality, Steven. You do horrid, horrid things to people. And yet you claim you would not harm Godric just because—"

He shook his head sharply, as if to clear his distasteful past, and snapped, "Enough! I do not need to explain myself to you. Come. A farmer's cart awaits below. You travel back to Ravenshire in high style, my lady.''

All of Eadyth's bindings were put back on, including the blindfold and gag, and she was forced into what must be the bed of a wagon, then covered with straw. Before they left, Steven told her, "Three days, Eadyth. Or you will receive my 'gift' to you.''

Several hides away from Ravenshire, the farmer stopped his wagon and released her. He pointed her toward the road, refusing stonily to answer her questions, then turned and went in the opposite direction. Eadyth began the long walk home and entered the keep through the hidden tunnel. She barred it from the inside to preclude any further unannounced visits from Steven.

Luckily, Eirik and John had not yet returned from Wessex. She had time to compose herself and make her plans. And, although skeptical, a frantic Wilfrid and the Ravenshire staff accepted her explanation that she had become lost when searching in the forest for Godric.

That evening, Eadyth sought out Britta to aid her in her plan. The maid, having suffered personally at Steven's hands, would understand Eadyth's need to take such drastic action. Leastways, she hoped Britta would understand.

"Are you daft?" Britta exclaimed after hearing Eadyth's story. "You want me to help you plan for your death, and John's?''

"Not our real deaths, just our false deaths. You, more than any other, know he means what he says. He will behead Godric if I do not do as he orders.''

"And he orders that you kill the Lord of Ravenshire?''

"Yea, and then wed with him.''

Britta shivered with distaste at the prospect. "But there must be another way. If you discuss it with the master—''

"Nay, I cannot. Steven would know and he would enact his revenge on me by hurting Godric. Furthermore, Eirik would go after Steven with even more furor, and I fear for his life, as well.'' Her last words were spoken in a bare whisper, and tears welled in her eyes.

"You love the Lord of Ravenshire, then?" Britta asked, laying a hand compassionately over Eadyth's.

Eadyth nodded, unable to speak.

"It would break the master's heart to learn of your death. He loves you so."

"Do you think so?" Eadyth asked hopefully.

"Anyone with eyes can see that he cares. How can you hurt him so, if you love him?"

"How can I not do this, if I love him? 'Tis best for everyone. 'Tis the only way." She swallowed the bitter taste of despair in her throat and took both of Britta's hands in hers. "I know that you love Wilfrid and that he wants to wed with you. Nay, do not protest. I know your concerns about your differing backgrounds . . . we will discuss that later. But consider if it were you in this position and you feared for Wilfrid's life, what would you do?"

"Oh, mistress!" she said softly, understanding completely that Eadyth had no choice. "How long would you have to stay in hiding?"

Eadyth shrugged. " 'Til Steven is finally dead."

"But that could be years and years."

She nodded dismally.

"And what if Eirik should decide to remarry?"

Eadyth gasped. She had not thought of that possibility. She pictured the years ahead . . . alone, bereft and desolate. She girded herself to be strong. "Then I would have to stay 'dead' forever, although John could return when he reaches his majority to take over Hawks' Lair."

"And how would he explain away his 'death,' and yours, then, when he returns from the dead?"

"Oh, I do not know. All these questions! I will worry about that when the time comes. Will you help me, Britta? You are my only hope."

Britta agreed reluctantly.

"It must be done soon. Mayhap on the morrow. The next day, at the latest. Steven only gave me three days."

"And what about Godric?"

"I think Steven will release him when he learns that John and I have died. Something he said makes me think he will not torture the boy needlessly. I believe Steven was abused badly as a child."

Britta eyed her skeptically. "And how will you 'die'? With the poison he gave you."

"Nay, there can be no 'dead' bodies for Eirik to examine. I had thought of fire, but that would be too devastating for Emma to go through again. Losing me and John will be hard enough on her and Larise."

"Drowning?"

"I had considered that, but there are no large bodies of water nearby, ones with currents strong enough to carry away evidence. And Eirik would search for our bodies."

"Then what?" Britta gaped at her in horror.

"I have heard there have been problems with marauding wolf packs in the hills. Do you think we could pretend to have been the victims of the wild beasts?"

"There would have to be evidence, would there not?"

"Yea, but if there were pieces of our bloody garments, and some bones—"

"Bones! What kind of bones?" Britta was backing away from Eadyth as if she feared she had lost her sanity. Mayhap she had.

"Well, I was thinking that perchance you could—"

"*Me?* What? What are you planning? Oh, Lord," she said as realization seemed to hit her like a lightning bolt, "you want me to rob some graves, do you not?"

Eadyth smiled mirthlessly. "Nay, even I would not go *that* far. I think if we used some animal bones from the kitchen butcherings, and mangled them a bit, Eirik might not question too closely." She looked hopefully to Britta. "What do you think?"

"I think you are daft."

They had no more time to discuss the plan then because Girta knocked on the chamber door, announcing happily,

"Riders approach carrying the Ravenshire colors. It must be Eirik and young John returning from Glastonbury. Hurry."

Eadyth pulled Britta into a hug, thanking her in a heartfelt whisper. "I will never forget what you are doing for me."

"Methinks I will ne'er forget it, either," Britta grumbled as she went off to gather bones.

Eadyth had just got to the bailey when Eirik and his retainers rode in. John jumped from his horse and rushed into her arms, talking excitedly.

While she hugged and kissed him over and over, he exclaimed, "You should have seen the funeral, Mother. There were ever so many people, and all of 'em cryin' for the king. And there were two hundred white horses with gold bridles. And Prince Edwy and Prince Edgar had their own ponies. And I learned to play dice . . ."

Eadyth shot a glare at Eirik, who was dismounting. "Dice?"

But John just rushed on, pushing his way with some embarrassment out of her continued embrace, ". . . and King Edred and some priest named Dunstan talked to me about Father, and they asked me about some man, Steven, I think . . . leastways, the king and this . . ."

John rambled on and finally Eadyth shooed him up the castle steps where Larise and Emma were waiting. Eadyth turned then and walked into her husband's arms, holding on to him tightly. She could not stop the tears which streamed down her face. Every moment that she had left with Eirik would be precious.

Eirik looked down at Eadyth with surprise. She had never been so demonstrative in public before. Well, she had been worried about her son's fate, and he and John had been delayed overlong with Dunstan's maneuverings. Relief, no doubt, accounted for her squeezing the very breath from his lungs and the profuse tears which wet the front of his tunic.

More than that, he hoped her embrace meant that she had missed him. As much as he had missed her.

I love her, Eirik thought with wonder. There was no question in his mind now. It had taken only one day away from her for Eirik to come to that realization, but he had not wanted to tell her in his letters. He wanted to see her face the first time he told her of his love.

I love her.

Eirik gazed down at his sobbing wife and smiled. It did not matter if she was shrewish on occasion—more than on occasion, actually, he thought with a rueful smile. And he could put up with her domineering ways—up to a point. Another rueful smile twitched at his lips. As long as she continued to match him in the bed sport . . . and tell him she loved him . . . and provide a warm family for him and their children . . . and . . . .

Eirik's thoughts trailed off as he realized, *I just love her. There is no logical reason. She has snared me good and well. The sharp-tongued, waspish witch!*

"Shush, dearling," Eirik said, kissing the top of her hair and pulling her to his side with an arm draped over her shoulder.

Wilfrid stepped forward. "There is much I have to report. That starveling Godric is—"

Eirik waved him aside. "Later. I would . . . comfort my wife first."

"But—"

Eirik ignored Wilfrid and the other servants. Larise and Emma were on the other side of the hall, held back by Girta. Later . . . later he would greet his children good and proper. For now, he wanted . . . nay, *needed* to be alone with his wife.

No sooner had the bedchamber door closed behind them than Eirik pressed Eadyth back against the door with his arms braced over her head. Her eyes were wild and darting about, refusing to meet his. And she whimpered, as if in pain.

"Eadyth, dearling," he said huskily, holding her chin in place, forcing her to look up at him, "have you missed me as much as I have missed you?"

"Desperately. I have longed for you desperately," she admitted without her usual inhibitions.

Eirik's heart expanded in his chest almost to bursting, and

his staff began to harden against her. He pressed himself against her belly to show her how desperately he "longed" for her, as well.

"No doubt there were many beautiful women at Edred's court," she said, tracing his jaw lovingly with a forefinger, then following its path with small kisses.

"No doubt," he said rawly. His blood thickened and his skin grew hot. As his loins grew heavy with want, he had to force himself not to throw his wife to their bed with undue haste.

She arched her hips upward against him, and Eirik gasped. He saw that she wanted him as fiercely as he wanted her.

"And no doubt those women were . . . available to you."

Does she really think I noticed other women after having her? "No doubt." To his pleasure, he saw her eyes flash with anger.

"And were they sweet and biddable?"

Is that my shrewish Eadyth looking vulnerable and insecure? "No doubt," he said silkily, smiling against her lips.

She nipped at his bottom lip with her teeth to show her displeasure.

He did the same to hers, continuing, "But I had an odd craving for tartness . . . and a woman who could turn *me* biddable. Do you perchance know of such a woman?"

"Mayhap." And she smiled against his lips.

Touching the tip of his tongue to her enticing mole, he traced the seam of her lips which parted on an involuntary sigh. "So tell me, my not-so-sweet and not-so-biddable wife, what would you *bid* me do for you?"

"Ease my ache," she said softly, surprising him. "Can you cure me of this sweet, hot ache which has overcome me?"

Eirik's knees almost buckled. He lifted her by the waist so her toes barely touched the floor and braced himself against the vee of her legs.

She moaned and arched her neck back.

"I am nigh blind, Eadyth, you know that—"

She made a growling sound of disbelief.

"—therefore you will have to show me where you . . . *ache*."

Through half-slitted, passion-glazed eyes, she gazed up at him. Holding his eyes, she boldly placed one of his hands over her heart.

And he almost lost his fast-slipping control. Gripping her head with both hands, he kissed her with savage intensity, unleashing all the pent-up longing of the past two sennights. Urgently, he claimed her lips, entreating her to open for him, then explored her mouth with his tongue. She almost shattered him with the hunger with which she yielded to his forceful domination, returning his kisses in equal measure.

He wanted to devour her. He wanted her to devour him.

He wanted to sear her with the heat that was burning him up. He wanted her to envelop him with her own hot fires.

He wanted to love her until the end of time. And he wanted her to return that love.

But all he could say was, "Eadyth," softly, wonderingly, over and over, between kisses and frantic caresses and an arousal that grew and grew and grew. Finally, he tore his mouth from hers, breathing raggedly. He could take no more. Lifting her into his arms, he walked a few short steps and laid her gently on the bed.

With jerky, urgent movements, they helped each other disrobe, sometimes tearing cloth in their haste. When they were both naked, gasping for air, Eirik leaned over Eadyth, straddling her body. He put a hand between them, touching the dampness of her maiden hair with familiarity.

"You are ready for me, Eadyth," he rasped out.

"For days I have been ready for you, my husband. Mayhap a lifetime," she confessed on a broken whisper.

"I have been thinking about us like this for days," he said gritting his teeth as he entered her moist silk, slowly, so slowly he could barely breathe. Her hot sheath spasmed around him in welcome, its folds shifting to accommodate his growing size. And hot woman dew gushed out of her body, anointing him with her pleasure.

Eadyth made a slow keening sound of pleasure-pain and wrapped her long legs around his waist.

He drove her with long, excruciatingly slow strokes to the point of madness—his and hers, both—then stopped, and started all over again. He knelt, still impaling her, and arched her body upward so her breasts met his thirsty mouth. As he suckled, then plucked gently with his teeth on the aching buds, she convulsed around him with violent shivers. But he would not let himself go.

He filled her. He consumed her. He wanted all she had to give and then more.

He was beside her, over her, under her, around her—touching, kissing, pressing. He could not tell where her slick body ended and his began. Her flailing, keening body called to a primitive side of his soul.

"Let it happen," she pleaded incoherently.

Desire roared in his ears like wild wind on a stormy sea.

He raised himself on straightened arms and arched his shoulders back. "Look at me, Eadyth," he demanded in a thickened voice. When she raised her eyelids only slightly, gazing up at him dreamily, he ordered, "Nay, open your eyes. *Really* look at me."

When he had her full attention, Eirik pulled himself almost completely outside her body. "I love you, Eadyth. Do you hear me? I . . . love . . . you."

Her eyes grew wide, misting with tears, and then she smiled. A beautiful, soft, heart-stopping smile, like a caress. "I love you, too. Oh, Eirik, I love you, too. Always remember that."

He gave himself freely to his passion then, pummeling her willing, spasming body with harder and shorter strokes until he embedded himself in the heart of her and filled her with his seed. He cried out once again, "I love you, Eadyth," before he fell heavily on her.

An amazing sense of completeness enveloped him as he slowly came to his senses, rolling to his side and taking Eadyth with him. This wonderful thing that had just happened to them was so much more than a physical act. He tried to find the words to tell Eadyth of his feelings as he stroked her smooth shoulder, her silky hair. But then he noticed that Eadyth was weeping silently, profusely.

He leaned up on one elbow to look at his wife, his *beloved* wife. "So this is how you react to my first words of love to you, Eadyth?" he teased, oddly hurt by her tears.

She tried to smile, and failed. Caressing his cheek, she murmured, "Your love means everything in the world to me, Eirik. Know that, always."

Always? The word had an ominous ring to Eirik's ears. He narrowed his eyes, scrutinizing her more closely. Damn his bleary eyes! He squinted and drew back slightly to see better. Dark shadows marked the undersides of her eyes and tension bracketed her tight lips. Had she looked like this when he arrived? Or had his lovemaking caused her dismay? Or worse yet, his words of love?

"Tell me what troubles you, Eadyth," he demanded, sitting up. "How have I displeased you?"

"Oh, nay, 'tis not you," Eadyth reassured him, then shifted her eyes away guiltily, as if to hide some secret. Even with his poor sight, he could see that she seemed to be gathering her senses. She told him about Godric being missing and how she had been lost in the woods. But she deliberately looked away when he questioned her icily about having disobeyed his orders and leaving the keep and about exactly what section of the forest she had been lost in.

"We will find Godric," he promised her and saw that her eyes darted nervously. He took her trembling hands in his and asked, "Is that all, Eadyth?"

She nodded, but her eyes had a faraway, unreachable cast.

"And you have had no more encounters with Steven?" he asked, lying back down beside her, tracing a fingertip lazily down her arm, then kissing the inside of her wrist.

She shivered, whether from his touch or the question, he could not tell. Then she shook her head. Eirik peered closer and saw that her face had flushed.

"Why would you ask about Steven?" she asked tentatively, and clenched her fists tightly at her sides.

Eirik shrugged, a dull ache of foreboding creeping over the back of his neck. "No reason. You just seem jittery and . . . frightened."

He felt her pulse jump in her wrist. Looking at her closely, he studied every telling reaction. "And that is all?"

She hesitated. "Yea."

And Eirik knew his wife was lying through her teeth. The woman to whom he had just pledged his undying love was keeping secrets again. A raw and primitive grief overwhelmed him.

Women and lies, the ageless combination! Bloody Hell! Would he never learn?

Chapter Nineteen

"They are both hiding something," Wilfrid told Eirik just past dawn the next morning as they broke their fast, alone in the great hall. He thumped his goblet down angrily, spilling some watered ale on the table. "Britta and your lady wife had their heads together all of yesterday. Whenever I asked Britta what it was about, she nigh trembled out of her skin."

"Eadyth is the same," Eirik said miserably. In his fury last night, he had been unable to bear the thought of making love to his wife again. She had lost her appeal after he realized she was involved in some new deceit, especially when she stubbornly refused to tell him the truth. He would not even share her bed, despite her tearful protests. Instead, he had laid his head on one of the hall pallets. But he had not slept.

"Mayhap they are just worried about Godric," Wilfrid offered unconvincingly.

"We all are, but I know there is more. God's Bones, did you hear the lame excuse Eadyth gave for being gone from the keep while I was away? I never heard so much stuttering and stammering and outright lying in all my life."

"So you do not believe she was lost in the forest?"

Eirik made a snorting sound of disbelief. "I am furious that Eadyth left the keep against my orders. The woman's willfulness staggers the senses. But, even worse, there are no forests close to the keep and none so thick that a person could not soon find a way out."

"Eirik, I know you are angry, but there must be an explanation."

"There is no excuse for lying. *None.* Eadyth knows how important honesty is to me, and still she deliberately deceives me, *again.*"

Wilfrid sat up straighter. "I just thought of something else. The Lady Eadyth has been behaving strangely in other ways since her return. She has been buzzing about the keep in a most frantic fashion—"

"She always buzzes," Eirik said, "or nags, or orders, or 'manages.' "

Wilfrid waved his hand dismissively. "Nay, I mean that she was making odd lists for one and all. A calendar of chores for each and every Ravenshire servant to complete for the next year. A list of repairs needed in the keep and the cotters' huts. Items to be ordered from Jorvik. Instructions on how to care for her bees and her bee products. 'Tis almost as if . . ." Wilfrid's eyes widened with shock.

"What?"

" 'Tis almost like a dying person putting his affairs in order," Wilfrid said.

Eirik laughed mirthlessly. "Eadyth is as healthy as a mule. A mean, stubborn, braying mule." *With the morals of a snake.* He considered Wilfrid's words, nonetheless, as he stroked his upper lip, deep in thought. "I am sure there is some connection here betwixt her and Britta conspiring, Godric's absence, her list making, and . . . I hate to say this . . . Steven of Gravely. You can be sure I will get to the bottom of this puzzle, but I will never, *never*, trust the woman again."

Wilfrid nodded gravely.

"See what you can find out."

Eirik was about to go up to his bedchamber and confront Eadyth once again when Wilfrid signaled him to come over to the door leading to the bailey.

"Bloody Hell!" Eirik exclaimed as he saw Jeremy, Eadyth's stoneworker from Hawks' Lair, driving an overloaded wagon through the gate. He and Wilfrid descended the stone steps and walked up to the building where the cart had stopped. There were enough woven bee hives, pottery containers for honey, straining cloths, candle molds and kitchen supplies to last Ravenshire for a year. "What in the name of all the saints is this?" Eirik demanded of the startled servant.

Jeremy shrugged, backing away from Eirik's stormy countenance. "My lady sent me to Jorvik yestermorn with a long list."

"A list!" Eirik and Wilfrid both said, giving each other speaking looks.

"And you drove all through the night to get here just past dawn? What prompted your haste?"

Jeremy shook his head uncertainly. "My lady said there was urgency."

"For honey pots?"

"My lord," Jeremy said impatiently. "I do what my lady orders. 'Tis not fer me to question."

Eirik told Jeremy to unload the cart, but not before the servant handed him a large, linen-wrapped parcel.

"What is this?" Eirik snapped.

"More fabric fer beekeeping veils. Wouldst you give it to the mistress? And tell her that her agent sez this be the last of it he could find in all of Jorvik. And he is sore angry with her fer demandin'—"

Eirik turned away rudely from the servant in mid-sentence, too angry to be polite. He headed toward the keep. Her agent was not the only one "sore angry" with Eadyth. He intended to confront his lady wife once again and get some answers this time.

"Here comes trouble," Abdul squawked when Eirik entered the bedchamber. In no mood for shrewish carping, whether from a parrot or his wife, Eirik threw a mantle over the cage. But the damn bird got the last word in, muttering, "Loathsome lout! Awk!"

Eirik saw that Eadyth was still asleep, though she tossed restlessly. No doubt troubled by her latest deceits, Eirik thought. He pulled a chair closer to the bed and slouched down with outstretched legs crossed at the ankles, his fingers steepled in front of his mouth.

He could not see her very well in the dim light, just the outlines and shadowy curves of her nude body barely covered by the bed linens. For once, he was not tempted—not by the exceedingly long legs, or the curve of her breasts, not even by the enticing mole above her lips. All he saw when he looked at his wife was deceit.

How will I ever be able to live with a woman who lies as often as she breathes? In truth, can I live with her at all now?

"Eirik?" Eadyth said tentatively as she opened her eyes sleepily and sat up in the bed. Drawing the sheet up over her breasts, she tossed her mane of silver hair over her shoulders. "You never came back to bed," she rebuked him in a trembling voice.

He said nothing, just stared at her, trying to understand her devious mind.

"Eirik, come to bed. Please."

"I will never lie with you again, Eadyth," he said, marveling that he could speak so calmly in spite of his fury.

She gasped and made a small whimpering sound.

"Unless you tell me the truth," he continued in a steely voice. *And mayhap not even then*, he added to himself.

She closed her eyes and rocked back and forth in misery, but would not speak. In fact, she bit her bottom lip as if to prevent the words from spilling out.

His desolate spirits sank even lower.

When she finally opened her eyes, he saw that they were filled with tears, pleading. He was not moved.

"I love you," she said in a small voice.

He stood and stared at her in icy contempt. "I do not care." *God help me, I wish that were so.* He threw the package of fabric Jeremy had given him on the bed. "Here. This just arrived for you."

Eadyth gazed at the linen parcel in horror and shoved it away from her. It fell down to the rushes. Then she began to keen loudly, "Oh, nay, please, do not let it be so. Oh, God, 'tis only the second day. Oh, God—"

"Bloody Hell, Eadyth, what ails you? 'Tis just the fabric you ordered from Jorvik. Jeremy brought it." He looked down at her with puzzlement. "What did you think it was—a shroud?"

Her violet eyes, misted with tears, blinked in confusion. "Fabric?" When she finally understood, Eadyth put her hand over her heart as if to still its wild beating. Then she pressed her lips together tightly and defiantly refused to answer his question.

Crushed by the defeat of Eadyth's silence, Eirik stalked over to the door and slammed it loudly behind him. Sigurd and Tykir were waiting for him in the hall.

"Good news finally, Eirik," Tykir informed him. "Earl Orm sent a message. We now know Gravely's hiding place in Northumbria . . . for a certainty. 'Tis a small manor about two hours from here, near Lord Cyril's estates."

Eirik closed his eyes and gave silent thanks that he might catch the evil Gravely at last. Nothing else in his life was going right. At least he would get this satisfaction.

"With any luck, we will find Godric at the same time," Sigurd said. They all nodded in agreement.

Wilfrid rushed up to Eirik then. "My lord, come at once. You will not believe what I have found."

"I have no time—"

"Believe me, Eirik, you have time for this."

Eirik ordered Tykir and Sigurd to ready their horses. "I will join you shortly." Then he followed after his seneschal, grumbling about the wasted time. They went through the kitchen and out to the courtyard, ignoring the working servants who stared at them with curiosity. When they got to Eadyth's crude shed for making mead, Wilfrid opened the door with a flourish.

Eirik's mouth gaped open with surprise.

A pile of bloody bones lay on the floor in the center next to the still. All kinds of bones—cow legs, cattle shoulder bones, the hipbone of a sheep, what appeared to be a pig's skull, eyeballs . . . *eyeballs!* They were piled almost waist high and beginning to emit a rank odor.

"What is the meaning of all this?" Eirik exclaimed. "I must be off with Sigurd and Tykir to capture Gravely. Why do you waste my time with animal remains? And why are they out here and not in the midden?" He wrinkled his nose with distaste.

" 'Tis a clue," Wilfrid announced, grinning with self-satisfaction.

"Have you lost your senses like everyone else in this keep? What kind of clue?"

"A clue to Lady Eadyth and Britta's plot."

Eirik put his hands on his hips and glared at his seneschal, tapping his foot testily.

"Do you not see? They have been hiding the bones in here for some devious purpose. Methinks it has something to do with Godric."

"Methinks you were knocked on the head this morn. Methinks 'tis more likely these are the secret ingredients in Eadyth's mead."

Wilfrid's eyes widened with wonder. "Do you really think so?"

"Nay, you lackwit, I do not think so. Get Britta and bring her here at once. I have had more than enough of all this nonsense. I will have answers and I will have them *now*."

A short time later, a clearly frightened Britta stood before them in the shed. Her red hair stood out in disarray, and her apron hung askew, as if she had hurried, or was flustered.

"I will give you an opportunity to answer my questions, Britta," Eirik said tautly. "One lie . . . one lie only . . . and you will be banished from Ravenshire. And do not be thinking your mistress will help you, because she may very well be traveling the road with you.''

Britta looked toward Wilfrid for help, but his arms were crossed over his chest. He scowled down at her, refusing to come to her aid. ''Tell the truth, Britta,'' Wilfrid said stonily, ''for if you are banished, I will not be able to come with you, or after you.''

Her eyes darted forlornly around the shed, like a trapped rabbit.

''Why have you and Eadyth been collecting these bones?'' Eirik asked, ripping the words out impatiently.

The maid inhaled deeply for courage, then exhaled loudly with resignation. ''So she and John can die,'' Britta confessed in a voice barely above a whisper.

Eirik's mouth dropped open, and Wilfrid's eyes almost popped from his head.

''Die? Die?'' Eirik grabbed Britta by the forearms and shook her. ''Stop blathering your foolish words. Why are these bones here?''

''I told you,'' Britta said through chattering teeth. ''The mistress needs to pretend that she and John have been killed by wild wolves, and these bones were going to be the evidence. Oh, Blessed Mary, now Godric will die. And you, too, Lord Eirik.'' She threw herself into the arms of a stunned Wilfrid, wailing loudly about poisons and drownings and human heads.

When Britta settled down a bit, they all sat on a nearby bench. Eirik forced Britta to disclose everything. After her lengthy, incredible story, Eirik stood abruptly, rigid with rage. ''She thought to fool me with cow bones and pig eyeballs?'' he asked incredulously. ''Does she think my vision is that poor, my brain that dull?''

''Oh, nay, master, we were going to mangle them a bit. Once we crushed the bones a few times with a hammer, you would not be able to tell . . .'' Her words trailed off when she heard his quick intake of breath. He gave her a sidelong look of utter disbelief.

"Britta, how could you?" Wilfrid sputtered out. "I trusted you. I asked you to be my wife. How could you?"

She began to wail again.

"And where was she going?" Eirik asked icily, spacing his words evenly.

"Normandy."

Eirik clenched his jaw.

"My lady's missive to her agent—the one with her orders for supplies—also had instructions for booking passage for her and John."

"And how did she intend to live?"

"Bees," Britta offered weakly. "She was taking a small hive with her to start a new colony."

Eirik rolled his eyes heavenward. "One last thing. Where is the poison Steven gave her to use on me?"

Britta looked uncertain. " 'Twas hidden above the door jamb in your bedchamber, out of the children's reach, but the mistress may have thrown it away by now. Oh, master, you never thought that she would actually use it on you, did you?"

"Nay. I am thinking of using it on her, though." He turned to Wilfrid and said, "I expect you to punish Britta for her part in this foolhardy plot. As I will handle my own faithless lady."

Wilfrid nodded, and Eirik turned, heading back toward the keep and his willful, deceitful, lackbrain wife. At that moment, he could have killed her without any compunction whatsoever.

Eadyth was not the only one with a talent for making lists. He began to make a list in his mind of all the ways he could torture her before doing the final deed. Mayhap he would start by rubbing her face in the bloody animal parts. Or make her swallow a pig eye or two.

Luckily, Eadyth was hidden behind a screen in his bedchamber when Eirik entered. He reached above the door jamb and retrieved the vial of poison. Then he locked the door behind him. Quickly, he dumped the vial's contents into a chamber pot, then rinsed it out and filled it with water.

He noticed the still-wrapped linen parcel on the floor and felt a momentary twinge of sympathy for Eadyth when he realized that she must have thought it was Godric's head. But her pain was naught when weighed against the kind of pain he would have felt on learning of her and John's deaths. *How could she?*

Eadyth practically jumped out of her skin when she emerged from behind the screen, fully clothed, and saw him leaning against the door, waiting for her.

"You came back," she said hopefully, reaching out toward him with open arms.

He sidestepped her embrace. "I am leaving with Sigurd and Tykir," he told her evenly, barely holding in check the angry words he wanted to hurl at her. "At last, we have Gravely within our grasp. I hope to inform you afore this day ends that the demon is finally dead."

"Oh, nay, you cannot go after Steven now."

"And why not?" He raised an eyebrow at her.

The hand she pressed to her lips shook, and she moved jerkily. The woman was clearly overwrought. She finally choked out, "Please. If you ever cared for me, do not go today."

"Why?"

"Because . . . because I have had a dream portending misfortune." She could not look him in the eye as she spoke.

Liar!

"And I am feeling unwell." Her eyes looked everywhere but at him.

Liar! "Are you worried that I would be unequal in a contest with Steven of Gravely?"

"Nay."

Liar!

"Do you think he may have captured Godric and that my precipitous actions may jeopardize the boy's life?"

365

She gasped, and her eyes widened with fright at his words, which must seem glaringly insightful to her. "Of course not, though you know how devious Steven can be, and, *if* he has Godric, he might use the boy in any way he can . . ." Her words trailed off as she realized that she was rambling and that he was staring at her with icy contempt. "Eirik, I beg of you, stay at Ravenshire today. There will be other days to go after Steven."

"Give me good reason to stay."

"Because I love you."

Eadyth's words cut Eirik deeply because he now knew she was a master of falsehood. If she lied about one thing, she would lie about another. He hardened himself against her entreaties. "Love and lies never go hand in hand, Eadyth."

Her shoulders slumped with defeat.

"Why are you trembling, Eadyth?"

She stiffened and clenched her fists, forcing her body to stop shaking. The woman's will was formidable. And her courage, too, he had to admit.

Eirik stepped forward a pace and nudged the vial in the rushes, where he had placed it moments before. "What is this?" he asked, picking up the container with mock puzzlement.

"Oh!" she exclaimed, turning deathly pale. "Give that to me. It must have fallen . . ." She looked quiltily up at the door jamb.

Eirik held it close to his face, sniffing. "What an odd odor!"

"Give it to me," she demanded in a near hysterical voice, coming closer.

He held it out of her reach and tilted his head questioningly.

" 'Tis a headache potion the village herbal woman gave me. I told you I have been unwell."

Liar! He widened his eyes with forced delight. "Wonderful! I have a fearsome headache." Then, before she could react, he unstoppered the vial and downed its contents in one long swallow.

She screamed then. "Oh, no! Oh, no! 'Twas poison, my dearling! Quickly, try to vomit it up!"

"You wished to poison me?" he asked, blinking his eyes with deliberate hurt at his deceitful wife.

"Nay, 'twas Gravely." She tried to stick her fingers in his mouth to make him throw up the potion, and he bit her, hard.

Pushing her aside roughly, he stumbled over to the bed and plopped down onto his back. With an exaggerated sigh, he closed his eyes, moaning, "My loving wife, I will miss you sorely," and, with all the drama he could muster, pretended to die.

He could have sworn he heard Abdul snicker.

But Eadyth would not give up. She threw herself over his body, trying desperately to lift him up. Then she attempted once again to pry his mouth open and stick her fingers down his throat and bring up the fatal contents of his stomach. The whole time she was weeping and telling him how sorry she was and that she loved him dearly.

He gritted his teeth, faking the death stiffening of muscles. When she was unable to stick her fingers into his mouth, she began slapping his face back and forth, trying to awaken him from the dead. She even took both his ears in her hands and shook his head mightily, up and down off the mattress. His ears were ringing from her shrieking, as well as the head pounding on the mattress. Hell's flames, he really was developing a headache now.

A loud knocking commenced at the door, and he could hear Tykir and Wilfrid and Sigurd shouting with concern. Apparently, they had heard Eadyth scream. Hell, the pigeons in Jorvik had probably heard her caterwauling.

Eadyth just ignored them all, keening like a banshee as she tried straddling his body and breathing her own air into his mouth. When she pinched his nose shut with the fingers of one hand, placed her mouth over his, trying to breathe air into his lungs, and bounced her rump up and down on his chest to restart his heart, he decided he had suffered more than enough. If he did not stop the wench, she would truly kill him.

Gasping for breath, he shoved her from his chest and rolled off the bed. "Save your ministrations, Eadyth. I want them not."

She gaped at him. "You are not dead."

"How observant of you!" He called out to the men still shouting outside the door, "All is well. I will be with you in a moment." He heard them walking away, grumbling.

Eadyth shook her head, much like a wet dog, as if to clear her senses. When comprehension dawned, she lunged for him and began to pummel his chest. "You beast! How could you play such a cruel joke on me?"

"Cruel? Cruel?" he lashed out with savage anger, taking her wrists in both his hands and holding her away from his body. "I will tell you what is cruel. Having no faith whatsoever in a husband and his ability to protect you. Lying whenever 'tis convenient for you. Planning to fake your own death and that of your son. Leaving the man you claim to love, mayhap for a year, perchance forever. Not caring about the grief you leave in the wake of your thoughtless maneuverings. That is what is cruel, my lady bitch." He released her hands and shoved her away with disgust.

Eirik knows. The message finally seeped into Eadyth's muddled brain. *Oh, Lord, will he ever forgive me now?*

"I am going after Gravely. We know where he is now. Finally. And, yea, my deceitful wife, I think I am capable of the task, despite your lack of faith."

"Eirik, I never doubted your abilities—"

He raised a palm to halt her words. "Naught you could say now will ever erase your actions. Do not seek to excuse them. And do not blame Britta for confessing your lackbrain plot. 'Twas unfair of you to involve her."

Eadyth nodded, wringing her hands with concern. "I worry about your safety, Eirik. Everything I did was out of concern for you and Godric."

"I want naught from you now, Eadyth. Not your concern.

Nor your affections.'' He stepped up to her and poked a finger in her face. ''You are not to step from this room 'til I return or you receive word that Steven of Gravely is no longer a threat. Do I need to tie you to the bed? Or post a guard at the door?''

She shook her head as tears of hopelessness streamed down her face.

''I love you,'' she whispered to his departing back.

''I do not care,'' he said flatly, without turning around.

Eirik refused to think about Eadyth and the pain of her betrayal as he rode toward Gravely's hiding place. He needed to focus his attention on the task at hand. Tykir and Sigurd accompanied him, along with three dozen armed men, all on horseback.

When they approached the abandoned manor from a circuitous back route, Eirik motioned the men to divide into four and cover all sides of the keep, which appeared to be heavily guarded. He would try to enter, alone, from the rear while Sigurd created a diversion near the main gate in front.

He tied his horse to a tree some distance away and crept stealthily to the back wall. It was not as heavily manned as the front since there was no rear entrance, just solid stone. He waited until the guard passed on his patrol and figured he had only a few moments. Tossing a loop of rope up, he tried to catch it on one of the crenellations. It took three tries before it caught.

He heard shouting and the clang of metal off in the distance and knew his men were trying to breach the front entrance. Quickly, he pulled the rope taut and carefully walked himself up the back wall. He smiled, despite the gravity of his situation. Wall climbing had been a feat he and Tykir had practiced innumerable times as youngsters under their grandfather's watchful eye at Ravenshire. It was a game they had soon mastered. Pray God the talent would carry him today.

He climbed over the top and found himself immediately in

peril. Two of Gravely's guards approached from different directions on the parapet, snarling obscenities. Pulling out his sword, Eirik immediately dispatched the one with a thrust to his huge stomach. The other was a more even match, and Eirik only managed a few nicks at his forearms and thighs. When Eirik backed up from one particularly harsh assault, he tripped over the leg of the fallen soldier and was soon backed up against the wall of the walkway.

Pressing a sword against Eirik's throat so that it drew blood, the burly soldier growled, "Who are you? Do you come from Ravenshire?"

Eirik refused to answer and felt the blade press tighter. "Prepare to meet your maker then," the guard threatened.

Eirik said a silent prayer for his immortal soul, figuring his death was at hand, but then he stiffened with determination when he realized that Gravely would escape once again. With renewed strength born of the need for revenge, he kicked the soldier's vitals. At the soldier's momentary gasp of surprise, Eirik shot both arms up and out against the massive chest. In seconds, the guard lay below Eirik, face up, with Eirik's sword through his chest, spilling his life's blood. Eirik pulled his blade out with distaste and wiped it hurriedly on the man's tunic.

He turned and almost jumped out of his skin.

Tykir stood leaning against the parapet, smiling widely. "Well, 'tis glad I am that I did not have to rescue you."

"Bloody Hell, Tykir, what are doing here? You are supposed to be with Sigurd."

"Do you think I could let you climb a wall without me? I was ever the winner in that contest."

Eirik shook his head hopelessly at his brother's teasing, knowing the ill-timed humor masked a deep concern for his welfare. Eirik would have done the same for Tykir.

A short time later, dozens of Gravely's men lay dead or dying in the bailey, inside the hall and in the corridors, but there was no sign of the demon lord himself.

When Eirik entered one room after another, searching, he

finally found Godric, tied in a remote chamber. After he released him, the weeping boy clung to him in fright, unable to speak. Other than being terrified, the child did not appear to be injured. Mayhap Eadyth had been right when she told Britta that Steven would not harm the young boy.

Holding him on his lap, Eirik asked softly, "Do you know where Gravely has gone?"

Godric's little body began to shiver violently and he clung to Eirik even tighter, but his eyes shifted involuntarily to a drape-covered alcove on the far side of the room. With seeming calmness, Eirik signaled to Tykir with his eyes and handed him the boy. "Best you find Godric some food before we take him home. No doubt, John and the other children will treat him like a conquering hero." He pushed them both toward the door and pulled his sword from its scabbard and a dagger from his belt.

When he flicked the drape aside, Gravely jumped out at him brandishing a battle axe. His blue eyes were wide and crazed. Froth dribbled from the edges of his mouth.

"At last!" Steven screamed, and having the advantage of surprise, swung the axe over his head toward Eirik's face. Eirik swerved, but not before the blade swiped a chunk of flesh out of his shoulder almost to the bone. With a curse, Eirik ignored the pain and parried his opponent's next thrust, managing to wound Steven in the upper abdomen.

Despite the illness which had racked Steven's once fine body, he was still a strong warrior capable of holding his own against Eirik's expert skill, at least in the beginning. Back and forth, they parried and thrust. Steven dropped the axe and picked up a sword with nary a blink. But then the ravages of his illness began to take their toll, and Gravely's endurance faltered. He grew careless and clumsy.

And Eirik lost the taste for the kill. Oh, he would destroy his evil enemy. He had to, if for no other reason than to stop his senseless assaults on any who crossed his path. But the man was clearly insane. His eyes were unnaturally wide and glazed with a berserk lust for blood. His mouth hung slack and trembling, like that of an aged man. Mayhap he had always been mad, but hid it under a calm exterior.

How can I feel pity for this man who has hurt me so?

Because you know he must have suffered greatly to have reached this sorry state, he answered himself.

With a mighty thrust, Eirik shoved him against the wall and held his sword horizontally against Steven's throat. " 'Tis over, Gravely," he snarled. "Finally, your evil will end."

Steven cackled madly. "Yea, but will you be able to live with my death, *brother*?"

A cold chill ran over Eirik. The room rang with an ominous silence. He should have known that, even facing death, Steven would find a way to leave destruction in his wake.

"Eirik, do not listen to him," Tykir called out from behind him. "Just kill the bastard."

Gravely laughed again, not even trying to break free any longer. "Have you never thought on the resemblance betwixt us, Eirik? Black hair. Blue eyes. Same height. You share my blood, *brother*. And you know it."

"It cannot be so," Eirik said, shaking his head in denial.

"Your father planted his seed in my mother the one time she was able to escape her husband, the notorious Earl of Gravely, the man most people thought was my true father. She returned to Gravely when she learned she was breeding."

Eirik shook his head from side to side, denying Steven's claims. He still held the sword blade against his enemy's throat.

Steven continued with his incredible story. "My 'father' never wanted me, and after my mother and then he died, I was left at age ten in the care of the most evil man in all Britain—Jerome, the Gravely castellan. And my brother Elwinus barely out of swaddling cloths. Oh, Lord," he moaned, and his eyes rolled back in his head at some memory so painful even he could not bear to think on it.

Then Steven seemed to calm himself. He looked Eirik levelly in the eyes, momentarily sane, and whispered brokenly, "Brother . . ." At the same time, he jerked his head forward, deliberately cutting his own throat. Blood spurted every-where, but still a horrified Eirik held Steven upright by the arms.

And Eirik could not see for the tears which misted his eyes for his most hated enemy.

Chapter Twenty

Eadyth looked at the parchment in her hands and read it again, trying to understand:

> *Eadyth,*
> *It is over*
>
> *Eirik*

What did it mean? Wilfrid had returned with the men that evening, bringing Godric home safely, thank the Lord. But Eirik had gone to Jorvik with Tykir, leaving no word for her when he might return to Ravenshire.

It is over. Did it mean the struggle with Steven of Gravely was finally over? Or did it mean he considered their marriage over?

Eadyth quizzed Wilfrid repeatedly and got no answers. Oh, Wilfrid had told Eadyth about Steven's last words, and her heart went out to her husband and to Tykir, who must suffer greatly knowing they shared blood with such a demon. Or mayhap they grieved as well because they had never been able to help Steven as a boy before his mind became twisted from abuse.

Eadyth replayed the events of the past few days in her mind. Should she have gone to Eirik and told him all, even at the risk of Godric's life and his own, as well? Eirik apparently thought so.

Would she have done things differently if she had a chance to do them over? Probably not, Eadyth admitted to herself. She was headstrong in her ways, just as Eirik had said.

Perhaps she could change. Maybe if she were able to remove all the objectionable characteristics Eirik had pointed out, Eirik would be pleased and grow to love her again. For the next few days, as Eirik stayed in Jorvik and sent no word to her, Eadyth deferred to Wilfrid in many matters regarding the estate, even when he looked at her oddly. Even when he performed his duties in a manner she considered less than satisfactory or in a way she could do better.

She did not raise her voice shrewishly, not once, even when Bertha belched loudly in the hall.

She spent more time with the children, tutoring them and telling them tales. Did that not make her more womanly, less mannish? Would that impress her husband?

If only Eirik would return, somehow she would make it up to him for all the ways in which she had wronged him. She ached for the return of her husband, for the love she had apparently lost.

And she ached for other reasons, as well. For throughout all those days that Eirik stayed away, Eadyth retched every morning, ate ravenously the remainder of the day, and wept spontaneously at the least provocation.

She was carrying Eirik's child. She was gloriously happy. And she was extremely unhappy that she could not share the good news with her husband. Would he even consider it good news now?

"Send a message to the lackwit in Jorvik and tell him of the babe," Girta advised. "He will come when he learns of your condition."

"Nay. I want him to come because he loves me, not because of my child."

"And if he does not return?"

"Oh, Girta," Eadyth cried, throwing herself into her old nurse's arms. "I could not bear it if he never came back to me."

Then an insidious thought began to creep into Eadyth's mind as a sennight went by and she still had no word from her errant husband.

Could he be with Asa?

Nay, he would not go to her. He told me he had given her up, that he preferred me, the other side of her mind countered.

But that was afore I lied to him.

Well, if the bastard prefers another woman, let him go.

Eadyth thought about that last possibility for only one moment. *Nay! Bloody Hell, nay! I will not allow another woman to have my husband.*

And Eadyth reverted back to her old ways. With brisk efficiency, she ordered Wilfrid to bring her horse, along with two guards to accompany her. She was going to Jorvik.

And then, being the ever-practical business woman that she was, she decided there was no sense wasting a trip to the market town without bringing some of her honey and candles to her agent. And mayhap she could sell some wool, as well. Therefore, she told Wilfrid to get the cart and a driver.

"And there might be a buyer for those extra cherries and the embroidered cloths Girta has been working on," she told Wilfrid. Soon the seneschal was rolling his eyes heavenward, but he muttered, " 'Tis good to see you back to your old self, my lady."

When she got to Jorvik toward evening, Eadyth headed directly for her agent's home, where she usually stayed on her trips to the city. She discussed her business affairs with Bertrand that night, and the next day she headed to the orphanage outside the city where Eirik's "Uncle" Selik and his second wife Rain, Eirik and Tykir's half sister, lived.

The happy pair greeted Eadyth warmly after she introduced

herself amidst the din of dozens of children screaming and crying and laughing. Eadyth could only gape at the striking couple. Rain was almost as tall as her Viking husband. Both were blond-haired and beautiful. They continually touched each other as they passed in their everyday duties, the love between them apparent to all.

Amazingly, Rain was a healer, an unusual occupation for a woman, and she ran her own small hospitium on the orphanage grounds. Selik owned trading vessels which traveled around the world to market towns. Eadyth soon realized she might strike an advantageous arrangement with him for carrying some of her bee products.

"I am sorry we could not come to your wedding," Rain said. "I was not feeling well at the time, and Selik was concerned about my traveling this late in my pregnancy." She patted her stomach, and Eadyth could not stop looking at Rain's huge belly. Eadyth's eyes welled with tears when Selik came up behind his wife and placed his hands lovingly over their unborn child, kissing Rain's neck. Eadyth had never seen a married couple demonstrate their love so publicly before, and she found herself filled with envy.

Seeing Eadyth's dismay, Rain asked Eadyth to sit with them. "What is wrong, Eadyth? How can we help you?"

"Have you seen Eirik?" Eadyth blurted out.

"About five days ago," Selik said with a nod. "He came looking for helpers to refurbish his ship."

"His ship?" Eadyth stiffened with annoyance. So, not only did her husband have a treasure room at home, but he owned a ship in Jorvik. And all the time she was jabbering away about her business ventures, he had his own trading ship. By the saints! If she did not want the lackwit so much, she might consider tossing him out on his ear.

Then another unsettling thought occurred to her. "Does he intend to sail himself?"

Selik looked uncertain. "He did not say." Then he looked Eadyth over appraisingly. "Tell us why you are looking for your husband."

Eadyth felt her face redden, but it was no time for pride now. She started at the beginning with her foolish charade and ended with Steven of Gravely's disclosure.

Selik and Rain looked at each other oddly, then embraced tightly. Rain explained, with tear-filled eyes, "Selik and I—like so many others—have reasons to exult in Steven's death."

"Hmmm. Now I understand why Eirik seemed so upset," Selik said. "He always was such a sensitive, somber boy. He takes things very seriously. And, no doubt, he hoped to spare our feelings."

"Eirik? Somber?" Eadyth laughed. "Nay, you must refer to Tykir. Except for when he is angry, Eirik is ever teasing, or grinning, or winking."

Rain and Selik both stared at her, gape-mouthed with amazement. Then Rain turned to Selik. "Have you ever heard Eirik tease anyone?"

"Never," Selik said unequivocally. "And I have known the boy since he was in swaddling cloths."

"And winking!" Rain laughed aloud. Then she took both of Eadyth's hands in hers and squeezed warmly. "He must love you, dear, if you bring out that side of his character."

Eadyth's heart was warmed with hope, but it still brought her no closer to Eirik and a reconciliation. Selik and Rain invited Eadyth to stay with them, but she declined, wanting to be inside the city, closer to Eirik.

It was only midday when she returned to Jorvik, so she decided to look for Eirik at the harbor. She had gone but a short distance when she saw Tykir talking to a group of sailors who were loading a ship. With regret, she realized that he was preparing for a trading voyage. Would Eirik be going with him? she wondered miserably.

When Tykir saw her, his eyes brightened and he ended his conversation, sending the sailors off on some errand. "Eadyth! How wonderful to see you!" Opening his arms, he pulled Eadyth into his embrace. Then Tykir held her at his side with an arm looped over her shoulder and took her onto his ship.

"Where is he?" she asked immediately. "Have you seen Eirik?"

"Yea, of course I have seen him. He works on his ship near here. But Eirik went to Wessex yestereve to see King Edred and has not returned yet."

"Will he be back today?"

He shrugged. "Eirik is not himself, Eadyth. He tells me naught."

"I worry about him. My lies and the things Steven told him . . ." She broke off, unable to continue.

Tykir brushed some wisps of hair off her forehead with brotherly care. "He was shocked by Gravely's disclosure. I will not deny that. We both were. But he has come to accept that he could have done naught to change the course of Steven's life. We did not know of Steven's existence when we were boys, and Eirik would have been only five when Steven was orphaned."

She nodded. "And my lies? Will he forgive those?"

"Eadyth, really, just give Eirik time. He is a somber fellow, but—"

"Somber! Somber! Why dost everyone refer to Eirik as somber? The man is a rascal and you know it."

"A rascal? Eirik?" He studied her for one long moment, then declared, "He must love you if he shows a rascally side to you and no other."

It was much the same thing Selik and Rain had told her. But then Eadyth alarmed Tykir and surprised even herself by bursting into tears. Well, she told herself on a snuffling hiccough, she had already retched up her stomach's contents this morning. Now she was crying her eyes out. And soon, while she sat on a wine cask on Tykir's deck, spilling her heart's contents regarding her missing husband, she ate three apples, four honey cakes and twelve dried figs.

He gawked at her, astounded at her appetite. "Does the loathsome lout know?"

"Know what?"

"That you carry his 'loathsome lout of a son'?"

She looked up quickly in surprise at Tykir's insightful remark. "Nay, and do not tell him. I will not have him return to me out of obligation."

An hour later, Tykir walked her back to her agent's home. On the way, Tykir stopped suddenly at an eastern merchant's stall, his eyes twinkling mischievously.

"I think I know the very thing to lure your husband home."

"What?" she asked suspiciously.

When Omar, the trader, showed her the product that Tykir requested, Eadyth's mouth formed a small "o" of wonder. "Do you think . . . nay, I could not . . . never . . . well, if you *really* think so."

Eirik did not return to Jorvik that night, nor the next morning, and Eadyth began to panic. Tykir had told her that he would make sure Eirik came to her the minute he arrived, even if he had to truss him up and carry him. Eadyth was growing quite fond of her endearing brother-by-marriage.

Was it possible that Eirik had returned to Jorvik and refused to see her? After all, Tykir could not really force Eirik to do something he did not want to do. Or perchance he had come back to the city and had never gone to his ship. What if . . .

Eadyth reeled with pain at the possibility that Eirik might be with Asa, his former mistress. She could not sit and wait any longer. Eadyth dressed carefully in a pale lavender gunna over a cream-colored chemise. She left off the wimple, but wore the sheer violet head-rail she had worn for her wedding. A thin gold circlet held her head-rail in place, matching the gold-linked belt cinching her waist. She thought she looked quite well, considering her inner turmoil . . . until she got to Coppergate and found Asa's jewelry stall, that is.

The petite, raven-haired beauty was a jewel. Eadyth felt like a lump of granite next to her. Wallowing in misery, Eadyth knew she could not compete with such a beautiful creature.

When Eadyth introduced herself, Asa's eyes widened and she invited Eadyth to step into her home in the rear of the market stall. Eadyth looked around quickly at the small but immaculate home, decorated with several finely carved chairs and tables—probably from Eirik's treasure room, she thought meanly. She tried to picture Eirik here with Asa, sitting before that fireplace, eating her food, going up to that cozy second-floor bedloft. *Oh, Lord.*

To her mortification, she burst into tears.

Eirik was thoroughly disgusted. He had just returned from Winchester where he had spent a day arguing with Edred and his advisors about their plans to invade Northumbria and all the shires who conspired against him with Archbishop Wulfstan and his uncle Eric Bloodaxe. His arguments had fallen on deaf ears. Edred would be waging a bloody war, and Northumbria would be the loser. Although Ravenshire would not be one of the targets, many of Eirik's neighbors would be hit, and Eirik found himself in the unenviable position of having to choose sides amongst friends.

He had to return to Ravenshire as soon as possible, and not just because of the threats posed by Edred. Eirik was beginning to feel guilty over his treatment of Eadyth.

Hell's flames, the woman was driving him mad. He hated her meddling, shrewish, managing ways. And he especially hated her lying to him about Steven of Gravely. But, Lord, he loved the woman to distraction. They would have to find a way to work out their problems.

He approached the harbor and saw Tykir loading his ship. He remembered that his brother would be leaving for Hedeby on the morrow. He would miss him sorely.

Tykir barely glanced up when he called out to him. Tykir's stiff demeanor bespoke a coiled anger.

"Now what?"

"Your wife is in Jorvik looking for you," Tykir informed him flatly when he finished handing some barrels to his crew members.

Eirik raised a brow quizzically. "Eadyth? In Jorvik? Looking for me?"

"Taking lessons from your parrot now, are you, Eirik?"

"Yea, and I need no lessons in sarcasm from you, my brother. Why is my wife looking for me?"

Tykir put his hands on his hips and glared at him. "You are a lackwit. Why the hell do you think she seeks you out? To tend her bees?"

"I do not care for the tone of your voice."

"And what do you intend to do about it?"

Eirik clenched his fists angrily and could not believe he was about to strike his own brother. Breathing deeply, in and out, he calmed his temper and asked with forced politeness, "Brother dear, why is my wife in Jorvik?"

"Because the mindless maid misses her loathsome lout of a husband, *brother dear*," Tykir retorted with equal sweetness. "And because she is worried sick about you." Tykir exhaled loudly with disgust and advised, "Go home, Eirik. Go home and make a family with Eadyth. I do not know why, but the lady loves you."

Eirik grinned. "Yea, I am a lovable lout, am I not?"

"It runs in the family," Tykir agreed, punching Eirik playfully on the arm. "Oh, by the by," he added casually, "do you have any idea why Eadyth has been practicing standing on her head?"

Eirik choked on a surprised swallow of air, and it took three harsh thumps on the back from Tykir before he could breathe again. "You lie, Tykir. I know you made that up."

"Did I?" Tykir said, examining his fingernails in a bored fashion. "Well, mayhap I misheard her."

The two brothers laughed, wrapping their arms around each other's shoulders. They went onto Tykir's ship and drank some of the excellent mead Eadyth had brought for Tykir's voyage. After they talked for a short time, Eirik informed Tykir of Edred's plans and expressed thanks that Tykir would be leaving Britain and the upcoming fray. Tykir told him he would be sailing at dawn, so he would not see his brother again before departing.

Tykir exclaimed with a snap of his fingers, "Oh, I forgot something." He went over to a chest and came back carrying a package.

"What is it?" Eirik asked suspiciously.

Tykir jiggled his eyebrows. "'Tis my wedding gift to you. I purchased it, with Eadyth's permission, in one of the market stalls yesterday."

"For me? Why would you need her permission to buy me something? Besides, you already gave us that damn parrot for a wedding gift."

"Nay," Tykir corrected Eirik with a laugh. "I gave the parrot to Eadyth. This is a special treat for you."

"Will I like it?"

"Eirik, you will thank me to your dying days for this gift."

The brothers embraced again near the dock. Eirik was just about to leave and go to the home of Eadyth's agent when Tykir snapped his fingers again. "Oh, there is something else I forgot."

"What? Another secret purchase?"

"Nay. I just thought you would like to know where Eadyth is right now." Tykir was leaning jauntily against a tall coil of ropes, and Eirik briefly considered picking him up and tossing him into the river. He just knew he was not going to like what Tykir had to tell him.

"Well?"

"She has gone to visit Asa."

Asa's jewelry stall was closed when Eirik arrived at Coppergate, and, at first, there was no answer when he knocked on her door. Finally, a servant answered. Recognizing him, she motioned him into the large hall. Eirik approached the small solar off the hall where the maid directed him, and then Eirik stopped mid-stride with horror.

Eadyth and Asa were sitting side by side on a bench at the window seat. Eadyth was weeping, and Asa had her arm around her shoulder, whispering words of comfort.

"Eadyth?" Eirik asked as he moved closer.

"Eirik!" Eadyth and Asa both said at the same time as they stood, Eadyth towering over Asa's much shorter figure. He had always thought Asa was the most beautiful woman in the world. He realized now how wrong he had been. Eadyth, his wife, was much more beautiful. Gloriously beautiful. And she was his.

And I love her.

He smiled warmly toward Eadyth, expecting her to smile back. Instead, she looked with pain-stricken eyes from him to Asa. Her violet eyes turned luminously angry. "Oh . . . oh . . . ," she sputtered and shoved him aside, running through the hall and out the door.

"Wha-at?" he asked Asa.

Asa just shook her head, as if he were the most dull-headed fool in the world.

Eirik spun on his heels and hurried after his wife, but she had already disappeared in the crowded street. He got his horse and rode toward her agent's house. By the time he maneuvered through the bothersome crowd, his mood had turned sour. He entered the agent's house without knocking.

A startled lady looked up—presumably Bertrand's wife—and Eirik asked rudely, "Where the hell is Eadyth?"

"And you are . . . ?" the buxom woman asked, approaching with a raised copper ladle.

"Her husband."

"Oh. The loathsome lout."

Eirik grimaced at the woman's words.

She lowered her weapon and jerked her head toward the stairs leading to an upper level. He thought he heard her say, "Mayhap now the maid will stop her constant weeping."

Eirik found Eadyth in one of the guest bedchambers, packing her belongings in a leather bag. "Good tidings, wife," he said in a silky voice, as if he had just returned from the exercise fields at Ravenshire a sennight ago, before all their angry words and separation, before Steven's death. He pulled the door shut behind him and turned the lock so they would not be disturbed. Then he leaned lazily against the wall, watching her closely.

She looked up at him through red-rimmed eyes and gave him a condemning, condescending look—the kind Eadyth excelled in, the kind she flashed at doltish servants and lackbrain husbands. Lord, he loved the woman.

"Are we going home?" he asked, looking pointedly at her traveling bag.

"I do not know where you are going, but I am returning to Ravenshire."

"Then we will travel together, I suppose."

"I do not need your company."

"But I need yours," he said softly.

Her eyes shot up at that. "Since when?"

"Since the day you barged into my keep, kicked my dog and started managing my life."

"I never kicked your dog," she protested. " 'Twas a soft nudge." Then his other words sunk in, and her face colored. "What about Asa?"

"What about her?"

"Do not play games with me, Eirik. You went to her house."

"And . . . ?"

"Eirik, I told you the first time we met that you could have your mistresses as long as you did not bring them to Ravenshire. Well . . . well, if that is what you want . . ."

"Eadyth . . . Eadyth . . . Eadyth," he said softly, shaking his head. "If you ever say again that you do not care if I have a mistress, I think I may just—"

"I never said I did not care," she declared vehemently. " 'Tis because I care and want you to be happy that I will not play the shrewish wife."

He raised his brows mockingly. "Really? I do not know if I like that idea. I have grown rather fond of . . . shrewish tongues."

She made a clucking sound, so like her usual self. He

Sandra Hill

wanted to squeeze her with sheer joy. "Eadyth, I have not been with Asa since before our betrothal."

She stilled suddenly, and he noticed the trembling of her hands as she laid aside her packing to study him. "Why are you here, Eirik?"

"Why did you come to Jorvik?" he countered.

Her eyelashes fluttered downward and she said, barely above a whisper, "To convince you to come home."

"Well, convince me."

She glanced up at him sideways, trying to guess his mood. "Will you come home?" she asked, lifting her haughty chin to the ceiling, as if anticipating a negative answer.

He pretended to ponder her question and moved away from the door toward her. He picked her traveling bag up off the bed and laid it on the floor, then sat down wearily on the mattress. He drew her down beside him.

Eadyth wanted to shake an answer from her husband, and she wanted to remain pridefully silent. More than anything, she wanted to save her marriage. "Eirik, I have made mistakes," she choked out, "but I think I could change."

Eirik grinned disbelievingly at her. And Eadyth's heart flipped over. Blessed Lord, he was a handsome man.

"I need to be able to trust you, Eadyth. I cannot abide lies. I just cannot."

"I know, and I am sorry. I thought I was doing the right thing."

"You always do." Fine lines webbed his eyes and the edges of his mouth. He looked exhausted and heart weary, and Eadyth cried inwardly that she had caused him so much pain.

Eirik took her hand in his and traced the betrothal scar at her wrist. Eadyth's pulse jumped under the tender caress. Then he entwined their fingers so that their two scars met. "Heart of my heart," he murmured, repeating their betrothal vows. And Eadyth's heart felt as if it were expanding in her chest. So many feelings unfurled and rippled through her senses. There was no way to express them all.

So, of course, she started to weep.

"What shall we do, Eadyth?" Eirik asked, wiping the tears with the fingertips of his free hand.

"I do not know," she said on a sob. "What do you want?"

He looked at her levelly. "A wife to love, who would love me in return. A family. A warm home." He held her gaze for a long moment, then added on a whisper, "You."

Eadyth's heart stopped beating for a moment. Then she threw herself at him, knocking him backward onto the bed as she kissed his face and neck and ears and hair, crying the entire time. Her head-rail slipped off and its gold circlet fell to the floor with a metallic clink.

"Oh, Eirik, I promise you will not be sorry. I am going to be the most biddable wife in the world."

He laughed with disbelief against her neck as he swept his palms up and down her back, from her shoulders to her thighs, over and over.

" 'Tis true, and I will never, never lie to you again."

Eirik held her face above his in the cradle of his two palms. "Eadyth, do not make promises you cannot keep."

Eadyth could see the pain in his wonderful blue eyes, pain she had caused with her dishonesty, no matter how well-intentioned. "I want to try," she said.

He nodded in acceptance of her pledge. " 'Tis good enough for now." He pulled her head down to his then and kissed her with all the pent-up passion of the past sennight of their separation. When he finally tore his mouth from hers, panting for breath, he told her in a thick voice full of emotion, "I have missed you, dearling, more than you can ever know."

"I never want to lose you, Eirik. You must help me, though. I have a tendency to try to take over and manage things, just as you have complained ofttimes. And . . . why are you grinning?"

"Because there have been a few times when your 'managing' has not been too difficult to abide."

Her eyes widened as she remembered the scandalous way in which she had "managed" a seduction of her husband one night. And she marveled at the changes this man had wrought in her cold life and disposition. Good changes, she decided.

Eirik's fingers were busy meanwhile with some managing of their own. He undid her belt and lifted her tunic and chemise over her head, stopping here and there to kiss a shoulder, to nip a breast, to touch the tip of his tongue to her mole.

When she was naked, he stood her before him and removed his own clothing, holding her eyes the entire time. "Can you see me in this dim light?" she asked tentatively, knowing how sensitive he was about his eyesight.

He chuckled softly. "Well enough to see the rapid rise and fall of your breasts. Well enough to see your nipples peak with their own sweet ache. Well enough to see your lips parting in anticipation of my kisses. Well enough to see the dew of—"

She stepped forward and put her fingertips over his lips, stopping his next words. Then she tried to loop her arms around his neck, but he put her away from him with a gentle kiss. "Not so fast. I want to open my wedding gift from Tykir first."

"Wedding gift? Oh!" she said, blushing hotly when she recognized the purchase Tykir had made for her in the market yesterday. "He told me it was a gift for me."

Eirik took the silken harem garment out of its wrapping and handed it to Eadyth. It was really only a series of transparent scarves draped together with tiny bells along the edges. "Will you dance for me, Eadyth?" he asked in a suddenly raw voice.

Shyly, Eadyth donned the flimsy costume for her husband, wanting to cover herself with her hands, but stopping herself from doing so when she saw the look of pleasure in Eirik's eyes as they swept over her.

"I cannot dance. I never learned how," she confessed. "But I could sit on your lap while you tell me one of your caliph stories."

Eirik thought that was a splendid idea.

But they only got through the beginning of his story before

the floor was littered with silken scarves. When he was buried in her woman folds, she held him close, forestalling the onslaught of spiraling passion which would overtake them soon. She cherished this oneness with her husband, this moment out of time, where only he and she—man and woman, husband and wife—existed.

Eirik seemed to cherish the special moment as well. Bracing himself on his straightened arms, he looked down at her adoringly and declared on a heartfelt whisper, "I love you, Eadyth."

"I love you, too, Eirik. Nay, do not move yet . . . oh!" She put her hands on both his buttocks to hold him in place, but closed her eyes for a moment until the spasms of sweet pleasure at their joining place stopped. With a sigh, she then took one of his hands in hers and laid it on her stomach. In an emotion-choked voice she told him, "With all the wedding gifts you and Tykir have given me, I have not yet given you any. Here 'tis, and I hope you will cherish it as much as I value all those you have given me."

At first, he just gazed at her in confusion. When understanding dawned, he smiled at her with such open love that Eadyth felt blessed by God. Then Eirik showed her with slow, slow strokes, and sweet kisses, and softly spoken words of love how very much he prized her love gift to him.

Much later, Eadyth lay cradled in her husband's arms, tracing her fingertips across his fine chest hairs, liking ever so much the idea that she had a right to touch him so. Eirik's gaze and his caresses went continually to her flat belly, as if in amazement that they could have created a child together.

Then, despite the lateness of the hour, they decided to head back to Ravenshire, wanting to be in their own home, with their children. As she prepared to step up onto the wagon seat with Eirik a short time later, their horses tied behind them, and several of Eirik's guards following after them, Eadyth remarked to her husband, "I was thinking, Eirik, now that I know you have a trading ship, and I have all these products to market, well, I was wondering—"

"You do too much wondering, Eadyth," he grumbled, whacking her softly on the bottom for emphasis. "I intend to keep you too busy to take on any more ventures."

She gave him a sidelong look of chagrin when he sat down next to her on the wagon seat. Under her breath, she muttered, "I think I could manage both."

But Eirik heard her and threw his head back, laughing. "I do not doubt that at all, Eadyth. Then he put his arm around her shoulder and drew her closer. "Yea, we will manage *together*."

**TIMESWEPT
PASSION...
TIMELESS
LOVE**

The Reluctant Viking

SANDRA HILL

*"Picture yourself floating out of your body—
floating...floating...floating..."* The hypnotic voice on the
self-motivation tape is supposed to help Ruby Jordan solve
her problems, not create new ones. Instead, she is lulled from
a life full of a demanding business, a neglected home, and
a failing marriage—to an era of hard-bodied warriors and
fair maidens, fierce fighting and fiercer wooing. But the
world ten centuries in the past doesn't prove to be all mead
and mirth. Even as Ruby tries to update medieval times, she
has to deal with a Norseman whose view of women is stuck
in the Dark Ages. And what is worse, brawny Thork has
her husband's face, habits, and desire to avoid Ruby.
Determined not to lose the same man twice, Ruby plans a
bold seduction that will conquer the reluctant Viking—and
make him an eager captive of her love.

_51983-6 $4.99 US/$5.99 CAN

THE OUTLAW VIKING

TIMESWEPT

SANDRA HILL

Winner Of The Georgia Romance Writers Maggie Award

As tall and striking as the Valkyries of legend, Dr. Rain Jordan is proud of her Norse ancestors despite their warlike ways. But she can't believe her eyes when a blow to the head transports her to a nightmarish battlefield and she has to save the barbarian of her dreams.

He is a wild-eyed berserker whose deadly sword can slay a dozen Saxons with a single swing, yet Selik can't control the saucy wench from the future. And if Selik isn't careful, the stunning siren is sure to capture his heart and make a warrior of love out of the outlaw viking.

_52000-1 $4.99 US/$5.99 CAN

FOR LOVE AND HONOR

FLORA SPEER

Bestselling Author Of *Love Just In Time*

Falsely accused of murder, Sir Alain vows to move heaven and earth to clear his name and claim the sweet rose named Joanna. But in a world of deception and intrigue, the virile knight faces enemies who will do anything to thwart his quest of the heart.

From the sceptered isle of England to the sun-drenched shores of Sicily, the star-crossed lovers will weather a winter of discontent. And before they can share a glorious summer of passion, they will have to risk their reputations, their happiness, and their lives for love and honor.

__3816-1 $4.99 US/$5.99 CAN

the ROSELYNDE CHRONICLES

ROSELYNDE

Roberta Gellis

"A superb storyteller of extraordinary talent!"
—John Jakes

In an era made for men, Alinor is at no man's mercy. Beautiful, proud and strong willed, she is mistress of Roselynde and her own heart as well—until she meets Simon, the battle-scarred knight whose passion and wit match her own. Their struggle to be united against the political obstacles in their path sweep them from the royal court to a daring crusade through exotic Byzantium and into the Holy Land. They endure bloody battles, dangerous treacheries and heartrending separations before their love conquers time and destiny to live forever.

_3559-6 $5.99 US/$6.99 CAN

Dorchester Publishing Co., Inc.
65 Commerce Road
Stamford, CT 06902

Roberta Gellis

"A superb storyteller of extraordinary talent!"
—John Jakes

Ravishing, raven-haired daughter of a Welsh prince, Rhiannon is half shy and half wild. It is said she can cast a spell over any man, but she is no man's prize.

Notorious for loving—and leaving—the most beautiful women in the realm, Simon is the court's most eligible—and elusive—bachelor.

Then the handsome nobleman meets Rhiannon, who drives him mad with fury and delirious with desire. While bloody rebellion rages through England, Rhiannon and Simon endure ruinous battles and devastating betrayals before finding a love so powerful no enemy can destroy it.

_3695-9 $5.99 US/$6.99 CAN

FORBIDDEN PASSION

THERESA SCOTT

Bestselling Author Of *Bride of Desire*

"More than Viking tales, Theresa Scott's historical romances are tender, exciting, and satisfying!"
—*Romantic Times*

Ordered to Greenland to escort his commander's betrothed to their Irish stronghold, Thomas Lachlann is unexpectedly drawn to the beguiling beauty he was sent to find. Bewitched and bewildered, Thomas knows that if he takes Yngveld as his beloved life will be forfeit—but if he loses the golden-haired enchantress his heart will break.

_3855-2 $5.99 US/$7.99 CAN

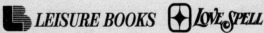